THE BONDS THAT TIE

Savage Bonds

Also by J Bree

The Bonds That Tie Series

Broken Bonds
Savage Bonds
Blood Bonds
Forced Bonds
Tragic Bonds
Unbroken Bonds

The Mortal Fates Series

Novellas
The Scepter
The Sword
The Helm

The Trilogy
The Crown of Oaths and Curses
The Throne of Blood and Honor

THE BONDS THAT TIE

Savage Bonds

J BREE

Savage Bonds
The Bonds that Tie #2
Copyright © 2021 J Bree

Cover & Interior Illustration by Emilie Snaith
Cover Typography by Bellaluna Cover Designs
Edited by Telisha Merrill Mortensen
Proofread by Samantha Whitney
Interior Formatting by Wild Elegance Formatting

Savage Bonds/J Bree – 2nd ed.
ISBN-13 - 978-1-923072-01-5

Prologue

NORTH

B lack curls of smoke writhe around Bassinger's body as he struggles against my nightmares, the disembodied limbs claw at his skin as I keep them from consuming him entirely.

He's a pain in the ass and I don't have time to placate him right now because not even Athena Bassinger's nephew can distract me from the cluster-fuck of incompetency and mismanagement that happened on the college campus this morning.

After we'd cleared out the front buildings, we were working our way through the courtyard when Gryphon got the call from Black to say that Oleander had been taken. It was only when we caught up with Gabe and Bassinger that we found out she'd left them behind the moment they'd turned their backs on her.

Once a runner, always a runner.

"She's my fucking Bond, you can't keep me from going to her," Bassinger snarls, and I have to force my eyes not to roll at him. It's the same bullshit he'd been spitting at me from the moment I'd had to disable him when the others had left.

I was too late to stop Gabe and if the little shit gets himself injured, I'll have him screaming in terror for the rest of his natural life for running after her. If she were a normal Bond, someone who actually gave a fuck about any of us, then I'd be more forgiving, but she proved how little she thinks of us all a long time ago. There are many names I've been called in my life but a blind fool isn't one of them.

I tug my tie away from my neck and let the silk slowly unravel. "You were never taught to share, were you? Your 'only child syndrome' is showing. She's our Bond and she ran off at the first signs of chaos, exactly like we all knew she would. Have you seen through her little charade yet? Or are you still so infatuated with the feel of her bond that you can't think past your dick?"

The tattoos on his neck stand out as he strains against the smoke again in a futile attempt to get free and, very probably, knock my front teeth out. We're locked away in my office, waiting on the signal from Gryphon and Nox for an evacuation, and with no witnesses around, I'm comfortable enough to grin at him in an animalistic baring of teeth. No part of me right now is the sophisticated councilman. No, I'm nothing but the *monster*.

The next Draven man in a long line of cursed men, never to know peace or comfort.

I watch as Bassinger's lip curls at me, no fear in him, which means he either has no idea of what I'm capable of, or that he thinks he can take me on. Either way, he's stupid and reckless, another liability in our Bond group.

Oleander is bad enough.

We're interrupted by a knock at the door, a hesitant sound that is easy to distinguish as my assistant in an utterly panicked state over everything that has happened in the last four hours. I let the calm and sure mask settle back over my features, the measures I'm forced to take to inhabit this world without being hunted in the night.

Little do they all know that I'm most comfortable in the dark.

"Come in."

Penelope looks terrified as she enters, taking a deep breath as she approaches me. Every inch of her body is shaking as she clears her throat twice before she can speak. "The Delta TacTeam has made their way through all of the students who were on campus during the attack. We have forty-two with injuries, but thankfully no deaths to report yet."

Her eyes flick over to where Atlas is being restrained and what little color her face was desperately holding on to vanishes until she's the shade of a fresh powder of snow. I take a half step in front of him and give her a reassuring smile. "Mr. Bassinger isn't thinking rationally. I've been forced to take extreme measures to keep him here but rest assured, he is both safe and unharmed."

She swallows again and her eyes flick back to mine as her chin wobbles just a little. She's new around here, the daughter of one of the more affluent families, and she's been sniffing around after me as though she thought that sleeping with the boss was the best way to get a cushy ride and easy paycheck.

I've been through dozens of assistants with the same attitude but none of them make it past this moment, the moment where the curtain is pulled back and there's no mistaking exactly what I am.

She clears her throat again and holds out a sheet of paper to me, her hand trembling a little. "There's also reports that Miss Fallows went after her friend, Sage Benson. She didn't attempt to run, despite the earlier... speculation. We spoke to Gracie Davenport and she was adamant that Miss Fallows went after her friend. I thought you'd want to know this information."

I find that very hard to believe.

My chest is still tight, my jaw aching from how hard I'm grinding my teeth together, and when she visibly gulps at me, I can't muster up the energy to placate her. She excuses herself and practically runs from the room, stumbling at the door.

Bassinger waits until it's shut behind her before he snaps, "See? Hate her all you want but you're wrong. She's not running from her Bonds. She's not running from *me*."

My phone starts buzzing in my pocket and when I fish it out, I find Gryphon's name flashing at me, GPS coordinates, and a single line to tell me he has Oleander and Gabe secured.

"Keep thinking that, Bassinger, and she'll lead you right into hell."

OLI

The only positive to the entire situation I've found myself in is that I'm not facing North Draven's wrath by myself.

We all watch as the plane touches down on the dirt runway, the engine roaring as it kicks into reverse to slow and finally come to a stop only a couple of hundred feet away from where we're all standing around. The moment my hands had stopped shaking from using my gift, Sage had come over to stand with me, holding Gabe up between us. She'd moved slowly at first, but it wasn't the same fear that Gryphon's TacTeam was throwing my way. Instead, she was being understanding of just how volatile bonds can be when their Bonds are threatened.

She was respecting the insanity of this entire situation

because she's the best goddamn friend a girl could ever ask for.

Gabe still isn't looking great, his face is green and he's swaying a little on his feet, but he has that same stubborn look on his face as always. I glance past him at Sage and she shoots me a look like she's praying for me to survive whatever the hell is about to come from all of this mess.

My gift hums in my chest like it's eager to be formally introduced to the rest of my Bonds. My legs still feel a little weak and my head is pounding. I need a nap to recharge from using my gift and I'm hoping that plane is as luxurious as the rest of North's possessions.

There's murmuring behind us and an argument between a couple of the TacTeam guys, but my head is hurting too much for me to really take in their words. When Gabe's arm tightens around my shoulder and Gryphon steps back up to my side, I make the calculated guess that my honor is being torn apart.

Like I give a fuck.

"You need a new fucking team," Gabe snarls and Gryphon shrugs at him, his eyes sharp as the back of the plane finally starts opening.

"I'm finding out who's loyal and who's not, adjustments will be made."

Jesus, he doesn't sound angry about it either, and I start to wonder how long he's worked with this group. Kieran and Nox are both standing with Gryphon and when the word *monster* filters into my brain again Kieran curses viciously under his breath and turns on his heel to ream the two squabbling team members out.

Gryphon glances down at me like he's expecting me to react to them, but I couldn't care less about their opinions.

I care about what hell North is going to put me through over this. I care about the way that Nox had reached out to my gift with his own, like he wanted to know exactly what I'm capable of.

I care that Gabe is still swaying on his feet with whatever drug he was dosed with.

"Any explanation for us yet, Fallows? Anything to say about lying to us all for months about what you can do?" he says, and Gabe turns to glare at him in my defense.

The eight-pack hottie is really growing on me, dammit.

When Gabe opens his mouth, I cut him off because there's no way I'm going to sit back and let him fight my wars for me, that just isn't my style. "Nope. Just because you're my Bonds doesn't mean I owe you shit. I'm *so* sorry you had to find out this way that you're stuck with a monster."

The sarcasm is dripping from my tone and I'm expecting him to react but he doesn't, his eyes still just staring me down coldly. From the corner of my own eye, I see the snarl on Nox's face pointed right in my direction, but fuck him and his shitty mood.

Gabe also moves to glare at me instead of Gryphon and snaps, "Don't fucking say that shit. You just saved us all. A monster wouldn't do that, and every last one of the people here that are saying that shit are ungrateful, spineless assholes who would burn their saviors at the stake just because they're stronger than them. Gutless and jealous fucking assholes."

Huh.

There's a nerve there that I didn't even know existed and when I take a second to look at the rest of my Bonds, it's clear on their faces as well. Something about what's being said about me is triggering them and I know for sure it isn't on my behalf, because Nox is looking particularly bloodthirsty about it and he really, really fucking hates me.

Gryphon is staring around at his team with cold eyes, taking in exactly what's happening around us. Kieran is still verbally tearing strips off of the men behind us and there are others watching on in disgust, but when my eyes hit the other students staring at me in horror, my blood chills a little bit.

Then I remember that they're all here right now, breathing and torture-free, thanks to me, and instead of feeling like shit about who I am and what I can do, I smirk and wiggle my eyebrows a little at them, taunting them.

I swear one of the girls nearly faints.

She would never have survived the Resistance and their camps.

The back of the plane finally opens completely and another group of TacTeam members, all clad in black, come streaming down the ramp and over to us, order being called out in code words that mean absolutely nothing to me. Gabe's arm tightens around me again, his jaw clenching as he stares out over the newcomers as though he's expecting another attack. I'm kind of hoping we're past that though, as past that as we can be, when I see two more figures descend from the plane that have me gulping a little.

I really don't have much fight left in me and North's particular brand of it isn't great, even when I'm at full strength. Right now, with everything I've had to do? Shit, we might just be scraping his innards off of the side of the plane if he so much as looks sideways at me, because my bond is not fucking around anymore.

I have my gift back and it's eager to come out to play.

I squeeze my eyes shut for a second just to take a deep breath and clear my mind, to find some sort of calm or peace or *something* to get me through this without destroying everyone around me.

"Fuck, he looks pissed. We're both in for it, Bond," Gabe mutters under his breath at me, and my eyes snap back open to find Sage cringing and looking terrified about the hell that's heading towards us all.

North starts off charging towards us but his footsteps slow as he takes in the damage lying all around us in the fields, all ninety-two of my victims writhing and twitching on the ground as blood pours from their eyes and ears as their brains begin to break down in their skulls.

Atlas doesn't miss a beat, his feet propelling him to me without a single glance in any other direction. Only at the last second does he seem to notice Gabe and the way that we're wrapped around each other, but he doesn't comment as he slams into me with enough force to knock the breath out of me and tears me away from Gabe, swinging me into his arms and clutching me close to his chest.

"What the fuck was that, Oli? Why the fuck did you take off without me? I would've come with you to find Sage," he murmurs into my hair and my arms feel as though they weigh a thousand pounds as I lift them to return his embrace.

I let out a shuddering breath as I let myself just melt into his arms, too exhausted from using my gift in such a huge way after years of hiding it. I let my face tuck into his neck as I mumble back, "There wasn't time. They already had her and I couldn't let her go without backup, that's not who I am, Atlas."

His arms tighten around me even more, constricting me until I can't breathe, but there's something so goddamn comforting about it that I'm willing to just die here rather than ask him to ease up. His hand cradles the back of my head as he whispers back, "I never doubted that or you for a minute, Sweetness. Fuck the rest of them, I already told you that it's us against the world."

I accept that I'm going to die here wrapped up in him and I'll never regret it, not even while I'm rotting six feet under and burning in the pits of hell for all of my sins.

"Bassinger, get off of her, we need to get her out of the open before the riot starts," North snaps, but his words make no sense.

Riot?

Why the hell would there be a riot and exactly which people would be starting it? But Atlas drops his arms away from me slowly, which is great because my legs give out on me.

He catches me and swings me back up into his arms, snapping at North, "She needs a healer, did you think to bring one? Fuck Ardern, he can wait. Over my dead body are any of you being attended to before my Bond."

And then he stalks forward with me still securely wrapped around him until he reaches Sage, dropping one arm to offer her some help if she needs it. When she shakes her head, he motions at her to follow him back to the plane, keeping my friend safe without a word from me, because even in the short time he's known me, he's figured out just how to reach my ice-wrapped heart.

I let my eyes slip shut, mumbling a quiet *thank you* even as I slip out of consciousness.

I slip back into some semi-consciousness as Atlas takes his seat and adjusts his hold on me, moving me around a little until I'm secure in his arms.

I feel Sage's hand slip onto my forehead as she murmurs with Atlas about finding a healer for me, but I manage to croak out, "I'm fine. Take me to Felix when we get home, I don't want anyone else to touch me while I'm out of it."

Atlas' arms tighten again and for a second, I think he's pissed at me but then my bond feels Gabe take the seat next to us, jostling me a little as he collapses there. When Atlas snarls at him, he snaps, "Give me a fucking break, I've just been drugged and had the shit kicked out of me."

My bond doesn't like that at all and my gift bursts out of me before I can stop it.

Gabe yelps as it hits him, scrambling up like he thinks I'm about to tear his mind apart. I don't have the energy to feel bad about it. I mean, they don't know about the other things I can do.

They don't really know anything.

Gabe figures it out first. "My headache and dizziness is gone."

I hear footsteps and my bond recognizes Gryphon as he approaches us, his voice low and gravelly as he snaps, "What the fuck was that? What the fuck just happened?"

I feel the Draven brothers both approaching and even in my paralyzed-like state, I tense a little and then Gabe speaks again, harsher than I've ever heard him before, "Don't take another fucking step near my Bond or I'll rip your fucking throat out with my bare teeth."

I wonder which one of the crew has been stupid enough to try to approach us because he cannot be talking to one of the Dravens like that, but then Nox says, snark dripping down his words, "She's my Bond as well."

Atlas scoffs. "No, she's your punching bag, your favorite victim. She's the default villain in every one of your stories. You move even an inch closer and I'll take the whole fucking plane out to stop you. No more warnings."

I struggle to get my eyes open, to prepare myself for the war about to break out because Nox Draven does not back down, but I'm too fucking tired.

Maybe it's for the best that I just die in the melee of what's about to happen.

There's a shuffling sound again and then Nox snaps, "Take her to the bedroom. We need to talk. Now."

Bedroom?

Of course North's plane has a fucking bedroom. Of course.

As Atlas gently lifts me in his arms as if I weigh nothing, cradling me against his chest like I'm precious, I hear the sounds of the plane filling with people and orders being shouted everywhere as they prepare for takeoff.

I don't know why he thinks I'm precious, I've just ruined dozens of people, and yet he is acting as if I'm even more important to him now than ever before.

He's steady on his feet, even with the throngs of people around us, as he walks us over to another room and then lowers me carefully onto a bed, pulling up blankets and tucking them around me as he brushes his lips against my forehead.

I'm almost pissed off that I can't acknowledge it or ask him for more.

I hear more footsteps shuffle into the room and then a door slides shut.

"Hurry up then, Draven. I want you out of this room and as far away from Oli as you can get on this fucking plane," Atlas snaps, and again, I try to pry my eyes open. Nope. Nothing.

Nox growls under his breath and footsteps get closer to the bed. "She just healed us all. You don't think we need to talk about that? You don't want to be let in on exactly what our little lying Bond just did out there?"

Gabe snorts. "Bonds can heal each other in dire situations, you already know that. Move the fuck on. You just want to argue over every little thing because you don't want to admit that you were wrong about her. Heaven fucking forbid you admit you were wrong. I saw the Resistance get a good look at her, Nox. They knew her. She's been *running* this entire time and now we know why. They want her because she can do something no other Gifted can do-"

Nox cuts him off. "She's more than just a fucking Gifted, that's what I'm trying to say. She didn't just heal us enough to survive, she fixed *everything*. Everything! My fingers are straight again, Gabe. She fixed an injury that happened *twenty fucking years ago*."

Oops.

I feel like my life is about to become even more complicated if that's possible, but whatever their answers are to that statement, I don't hear them. Instead, my mind finally catches up to my body and I pass out into nothingness.

J BREE

I wake in a bed I don't recognize, in a room that is definitely not the airplane, feeling both well rested and sick to my stomach.

It's far too luxurious to be one of the dorm rooms, there's no mistaking the wealth behind every piece of furniture, right down to the softness of the pillows behind my head.

I'm instantly freaked the hell out.

"You're safe, Oleander. Atlas and Gabe stepped out to shower and find food. I told them I'd watch you."

God-fucking-dammit, I know exactly whose mansion I'm in.

I look over to find North sitting in a plush chair on the far side of the bed, his jacket off and his dress shirt unbuttoned partially down his chest. The sleeves are rolled up to show off his forearms and I think this is the most casual I've ever seen him, except for that one time I'd seen him shirtless but I can't think about that without drooling a little.

His eyes are as intense as ever.

I can't believe that he managed to talk Atlas out of this room, and I'm a little bit pissed that I was brought here in the first place. What's the point of giving me a room here if I'm just going to be shoved into random beds when everything goes to hell?

North continues watching me, his eyes getting sharper the longer I stay silent. "Do you need anything? Water or the bathroom? You've been asleep for forty-eight hours, we were starting to get worried."

Yes to both, but it feels weird to talk about peeing with this man. Gah. I shake my hands out to stop them from shaking before I push the blankets aside. He watches my every move and when I pause for a second to get my bearings and clear my spinning head, he stands to walk around and help me.

I can't deal with his hands on me at any time, let alone while I'm feeling this terrible, so I wave him away. "Just point me in the right direction and I'll be fine."

He scowls at me, his eyebrows drawn in tight, and then waves a hand at the far door. "We need to talk once you're out. I'll get you some water."

I bite back a groan and get moving. The bathroom is stunning, all marble and expensive fixtures, and I feel like I'm in a freaking palace. When I wash up after I take the longest pee of my life, the soap is lightly scented, and I close my eyes as I take in a deep lungful. Something settles in my chest, like my bond is happy about this smell being on me, and then I realize it's *North's* soap and *North's* scent.

Well, fuck.

Of course he would bring me back to his goddamned bedroom and of course he lives in this level of luxury. *Of-freaking-course* this is all his. I try not to flinch as I amp up the heat of the water to try to clean some of the smell off. Doesn't matter that my bond is craving it. Doesn't matter if it feels *right* to smell like him.

He hates me, all the way down to my core, and I'm not a fan of his either.

I need to grasp at the distance so my heart doesn't get ripped out any more than it already has been.

I try to tame my hair a little and then when that doesn't work, I smooth a hand down my silk pajamas.

Uhm.

Wait, what?

Silk. Fucking. Pajamas.

I'm wearing a pinstripe, luxurious-looking, long-sleeve pajama set in a deep navy color that makes my skin look amazing. Hell, even the silvery tones of my hair look gorgeous against this color, but all of that shit is besides the point here. Who the hell changed me? I check and, nope, my underwear is gone too. Someone got me *naked* while I slept, the fucking perverted bastards.

I charge out of the bathroom ready to yell at North, however terrifying that may be, only to find all of my Bonds there now.

Atlas and Gabe are both on the bed, Gryphon has taken North's seat on the far side, and Nox has pulled up another to sit beside his best friend, scowling at me like he always freaking is. North stands at the small table by the door, pouring out a coffee that has my heart thumping a little off kilter in my chest.

Coffee.

"Take a seat, Oleander. I think we can both agree that there's a lot we need to discuss."

Joke's on him, there's absolutely nothing I have to say to him right now… or anytime in the foreseeable future. Even if I trusted him, I wouldn't tell him a single thing about myself, and with all of the shit he's put me through, there's no chance I'm telling him anything.

My skin prickles at the five sets of eyes that take me in with varying degrees of interest and a little disgust, but it's no surprise to me that Nox is throwing that shit my way.

I grumble under my breath as I stalk back to the bed, crossing my arms over my chest to try to hide the fact that I'm sans bra.

Atlas grins at me, ignoring the presence of the others as though they're all beneath him, and he lifts the blankets and tucks me back into the bed beside him. His arm comes up and around me as if I was made to be molded against him. I glance around the room again and suddenly I'm glad he's all over me like a hot rash. There's too much intensity in the eyes of everyone around us. They're all too focused on me.

I hate it.

North hands me a glass of water and I frown at it. "I'd rather have a coffee."

"You've been unconscious for two days. You can have the coffee after you've had the water."

I feel like if I murdered this man right now, I could argue my case in court and have it be counted as justifiable. I have to force my jaw to unclench to force the water down my throat, but I down the entire lot in one go. When I hand him back the glass, his eyes narrow at me and Atlas' arm tightens around my shoulders as he pulls me in closer to his side.

Finally, North takes a step back and grabs another chair from the huge walk-in closet to sit where he can watch my face. I'm always a fucking subordinate to this man. If I could run screaming from this room and find some sort of escape, I would do it. In a heartbeat, I'd freaking do it.

I also realize that right now, even with two of my Bonds sitting on the bed with me, I'm outnumbered because I'm sure Gabe and Atlas want some answers as well.

North's eyes flick over to Gryphon's and when he nods, North starts in on me. "Right. There are a whole list of questions we have for you, Oleander-"

I cut him off. "Can we not? I'd rather just go back to the way it was before I was taken. You ignore me and I go to my classes like a good little slave. Sorry I got jumped when I went after Sage, I'll do my best to never let it happen again. Are we good?"

His eyes flash at me, the first sign he's pissed. Good, I'm fucking livid right back at him.

"No, we're not *good*. You lied to us. Again. You knew you were Gifted and lied to each and every one of your Bonds. This is going to stop. Right now. What else are you keeping from us?"

Gabe shifts uncomfortably beside me and I can't look up at him. I don't need to see the hurt in his face when I never owed him the truth about myself.

This isn't about him.

I pull away from Atlas to carefully climb out of the bed and gesture at the pajamas. "Who did this? Which one of you got me naked while I was unconscious?"

Atlas rolls off the bed as well and grabs a bag from where it's tucked under the end of the bed. I hadn't even noticed it there.

He grabs my hand and says, "North did it. We got back here and he just took off with you, refused to put you in your own bed, and made Felix heal you here. When I questioned him about your outfit change, he said it was no big deal."

North doesn't even flinch under the savage glare I level at him. "Good to know my naked, non-consenting body is *no big deal.*"

North's jaw clenches. "Fallows-"

Great, back to Fallows. "No. You don't get to sit there and tell me how bad I am for keeping this from you, when everything I've done has been to keep us all safe. That's it, that's all I'm saying about this. If you want any more information, then I'm sorry to say that you're going to be left hanging."

I step towards the door, forgetting for a second that Atlas is holding my hand, until I accidentally tug him along with me. He doesn't hesitate though, just steps up with me to leave this ridiculously perfect room.

"Fallows, you can't just walk out without telling us anything. What exactly is your gift and what else can you do? Why did you hide it from us? How did the Resistance know about it?" North snaps, his voice getting deeper the angrier he gets, and I almost slam into the wall that Atlas makes behind me as I spin around again.

I point a finger at him, ready to tear into him, when Nox cuts me off. "Leave it, brother. She's still just a pathetic little child who runs away the second it gets hard."

I hate him.

I hate him so fucking much and it only grows stronger when his eyes flick back up to me as he drawls, "Go on then, scurry away to find a little dark hole to hide in. You're the same worthless Bond we had a week ago, only now we know you had the option not to be. You could have really been something and instead, you chose to be *nothing*."

I could kill him.

My bond even considers wiping him from the face of the Earth, no matter the connection between us, but instead, I turn on my heel and stalk out.

I instantly regret storming out of the room when I find myself in a hallway that I've never seen before with no idea of how to find the room North assigned to me.

When I blanch, Atlas immediately scoffs at me and takes the lead, shaking his head with a grin. "You really have no sense of direction, do you?"

I shrug and focus on keeping my legs steady under me

because my stomach is still churning a little, even though I also feel starving and cranky and, fuck, okay, I feel a lot of conflicting things right now.

Right as we turn the corner at the end of the hallway and I find myself staring at my own door, because of course North has me sleeping within a second of his own room like the utter control freak he is, I hear his door open and slam shut behind us.

I don't want to deal with whoever is coming after us right now.

I don't want to go another round with North or to have some more barbs thrown at me by his charming brother, and if Gryphon shows up here to stare at me until I crumble and start crying, I might just throw myself out of the window to get away from all of this.

Atlas presses a key into my palm as he covers my back, checking behind us as I find that it is actually my copy and get the door opened.

He scoffs. "We don't want you here, Ardern. Go find some catnip to keep yourself busy."

I let out a breath of relief that it's Gabe and not one of the others as I get the door open and walk into the room. It doesn't feel like my own, not really, but there's a lock on the door and one of my Bonds has a copy to get in without my permission. I'll take one over five of them any day of the week, even if it is North.

Atlas moves to fill the entire door frame, blocking Gabe from my view right as he says, "I think I'll hear from my Bond whether or not she wants me here. You don't speak for her, and you definitely don't get to tell me what to do."

Great, they're no closer to being amicable, even after they'd joined forces on the plane against the others.

But I don't want them arguing and even though I distinctly remember healing Gabe on the flight, I'd still like to get a look at him properly to know that he's okay.

"Let him in, Atlas. As long as neither of you harass me about my gift, then you guys can stick around."

He doesn't argue with me, just turns and walks into the room. He's already been in here before and slept in the bed with me, so he just walks over to drop his bag on the bed and start rummaging through it.

Gabe shuts the door behind himself and locks it, wiggling the handle a little to make sure it's secure before he starts looking around at the room. I've done nothing to the space at all, and my tiny little duffel bag of clothes is stashed away in the closet, so it just looks like a very well-decorated spare room.

I take a breath and then the wiggling of my chest reminds me that I'm still in the freaking pajamas without a bra, so I take off towards the ensuite. "I need a shower. We can… hangout or whatever once I'm clean. Try not to break each other or any of the furniture while I'm gone."

They both make some kind of noise in agreement, that total boy way of agreeing without actually saying they do, and I leave them behind to scrub myself down.

I'm happy to see that North didn't actually clean me, he just changed me out of the filthy workout clothes, because it seems so much more invasive to think about him washing my naked body while I slept.

I'm also just a little bit pissed that my bond was totally fine with what he was doing and didn't kick in to wake me up or shove him away. I'm going to pretend that means he was respectful because if I find out he wasn't... murder. Pain. Chaos and bedlam until the world burns down to the ground around us.

I'm happy to find that the soap in here is different to North's soap, so even though my bond gets sulky about it, I get to clean away the smell of him from my body. I scrub out my hair as well, the scent of smoke still clinging to me a little, and by the time I step out of the stall, my body is pink and practically sparkling with how clean I am.

It's a freaking amazing feeling.

I scrub my teeth twice and drink down another huge glass of water that also feels pretty lifesaving. I'm still starving, but the idea of leaving this room is abhorrent to me right now, so I guess I'm just going to continue starving until tomorrow.

When I finally step back into the room, wrapped up in

a towel because I forgot to grab clothes before I went in for the shower, Atlas and Gabe both look up at me the second I step out.

There's way too much going on in both of their gazes and I'm instantly trapped by them, frozen to the spot until Gabe gulps and breaks the spell.

"Sorry— I forgot— just give me a second!" I sputter as I dart over to the closet and start rummaging through my bag for something to cover up with. There's no door on the closet but I'm tucked around the corner well enough that I can throw on one of Gryphon's sweatshirts and a pair of yoga pants without flashing the two very hot-blooded men sitting around in my room.

Lusting after me like I'm their next meal.

Look, I get it. I mean, I've been staring at all of them for months like they're my last meal on death row, but it was easier to ignore it when I hated them all and when they all thought I was a useless, giftless reject.

That's not the way things are going anymore.

Those two definitely don't hate me, and I'm not willing to admit how much I want them right back.

Gabe came after me.

Atlas attempted to as well.

Both of them stood up for me against the others, Gabe took on the Resistance to find me and bring me home, and both of them shielded Sage when things got rough.

It doesn't mean I can Bond with them or give them any answers, but it means *something*.

When I step back out of the closet to find Gabe standing with his back to me as he stares out of the window and Atlas lounging on the bed with his phone in his hand, I feel awkward as hell as I walk back over to the bed, trying not to feel self-conscious in the baggy clothes with my hair still dripping down my back while both of them look as though they've just stepped out of a magazine for sports models.

They're both really freaking hot, okay?

"Come lie back down, you're as white as a sheet, Sweetness," Atlas murmurs to me as he shifts over and pulls back the blankets for me. I feel like after two days of sleeping I should be totally sick of being in a bed, but it's too tempting to crawl between the sheets and just die there.

Gabe watches us both with a sort of seething jealousy, but he doesn't say a word as he pulls one of the huge, ornate armchairs over to sit beside me.

Neither of them say another word and I start to think I'm going a little crazy. "I'll be fine here, guys. You don't have to babysit me. I'm not going to run off, I swear."

Gabe huffs and I get ready for him to say something particularly cutting to me but instead he snaps, "Neither of us think you're a runner, Oli. Nox is a fucking asshole, he's projecting like a motherfucker right now. If he speaks to you like that again, I'll kill him."

Atlas scoffs back at him. "Oh really? How exactly is a shifter going to go up against a Draven and his nightmares? If either of us are going to kill him, it's me."

I really don't want another pissing contest to start up but if I let them both run their mouths, then I might actually find out what Atlas can do without having to ask him.

I'm not sure why I'm still so against speaking to them about what they can do, probably because if they ask me anything about my own gift, I'll feel like an utter bitch for refusing to tell them a thing.

It turns out I don't have to wait long.

"Being strong won't help with the nightmares either. You can't wrestle them into submission, they'll just consume you," Gabe snaps, and Atlas chuckles at him.

"I'm indestructible. They can consume all they want, it won't hurt me or do a goddamned thing to me. I'm fucking bombproof."

Huh.

That's handy.

I'm also very clearly such a broken and terrible person because instantly my gift wants to test his theory, test whether or not I could take him out.

I have to shove it away and remind it that we *do not* hurt the Bonds and we *definitely* don't hurt the two Bonds sitting here with me.

Before Gabe can reply with some new jab as they work out who is the alpha around here, there's a knock at the door and we all turn as one to look at it.

It's not one of my Bonds, I can't feel them there at all, but I still don't want to face one of the staff members either. What if North sent them up here to collect me for another round of questioning?

No, thanks.

"Don't open it," I mutter, but Gabe gets up and braces his shoulder against the wood like he's planning on physically holding down the fort.

More points to him.

"Who is it?" he calls out.

A small voice replies, "Kitchens. Mr. Draven sent us up here with food for Miss Fallows."

Thank God.

I don't want to give him a point as well, but my stomach growls at the very mention of food and Atlas jerks his head at Gabe to get him to let them in.

Dish after dish of seafood and fish are rolled into the room and I swear to God I almost orgasm at the mere smell of it all.

I eat enough for three people.

Atlas and Gabe don't touch a thing until I'm done.

I spend the entire evening with Atlas and Gabe, trying to play peacekeeper between them and failing miserably. It becomes very clear to me that they'll only agree with one another when I'm in danger or they're dealing with the other Bonds.

When we're alone like this, they just bicker and pick at each other until I want to murder them both.

When I finally decide to pass out for the night, neither of them will leave the room and, as much as I don't want to admit it, I don't really want them to. Atlas takes a shower and comes out to climb into my bed in just his boxers.

Gabe strips his shirt off and makes a nest of pillows and blankets on the floor next to my side of the bed without a word to me about it. He's had a hell of a lot to say to Atlas about everything all night but not a whole lot to say to me. I don't know if it's guilt or if he's just waiting to speak to me alone but it makes me feel jittery and nervous.

Atlas is respectful about keeping his distance from me in the bed but his hand finds mine under the sheets before I turn the lights off.

When we wake up the next morning, I feel like I was hit by a freight train, but I keep that little nugget of information to myself because there is absolutely no way I'm staying in this freaking mansion all day today. I'm going to class and I'm going to take advantage of what little freedom I still have. I need to see Sage and check up on how she's doing after her abduction. I need to thank Felix for healing me just because I asked for him, he definitely didn't have to do that. I even need to find Gracie and thank her for yelling about Sage and letting me find my best friend when she needed me. I'm eating lunch with all of my friends, dammit!

"I don't like this," Atlas says from the doorway of the closet, his back to me as I change but still sticking close with me. I tell myself it's a Bond thing and not at all because I must look as freaking terrible as I feel.

Gabe had disappeared to grab a shower and get dressed in his own room, which is when I found out that he also has a room here. Technically he doesn't live here, but apparently when North had found out about me and who

I was the Central Bond for, he'd put aside rooms here for us all.

Controlling asshole.

I pull one of Atlas' shirts over my head before I tug on one of Gryphon's hoodies, the last one that still smells like him. I need to figure out a game plan on how to get some more off of him... or return the others to him to get his scent back on them.

Would it be totally pathetic to get Gabe to help me out with it?

I wonder if he has some shirts I can steal as well?

Jesus, focus, Oli!

I clear my throat as I pull on some jeans that have seen better days but still fit me well enough. "I need this. I really just need to get back into my life and let things settle."

When I'm covered completely, I press a hand to his back to grab his attention and he turns to give me a grin, his eyes bright on mine. "You look fucking perfect in my clothes, Sweetness."

I blush, which is stupid, and snark at him, "What are you talking about, you can't even see it! Are you going to be like this over every item of clothing I steal from you because my bond is fucking weird about smells and... I think this is going to be a regular thing."

He shrugs and wraps an arm around my shoulders as Gabe lets himself back into the room with my key that he'd swiped. "Take whatever the hell you want from me, take everything. You want my car too? That one might hurt a little but only if you're shit at driving."

I cringe and when I glance at Gabe, he's still looking at Atlas like he wants to rip his throat out which makes it even harder to speak, but I find my voice, "I don't actually have my license, so you can keep the car. The TacTeam took my fake ID and, thanks to North, everyone on campus knows who I am, so there's no getting around it."

The grin on Atlas' face falters a bit but then he swoops down and kisses my cheek softly, a tiny brush of his skin against mine, but my bond keens for him like a sulky bitch in my chest.

"I'll add it to the list of stuff we have to sort out for you, it'll be right up there with the GPS tracker and getting you a job, if you still want one."

I blow out a breath and muster up a smile. "So... totally achievable shit, nothing that'll piss North off so much that he chains me to his fucking basement."

Atlas' eyes narrow but I don't want to get into that whole can of worms, so I step around him and over to the bed, shoving the last few notebooks into my bag. I need to find my shoes, because I only have two pairs and one set is over at the training center.

The other pair were taken off of me by North.

Fuck, I don't want to think about that man anymore today.

Gabe walks over to me quietly, hesitant, but I don't know why until he holds out a bag to me. "Gryphon gave these to me this morning. He said… fuck, it doesn't matter. They're yours."

I frown at his awkwardness but then when I take the bag and look in, I find my leather boots. I find my motherfucking thrifted, perfect pair of stunning leather boots that I thought had been left behind when the TacTeam grabbed me and I cried over them for *days,* and yet here they are in this little bag.

I burst into tears.

It's so freaking ridiculous and Gabe stares at me in the type of horror that says he's pretty eager to run away from me right now and scrub this moment from his memory forever. Except then he grabs my elbow and pulls me into his chest for a hug, the halting but secure kind that guys do when they're afraid they're going to crush you.

I sob all over him.

I keep my face pressed against the rock hard surface of his perfect chest as I mumble, "They're the best shoes I've ever had and I thought I lost them. Fuck, this is so embarrassing! Both of you need to leave and forget this ever happened. Promise me we'll never talk of this again."

Gabe hums at me, rubbing a hand down my back

like he's still worried I'll scramble his brains if he does something wrong. "You should've just asked him about them. He's not a Draven, he can be reasonable, you know."

I snort at him, probably a mistake with the mess I am, and pull away from him to grab the boots and slide them onto my feet. I instantly feel put together and cute, instead of the haphazardly thrown together kind of sloppy I was feeling three minutes ago.

Gryphon just handed me heaven and the man has no freaking clue.

"Right, so shoes are the way to your heart, got it," Atlas drawls and I glance up at him with a watery smile.

We all grab our bags and head out, locking the door behind us. "Tell me I don't look cute right now, I dare you! I could kill a man today. I could walk into Nox's class and skin the asshole alive wearing these shoes."

Gabe shakes his head at me. "Maybe you shouldn't wear them, now we all know you can back up those threats with action."

It's the first time either one of them has mentioned my gift but he doesn't say another word about it, no pressure or lingering looks about it, so I don't immediately run off into the sunset over it.

I follow the guys down the hall and into the elevator, trusting them to get me out of this rabbit warren of a house because I, once again, have no freaking clue where I am.

Seriously, I need someone to get me a map.

When the elevator doors shut, Gabe hesitates over the floor choice for a second, glancing down at me. "Are we going down to breakfast, or to the garage and eating at the dining hall?"

My nose wrinkles. "Is there a third option?"

Atlas leans forward and chooses the basement. "Yeah, the cafe down the road from campus does good coffee and breakfast burritos."

I open my mouth and he cuts me off, "Don't say a word to me about money right now, Oleander, or I'll go rip North a new asshole for making you feel like shit about this. I know exactly who you are and where you've come from, I'm not worried about covering whatever you need until you're settled in."

I still don't want him to pay for things for me, but I also really don't want to see North this morning, so I just duck my head and nod, staring down at the perfect leather boots again. I worked for the money to pay for them. I hunted in thrift stores with a fistful of dollar bills shoved in my pocket until I found them.

I tell myself that I'll just keep track of what he's paying for and then pay it back the moment I can. If these two are fine with me getting a job and Gryphon said he'd back me, then North has to ease up on it, right?

It's not like he's the boss of us all… right? Jesus, why

is this all so messy?

When the elevator doors open up at the garage again, we walk over to Atlas' Hellcat and Gabe opens the passenger side door for me, seeing me settled and belted up before he climbs in the back.

Atlas raises an eyebrow at him but he just shrugs back. "I'm not leaving Oli's side. I'm guessing you're feeling the same way, and we can't all fit on my bike, so your car it is."

The breakfast burrito is the best thing I've ever put in my mouth and when I moan at the first bite, Atlas roars with laughter at me.

Gabe focuses on his food like a man with a mission, slurping down his coffee in two gulps and then taking out his food in about three bites. I get that he's the size of a small mountain, but it's still so impressive to me how much food he eats, even when it is just the rabbit food he usually sticks to.

"You keep that up, we're not making it to class," Atlas says, directing the car back into the campus rush hour traffic.

I scoff back at him. "We're not making it because no one here knows how to park in a timely manner."

I've never noticed how bad it was before because I'd always walked with Gabe, my attention on how much I didn't want to be around him, but we spent more time trying to get into the parking lot than we did waiting in line at the cafe.

It's ridiculous.

I text Sage to let her know we're here and she replies straight away about heading to us with Sawyer and Felix. I don't even question that the healer is tailing her, after such a close call I'm sure he's been all over her ass.

My opinion of Riley hits a record low because he doesn't feel the same way.

It occurs to me that if Gabe and I are really friends, I now have another ally on team Riley-needs-to-die and I turn around in my seat to give him a look. "What's your take on Riley? I want your opinion before I scramble the dickhead's brain and watch him convulse until he dies."

There's a moment of silence in which I'm sure both of them regret being my Bonds, but then Gabe replies, "He's a fucking dick. He used to fawn all over Sage when we were growing up and I knew they'd be Bonds. You can just tell sometimes, and he was like a protective shield over her at all times… then Giovanna shows up and he drops Sage like she's nothing, I have nothing but hate for him."

I want to point out that he used to defend the guy to me all the damn time but that seems counterproductive right now. It doesn't matter, he realizes he's being a hypocrite and cringes at me. "I know. I know what I said. I was fucking furious that you were insta-friends with Sage the second you got here. You still look at me like I'm the worst thing you've ever seen, but you loved her right away."

Oh God.

A wave of guilt hits me and I force myself not to look at Atlas because he's probably sitting there feeling smug over how easily I accepted him when he arrived too.

I really am the bitch Gabe thinks of me.

When Atlas parks up, I ask him to give Gabe and me a second and he gets out without a word, squeezing my hand and walking over to meet with Sage because he's actually too freaking perfect.

Deep breath, Oli, don't puss out now. "I'm sorry. I needed to keep you away from me because I can't Bond with any of you. Not you, not Atlas, not any of you. What I can do... it can't be allowed to get stronger. That's all I can say. It's terrifying, Gabe. I can feel it even stronger now, and if I let it grow just because I want you all, well, I'm not that selfish. I can't put myself ahead of everyone else like that."

He stares at me for a second and then his eyes flick down to my hands. They're rock steady right now, my gift sitting harmlessly inside of me and my bond content with the smells of them all around me right now.

His voice is low and even as he asks, "That's it, that's the only reason you don't want to Bond? You're afraid of what'll happen if you do?"

I nod and glance out to see Sage smiling at something Sawyer has said, all four of them acting as though they've been friends for a million years and we weren't just abducted by a crazed bunch of militia Gifted.

"I'm not going to force answers out of you. I want them so goddamn much but... but maybe our problems have been because I was making my mind up about how things should be and not just letting us figure it out for ourselves," he says in that same low tone as he watches the others as well. He sounds freaking miserable and I still feel like that worst type of person for doing that to him.

I need to remember that he was a dick too, that this doesn't all land on me. He's made a change and is seeing it through, but that doesn't erase that he was a giant dick to me.

I clear my throat and grab my bag. "No more talking about gifts and Bonds, let's just be friends and get on with... passing all of our classes without killing everyone. We can totally do that, right?"

He scoffs at me and gets out, moving so quickly that he has my door open before I get the chance to get a grip of the handle. I grab his hand to get out of the car but let it go the moment I'm steady on my feet.

There's no point tempting fate.

Sage watches me take two steps towards them before she launches herself at me and my legs buckle under us both, almost taking us to the ground. Almost, because Gabe catches us and keeps us both steady.

Sage squeezes me so hard that my ribs creak as she says, "I can't believe you slept for two whole days and now you're just showing up for class! I'd be locked away for at least a week if I were you."

I laugh and pull away from her to get a good look at her. She's fine, not a mark on her, and I'm sure we have Felix to thank for that. "There's no way I'm going to stay holed up with these two fawning all over me. Can you imagine? I'd end up killing someone... or drinking myself to death."

She giggles and throws Gabe a tight smile. "I forgot to say thanks for calling my parents from the plane. I'm grounded for the rest of my life, or I would be if I wasn't a fully formed adult with my own car, job, and money. My dad tried to follow us to campus today, he was going to just hang out in the back of our lectures all day like a creep. Sawyer had to talk him down."

Sawyer grins at us both and gently pats my shoulder. "We now have a 'Sage and Oli protection' roster. Get used to these faces, girls. We're never leaving either of you alone again. Even Gryphon has a copy of it, he's got a few time slots as well."

Oh God.

I glance at Gabe and he shrugs. "I made him agree not to tell the Dravens."

I scoff at him and try to ignore the looks we're getting from the other students as they pass us all. It's beyond creepy how much they're all whispering and pointing at us, but I'm sure the novelty will wear off eventually. "And you believed him? Those three are all in each other's pockets, there's no way he's going to keep them out of your little plans."

Gabe just shrugs again and scowls at the passing group of girls all talking a little too loudly about the new rumors circulating about me. They're true for once, so there's nothing I can say about it.

Sage glances between us again and then tucks her arm into mine, tugging me along. "I need to stop off at the admin building. I need to sign some paperwork about my class changes now that I'm enrolling in TT."

It takes me two whole steps to process her words and understand them before the squeal rips out of my body. "You're joining TT?! Sage, I love you, but are you sure?"

She giggles at me, both of us ignoring the way the guys are all falling into some weird formation around us as we head off towards the campus. "I told you before that my parents wanted me in the class but I was too scared to do it... well, now I'm too scared not to."

She glances up at Atlas who is at my side, but he doesn't try to interrupt her, just nods at her like he agrees with her decision.

I knew there was a reason he's one of my favorites.

"Oli, if you hadn't— if you didn't come after me, I already know that I'd be dead. You already know that I'm not going to ask questions about how you knew what to do, or how you kept your head about you, but I need to learn that for myself. Plus, Felix and I are pretty sure Vivian has a soft spot for you. I'm pulling the friend card and asking you to get us put together in all of the simulations and scenarios. We'll be unstoppable in there, you scrambling people's brains and me setting them on fire."

I laugh at her a little too loudly, but she's absolutely right.

We're basically super villains in the making and I'm almost pissed that Zoey won't be around to get her ass kicked by us.

Sawyer starts telling Gabe some story about the new guy on their football team, the two of them pairing off behind us even as they watch our surroundings obsessively. I feel better having them both there, knowing that our backs are covered.

Atlas grins at the bloodthirsty look on my face and slings an arm around my shoulder, leaning in to murmur to me, "You'd better get me on your team as well. I can't be left unattended around these people or there'll be hell to pay."

I scoff at him even as the blush climbs up my cheeks at his closeness in front of everyone. He has a casual way of interacting with me, a complete disregard of whether it's appropriate to be touching me, which is both refreshing and terrifying.

My bond likes it a lot.

My brain is once again screaming danger because I can't forget that Bonding is still firmly off the table.

No matter how badly I want them.

J BREE

*M*onster.

The word follows me through all of my classes and the dining hall for lunch. Atlas, Sage, Sawyer, and Felix all follow my lead and just ignore it all. I don't care about any of these people. None of them have tried to be even a little bit tolerant of me, even when they thought I was a giftless reject, so why should I care now that they're all hating me?

I keep my temper in check and just get on with my day. Gabe doesn't.

The moment we step into the building and the whispers start, he glues himself to my side, gently maneuvering Sage out of the way because he knows better than to try to engage with Atlas at this point. He's on edge and watching everyone down the halls and in every lecture hall as though he's waiting for us to be jumped.

I want to believe that he's overreacting but I've lived through too much at this point to brush this off. So instead, I watch everyone with him. I watch all of his friends hesitate before they greet him, keeping a healthy distance away from us. I watch the girls who have all been drooling and fawning over him for months avoid his eyes as they pass us and talk shit about me. I watch everyone who had treated him like the golden child on campus the entire time I've been here turn on him, thanks to me.

It makes my bond and my gift *very* twitchy because I don't really give a fuck about what these idiots think of me, but to treat my bond like that just because he's stuck with me? Nope. Don't like that, not one bit.

When we leave History and head towards the dining hall for lunch, Gabe murmurs with Sawyer until they get Sage secured on the other side of Atlas so that she's sandwiched between him and her brother. I give Gabe a look and he leans down to murmur to me, "Bassinger is indestructible. Who is better to protect you two than a guy who can be a human shield without dying?"

Okay, so when I manage to get the GPS out from under my skin without my brain exploding, I'm going to have to take all of these people with me. There's no question in my mind that I'm going to be finding a bus to fit us all in because maybe we haven't had the best start to our friendships, but I can feel it now, we'll all be rock solid by the end of all of this bullshit.

When we arrive at the dining hall, it's packed and the only good menu option is in high demand, so we get stuck in a line. Atlas jokes around with Sawyer about sport stuff I couldn't care less about and Sage goes over our options for the next history assignment that's coming up. She's way smarter than I am and I'll take all of the help I can get for this one because I know exactly nothing about the Gifted riots in the seventies. The line moves so slowly that by the time we make it to the pizza, there's only a couple of slices left.

Atlas grabs them, plating them up and questioning the server about the wait time for more. When she replies that they're almost ready, he holds a plate out and nudges me to go grab a seat.

I blink at him like an idiot and he grins back. "As if I'd eat before my Bond, go with Ardern and I'll meet you guys over there."

I glance over and find Gabe already sitting there, glaring around at everyone like he has all day. With a sigh, I walk to him, weaving through the crowd, although it's made easier by the sheer amount of people who jerk away from me as though they're afraid to touch me.

I like that.

Gabe has his usual plate of sadness in front of him, salad and protein like a good growing boy, and I take the opportunity to question him now that there's less ears around us for the moment.

"Why do you all care so much about what they're calling me? What do I care if they think I'm a monster?"

He grimaces and glances over his shoulder to where Atlas and the others are all standing together, chatting happily. Atlas meets my eye and smiles at me, checking in on me, and I smile back brightly so he doesn't rush over here and interrupt this.

I need some answers.

"North and Nox have the same dad but different moms, did you know that? Their dad was the Central and he had the nightmare creatures too. Their dad... well, none of us really know what happened, but their dad killed North's mom with his power. He was put to death over it. William Draven, their uncle, took over their seat on the council until North was old enough to take it."

Jesus. That's a whole can of worms I was not expecting from such a simple question. Even though my stomach is roiling at the thought of food right now, I shove some pizza in my mouth just to give myself something else to think about.

Gabe winces at me and then clears his throat to continue, "Other shit happened too, but I'm not— it's not— fuck, I shouldn't be the one to tell you and I probably have half the details wrong anyway. All that matters is that when everyone found out that North and Nox both have the same gift as their father, there was a lot of talk at the time because of it. More than talking, the Council had to intervene. Then... well, Gryphon's power has people on edge. Mine is just as bad. When we all found out that we were in the same Bond, it made a lot of people nervous."

A healer and a shifter made people nervous? They're run-of-the-mill gifts, it makes no sense to me. Except then Hanna's words filter back to me from weeks ago, when her gift had shoved me away from her during TT.

Gryphon Shore is not someone you just decide to piss off on a whim.

I mean, if that isn't a warning that I've misjudged him, I don't know what is.

Gabe glances back and the others are finally getting served, the fresh smells of hot pizza wafting over to us.

He turns back to me and pitches his voice low so they don't overhear him as they head our way, "Nox was barely more than a kid when he was brought back to North when his mom died. There were riots in the community about letting him go to school here. It doesn't matter that their name is on the building, people hate them for what they can do. They hate all of us, Oli. Why do you think we were all so sure you'd been taken when you disappeared? Why do you think North has your every move watched? It's not just because you're a flight risk."

Jesus.

Have I really read this entire community that badly?

Atlas takes the seat next to mine, still laughing with his new best friend Sawyer, and I pitch my voice low just for Gabe again, "I thought everyone here loved you? I was feeling crappy about having them all turn on you for me."

Sage overhears me and gives me sad eyes but they're different these days. Mostly because I know that she's a rock-solid freaking badass under all of that amazing empathy and quiet wit of hers.

She glances around and then murmurs across the table at us, "You mean you didn't know that everyone here are backstabbing, gutless, social climbers who would happily suck up to Gabe when they thought it would help them with their grades and future prospects because of your Bonds, but now that they've been reminded that all of you are like *the* strongest of the Top Tier Gifted, they're back to talking trash like the spineless pieces of shit they all are?"

Even Sawyer stops talking to blink at his sister, the venom dripping from her words because she's clearly so fucking over this place. I'm right there with her, and there is something extra vicious in me at the thought of these people using Gabe for the others.

Maybe the shoes were a terrible idea after all.

I lean back in my chair, grinning at Sage. "Should we set them all on fire or take the ceiling out so that they're all crushed under it? I'm not sure I have enough control yet to fuck them up without hitting one of you guys, sorry. I'm pretty much useless."

I'm loud enough that the table behind us starts packing up and moving out in a hurry, not fucking around with my threats because apparently they must have brains in those skulls of theirs.

Gabe glances at me. "You can't just threaten people, Oli. Not when they all know what you can do."

I watch as Zoey passes our table, her eyes locking on mine, and I make sure she hears my answer, "They don't know half of what I can do, Bond. If they did, they wouldn't dare call me *or* mine a monster."

The whispers stop immediately.

Gutless fucking idiots.

Sage offers to stick around in the library after our classes to start working on our history assignments. I'm nervous about this one, it's the first time I've really felt out of my depth, and I take her up on it with so much relief written all over me that she starts a list of extra readings for me to do once I get back to the Draven manor.

Gabe, Sawyer, and Felix head off to football practice but only once they're sure Atlas is fine to watch us both alone. Felix is particularly vehement about making sure we don't just leave Sage behind when we're done and Sawyer has to remind him that I'd run off into the arms of the Resistance after her the moment I'd heard she was taken.

He grins at me sheepishly but I wave him off with a laugh.

Once they make it back to us, we all split off for the night, Gabe and I piling into Atlas' car with an easy and calm air around us all. It's a million times better than life was even a month ago and I find myself happy, even with every fiber of my being aching.

I pushed it too hard today and I'm feeling it.

When we get back to the manor, I'm ready to eat and pass out and to hopefully avoid any of my other Bonds in the maze-like hallways. There has to be advantages to how colossal this place is, dammit!

When I say this to Gabe, he cringes at me and scratches at the back of his head. "So North messaged earlier and has moved the Bond dinners to Mondays because he's got some council shit on Fridays now."

I blink at him for a second before I find my words. "So you're telling me that I can't just shovel some pasta or bread in my face as I run up to my room because North has decreed that I have to see everyone tonight? I hate that man."

Atlas slings his arm over my shoulder and leads me over to the elevator. "Let's just skip it then. We can order something to be delivered and do our own thing for the night."

I desperately want that.

I also know that North was willing to rip me out of Atlas' bed and drag me here in the middle of the night for daring to disobey him, so it'll never work. "It's fine, better to get it over with now and get Friday nights back. Atlas, I hope you're ready for the most uncomfortable meal you've ever eaten in your life because this is about to get rough."

Atlas scoffs but tugs me closer, pressing his nose into my hair like he needs my scent just as badly as my bond is craving his. I wonder how strongly they all feel the pulls of our connections, whether they crave me as much as I crave them? I doubt it, because they all seem to find the distance between us much easier to handle than I do.

Damn them.

When we get to the dining room, we're the first ones to arrive, small mercies, and we take our usual seats, except now I have Atlas on my other side. I'm hemmed in by the two of them and isn't that just freaking perfect?

"I feel like we're at a wake, except it's just our wills to live that are dead," Atlas murmurs as the kitchen doors open and the house staff begin to serve us dinner.

They usually wait until North is here and summons them. I feel so uncomfortable with them walking around and carrying out a dozen different kinds of foods for us, but the other two just start filling their plates up.

Gabe hesitates for a second before grabbing my plate and filling it for me, grabbing all of the foods he's figured out are my favorites and adding in some of the healthy stuff he lives on. The servers all stare anywhere but at us, which feels a little too much like the students today for my liking.

Now seems like the right time to get information out of him while he's distracted, so I lean over in my seat until I can whisper to him without the server hearing me, "Why is a shifter so scary to them? What are you hiding from me?"

He stiffens in his seat, his fork hovering halfway to his mouth as he freezes, and he clears his throat before he answers, "Why should I tell you anything about my gift, if yours is off limits? I'm happy not to push but you're asking a lot, Bond."

Dammit.

That was the whole reason I haven't already tried to ask him, but thanks to him dropping little hints about how terrifying they all are, I'm now insanely curious.

I pout.

Now that we've found this sort of weird peace between

us, a friendship that's both a lot more than that but not at all a relationship, I feel comfortable enough to do that and know he's not going to call me a spoiled brat or a sullen child like some of my other Bonds would definitely do.

Instead he chuckles at me and murmurs, "If you tell me one thing about your gift, one thing that no one else knows, I'll answer all of your questions. See? I can be generous too."

Ah, so Atlas' little dig about covering things for me has really taken a hold under his skin. It's fine, I can't stop them from fighting or make them be friends, but it's also a little like watching all of the problems we're going to have down the track start to brew.

It might make me the biggest bitch in the world but I'm absolutely going to take it and use it to my advantage here. I have so little power in this Bond with all of these men, not with a gift that could end us all and the Resistance looking everywhere for me, so I need to just use what I can and let the cards fall where they may.

"Deal. Not right now but… later, I can do that."

He smirks at me right as Gryphon walks in covered in mud, a bruise blooming on his cheek. My bond immediately takes offense at the sight of it, my gift bursting out of me to heal him so quickly there's no stopping it. Gabe startles but doesn't yelp and dive away from me, which I'm taking as progress.

Atlas watches me and carefully moves his hand on the table closer to mine so that we're not quite touching but he's showing me he's here if I need him.

I don't say a word and the moment my gift settles back into me, I pick up my fork with a shaking hand, ignoring how ridiculous I must look trying to eat like that.

"You didn't need to do that," Gryphon says, taking a seat in his usual spot down the table from us.

I shrug and try not to look as shaken as I feel. "I can't help it. My bond doesn't like seeing you guys injured, even if it is just a bruise."

I can feel all three sets of eyes on me but I start in on my food, ignoring them as best I can.

Less than a minute later North stalks in, a savage look on his face as he takes us all in, but his eyes stay glued to the plate in front of me. I glance down at it but there's nothing wrong with the food there, no contraband that he could get pissed off about sitting amongst the peas and corn, so I just keep my eyes down and get to finishing off the plate.

"What happened? Why is Oleander using her gift?" he says, pulling out his chair and taking a seat. He looks so agitated, I'm not sure how he thinks he's going to be able to eat in that state.

I shove a forkful into my mouth so I don't have to answer him but Gryphon is quick to supply, "She healed me and she didn't mean to. We should all make sure we're not showing up here injured or pissed off until she has more of a handle on her gift, now that she's got it again."

He says it all in such a matter of fact way that North doesn't question it at all and just turns to look at me like I've grown a new head or suddenly started speaking a dead language.

"Noted. I'll speak to Nox about it later as well, he's… tied up."

Tied up.

There's a whole lot of nope behind those words and I don't want to know about it at all. It's not until we're all eating again, North and Gryphon talking about council business amicably, that the door opens again, because of course I'm not going to get through this dinner without facing them all.

Of course.

Nox stalks in with one of his usual girls, Lana, tucked in under his arm and once again, my bond ignores it. He's really managed to piss it off, which is helpful because he's not easing up on his dickish behavior at all.

When Lana tries to grab the chair next to Gryphon, he stops her and snaps, "Out. You're not welcome."

The room falls quiet and Nox's eyes shift between Gryphon and me. I try not to look guilty, which should be easy because I've done nothing wrong, but I think I fail miserably.

Lana giggles but it's an awkward sound. "But Nox invited me, you just want me to leave?"

Gryphon raises his eyebrows at her and I've never been so uncomfortable in my life. "I'm not asking you, I'm telling you to leave this house right now. Either you do it yourself, or I make you."

She takes a step away from him slowly, as though she's afraid he's about to strike with... whatever the hell he can do.

Am I the only person who doesn't know what all of my Bonds are capable of?

No one says a word to intervene, and North even picks his knife and fork back up to get back to his meal, the clearest dismissal of this entire mess that I've ever seen. Nox watches as Lana walks out, her shoulders slumped in a way that should make me feel sorry for the girl, but also fuck her because she knows he has a Bond. She knows and she came here in an attempt to rub their sex life in my face.

Shit.

Don't think about any of them having sex lives without you, Oli. Your bond is already feeling delicate and volatile!

Sure enough, my fingers tremble with the power of my gift swirling through my veins, ready to strike out at any of them who might dare to want another woman instead of me. I shift in my seat, shrinking back from Atlas and

Gabe so I don't accidentally destroy one of them with my jealous bond.

I squeeze my eyes shut and take a deep breath, my head swirling with all of the emotions I won't let myself feel but that my bond is writhing with. Jealousy, anger, wrath, blood, pain, *destroy them all*.

Fuck, my periods are going to be next level now that my gift is back, I can freaking tell already.

"That's why you need to quit provoking her until we know what she can do. No more women. No more, Nox."

My eyes snap open at the sound of Gryphon's voice to find him pointing at me with a glare pointed in Nox's direction. I'm so focused on the two of them that I startle when Atlas' fingers slide against my own, threading them together until he's got a hold of me. I glance down at them and look at him with all of the shock and fear that I'm feeling at him willingly touching me.

He smirks at me, then leans over to murmur in my ear, "Bombproof, remember?"

God, I hope he really is.

I hope he'll survive me.

The rest of dinner is uneventful but uncomfortable as hell, thanks to Nox's antagonistic presence. I've never seen North or Gryphon go head to head with him before, or even just attempt to rein him in a little, so it's almost amusing to watch them shut him down every time he so much as looks in my direction.

The very idea that they could've been doing this for me all along but chose not to is like an itch under the skin, niggling at me and impossible to ignore.

I don't want to eat dessert but when North slides a slice of the baked cheesecake in front of me before heading out for another one of his meetings, all of my plans to run back to my room disappear because, my God, does his chef know how to do desserts right.

Even Atlas takes a second slice.

Once we're done, Atlas and Gabe head back to my room with me, both of them fussing over me when I stumble a little getting into the elevator. My feet feel as though they weigh a thousand pounds and it's hard to make them work right. Gabe offers to carry me, grinning and joking around, but I'm also pretty sure he'd do it if I actually said yes to him.

As we get to my room, North comes around the corner from his end of the hallway, the fact that his room is only a few feet away from mine popping back into my head.

Jesus, don't think about that, Oli.

I'm perfectly ready to just duck into my room and pretend that we haven't crossed paths here, but right as I get the keys into the door, he stops in front of us and says, "Oleander, a word."

No please, no explanation, no attempt at telling me what it is that he wants, just another command that I'll be hearing him out.

I turn to face him but Atlas is already drawling, "Unlikely, Draven. I'm not spending the rest of the night dealing with whatever bullshit you're here to throw at her this time."

North's eyes cut across to him as he snaps, "I will speak to my Bond, in private, for a minute and then she'll be free to spend the rest of the evening with you two. There's no ulterior motive here."

Atlas steps in close to my side, shifting so he's covering me just a little and a half step away from shielding me completely. It's such a casually protective move, something he does on instinct but that makes me feel absolutely safe and... loved.

I haven't felt loved in a very long time.

"I know exactly what happened the last time I trusted her to your care, so no, I don't think I'll take you at your word, Draven."

Gabe's eyes flick to mine but I instantly look away. I don't want that on me today, I don't want their opinions of what happened and their judgements of me. I know that Atlas believes that I'm absolutely a victim, which isn't true, but I also know that North probably thinks his brother did nothing wrong, which is also not true.

A mess.

Everything is a fucking mess.

North's jaw tightens and then he looks back over at me. I can see just how angry he is under all of that carefully put together calm of his, all of the tightly restrained rage at having Atlas question him and call him out.

I don't want things to get worse. I grab Atlas' hand and give it a squeeze. "It's okay, I'll be a minute. Grab a shower and we can study afterwards."

Gabe opens the door and holds it open for Atlas, a

clear sign that he's happy to take my word for it, but Atlas takes a second before he steps away, every inch of his body practically vibrating with rage and frustration.

He leans down to brush his lips against my cheek softly, a small lifeline to let me know that none of his attitude has anything to do with me, and then he stalks into my room, shutting the door firmly behind him.

I force my hands into my pockets so I don't fidget with them and give away just how nervous I am to be standing here with him. I'm not scared, nothing about North scares me, but I'm also sure that he would be able to destroy me with only a few carefully chosen words and I'm so tired, so bone-achingly tired, thanks to the long day on campus.

I'm desperate to just pass out.

"You look exhausted."

That's not at all what I was expecting out of him and words tumble out of me without thought and harsher than I intend them to be, "I am, but I have no choice but to pass, right? This is what following your orders looks like. Is there a real reason we're talking, or are you just hoping to pick me apart? If you don't like my outfit, you'll have to go to Gryphon. He's the one who refuses to wear a little color."

His eyes flick down to the black hoodie I'm drowning in but he doesn't rise to my bait. There's something in his eyes that makes me feel defensive, something that says he's not happy about me wearing my Bond's clothing, and I have to remind myself that Gryphon never came to my room without leaving something behind for me. He's seen me wearing them, he's never said a word to me about it, it's not like I stole them.

Jesus.

North probably thinks I *did* steal them and is going to bitch me out about that too. Why isn't he saying anything? Why is he leaving me here to spiral about all of the possibilities of what this could all be about?

"If you need a tutor or more help with your classes, I will provide you with it. Whatever you need to succeed, you'll have it."

I try to keep the frown off of my face. "I'm handling it. I can do it, I'm not stupid. Is this... it? Are you just checking up on me or is there something you need?"

He scowls at me for another second and then shakes his head. "Bassinger is making a problem of himself on your behalf, he wants you to have access to a job and money of your own. I still don't believe that it's a good idea, but you've convinced enough of your Bonds that you have good intentions, so I'm not going to stop you anymore. You will be at dinner on Mondays and your grades are to stay stable but as long as you're within your curfews and perimeters, then you can spend your afternoons and weekends however you want."

My mouth drops open and I'm sure I look like an absolute idiot, but he just turns on his heel and stalks back in the direction he came from without a word.

A job.

Money.

Freedom, a new wardrobe, buying my own breakfast when we're avoiding eating around my Bonds, this is the greatest gift anyone has ever given me.

I turn back around to my door, the key still sitting in the lock, thanks to Gabe's forethought, and when I get into the room, I find Atlas standing there, waiting for me with an agitated look on his face.

I launch myself into his arms.

He has great reflexes and catches me, pulling me up and into his chest so that we're fused together in a way that my bond likes a little too much.

"What happened? What did he do? I'll kill him," he mutters, his hands clutching at me in a very respectful, but desperate, sort of way. Like he's groping at me, but not in any of the places that would make it sexual, which is both a terrible and great thing.

"Nothing. He's— I can get a job, Atlas! I can work and earn money and buy a pair of jeans that actually make my ass look good," I ramble at him, close to tears but holding it together.

He chuckles at me and slips his hand down to give my

ass a quick squeeze, the tiniest stretch of the boundaries he's been so good about respecting. "I dunno, it already looks fucking perfect to me. I'll be spending all of my time in cold showers if it gets any better."

I scoff at him but only squeeze him tighter because he gave me this. He came here after I ran away from him with nothing but acceptance and a willingness to fight for me when I have nothing to offer him.

If I could do it without risking everything, I'd Bond with him right the hell now. I'd do it without hesitation, ready to commit to him for the rest of our lives, because this is a good man and, fuck, do I need one of those.

"Do you two need a minute?" Gabe says, sarcasm dripping but with the sort of hesitance where it's clear that he's expecting us to kick him out.

I break away from Atlas, a blush creeping up my cheeks, and mumble, "I need a shower, it's been a long day."

I hear the sound of someone getting punched and Gabe grunting, but I don't look back to see them bickering again.

I wake up to the first knock on my bedroom door and I know instantly that it's one of my Bonds out there, waiting impatiently to come in as they knock again. Gabe grunts in his sleep and shifts but doesn't actually wake up from his nest on the floor while Atlas rolls towards me like he's planning on physically covering me again.

I can't hide from them forever, no matter how much I might want to.

"Wait here, I'll see who it is and what the hell they could want at this time of the morning," I murmur. He must be tired because he just mumbles agreeably as he sinks back down onto the pillows.

I'd crawled into bed straight after the shower last night but since it was so early, Gabe had put a movie on and climbed into the bed with me and Atlas, sandwiching me between them both. I'd drifted in and out of sleep for hours, comfortable and completely at peace with lying around with the two of them.

I have no memory of the two of them getting ready for bed or Gabe moving onto the floor and as I carefully step around him to get to the door, I decide that we need to figure something out because he can't keep sleeping down there.

When I get the door cracked open, the hallway light almost blinds me and I'm sure I look terrible as I blink and squint at Gryphon. He looks perfectly awake and put together, except for once, he's not dressed in his usual attire of jeans, a jacket, and biker boots. Nope, there he is in shorts, sneakers, and a hoodie.

He looks delicious.

"Wha— what time is it? Is the world ending? Why are you here at the ass-crack of dawn looking like *that*?" I croak, and he glances down at himself but doesn't comment on it.

"I'm taking over your training. Go get dressed in your workout gear, we're going for a run."

I groan, because why— why?!— but I do as he says, trying to move quietly around the room. He holds the door open and watches as I disappear into the closet and then when I come out and murmur to Atlas where I'm going.

I don't want him assuming anything or giving Gabe shit about being on the floor, so I crouch down to him as well, attempting to wake him up but when he snores through it, I just kiss his cheek and head back over to Gryphon.

His eyes are a little too intense for me this early in the morning but, as always, he doesn't say anything, just leads me to the elevator and then out of the manor.

It's still dark out and I'm a little worried about ending up flat on my face on the asphalt but Gryphon doesn't seem so concerned about it.

"Keep up, I don't want you getting lost."

I huff and roll my eyes at him. "Well don't forget that your legs are twice as long as mine and I'm sure we'll be fine."

He takes off and sets a brutal pace, I'm sure as

punishment for my smart mouth, but there's no better way to get me to follow orders than by suggesting I'm incapable of doing something.

I'll keep up with him if it fucking kills me.

It might, his breath barely changes and when we finally come across a gym and slow down, I'm gasping and sputtering like a fish out of water. I think I can taste blood. That's bad, right? Fuck, my lungs have probably just exploded in my chest and I'm about to die out here.

Gryphon stands there and watches me gasp for air for a second before he says, "This is where we'll be training. From now on, you'll meet me here at five each morning."

Five in the morning.

He's got me awake and running down here for a five a.m. start? I'll murder him. Fuck the consequences, I'm scrambling his brain. Except my gift is also exhausted from the run, or a little in love with the sight of Gryphon's ass in those shorts, because even with how bloodthirsty I'm feeling, it's oddly absent.

Maybe it's picking favorites.

Gryphon leads me down the path towards the gym and then uses a swipe card to get in. He hits the lights and I get to take the space in while he walks around opening it up and getting the AC running. It's on the smaller side, but all of the equipment is brand new and in great condition, everything is high end and meticulously laid out.

It's exactly the type of place I'd imagine Gryphon working out.

"Get on the mats and stretch out, we're going through your stances and control issues today. Once I'm sure you won't lose control and fry me, we can move on to more advanced training."

Stretching sounds lovely and I all but collapse onto the mats. I'm thorough about actually doing the stretches though, I learned that shit the hard way after my first TT class when I'd just gone home and then couldn't walk without crying for three days.

He watches me, critiquing me and making adjustments to what I'm doing with a blank face. He's so hard to read, impossible really, because he's so goddamn calm and calculating. He just watches my every move and then makes his assessments.

"Alright, that's enough. Up and show me what you remember of your stances. Your foot positioning needs some serious work."

Still, I keep my mouth shut. What's the point arguing with someone who actually knows what they're talking about? Plus, he's not being intentionally cruel… he just has no idea that hearing that I'm inadequate from any of my Bonds is literal torture and that I'd rather die than continue this.

I start working through the stances Gabe had talked me

through as Gryphon strips down to just his workout shorts, his chest already glistening with sweat from the run over here, and immediately my bond fills my brain with all sorts of prohibited ideas. Prohibited because there's no way I can shove him back on the mats and run my tongue up his pecs, grab a fistful of his hair, and shove his face between my legs and—

"What the hell are you thinking about? Your bond is humming right now."

I blanch and turn around on the spot, groaning and smacking a hand over my face. "It's your fault! My bond is a whiney, horny little bitch and you're waving a goddamn red flag at it right now. Put a shirt on!"

I cringe, cursing my fat mouth for just blurting that out, but then he starts laughing and I'd like to just die now, please and thank you. There's nothing quite like telling your Bond that you're thinking about fucking them and having them *laugh* in return.

Fuck this.

I can totally find my way home.

I make it one step before he hooks a hand around my elbow and drags me back. "You're not getting out of this just because your bond is acting up. Move into the next stance."

I want to kick him in the nuts and run for the hills but instead, I just grit my teeth and do as I'm told, muttering under my breath, "No, it's fine. I love being laughed at. This is fine."

He scowls at me and tells me to adjust my stance, walking around the mats barking out more orders until he reaches a duffle bag over by the weight machines and bends down to grab a shirt.

I don't know whether to be relieved or furious that he's covering up, but it sure does help my concentration.

He doesn't let me leave for a full hour of working through those stupid positions and when we're done, there's no choice but to run back to the manor together.

The sun is up and I do my best to actually take notice of where we're going so I have a chance of getting back here tomorrow. Gryphon doesn't say anything else to me and when we get back to the manor, he heads to the opposite side of the house as where my room is.

It takes me three attempts to get back to my room and I start to think that maybe the walls here move as well, because how can it be *this* freaking hard?!

I have to knock on my own bedroom door because I forgot to grab the keys, but Gabe opens the door for me with a smile that drops when he gets a look at me.

"What the hell happened to you? Shit, did you run into Nox on the way back up?"

I huff and stalk past him towards the shower, avoiding Atlas' eyes from where he's pulling on a jacket by the bed.

"Nope, thank God. I just got humiliated by a man who gives zero fucks about my feelings. I played nicely, I didn't deserve that shit. Excuse me while I drown myself in the shower."

Hot water fixes most things, and when I step out to brush my teeth in front of the mirror, I force myself to watch my reflection and take everything in. The silvery strands of my hair falling in wet clumps over my shoulders now that the lavender rinse has washed out again. The bags under my eyes because my body has been pushed too much lately and I need to try to sleep a bit better soon. The paleness of my skin that is worse than normal.

No wonder they all find it so goddamn easy to steer clear of me.

I'm a mess.

I give myself the time it takes to blow-dry my hair to wallow in self-pity and then I put on a brave face to walk back out and get dressed. All I need now is for Atlas to charge downstairs to beat Gryphon up over my honor to really make this day something special.

No thanks.

I step out of the bathroom wrapped in my towel again but this time, neither of them react as I duck into the closet to get changed. I pull on panties, jeans, and a bra easily but when I go looking for a sweatshirt, I find that they're all gone.

All of them.

I panic a little, my bond causing chaos in my chest, and when I tug open the drawers, I find them there. All four of Gryphon's sweaters and hoodies, folded neatly because the maids have washed them.

I burst into tears again.

This shit is getting fucking ridiculous, why has my gift turned me into a blubbering mess?

"Sweetness, if you're not decent, you need to grab something, and fast, because I'm coming in there," Atlas calls out and I barely get the towel lifted back up to my chest before he ducks into the closet with me, his eyebrows pulled down tight. "What's happened? What's wrong?"

I hold the hoodie up but I have no words left. Nothing.

Gabe steps into my view, more hesitant than Atlas, but still just as concerned for my mental state. Jesus, they're stuck with a crying, murderous, monster Bond.

Atlas glances back at him and says, "Give her your shirt."

Gabe scowls at him for a second and then glances over to where I'm sitting, still miserable at the sight of Gryphon's washed and neatly folded sweatshirt. I'm surprised Atlas figured it out that quickly but he's been too attentive from the word go.

Gabe swallows and then strips off his shirt obediently, handing it over to me and then watching with a kind of awe when I tug it on over the towel before letting it drop away, taking a deep breath, and letting my bond calm the hell down in my chest.

"I'm sorry—" I start but Atlas cuts me off.

"It's the Bond. This isn't you, Oli. It's your bond wanting us all to stay close to you since we're not Bonded. Don't cry, we'll fix this."

Gabe's eyes flare and he blows out a breath, running his hand through his hair and tugging at the ends a little. He looks as messed up as I feel about it, but at least Atlas is thinking clearly.

"Okay. You know where everyone's rooms are, right, Ardern? We need clean, but worn, shit from them all. We can ask Gryphon, but get shirts from the other two, shit that's easy for her to hide under sweatshirts and hoodies from the rest of us," Atlas says, immediately going into protective Alpha mode and for once, Gabe takes it on the chin, nodding and rummaging in his bag for his football jacket to pull on.

I eye it off because that one looks cozy too, but it would also come down to my knees, so it's not exactly practical.

Gabe gives him a nod and then turns back to me. "I'll grab them. I have another idea too, but I'll sort it out, Bond."

Fuck, I hope so because this feeling in my chest is unbearable.

I need to get out of this fucking house now.

There are two cafes open close to the campus that *aren't* owned by Gryphon's sister and when I ask Atlas to stop by them both so I can hand in my resume, Gabe insists on coming in with me. Parking is a bitch so even though I know Atlas wants to be with me, watching my every move and supporting me through every little moment of my life, he has to drop us off and drive around the block.

I try to argue with Gabe about coming in, I'll only be a couple of minutes, but I get shot down by them both.

"Do I have to remind you both of what I can do? The very tip of the iceberg is destroying people's brains, I think I can walk into a cafe by myself," I snark at them both, but it's no use, they only really stop arguing with each other when it comes down to my safety and overall well-being.

Gabe ignores me and grabs my door, flipping off the car behind us when they blast their horn at us for stopping. This entire campus is stupid, I'm hating it more and more as the days go on.

We weave through the cars and crowd together, the paths are busy this time in the morning, and I try to ignore the way that people scatter away from me as though I'm here to kill them all and drink their blood for breakfast.

"Gloria owns this place, I can talk to her if you want," Gabe says as he pushes the door open, holding it and waving me through first.

I try not to get flustered and shy about him acting chivalrous again. "No, I want to do this myself. I need to."

He nods and steps into line behind me, looking at the muffin selection as though he'll actually eat one. He's so unpredictable about food that maybe he will, but I also won't be surprised if he orders a salad to go.

My stomach explodes with butterflies when it's finally my turn and I ask the girl to speak to the manager about any openings. She looks me up and down, huffing before she calls out for Gloria. I step to the side and let her serve Gabe, forcing my face to stay neutral when she starts flirting with my eight-pack hottie.

Yup, I said it. He's mine, my bond is very attached, and even though I can't do a thing with him, I don't want some hot cafe girl giggling and batting her eyelashes at him.

He's polite but firm as he turns her down and orders coffee for us all, plus some of the muffins. When he orders the triple choc one, I start to plan out how I'm going to force a bite of it out of him without using my gift to scramble his brain. I need that sugar rush.

My bond is messing with my head so bad right now, I feel like I'm permanently PMS-ing.

I'm still fantasizing about that muffin when the kitchen door swings open and a curvy older woman walks out, her apron covered in flour and powdered sugar. She smells like cake in the best possible way.

"You're looking for a job? Have you got a resume?"

Straight to the point, she just raises an eyebrow at me and holds out a hand for me to pass her the newly-updated resume Atlas had printed out for me this morning. He'd officially moved into the Draven manor, giving up the lease for his apartment and moving into the room next to Gabe's. He'd fought with North over being closer to me, but there's only three rooms on the third level and North wouldn't budge on it.

Atlas had enjoyed pointing out that it doesn't matter anyway, he's the one sleeping in my bed every night.

"Oleander Fallows… you've moved around a lot, are you planning on staying here, or am I going to lose you in a month's time?"

Oh God. "No ma'am, I'm attending college here at

93

Draven. I'm not going anywhere anytime soon."

She nods but her face is still pretty stern-looking, like she's not impressed with me at all. I try not to take it personally or get disheartened. There's other options out there.

"I run a tight ship, it's a busy shop. If you're hoping for an easy ride, you'll need to go down the road to Fleur's place."

I clear my throat and choose my words carefully, "I'm a hard worker, I'm not looking for a handout. If you take me on, I'll make sure you don't regret it."

She just stares at me for a second with her eyebrow raised and I start to sweat a little. I definitely want to prove myself to her, prove that I'm not a flake or just some lazy college student looking to take advantage of her.

"I have some time this afternoon to train you, be here at two, ready to impress me," she says finally, turning around and heading back out to the kitchens without another word.

I blow out a breath and head back over to Gabe who is drinking his coffee and wincing when it burns his tongue. He smiles tightly to the girl behind the counter when she calls out a goodbye to him and then he ushers me out of there quickly.

I murmur to him, "That woman is terrifying."

"Kitty? She's a nightmare, keeps trying to touch me like I don't know what power she has. Someday she's going to go down for assault."

We stop at the bus stop and wait for Atlas to make his way back down the street to us. "I meant Gloria, she didn't really want to employ me. Wait, what can Kitty do? Is she the cashier?"

He grimaces and hands me my coffee. "Yeah, she's a Neuro. Not really strong though, she has to be touching you, but I've seen her making out with guys at parties in front of their girlfriends just to get back at them for other shit. The guys had no idea what she was doing or what had happened until their girlfriends told them."

I look back at the cafe as though I could take her out from here just for attempting to touch him. I mean... I could. Maybe that's the truth I'll give him in exchange for knowing all about what his gift is.

"She kept trying to touch my hand, she's been after my number for a while. I've never given it to her or her friends, obviously."

I clear my throat and glance down at our feet. "I'm going to say something and it's absolutely not my bond talking, Gabe. She touches you, manipulates you like that, I'll kill her. My gift would do it without my control for sure, but even once I have a handle on it again, I'll have her bleeding out of her ears in a fucking heartbeat."

He turns to stare at me, still unsure of me. "I've bragged about girls before and you've watched a dozen girls come to dinner with Nox. I didn't take you for the jealous type."

I shrug and wave at Atlas as he gets closer to us to make sure he sees us in the crowd. "I am. I just don't have a leg to stand on, half the time. Am I allowed to tell you guys that if I see someone smile at you I want to gouge their eyes out? That sitting at that stupid council dinner with North wasn't so bad until I realized he'd fucked the lady next to me? I'm a hypocrite, I can't bond—"

The car pulls up but Gabe grabs my arm to stop me from climbing in. "Oli, the Bonding is the least of my issues here. I thought you didn't want us... I thought you didn't want *me*."

I open my mouth but then the car behind Atlas honks their horn and we have to get in. Everyone on this damned campus is impatient as hell. Gabe gets my door for me even though it'll take longer because he doesn't give a shit about making them wait. When Atlas pulls back out and drives extra slow just to piss them off a little more, I roll my eyes at him, gulping down my coffee. Gabe hands Atlas one and then hands me the bag of muffins.

I stare at it for a second and he scoffs at me. "Like I didn't know you'd want the chocolate 'heart attack in the making' muffins, Bond. I'm sure the sugar high will get you through class today without gouging any eyes out."

They just might.

When I pull on the apron that Gloria hands me, she taps her foot, impatient even though I'm moving quickly and confidently. I've worked at a dozen different cafes over the last five years, this is going to be a breeze for me. I'm hoping it's as busy as she says it's going to be, because there's nothing I love more than a challenge and being so busy that five hours pass like they're nothing.

The moment I told them both about my trial shift, I had forbidden Atlas and Gabe from being here and it had taken the entire day to get them to agree. Surprisingly, Atlas gave in first, mostly because I once again pointed out to them both that I could kill anyone who looked sideways at me and I would. I absolutely would. Gabe literally just watched me ruin a hundred Resistance to save our asses, like I wouldn't do it to someone who was stupid enough to attack me at the cafe.

So I get to work without the protective shield that the two of them have become, but also without the pressures of them watching. It's easy to slip into being Oli-the-worker again, the girl who scrimped and saved and made her own way in the world, even when it was so fucking hard that I slept in my car on the streets sometimes because I couldn't make rent in any of the share houses I could find.

After only an hour, I get a handle on the way this place runs and confidently start serving customers, running the counter and taking the food and drinks out to the tables without any trouble. A little after four, a group of professors from Draven walk in together and grab a booth. I sigh with relief that Nox isn't with them just a little too soon.

He arrives a minute later, sneering at the very sight of me.

Kitty takes their orders, grinning and flirting away, but they all seem to know her game and avoid her touch. It's gross to me that they know what she does and yet she's still out here in the community being a danger to everyone.

Something to snap at North and the useless council about later.

When their orders are up, I don't want to serve them, but I also really want this job, so I paste a smile on my face and bring them their coffees, the picture of professionalism even when Nox's lip continues to curl in my direction.

I hate him.

His co-workers don't comment on it or treat me badly. I don't have any of them as professors but I've seen them around campus enough to be sure that they definitely teach there.

I get back into the afternoon rush and almost forget they're even there. Well, except for whenever I accidentally glance that way and catch Nox seething in my direction, then I certainly remember he's there and hating every second of me being here.

I almost got through my entire shift without incident, almost. Half an hour before closing, a group of footballers and frat boys come in and order enough triple shots to kill a man. Kitty is in heaven with all of the testosterone in the room but I do my best to skirt around it. They all notice me working there and I hear a few comments, but I block it all out like a pro.

When I head over to clean one of the newly vacant tables, one of the frat boys stands up and moves into my path, so quickly that I almost smack into him but, again, this isn't my first rodeo and I spin around him without missing a beat.

"Where are you heading off to? I'm trying to ask you out. We haven't seen you at any of the parties on campus yet, does being a part of the Monster Bond mean you're too good for us 'lower tiers'?"

I put the tray on the service counter and meet Gloria's eye through the window. I keep the smile on my face because I've sat through bond dinners with Nox and North tearing strips off of me before… does this guy really think I'm afraid of the word monster?

I know exactly what I am.

"I'm not the partying type, but thanks for asking. I'm sure Kitty would love an invite, I'll pass the invite on to her," I say brightly, moving around him to clear up the next empty table, but his hand shoots out to grip my arm.

Oh, so he wants to die? Perfect, my gift is hungry.

Nope, I need to stop that. I can't even joke about it right now because I'm too raw at the moment and my gift is just looking for a reason to lash out.

I try to tug my arm away but he doesn't let go. "You really should let me go—"

He leans into me, his bond reaching out to mine like he's testing me and, goddamn, does my bond hate the feel of it. "Why, what are you going to do to me, monster?"

There's a gasp behind us but I can't look away from the frat boy because I don't know his gift, he could have something physical.

I really don't want to get punched or bitten right now, thanks.

Then I see the black smoke curl round his arm, sliding up towards his neck before it coils around him until he lets me go, clutching at it as though he could possibly stop Nox's gift from cutting off his airway.

When he drops down to his knees, I take a step back and find myself pressed against my Bond.

This is bad.

The entire room is silent, only the quiet music over the speakers to be heard, and then Nox steps around me to crouch down over the frat boy, his eyes black voids, so like my own.

He uses his professor voice on him, that calm and professional tone that screams disciplinarian. "Branson, let this be a lesson to you that you should never provoke monsters. Miss Fallows is just trying to work. There's no reason for you to be harassing her, and if I find out you've been in here again, I'll do a lot more than choke you."

Branson nods, a small jerk of his head as his cheeks turn purple, and then the smoke fades away to nothing and Nox's eyes shift back to their usual dark blue hue.

I step away from them both, setting my tray down on the cluttered table and beginning to clear it up. I'll fake it until I make it, forcing myself to act as though this is nothing and hope that the rest of the cafe does the same.

As I begin to wipe the table down, I hear the bell ring over the door as Branson leaves and then, slowly, people get back to their coffees, murmuring to each other about Nox Draven and his Bond.

I take a deep breath before I head back into the kitchens, fully prepared for Gloria to fire me on the spot for bringing this drama into her business.

Nox is already in there getting the talking to of his life, I'm sure.

"— and of all the ways to defuse the situation, you chose to use your gift? Really, that was your only option? I've seen you throw a punch, you should've just knocked the little asshole out."

Okay, Gloria knows what's up. I like her a little more.

I place the tray down by the sink, starting to load the industrial dishwasher up and rinsing off the plates as I go. She turns to me and says, "You handled that well. You're doing a great job, keep your head down and everyone will forget who you are around here soon enough."

I swallow and nod, ducking my head and getting back into the task in front of me. "Thank you, I'll do that."

I finish up the closing shift, scrubbing down every single surface I come across and getting the floor to shine. I feel really good when I walk out of there, my apron and all of the employment paperwork in my hands, because the job is mine.

It's late enough that the sun is setting, the colors of the sunset beautiful and haunting across the sky, and I'm distracted for a second taking a photo on my phone, so I miss Nox stepping out in front of me until it's too late and I crash right into him.

"Oof, Jesus, sorry— oh. What are you doing here?" I ramble, bending down to grab my phone from where I've dropped it.

He sneers at me and flicks an arm out at the mostly-empty street. "Making sure you don't get jumped and lose control over yourself all over again, obviously."

I glance down the street but there's no sign of the

Hellcat or Gabe's bike to be seen, so I guess I'm not about to be saved here. Might as well do the right thing so it doesn't get thrown in my face later, though the high road sucks ass. "Thanks for helping me out. You didn't have to but I appreciate that you did."

He huffs out a cruel laugh. "I wasn't helping you, I was stopping North from shutting the campus down over the riot you would've caused when you lost control, Poison."

Poison, monster, I really am collecting a whole bunch of new names since I came to Draven.

I roll my eyes at him. "Like your nightmare creatures aren't going to start a riot, don't pin this on me."

He leans into me to murmur, "Everyone here knows exactly what I can do. There wasn't a man, woman, or child in that cafe who didn't know exactly who I was. You're the mystery, the anomaly, the rumor of madness incarnate. If you had confirmed all of their fears, then it would've taken more than a TacTeam to clean the mess up."

I really don't want to stand here and listen to this bullshit. With his bond reaching out to mine, it all feels as though he's fishing for information, trying to get me to slip up and tell him something vital.

The worst part is... I want to. I want to tell him about every person I've ever used my power against, just to prove myself to him, to prove that I did the right thing when I went on the run and stayed the hell away from this place.

"I've never met someone whose eyes turn black, not outside of our family anyway. It was our curse. I wonder who's curse you're holding, Poison?"

Curse? That seems a little too mystical and magical for me. It doesn't matter that I can literally manipulate souls inside of living beings, I don't believe in curses.

That's childish bullshit that people play make believe with to ostracize and villainize people with.

"Well… thanks for stepping in and saving me, even if it was just for North. I need the job and it would have sucked to lose it before I even got the chance to work."

He ignores me, stalking over to the Bentley at the curb and opening the driver door. "Get in. I already told Ardern that we're on our way home."

Jesus, that's going to go down well. We might not even have a manor to return to if Atlas has caught wind of this, but I slide into the car with him and seal my lips shut, even as his bond slides over my skin like a pointed caress.

I give him nothing.

My phone pings and I check to find a message from Atlas waiting for me.

He touches you, he dies.

I blow out a breath and let my head fall back against the seat with a thump. There's movement in the air around my hands and I look down to see a little creature of smoke sitting on my lap. It should not look as cute as it does but

I've always had a soft spot for Dobermans and the puppy curling up there is freaking adorable.

Is it bad that I think it's adorable?

"Is this thing about to bite me or consume me or something?"

He ignores me and then drawls at me, "Tell Bassinger that he can drop the savior act. You didn't say no and you didn't use your gift to break me. There's no way he can say a fucking thing about it anymore because you weren't some little giftless Bond, were you, Poison?"

Oh God, I would rather open the car door and throw myself into oncoming traffic than sit here and have this conversation with him.

Wait.

"Your little creatures are spies? Wow. Get off me then, you little cretin!" I attempt to flick the smoke creature off of my lap but my finger just passes through it, the smoke splitting and then coming back together as if nothing happened.

Nox ignores me but when he changes gears, the creature glides across the car and then tucks under his ear until it's obscured by his hair. It's just a bit too freaking adorable for me to get my head around. The man who loathes me and tortures me at every turn has a little smoke friend hiding in his hair.

I want to giggle.

I can't, he'll spit more fire at me and ruin my whole goddamn day.

When we pull up to the manor and the garage door opens, we find the rest of my Bonds standing there in a very heated argument that only stops as they all turn as one to look at the car.

The second the engine cuts off, Atlas starts towards the car, only stopping when Gryphon plants himself in front of him. I can see his lips moving but no sound makes it through the car to me.

Nox mutters at me, "More trouble than you're worth, Poison."

I don't attempt to answer him, there's no point because he isn't known for listening to reason, but when my eyes catch North staring through the tinted window at me, I gulp. He looks murderous and I have no idea what I could've possibly done to get him staring at me like that.

I didn't fry the guy who grabbed me, that is all on Nox.

Gabe gets my car door open and pulls me out of the car in the time it takes me to unbuckle my seatbelt. Nox's face shifts from the quietly seething displeasure he had while he was driving, to the openly vicious sneer that I'm used to seeing on him at the dinner table.

"Just stay behind me and don't freak out," Gabe murmurs and I'm insulted for a second before I realize that he's watched me cry twice over *nothing* in the last week and this is his way of discreetly reminding me to keep my shit together.

Right.

Don't get emotional over this shit, Oli. Don't look at your Bonds all coming to blows over you because two of them hate you, two of them like you, and the fifth one is a constant mind-fuck of changing opinions.

Don't think about it.

Gabe rocks on his feet, as though he's getting ready to shift and throw himself in the middle of a fight and, sure enough, Atlas and Nox kick off with vicious jabs.

"Bassinger, either learn to share or—"

"Don't fucking speak to me or I will—"

"Kill me? I'm shaking, honestly, you're so terrifying to me," Nox drawls back and yeah, maybe I shouldn't be around this.

I take another step away from Gabe and clear my throat. "I need to get out of here. I can't be here for this. If they actually fight, I'm going to lose control."

I'm not speaking to anyone in particular, but North

hears me loud and clear, stepping over to me and taking my elbow with firm but gentle fingers as he tugs me into his side. "Shut your eyes."

He doesn't give me time to argue or even follow his demand before his hand drops away from my arm and the smoke explodes around us, all-consuming until even with my eyes open, I can't see a thing. I don't realize that I'm reaching out for anything until a hand grabs mine out of the air, our fingers threading together and holding firmly.

I don't even know whose it is.

"Fucking Dravens! You can't just use your gift every time your brother fucks up or I'll start using mine," Atlas snarls, and I can't even tell which direction the sound is coming from, the smoke distorts everything.

Fuck this.

I call on my gift, just enough that my eyes glow and the inky darkness around us clears away from my vision.

North has them all wrapped up tightly with long, sentient black coils, darker and more solid than anything else around us. Gryphon isn't struggling or looking concerned but Atlas is fighting it, furious and determined to be let free.

Nox's eyes are black and he looks just as pissed as Atlas but he's not fighting it. Nope, his eyes are on me as he curses me out again.

It's getting old.

"You were all told to keep a hold of yourselves around Oleander until she's got her gift under control. If you don't like it, then learn some restraint."

My hand tugs and I look down to see that it's North holding it, pulling me to lead me through the smoke because he thinks that I still can't see through it. I glance back and see that Gabe is also wrapped up and while he's sweating about it, he's not struggling or looking anything other than a little sick at being confined.

I let North lead me through the garage, past each of my Bonds, without a word to any of them. When we get past Nox, the closest to the door out of everyone, I see the puppy-like creature poke its head out from behind his ear. It sniffs the air and I can tell that it doesn't like North's creatures by the way it moves, but it climbs down from his arm and trails after us anyway, doubling in size until it looks like a normal-sized puppy instead of the teeny tiny pup Nox had hiding in his hair.

When North gets us both through the door and into the hallway, he doesn't let go of my hand as he stalks through to the elevator. I try not to giggle at how ridiculous he looks with the puppy weaving through his feet with every step. It's playful and cheeky the same way a real puppy would be, snapping at his shoelaces that are bouncing as he walks.

When we stop at the elevator, waiting for it to arrive,

he finally notices the puppy and frowns down at it.

I let go of his hand and shift on my feet a little, anxious to be standing here with him while my bond is feeling so volatile, and he reads the action incorrectly.

"He's not mine, he doesn't usually leave Nox's side."

I shrug and bend down to let the puppy sniff my hand. "I'm not worried about him. He's a spy, but there's nothing he can find out about me that Nox can kill me over, so if he wants to tag along, then he can."

North scowls at me, staring at me like I've just announced that I'm secretly a clown on the side, but I just stroke a hand over the puppy's back. It's strange because he feels solid under my hand when I'm being affectionate with him but when I'd attempted to flick him in the car, he acted like smoke.

Curious.

"Does he have a name? You're awfully cute. If Nox named you something stupid I'll be pissed on your behalf. Oh God, it's Brutus or Octavius, isn't it? He picked something stupid, I can tell."

The elevator opens up and when I straighten up to walk in, the puppy jumps up to crawl up my arm and tuck into my hair, the same way he had with Nox earlier. There's no weight to him at all, but I can feel him moving there all the same.

North pushes the buttons for the third floor and then

shoves his hands in his pockets again, scowling at his shoes still. It makes me feel self-conscious, like I've done something wrong here, even though I know I haven't, and I force my mouth to stay shut.

My nervous babble will make things a million times worse right now and I don't need that.

"He doesn't have a name… or at least, not one Nox has ever told me before. He doesn't usually leave Nox's side."

He keeps saying that, I'm not sure which one of us he's trying to convince here. "You know what? Brutus is actually kind of cute. Will he ever grow up and become a fully fledged nightmare?"

North shakes his head as though he's trying to clear it. "They don't age, they just… are. Why aren't you afraid of it? Gryphon told me you saw what they did to the Resistance, you know that it isn't actually a little puppy."

Well, that should be obvious. It doesn't matter what it's capable of, the puppy has been asking for attention and pets. Why on Earth would I be scared of that? It's officially the only tolerable part of Nox that I've found.

The elevator doors open and I start off down the hallway because I'm very proud to announce that I've worked out how to get to my own bedroom… but only from that one elevator. If I use the other one, I'm screwed.

North says, still at my side, "I'll let them go once you're in your room, you don't have to let Bassinger in if he's still being an idiot about this."

I sigh and nod my head because it's easier than explaining that Atlas is never an idiot and he's very respectful about my boundaries, better than the rest of them put together.

When I slide my key into the lock, I look back at him, ready to just say goodbye and be done with him, but North is just standing there looking hesitant and it's freaking me the hell out. "Are you okay?"

He scowls again and then says slowly, "If Nox did something, I need you to know that I would take care of it. If he was— if he hurt you—"

Jesus, why does everyone keep trying to talk to me about this today? "He didn't. I'm fine and I could've stopped him if he tried."

I mean both times, but North is still looking at me like he's expecting me to cry. Little does he know that I'm currently a mess and cry at stupid shit, so he's not that far off of the mark.

I duck into my room before I have to talk about this anymore. Maybe someday I can have a real conversation with Nox about what happened, about which parts of it were wrong and which parts I did actually have some control over, but the very idea of them all questioning it and picking it apart when they weren't even there just… it pisses me off.

Why do I feel as protective of that moment as I do the little puppy in my hair?

Bonds are fucking crazy.

By the time Gabe and Atlas get up to the room, I'm clean and in my pajamas, texting Sage about the incident at the cafe. She's already heard about it through the Draven grapevine, and someone in North's camp must be playing spin-doctor because everyone is talking about how heroic Nox is for stepping in to protect his beloved Bond.

I could die of laughter at that and Sage is just as incredulous about it.

Atlas orders Chinese food and we spread out on the floor to eat while we study. Well, I study. Atlas seethes quietly and Gabe watches videos on his phone with his earphones in so he doesn't disturb me as I slowly cram as many dates and historical events into my brain as possible.

A little before midnight, I finally call it quits and head off to brush my teeth, giving Gabe a curious look when he grins at me. Atlas stands with me in the bathroom, scowling still, but it's only when I catch sight of Brutus snoozing on my shoulder, his body mostly obscured by my hair, before I realize what he's pissed about.

"He's not hurting me or upsetting me. He's… kind of cute," I say as I rinse.

Atlas gives me a curt nod but doesn't say anything else, so I let it go, it's not my fault or my problem. My Bonds need to figure their own shit out amongst themselves.

When I climb into my bed, I immediately know what Gabe was looking so smug over.

My pillows have been switched out and the new ones all smell like my Bonds.

He's taken pillows from each and every one of them and now my bed is like a delicious melting pot of all of them. My bond is writhing in my chest with joy, my skin tingling, and every last one of their scents is mingling together in an orgy of perfection. Literally, it's as though they're all lying around naked in my bed and I'm about to dive into that, my bond is practically orgasming with joy.

Atlas finally smiles back at me as he lifts the blanket on the other side like he's about to climb in with me. "Well, shit, Ardern came through. You're practically glowing."

I panic a little and hold out a hand to stop him. "You can't get in, what if you ruin the smells?"

Gabe bursts out laughing and Atlas shoots him a glare before turning back to me. "What if I only touch my pillow, can I get in then?"

Logically I want to say yes, because I like having him close to me, but my bond is being a complete nightmare right now, possessive and just freaking crazy about this.

I cringe a little. "I can't help it."

He stalks around the bed to me, holding out his hands. "Sweetness, I'm not angry. Don't let your bond make you think that, I just need to know what you need."

Jesus, am I about to cry *again*? "What I need is to fix this because I'm not an emotional person normally and this is fucking stupid! Why do I feel like this? Am I going insane? I need to get out of this fucking house before it ruins me!"

I tuck my arms around myself and Atlas stays within reach but doesn't pull me into his arms, which is good because I think I'm about to have a panic attack and lose control of my gift. Gabe slowly walks over from the bathroom where he was washing up but he doesn't speak, his eyes a little too wide for me to believe he's as calm as he looks.

Atlas holds out his hand to me again. "I'll sleep on the floor."

Gabe looks between us both and then scrubs a hand over his face. "We need to tell the others about this. It's getting worse and as much as I don't want to rock the boat here, we can't let it go too far. What if Oli loses control and hurts one of us?"

A chill runs down my spine because that cuts just a little too close to home, but Atlas glares over at him. "You want Nox fucking Draven to be around her? Because I certainly don't. We can get a handle on it. This will work."

The pillows do work.

I finally wake up feeling well-rested, and with one of North's shirts on underneath a sweatshirt of Gryphon's and the puppy still hiding in my hair, I breeze through my week.

The five am training sessions with Gryphon get easier, especially when I learn to just keep my mouth shut and focus on what we're doing. I progress to hand-to-hand combat quickly and it's easy enough because it, once again, starts with positioning and learning how to fall. I'm sure I'll struggle a little more when I'm forced to be all over him but for now, I'm okay.

I arrive at my first TT class with Sage and Atlas with a bounce in my step and a huge grin on my face. Sage smiles back at me but she's a little pale, the mousy tones of her hair that usually frame her face perfectly are pulled back into a harsh ponytail and complete her harried look of the day.

I gently poke fun at her while we get changed, and for once, I don't give a shit about my ill-fitting uniform or the looks from the other girls.

"I get paid after my shift tonight, we should go shopping this weekend."

Sage grins at me as she tugs on a tank top that makes her look like an athlete. She's probably one of those naturally sporty kinds of girls who'll breeze through this class and I'm both jealous and relieved for her.

I hope she kicks everyone's asses.

"The best mall around here is outside of your perimeter, do you think North would ease up on that if you bring Atlas and Gabe along? We could catch a movie too, make a whole day of it."

I wince a little and shrug. "Who knows, he's been a little less… pissed lately, I guess. I think he still hates me and definitely doesn't trust me, but he also let me get my job so... maybe? Jesus. Maybe we should get Gabe to ask him. He could spin it as a date or something."

Sage giggles at me and knocks her shoulder into mine as we walk out together. "Maybe it should be a date, he's not even trying to hide his obsession with you anymore. It was obvious enough before but now? God, he's really in the Bond haze."

The Bond haze. Fuck, I forgot that was even a thing and here I am, right in the middle of it myself. It's weird to even consider the guys feeling the same way but I believe Sage. She wouldn't lie about something like that and it's probably easier to spot from the outside.

I can't see past my own obsessive need to scent them constantly.

I want to rub myself all over Atlas and Gabe the second we stand with them, just to get their smells back on me because my gym clothes just smell clean. I refrain from it, but I stand close enough to Gabe that our arms brush each other.

Vivian stalks out from the back room and calls out in his booming voice, "Right, we have some new faces today, so we'll be going through the course once you've all warmed up. Everyone hit your workout. Fallows, you're on your usual circuit. Bassinger and Benson, come see me and we'll get you both sweating in no time."

My usual circuit starts with the treadmill and then moves on to weights, so I head right into it. Within minutes, Sage gets sent over to join me and we keep a great pace together.

Thanks to my morning runs down to the gym, I get through my time on the treadmill without too much pain and then when I start on the weights, I get to watch Atlas demolish the challenges Vivian throws at him.

It's freaking hilarious.

It also captures everyone's attention quickly. One by one, he breezes through all of the warmup machines and then when Vivian gets an attitude at him and throws him onto the mats, we get to watch as he beats the shit out of the shifters and the other physically gifted in the class.

Gabe refuses to go up against him.

When one of his football teammates tries to call him out on it, he just smirks and shrugs at him. "My Bond will take the entire room out if we fight. I'm saving your life right now, Matt."

Even Vivian pauses to look over to where I'm sitting on the rowing machine, and when I grin at him and throw in a wink for good measure, Gabe throws his head back to laugh at the unease on everyone's faces. If they all want to talk shit about me being a monster, then they can deal with my teeth when I rip their throats out.

Metaphorically, of course.

I'll leave the animalistic deaths to Gabe.

"Fine, I'm done trying to break Bassinger, so get your asses out to the obstacle course. You know the drill; two teams, first group to get everyone through wins. If you lose, suicides for an hour after class."

Oh God.

Sage turns to me and mutters, "Now's the time, Oli. You need to make sure we're all in the same group."

I scoff at her because there's no real way that I can talk Vivian into anything, but I guess it's worth a try. I wait until we move into the holding room filled with the security cameras. There's TacTeam guys already in there, drinking coffees and chatting amongst themselves. Gryphon isn't there but Kieran is, and when he spots me, he actually dips his head at me in respect.

I'm so shocked that I stumble over my feet a little.

I keep my eyes away from him and head over to where Vivian is frowning over the class list, making adjustments to where he's placing people into the teams.

"Fallows, good to see you're still alive after your little trip."

I forget for a second that we were even taken by the Resistance, so I stumble over my words, "Trip— oh. Right, it was fine. Obviously."

He raises an eyebrow at me and taps his form with the pen. "You're coming over to get put into a specific group, aren't you? What makes you think I'll just pop you in where you want? I don't do favoritism."

I grin at him, completely unrepentant. "We both know you do, just a little. Actually, it was more of a heads-up kind of thing. Gabe wasn't talking shit earlier, I've been having some... control hiccups. I might need to sit this one out if I'm not with my Bonds and Benson."

He turns to face me fully and I can read the look of what-in-the-bullshit-is-going-on-here all over him. "And what does Benson have to do with your Bond, Fallows? Why am I sticking her with you to save lives?"

I glance back to where Sage is definitely freaking out over this, but Gabe is biting the inside of his cheek over my antics.

I turn back and lean in to whisper to the old man, "Didn't

you know? I ran off after Sage. I'm extra protective of her, and my bond is super attached to her too."

The puppy, who is still playing in my hair, takes the opportunity to poke its head out, and while Vivian startles, he stays strong at the sight of it.

The TacTeam guys don't.

Three of them jump to their feet and Kieran curses viciously, putting down his coffee cup and grabbing his phone. He's probably going to tattle on me to North or Gryphon, but it's not like I did anything wrong.

It's Nox's nightmare, not mine.

Vivian snaps at me, pulling his phone out of his pocket, "What the hell is a Draven nightmare doing here? When did Nox give you that little shit? I remember him well enough from teaching that asshole."

I grin again and push Brutus back into my hair. "I told you, my bond is all over the place. I can totally sit this one out though."

He shakes his head at me and snaps, "My ass, kid. You can have your little bunch together today, but you better get a handle on your gift soon."

I take the win.

I hate this freaking course.

Gabe knows it too. The moment the door opens and everyone else starts sprinting, he stays back with me without a word as I set the pace at a slow jog. Sage stays close to my side, her eyes just a little too wide as she stares out at the artificial woodlands we're being funneled through, and Atlas walks on her other side, looking relaxed but alert.

"If this is a race, shouldn't we be trying to get ahead of everyone else?" Sage mutters to me, but I shake my head back at her.

Gabe glances behind us as he answers her, "You have to survive the woods first. If you go too fast, you miss the warning signs."

Sage glances over at me, but when I just give her a lopsided grin, she mutters, "Why does this feel like a horror movie intro? I guess the positive here is that we're both all-natural so we're not prime bait."

I cackle at her but my answer is swallowed up by the screaming and yelling that starts up further down the path from us.

The first batch of students to fall.

"Uhm, I need to know exactly what I'm about to run into because I'm feeling a little panicky and my gift wants to set fire to the woods right now to escape this," Sage gasps, and I slow our pace even more.

"Okay, the aim is to get through first, but this entire place is basically one giant booby trap. They change too, so it's not like Gabe and I can just lead you guys through it. Basically, the trees all have ears and eyes, so don't trust them—"

"Ears and eyes?! Oli, what the fuck?!" Sage screeches, and that's when I learn she's a little squeamish about that kind of thing. I don't blame her, it's a fucked up thought.

"Not like that, I mean that they're-- I mean, the course knows what we're saying and doing, so it'll change to mess with us in the worst ways."

Atlas' eyes get even more shrewd as they take everything in, and Gabe clears his throat roughly. "The first time I did the course, I broke my arm in three places.

I got taken out by one of the rolling logs towards the end, I missed out on three weeks of football thanks to it. Oli has breezed through it."

My bond preens in my chest over the compliment, but there's also an uncontrollable urge to check him over for scars or any signs of those injuries, as if there's some chance that he still feels an ache over it that I could fix for him.

Atlas moves Sage out of his way and snaps at Gabe, "Stop talking about being injured, Ardern. Take a breath, Sweetness."

Shit.

I'm glowing.

Gabe curses under his breath and then murmurs, "No pressure, Oli, but Gryphon reviews the tapes of TT to look for TacTeam candidates, so if you don't want them all knowing about your... Bond haze teething issues, then you need to keep it together."

I grit my teeth. "You're the one who talked about being hurt. Clearly, I'm not good at hearing about that stuff. I need all of you to just wrap up in cotton wool for a little while, okay?"

He grins back at me, gloating like a motherfucker, but then it slides right off of his face as we make it to the clearing.

There's bodies everywhere.

"Jesus fucking Christ," Atlas mutters, slowing down to a brisk walk. I nod in agreement, because it looks like a bloodbath.

Okay, they're all still breathing and only two people are unconscious, but there's definitely some severe injuries here.

"How is this allowed to happen? It's a college class for gym credits, for fuck's sake!" Sage hisses, a little more mouthy today; I'm loving it.

Gabe walks over to one of his football teammates, the same one who'd attempted to give him shit earlier, and drops down into a crouch to get a good look at him. "How many times do you have to get demolished in here before you learn that running through it isn't the way to go?"

The guy, Matt, coughs and splutters, "Like you can talk, you're only lagging behind for your Bond. Is Hanna okay? She was with me when the swinging log fell."

God, the swinging logs. They're the worst thing in this course, and when I start searching through the mud for Hanna, I make sure to look out for the next wave of them. They're hard to spot but the creaking of the wood and the whistling of them flying through the air is unmistakable.

We just have to hear them over the screaming and groaning of the injured.

"I got her! Hanna, can you hear me?" Sage says from where she was searching the other side. I rush over to her, quick to drop down to my knees in the mud and help get the girl conscious again.

I remember her straight away, the girl who'd accidentally shoved me away from herself with her gift while we'd sparred against each other. She's taller than Sage and I, broader, and with an athlete's physique, she's definitely the type of girl who belongs on a TacTeam.

She's also bleeding from her temple.

Her arm band is the same color as ours, we're on the same team here, and so there's no point for us to continue without her. We lose if we're not all across the line.

Atlas walks around the groups of groaning students, then over to the quiet one, and calls out, "They're all the other team. Is there a flare to send up for Vivian, or do we just leave them?"

It sounds awful, but it's also the whole point of the course. "We leave them. Vivian will step in if they need it, the whole course is monitored."

He nods and continues walking around the clearing, looking over all of the signs of what happened here. There are deep gouges in the dirt and broken branches littered everywhere. It's shocking that this is only the first stop, that there's still more to come for us to get through.

"Hanna? Matt, can you heal her a little? Just enough to wake her up, and then Oli and I can help her through the rest of the course," Sage says, and I'm proud of her for jumping straight into it.

Matt nods and groans as he pushes himself up onto all fours, crawling over to us, even with his leg dragging a little.

"Healer?" I mumble, and Sage shakes her head.

"He's her Central. He should be able to get her awake. They're Bonded."

Ah, even better. Gabe grabs my hand to help me up, pulling me into his body instinctively. I move into him without hesitation, enjoying the smell of him even with all of the mud and sweat clinging to us both.

Matt leans over her and I watch as he starts to glow, his eyes turning white as his bond flows through him and into Hanna. It's cool to watch, to see the process that I keep accidentally doing over the tiniest things.

Hanna's eyes flutter open right as I hear the sound.

The groaning, whistling sound of our doom.

I don't know whether to drop to my knees to avoid it or to run, but Gabe immediately catches my waist and drags me backwards. I want to fight him off but he's stronger than I am, and he's also got Sage's elbow to drag her away too, so at least we're all going together.

Except for Atlas. I frantically look for him as time slows around us all. I find him standing in front of Matt and Hanna, watching as the log swings on the chains towards them, the length of a semi and weighing more than a freaking elephant. He's going to die if he doesn't move. He needs to move, why isn't he—

Atlas catches it with one hand.

The wood groans and splinters in parts, bark falling all around him as it comes to an immediate halt. He doesn't so much as grunt as he takes the force of it, his feet shifting back a little, but no signs of strain or pain at the insanely difficult act he's just done.

I've never been so turned on in my life.

"Indestructible and strong. I can see the appeal," Gabe mutters into my ear, and I shiver at the sound of it and the feel of his breath down my neck while I'm already worked up.

Atlas looks over at us and grins. "We should get moving before I have to save your asses all over again."

I scoff but my legs are still like jelly with the leftover adrenaline, so Gabe keeps me braced against him while we walk back over to Matt and Hanna.

They're both staring at Atlas like he's a god.

My bond isn't such a fan of that, but I help Hanna to her feet, ducking under her arm while Sage does the same on her other side. Gabe gets Matt walking and we start back down the path to get out of this stupid place.

By the time we cross the finish line, Atlas has a student slung over each of his shoulders, walking as though their weight means nothing to him, while Sage and I struggle to keep Hanna up between us. Gabe and Matt were faring a little better until we found Martinez knocked out cold, so they literally had to drag him the last mile.

But we do it and, for the first time since I joined the class, my team wins.

I'm lucky that I didn't get injured during TT because I work at the cafe straight after the class, with only enough time for the quickest, and coldest, shower in the changing rooms in-between.

The afternoon rush is the busiest time according to Gloria, and I have no doubt that if she added dinner to her menu, she'd be packed out all night as well. Her baked goods are to die for and the coffee is the best on campus, only rivaled by Gryphon's sister's cafe.

I try not to think about it too much.

Atlas drives me over to work while Gabe goes to football training, groaning the whole way over there. I'm expecting Atlas to leave me here but he walks me in, orders a mountain of pie and coffee, and then takes up a booth with his laptop and the assignments he needs to catch up on.

I'm expecting to feel awkward about him being here while I'm busy serving people, but he basically ignores me the whole time and I just get on with it. Every time his coffee cup empties, he orders a new one, and when Gloria raises an eyebrow at me over him, I cringe a little.

"I can ask him to leave," I say as I rinse dishes and load the dishwasher.

She shakes her head at me. "I'm surprised they're not all here taking up space after what happened last time. It's no problem, he's ordering and keeping to himself, I don't mind losing a table for the shift if he's respectful about it."

I sigh in relief and shoot her a grateful smile, pushing myself to work even harder in thanks for her understanding. Kitty is still a nightmare as she takes orders, but I get better about both dodging her and working around her.

When I feel one of my Bonds arrive seconds before the bell rings over the door, I feel a flutter of nerves that maybe it's Nox here again and he's going to have another showdown with Atlas over being here.

I sigh in relief when Gabe walks in with Sage, Sawyer, and Felix; all of them looking exhausted but laughing and joking. They greet me and order drinks, sliding into the booth with Atlas and taking over his study space without an argument.

Gabe orders two of the triple choc muffins, one for now and one to go, and I grin at him when I deliver them to the table. "If that one isn't for me, you might need to make some quick life decisions, Ardern."

He smirks back at me for the sass, and Sawyer gags at us dramatically. "I knew you'd be boning in no time, just get it over with so the rest of us don't have to choke on all of this sexual tension."

Sage stomps on his foot under the table and shoots him a savage look. "Stop gossiping and being dramatic just because you're pissed about Gray. People are allowed to *exist* and be happy, you know, Sawyer."

Hold up. "What happened to Gray? Shit, is he okay?"

The cheeky facade melts away from Sawyer and he suddenly looks devastated. "He's fine, he's just been pulled out of school and locked up by his parents. They're jumpy, thanks to the abductions, and they're holding his trust fund over his head to keep him out of public for a while."

Jesus Christ. "Is it really that bad? I thought things had died down since… the last time."

Sawyer scoffs and pegs me with a look. "You mean when my sister was taken and you walked into a camp and brought her home like it was nothing? Not everyone has a bestie with brain melting powers to watch their backs. His parents have already lost two kids, so they're not fucking around when it comes to him and Briony."

I blink a little at him because that's a lot of information all at once. I'm still trying to come to terms with the fact that he's not pissed at me, because his tone seems like he is.

Gabe thinks so too. "Don't speak to her like that, man. I get that you're pissed, but you just said it yourself, she saved Sage. I was there, I saw exactly what she did for your sister. I also saw her threaten Black when he tried to use Sage against her. Oli isn't the problem here."

I look around and do a quick check of the room to make sure that there's no new customers or tables for me to clear off before I clear my throat. "I'm in this for the long haul with all of you. I don't need to know Gray to know that I'd run after him too. I… haven't been able to have friends before. I'm not going to ruin my chance to have them now. All in, Sawyer, even with your Ice Hockey Hottie."

He blinks at me a little and then clears his own throat, grabbing his coffee to hide behind it as he takes a sip.

By some miracle, Gabe gets me an exemption from North to go to the mall with our friends.

Okay, so we have to be escorted by a TacTeam and Gabe has to be within arm's reach of me at all times, but we're allowed to go. Atlas is pissed that North has openly stated that he doesn't trust him not to take me and run, but I'm not surprised in the least.

All I care about is new jeans and maybe some cute shirts, and maybe another pair of sandals or sneakers, if I can stretch my first paycheck that far.

We have to take three cars because everyone comes, including Gracie because Felix wasn't quick enough to think of a good excuse to leave her behind. He's a good brother, but he's also very aware that his sister is trying to bone at least one of my Bonds.

She also looks at Atlas just a little too fondly for my liking.

The second we arrive, Sage pulls her aside to let her know that drooling over Atlas or Gabe is both a despicable and, most importantly, life-threatening act and that she needs to get her shit together fast. She takes it better than I expect and, while she doesn't attempt to apologize to me for drooling at my Bonds, she does pull her head in.

We stop and grab a bubble tea first to drink as we shop, and I'm surprised that the guys are all so relaxed about spending hours walking through every clothing store in this place just so I can update my wardrobe.

I make it my mission to shop until I drop and with Atlas' arm slung around my shoulders, and both him and Gabe willing to carry all of my bags, I make a good run of it.

Sage helps to judge everything I try on, vetoing the guys when they say yes to everything just because I'm wearing it, and when we stop for an ice cream coma lunch, I check my bank account to see that I'm almost tapped out of funds already.

I've never been tempted to use Gryphon's card before but, God, would it be nice to just keep spending right now. I won't, obviously, but I might be spending all my paychecks on clothes for the foreseeable future.

The guys all get real food, scoffing at Sage and me for indulging in our treats, and even Kieran grabs a coffee to sit with us and drink. He hasn't said a word to any of us all day, except to tell Gracie to back off, but he's still attempting to be more civil with me. It's a win.

Sawyer takes a video call from Gray and immediately turns the screen around to introduce us, ignoring the fact that I have a mouthful of chocolatey-goodness. "Gray, this is Oli. She's a badass, and if we're all taken off of the street today, my vote is on her to get us out."

The guy on the screen laughs, his eyes twinkling at Sawyer, and I'm instantly furious at the Resistance for keeping them apart. I wave at him like a child, a stupid grin on my face that I'm sure is inspiring all sorts of confidence in my ability to hold my own in Gifted warfare.

Gray waves back and rolls his eyes a little. "No one is going to be taken with that many TacTeam guys around you. My family is just stupid about this shit, I can take care of myself."

Sage shoves a spoonful of ice cream in her mouth and then speaks around it, "Like I can when I was taken? Yeah, maybe you should cut your mom some slack. Maybe we should introduce her to Oli, if she gets a look at Brutus she might ease up a little… knowing you're hanging out with a Draven Bond and all."

Atlas huffs quietly under his breath and I slip my hand into his. I already know he's pissed that we've been dubbed that by the community, taking on the most influential name of our Bond, but I'm happy to take it if it helps my friends stay together and happy.

"What the fuck is a Brutus? If that's your nickname, Oli, I'm going to be worried for Gabe." Gray scoffs, and I share a look with Kieran. He does *not* look impressed. Fuck it, what's the worst that could happen?

If his TacTeam are afraid of a smoke puppy, that's their own issues.

I hold my hand out and Brutus scampers down my arm to sit on my palm, balancing there unnaturally and making me look far more impressive than I am. Sage giggles at the looks they all give me, but I'm proud to say that all of our friends react far better than the trained and armed people Gryphon works with.

I'm not sure if that's a good thing though.

"You mean to tell me I've been walking around all day with a Draven nightmare and I had no fucking clue? We need to find a bar, I need some shots," Sawyer says, his voice a little hoarse.

I forgot about all of the history with these creatures and immediately I want to protect Brutus, to shield him from them all thinking bad things about him. He's cute and little and I love him.

I *love* him.

I lift him back up onto my shoulder and he blends in with my hair, disappearing into the silvery strands.

"Don't call him a nightmare. He's adorable and I would kill for him."

Even Gabe blinks at me like I'm stupid, it's a little insulting. "That's a nightmare creature, Oli. That's literally what they're called. I don't care if it looks like a puppy, it will *eat you* if it's commanded to."

I pull a face at him. "Brutus would never. You maybe, but he loves me. I know it."

Atlas squeezes my fingers and doesn't argue, bless him, but Gabe doesn't let it go. "He's literally a part of Nox, do you really trust Nox that much? Because I was under the impression that you hate him. You cringe when he walks into rooms, you duck behind Atlas and me if we run into him at Draven, you haven't once given a shit about him bringing girls to dinner. Am I mis-reading all of that?"

Ugh. "He's not… my favorite."

I don't want to say I hate him, not to everyone here, and certainly not with Gracie and Kieran present.

Atlas smirks and says with complete confidence, "I

am. Tell them I'm your favorite."

I grin back at him and point at my hair. "Nice try, but Brutus is my favorite, followed closely by Sage."

She giggles at me and clutches at her chest. "I've been replaced by a smoke puppy? I guess that's fair, he's pretty cute."

Sawyer rubs a hand over his face. "Don't you start, it's a fucking *creature*. No calling it cute!"

He pointedly doesn't call him a nightmare but it's hanging in the air around us. I'm not sure why it bothers me so much, but these words— monster, nightmare, cursed— I don't like them. I don't want them pointed at my Bond in any way, not even the little puffs of smoke that I'm very aware are deadly. If Brutus keeps Nox alive, keeps all of us alive at Nox's command, then he deserves respect.

And I'll be damned if he doesn't get it.

SAVAGE BONDS

I should be able to spot it from a mile away, but we enter the calm before the storm and, like an idiot, I let myself just enjoy it. Gabe and Atlas start to take turns sleeping in my room with me on a mattress on the floor. I marinate in the scents of my Bonds on the pillows, then spend all day wrapped up in their scents with whatever shirts Gabe can steal for me without being too obvious. It keeps my bond calm... not exactly happy, I don't think I'll ever really be happy with having them so close but not being Bonded, but I'm level and able to keep my gift under control.

The students all calm down about me being a *monster,* and the rumors of the nightmare creature hiding in my hair eventually go away. I start to win every week in TT, thanks to my friends and Bonds having my back. Gryphon still won't talk to me in our training sessions but I don't exactly bother trying either. We move on to hand-to-hand, and he spends his time tearing me down because I know nothing about punching people correctly.

I'm more of a skilled amateur who gets shit done through sheer force of will. It works.

North is too quiet around me, his eyes a little too keenly observant, and I find myself getting even more nervous around him as the days go on.

Nox stops coming to the Bond dinners altogether.

I stop seeing him in the hallway and at the cafe, and if it weren't for his scent on the pillows and the hour per week I spend in his class, I would think that he'd disappeared into thin air.

Again, this should be an amazing thing and a total win for me, but my bond is Not Happy with his absence. Even with the stack of soft, worn shirts Gabe found of his for me to wear, it's like an open wound.

I start getting more assignments back and I find myself comfortably passing all of my classes. I'm definitely not in the top five but I'm way above the bottom, so my panic about my grades eases up a little and I stop studying way into the night.

After the first few weeks of Gabe sneaking off to football games without us, I finally ask North about going to all of the home games to support him. He's slept on my floor every other night, stolen clothes and pillows, sat in a booth in the cafe for hours to keep an eye on me, and tagged along to every shopping trip I've demanded to get my wardrobe situation under control without a single complaint. He's been more than a good friend to me since he called in a truce.

He's been a perfect Bond.

The least I can do is show up to his football games in a Draven shirt and face paint to yell at a game I barely have a grasp on the rules and regulations of. It costs me a fortune but I also buy a season ticket for myself and offer to get one for Atlas as well. He declines and pays for one himself but I didn't want to force anything on him, even though I'm keenly aware that he would never let me go alone.

Sage is *thrilled*.

We pick her up in the Hellcat because there's no way I'm going to just meet her there, no matter how calm and boring life has become since we were taken. She climbs into the backseat in a jersey of her own, giggling at the war stripes on my face, but I have much, much bigger fish to fry here.

"Uhm, Sage Benson, I'm fairly sure your brother's number is sixty-nine. Actually, I'm sure it is because I've heard just about every dirty joke possible about it, so why are you wearing a big old number four?"

She blushes and ducks her head a little before she

clears her throat. "Felix asked me out and I've decided to just give it a go. I'm nervous as hell about it and feel like I might die if he gets the call up for his blood work anytime soon but… yeah. I'm wearing his number tonight."

I squeal so loud that Atlas winces a little, but he's grinning just as wide as I am about it, which is all the more points in his favor. He gets us back on the road and racing down the highway to the stadium in no time.

Even *thinking* about Felix getting a call for a match to his blood work makes me feel sick. Most families in the Gifted community have their children's blood drawn and entered into the blood directory when they're born, waiting for the day that they'll be matched with their Bonds, but there are still thousands of cases of people not being entered until much later in life.

Myself included.

I never had the chance to ask my parents why they decided to wait, and my chest aches a little to think that I'll never have an answer for that question, as well as a million other things I'll never get to know.

Atlas notices how quiet I've become and threads his fingers through mine as he drives, a silent comfort to me that I'm pretty sure has become vital to my survival at this point.

When we arrive at the stadium, we head straight up to sit in Sage's ideal seats, Atlas laughing over how excited and bouncy she is as we get up there. Her parents sit directly in front of us and this time, they're actually nice to me.

Her father tears up as he thanks me for saving his daughter, shaking my hand and clutching at it so desperately that Atlas has to quietly intervene to get me out of his grateful, but forceful, grasp.

I share a look with Sage over it, and she's cringing like crazy, but if her parents ease up about us being friends, then I'm fine with a little crazed gratitude.

When the players run out onto the field, Sage and I cheer so loudly that people around us stare and whisper, but neither of us give a shit about it. Atlas buys us all hot dogs and drinks, then holds them so we can cheer as the game gets underway. Sage talks the whole time, giving me every stat about the team that could possibly exist, but it just makes it even more fun to watch.

Until it's not.

I feel the hostility in the air before the first signs of something being wrong.

At half time, we're up by six points, and there's a small moment of quiet that no one else seems to notice, but my gift is singing through my veins, coming to the surface as though it's about to take over my body to keep me safe. The teams run back onto the field and get ready to start the second half, but I want to vomit.

I glance at Atlas, but he's still laughing with Sage over

my head, completely oblivious to the *wrong* in the air. No one can feel it, no one but me as I sit in a crowd and try not to lose my goddamn mind over it. I start to shake uncontrollably.

"Oli? Sweetness, what's wrong?" Atlas says, and Sage immediately grabs my hand.

Then the music cuts and the teams go back into their locker rooms, the field clearing quickly as the crowd grows quiet.

There's a small pop sound and a disturbance in the air next to us before Keiran is suddenly there, standing over Atlas in the aisle.

He doesn't waste time with niceties or explanations. "Fallows, we need to leave. Benson, go with your parents to the north exit. Straight down and into your car, call Atlas the moment you're home safe."

Sage's parents don't hesitate to grab her and get moving, so I give her a quick hug and then I'm moving in the opposite direction. The people around us in the crowd call out to Kieran, his TacTeam gear making him an easy target for their fear and confusion, but he just leads the way down towards the tunnels to the locker rooms.

I have no idea what's going on, but I'm worried.

When we get to the second floor, there's a huge crowd of people already trying to get out, yelling and screaming about a bomb, and then I officially start to lose my cool.

Atlas pulls me into his arms and covers my back entirely and I know he's preparing himself for an explosion, just in case he needs to shield me. It doesn't help my freakout. If anything, it makes it worse.

Brutus starts growling at my ear, not a sound, but a *feeling*, like a rumbling deep in his chest.

The last staircase to the tunnels is bad but when we make it down there, we reach the lowest point of the stadium and the smallest space so far. There are people everywhere, bodies crushing up against mine as we move, and even with Atlas' arms tight around me and Kieran walking in front of me in an attempt to clear a path and get me *the fuck* out of here, it's unbearable to me.

Someone bumps into Atlas and because he's not using his gift, he jostles me a little, apologizing into my ear as he snarls at everyone around us. The problem is that I don't care about people bumping into me, I can even talk myself down from freaking out about being crushed, but there's no way I can handle my Bond being shoved.

I feel my bond take over even as I desperately try to claw it back. It's no use, in times of danger we're nothing but instinct and a very animalistic need to *fight*.

Kieran curses under his breath as he glances back at me, rubbing at the center of his chest desperately. When he lifts his phone to his ear, I already know who's going to be on the other end of the line.

"Where are you? Fallows is about to take everyone in the tunnels out, I need to move her... copy, we're on our way."

He reaches out with one hand to grip my wrist, his eyes flashing white as he calls on his gift of transporting. He doesn't grab Atlas. I don't know why he doesn't grab him, and I hear my Bond's snarl as I'm ripped away from him and transported away, but there's nothing I can do about it.

My stomach clenches and revolts at the sensations and when my feet finally hit solid ground again, I lurch away from him, sweat breaking out over my forehead.

I vomit all over the carpet, shaking like a leaf, and I hear the shrill sounds of someone getting pissed about it, but then I look up and they all see the color of my eyes and shut the fuck up.

I'm in an office with North, Nox, and a woman in a skirt suit and heels. She's got a hand over her mouth and her eyes are wide but that's not what upsets my bond. Nope.

She has a hand on North's bicep.

"Jesus fucking Christ, where is Shore? He told me to meet him here, she needs to be—"

The door crashes open so forcefully that it bounces off of the wall and ricochets back at Gryphon as he stalks into the room in full tactical gear, a helmet in his hands, and a neck gaiter pulled over his mouth and nose. He tugs it down and snaps, "Get your hand off of him if you don't want to have your brain turned into soup, Pen."

The woman startles and snatches her hand away from North, stepping away from him and stumbling over her feet a little. It doesn't make me feel any better.

Who is she and why does she think she can touch what's mine?

Kieran groans behind me. "Fuck, I can feel it in my chest again, Shore. If you don't do it soon she's going to go off."

And then everything turns black.

My bond is *livid*.

I come to in my own bed this time, thank God, but I know before I even open my eyes that all of my Bonds are in here with me. The tingles and little shoots of electricity running through me are ridiculous because there's a lot of shit in this room I don't want them getting a look at.

Like my bed full of their pillows or my closet that's overflowing with their stolen shirts.

I don't want to open my eyes and face them. I don't want to lose this little haven of smells that Atlas and Gabe built for me, and I really don't want to deal with the aftermath of them being in trouble for helping me.

A hand grips mine and squeezes a little before Atlas murmurs, "I can tell you're awake, Sweetness. How are you feeling? Tell me you're okay."

I groan and then blink a little as I look around at each of them quickly, just to get a handle of where they all are and how angry they look. Atlas is beside me on the armchair pulled up to the bed, holding my hand. Gryphon and Gabe are standing together in front of the closet, watching me so closely that my skin prickles with it, and Nox is sitting on the other armchair by the door with a sneer on his face.

That just leaves North, who is standing at the end of the bed looking furious.

It's nothing new but also, he's usually cold and cutting when he's angry. This is scarier than that, this is the white-hot seething sort of rage that I've come to expect from his younger brother, not the cool, calm, and collected councilman.

"She's been like this... since she came into her power again. Months, you've been lying to us about her and what she needs."

Gabe winces but Atlas just leans forward in his seat to rub a hand over my hair, smoothing it back. "Oli doesn't trust any of you. Why would she talk to you—"

"This isn't something trivial, she almost used her gift against a dozen people today!" North cuts him off with a snarl, and my heart jumps into my throat.

I turn away and bury my face into the pillow, but no matter how many deep, gulping breaths I take, it doesn't stop the panicked swell of power within me.

I hear Atlas stand up and move towards me again, snapping at North, "Like I give a fuck about them."

There's footsteps around the bed and then Gryphon walks into my eye line, muttering under his breath, "Spoken like a true Bassinger. I wondered just how alike your aunt you were, guess we all know now."

I don't know what that means either, but my bond zeros in on the tiny patch of skin showing at Gryphon's neck and I feel my eyes shift, my vision becoming clearer and more focused.

I want that.

I need it.

"What the fuck is she doing?" Nox mutters, but it only catches my attention and yes, I want that too. I want more than the crumbs I've been living on. I want more, everything, give me all of it.

I move with an unnatural speed to him, vaguely aware of their reaction to me doing so, everyone jumping to their feet around me and Atlas scrambling after me, but all I care about is his scent.

When I land on Nox's lap, I feel Brutus leave my hair and stand beside us like he's monitoring me, waiting for the moment he needs to strike, but when I start clawing at

Nox's shirt to shove it up his body, Brutus just pads over to curl up at his feet like I'm not stripping his creator.

Nox freezes and doesn't exactly let me manhandle him but he doesn't stop me either. He just stares at me with a startled, horrified look as I duck down to wrap myself around him and press myself into the newly-exposed skin.

The need in my chest settles for a second and then doubles. More. I need more.

"Get. Her. Off. Of. Me," Nox says through clenched teeth, and his heartbeat under my temple is so loud, it's as though his heart is trying to pump right out of his chest.

He's panicking.

He doesn't want me, he doesn't want this Bond, he really doesn't want—

"What the fuck is your problem—"

"Shut up and grab her!"

"Fuck, get her off of him before his nightmares come out. Oli, just let him go."

"*Oleander, let him go.*"

But I don't want to, I want more. I want him all over me until he's seeping into my skin and soaking into the very core of me and there's no chance of anyone ever getting between us. I need to wear him like a warning, a shield, so they all know. They all need to know.

North's face appears and blocks everything else out. "They do, everyone knows, Bond. Let him go. I'll give you what you need."

He won't though, he's covered in clothing and I don't want want any more shirts and sweaters and pillows, I want—

Skin.

More skin, skin that smells warm and male and *mine*. He doesn't tense or fight me as I move over to him, his arms take my weight as I wrap myself up in him and burrow into him. I can't get as close to him as I want to, but with my face pressed into his neck and my arms banding around him, it's a close second.

The door opens and closes, but I barely notice because there's so much skin under my fingertips and when I move to press my nose into his chest and take in another lungful of him, every inch of my body comes alive with the Bond. He's perfect and he's mine. He doesn't stop me, he doesn't flinch at the madness in my hands as I clutch at him to get him closer to me.

I need more.

North carries me back over to my bed to sit there with me in his lap and my bond likes that. I like him taking care of me and taking me back to where I need to be. I need to be naked, and he needs to get rid of his pants because I need to Bond now, I need—

"You take this any further, you're as bad as your brother. She has no fucking clue of what's happening right now. She's not even in there right now."

I don't like that.

My eyes flick over to where Atlas and Gryphon are hovering next to us, watching me as though they're watching a rabid animal, and I don't like that either. Nox is gone, but Gabe is sitting in the armchair over by the door watching me like he's heartbroken, and it doesn't make any sense to me because this is what I need.

"Knock her out again. Do it properly this time, and let her sleep the frenzy off," Atlas says, but Gryphon shakes his head.

"I can't."

North catches my hands from where they're slowly heading south, trying to find all of the skin I could possibly need. "You need to. She's not calming down."

Gryphon grits his teeth. "I'm not saying I won't, I'm saying I can't. It took everything to get her out the first time. I'm tapped out."

North tenses and I whimper without meaning to. I don't want him to stop me, I don't want him to flinch away from me. I can't have another one hate me—

"I don't hate you, Oleander. Take a breath. We're going to lie down, and you're going to rest. You need to sleep."

I don't want to sleep but his hands are firmly coaxing, moving me and stroking over me until he's under my blankets with me, my head over his heart and listening to the reliable and strong beat of it.

It's quiet for a minute as they all find their own places to sit and watch over us. My bond isn't super happy about the fact that North won't Bond with me but his arms are tight around me. He's solid and not moving away from me, so it's enough to settle my bond down.

I don't feel the moment my bond releases me but the relief in the room is palpable. Gryphon even lets out a breath, like he's been holding it this entire time. My eyes drift closed to the sound.

"What do you mean you're tapped out? Did she pull your power? Knocking people out is a low level ability, you've been doing it since you were three," North murmurs low, but the incredulous tone is clear enough.

I can just barely hear Gryphon's reply. "She didn't pull it but… she's stronger than she makes out. Whatever level you've guessed she's at… double it. Triple, maybe. It was easier to get into your head than it was for me to knock her out. That's a lot of fucking power, North."

I wake up with a total recall of everything that happened yesterday and the wave of shame that hits me is— well, I consider slitting my wrists in the bathtub so I don't have to face anyone this morning. Okay, that's a little dramatic but, fuck, I don't want to have any conversations right now. I don't want to look anyone in the eye. I just want to melt into a crowd and disappear into nothing.

I'm almost willing to risk my brain exploding to get the chip out of my neck.

My room is still dark but my eyes are adjusted to it and I can tell that Nox is the only one still missing. Brutus is stretched out on the bed next to me but his little smoky body barely takes up any space. North is still in the bed, shirtless and frowning in his sleep with an arm still over my waist. I refuse to think about how hard his dick is as it rubs against my ass because it has everything to do with morning wood and nothing to do with who is in his arms.

I can't believe he pretended to give a fuck about me to get me to calm down.

Gryphon is asleep in the chair at the end of the bed, and I can make out Gabe on the mattress by the bed.

I can't see Atlas, but I also desperately need to pee, so I wriggle out from under North, carefully so I don't wake him, and then start to creep around the bodies to get to the bathroom.

I find Atlas already in there, shirtless and sitting on the bathroom counter with his phone. He looks exhausted, and I instantly feel guilty.

When I ease the door shut behind myself, he jumps down and pulls me into his arms, his cheek pressed against the top of my head as he lets me soak him in.

"How are you feeling? What do you need?" he murmurs, and I choke on a laugh that sounds more like a sob.

"You mean other than to pee? I need to never look at anyone ever again. I need to get out of here before this gets worse and I need to never have to face either of the Dravens again."

He doesn't laugh or try to placate me, his hand gentle as he rubs my back and we stand there in silence, wrapped up in each other, until my bladder can't take it anymore.

He doesn't want to step out to let me pee but there is absolutely no fucking way that I can pee with him in here, even if he turns his back. He goes as far as the other side of the bathroom door, leaving it unlocked because while my bond frenzy might be over with, the damage it caused is still there, waiting to be dealt with.

The moment I turn the tap on to wash my hands, he comes back in, watching over my every move as I do my morning routine of washing up and brushing my teeth.

"There was a bomb under the stadium. One of the techs sensed it and found it with enough time to get it disarmed and everyone out. When North heard about it, he sent Black to get us out."

I scrub at my face with my cleanser, the new one I got on our shopping spree that smells divine, and mutter, "Why didn't he grab you as well then? Why did he take me by myself?"

He blows out a breath and hops back up onto the countertop, his muscles bunching and flexing in a very delicious way. "He was trying to get to Ardern to take all three of us at once. When your bond reacted to the small space and the panic, he changed plans. I went to Ardern and drove us both back here, and the others met us here with you."

I nod slowly, rinsing off and then patting my face dry.

My skin is soft and dewy, but it almost feels self-indulgent to be doing this while my Bond is sitting there looking like death warmed up. I clear my throat and lean into him. "Did something... else happen? Did I do something wrong? More wrong than pawing at you all like a fucking—"

He catches the back of my neck in one hand and pulls me in, pressing our foreheads together and squeezing his eyes shut tightly. "You did nothing wrong, Sweetness. You just— I'm just getting my head around what's about to happen because the little haven we've built here? It's not going to work anymore and not just because North and the others know you're struggling. Your bond came out because she wants more. That's what you were saying last night, over and over again."

I whimper, not because of my stupid bond for once, but because of the relief that floods my veins at the thought of this terrible longing I've been living with finally being dealt with.

Except it can't.

"What if I get stronger, Atlas? What if... I can barely keep it contained now, I can't get any stronger!"

He takes my face into his hands and holds me still, his eyes still screwed tightly shut. "If you burn, I burn with you. You're not alone, Oli, not for one second. I told you before, I'm not afraid."

I am, though, I'm terrified, and the moment my heart

starts to race in my chest, I hear the others start to wake up. Brutus comes bounding through the closed door, the smoke moving through the wood as if he's a ghost or something, and then he climbs up the backs of my legs to blend into my hair again.

I hold my breath when there's a knock on the door, Gryphon calling out, "What's going on in there? Why is Oli upset?"

Atlas blows out a breath and scowls at Brutus as his nose pops out to brush against my cheek, the one little action he has to check in with me. He's usually quiet about it but my heart is still thundering onto my ribcage like it's out here to break bones, and I'm not surprised everyone is freaking out about it.

"Bassinger? What the hell is going on?"

Atlas grabs my hips to push me backwards a little, only enough that he can jump back down from the counter, and swings the door open, snapping at Gryphon, "None of your fucking business is what's happening. Oli is allowed to brush her fucking teeth without answering to you assholes and if you don't back the hell up right now, I'll throw you out of here. All of you. Now fuck off and let her come out when she's goddamned ready."

He moves to slam the door shut again but Gryphon shoves his body into the doorframe, taking Atlas by surprise as he shoves his way in. "She doesn't answer to me but you don't get to speak for her either. She's freaking out and I don't think any of us want a replay of last night. What's wrong so we can sort it out before another frenzy happens?"

Jesus.

Of course he doesn't want that, none of them do, but he was also the guy laughing the last time my bond took a real interest in him and *oh my God* can the ground just open up and swallow me whole now, please? I practically assaulted two of my Bonds last night just to get their skin on mine.

Why didn't Atlas or Gabe just help me instead? Why did North have to lie to me and let my bond get even more attached to him? It's easy for them, they just want their powers from me and they don't have to live with the consequences of being Bonded.

They don't have to become the monster that everyone knows I'm going to be.

I take a breath, and then another one, because over my dead fucking body am I going to let myself go into another frenzy and have these men responsible for calming me down. I can't have them treating me as though they care.

I can't have them pretending that they want me for anything more than a completed Bond.

"I'm fine. I have it under control," I croak, my voice hoarse now that I'm trying to hold everything in.

Atlas glances over his shoulder at me and whatever

determination is in my eyes now has him nodding at me, his shoulders still tight with anger at Gryphon's insistence on coming in here. I glance down at myself but I'm still wearing the jersey with Gabe's number on it and jeans from last night.

"I'm going to have a shower and get cleaned up. I'll skip out on the training session this morning, Gryphon. It's not a great idea for me right now. I'll spend today studying and getting my head together and we can all just do what we can about forgetting last night happened. It won't ever happen again."

I'm proud of how calm and sure I sound, and neither of them attempt to argue with me as they step out of the bathroom. I scrub myself clean of the shame and humiliation of what happened and when I get myself dry and wrapped up in a towel, I pause for a second before I walk out.

Two Bonds in my room, so my guess is that North and Gryphon have gone and it's only Gabe and Atlas left out there, thank God. Facing Atlas wasn't so bad and I'm sure I can get comfortable around Gabe again, just so long as I don't think about how he looked at me last night.

I push the door open and find that it's actually Atlas and North still here arguing quietly, hissing at each other like they're trying not to disturb me, and I come to an abrupt halt as I clutch at my towel. They both turn to stare at me as one.

Atlas recovers first, stepping over to me and ushering me into the closet like he's covering me from North's eyes. It's sweet, but then my stupid brain reminds me that he's already seen it all before and obviously wasn't impressed.

Jesus.

I clamp down an iron-like control over my bond and force it into submission, the same way I had to when I escaped the Resistance, and even with the extra juice it has now that we're surrounded by my Bonds, I manage to get it to heel.

"Everything is fine, Sweetness. Get dressed and we'll go find something to eat. I called Gloria to tell her you were under the weather, she was happy to cover you," Atlas says, turning his back as he stands in the doorframe while I get dressed.

I grab whatever is closest and most comfortable, a shirt from Nox and one of Gabe's hoodies with a pair of yoga pants. I shove my feet into some sandals and try not to feel self conscious about looking just a little bit homeless.

Atlas never seems to mind.

When I step back over to Atlas, he slings an arm around me and then turns me to face North again. He's back in his suit, a little creased looking thanks to his night with me draped all over him, and I force myself not to cringe or freak out about it.

I force my bond not to react to him.

"Dinner tonight. Everyone will be here and we will discuss this. If either of you have any more secrets you're keeping from us, this is the time to say so. If you choose not to, I won't be so forgiving about it."

I spend the day desperate to act as though everything is fine and totally normal and definitely not as though the walls are all crumbling down around me.

Atlas buys me breakfast and then drives me to a park at the very edge of the perimeter that North had given me to stay within, a clear pushing of boundaries because whatever was said between them this morning while I showered has pissed him off. We sit together and eat in silence, not uncomfortable but definitely charged because there's too much in the air around us.

When we get back to the manor, I keep my head down the entire way back up to my room and just focus on staying calm. Atlas puts a movie on but spends most of his time on his phone to his parents, the news of the bomb scare reached them all the way on the East Coast. I'm sure they're hating me now for taking their son away and putting him in so much danger.

I throw myself back into studying because it's a great distraction.

Gabe doesn't come back to my room until after lunch, his textbooks in his arms and his eyes on the ground as he walks in. Guilt floods me but I plaster a smile on my face and welcome him into my little study bubble on the floor. He's a little stiff and formal, none of the easy friendship we'd worked so hard to establish, but after an hour or so, he calms down and slips back into our usual routine.

I can feel the hours as they pass, the tension slowly heightening as we get closer to dinner time, and when Atlas finally shoves his phone away and sighs at me, I know I can't put it off any longer.

"Oli, it's not that big of a deal," Gabe mutters as I start stacking my textbooks up and clearing away the study mess.

I scoff at him. "You wouldn't even look at me when you first came in. Sorry I'm not so keen on facing Nox after I practically threw myself at a man who loathes the very sight of me."

Gabe's eyes flick down to my hair as though he's looking at Brutus but the smoke puppy is still tucked firmly away behind my ear. It's hard to explain how I know that he's there, it's a feeling… but not at the same time. I just know it, the same way that I know my heart is beating or that my hair is silver. It's just the way it is.

"I don't think that's exactly what happened, but I'm sorry I made you feel like shit about it. I was just… it was hard to see you like that. I'm sure it was also hard to be in that state."

That state.

What a lovely way of putting it. I force my face to stay a blank slate but Gabe realizes and curses under his breath again, scrubbing a hand over his face. "I'm getting this all fucking wrong again. I meant that I knew how badly you didn't want any of them to know about what's going on. I knew you didn't trust them. I knew that you would've been horrified at what was happening and had no control. I didn't know what to do because I don't know exactly what your gift is capable of. I was completely fucking powerless because if I tried to intervene, it might have gotten worse for you. I would've though, if anyone had tried to Bond with you, I would've stopped them but… now I feel like I should've stepped in sooner. I feel like I've failed you all over again."

We're really getting good at hurting each other, aren't we?

I clear my throat and push myself up to my feet to hug him, a quick squeeze of my arms around him as I blink at the ground for a minute longer. "I'm fine. I'm mortified and scared of what's going to happen now, but that's not your fault. It's no one's fault but my own."

He pulls me in tighter, keeping me against his body even as I'm ready to pull away from him. It's as though he's desperate to find our normal again, desperate to have something return to the little moment of peace that we'd found together, but I already know that it's not.

The dinner is going to ruin everything.

Atlas wraps an arm around my shoulder and holds me tight as we walk down and Gabe keeps a hold of my hand. I'm once again irrationally angry about my bond acting up. Why can't this be enough? Why can't I just soak up these two and have everything stay the same?

When we get to the dining room, we're the last ones to arrive and North is sitting with his assistant at his side as he signs paperwork. Nox is sitting in his usual seat with a glass of whiskey already in front of him and a sneer on his face that makes me want to die a little bit more than it usually does.

Gryphon grimaces as we walk in and my chest tightens until he snaps, "Pen, you're done here. Anything else can wait until the morning."

Ah.

He's afraid I'm going to lose it at the mere sight of this woman working closely with North because I'm a sensitive little bitch now thanks to my horny, nightmare of a bond. I can't even blame him, it's kind of true.

The assistant looks up at me and startles as though she didn't notice us walk in together. I don't smile or acknowledge her, I just take my seat and avoid everyone's eyes as I take in the food selection for the night.

There's salmon and lobster. Someone is really looking out for me at the moment because there is nothing on this Earth as good as salmon and lobster. I could possibly, maybe, potentially deal with this dinner if that's the food I'm getting to ingest while it's happening.

North gathers the papers up and hands them over to the assistant, nodding at her as she does one last check to see if he's happy for her to leave. Gryphon death-stares her from across the table as though he's insulted she didn't run out of here screaming at his simple command.

It's a little bit amusing.

Just a little.

North takes a plate from the stack next to him and I don't even bother to question him when he starts piling it up. I already know it's for me. We all do. No one else moves to grab food, they're all waiting until he's done deciding what I'm eating for the night and exactly how much I'm getting.

He's lucky that he's filling it the way I would anyway.

Atlas' jaw clenches tightly but he doesn't argue with him yet. I say yet because I know it's brewing inside him right now. I know that at some point tonight, North is going to say something and it'll trigger some invisible trip line inside Atlas and he'll snarl something vicious and hateful at the Dravens as a whole.

The only person safe right now from his acidic tongue is me.

North waits until I'm eating dinner and everyone else is dishing themselves up food before he starts in but, as always, he goes right for my throat. "We can't just wait around for you to grow up and get over this little rebellious phase of yours. There are going to be changes made from tonight to ensure your bond doesn't lash out again, Oleander."

Rebellious phase.

Atlas very slowly and carefully places his cutlery back down onto the table, but I slip my hand into his to stop him from whatever he's planning on doing here.

I swallow the mouthful of decadent seafood. "I don't think it's so much to ask for a little respect before I just… spread my legs for you all. That's what your plan is, right? I just lie back and let you all use me for power? Why doesn't that register to you as something I might object to?"

Gabe stiffens in the seat next to me but he attempts to cover it by grabbing his glass and gulping down some water. I'll need to have yet another check in with him over this, I'm sure, but what I'm saying isn't wrong.

That's what they want.

North has to visibly unclench his jaw to answer me. "What I want is to get through the week without the fear that you're about to render everyone in our community braindead because you're throwing a tantrum. I'd like to know that you're going to be responsible enough and an adult about telling your Bonds when you're struggling and need something, even when it's something that's your own fault, like this."

Ah, there it is. The shame for daring to be biologically required to complete the Bond with them.

I look around at everyone, even though I'd rather die, and Nox is goddamn smirking at our argument. Smirking because this is so funny to him.

I want to kill—

Nope.

Don't think that, Oli. We're still in the danger zone here.

I look down at my barely touched plate. "What are you suggesting, because I'm no longer hungry. I'm going to bed early for classes tomorrow."

North's eyes flick down to it too. "You need a closer proximity to all of your Bonds. You didn't react to Gabe or Bassinger last night because you're already getting what you need from them. We're going to arrange a schedule and you'll be sleeping with one of us each night. If that doesn't work, you're going to have to start considering the logistics of Bonding with us, otherwise you're a danger to us all."

Abso-fucking-lutely not.

No way.

He can't be serious?!

But as I look around the table, I find that not only is he serious, he's already convinced everyone at this table that it's a good idea… if not the only solution available to us.

Fuck.

"Why can't I sleep in my bed and you all take turns to sleep there too? Why do I have to go to you?"

This is not my biggest concern, but it's the only one I can voice right now with all of them staring at me with varying levels of disdain and contempt.

Okay, so that's mostly Nox, but still, it makes it hard to even speak.

North gets back to eating his dinner as though he's not ruining my entire life, speaking in his usual clipped tone, "Gabe said you've needed a lot of scents, clothes that have been heavily worn are preferred, so sleeping in our beds makes more sense. Maybe once your bond has settled, we can revisit that idea but for now, this is what we'll do."

Right.

North Draven, the Councilman, has spoken so of course that's just how it'll be. I've had such a good grip on my bond all day and now I can feel it straining against me at the gall of this man. I can't let it out though, no matter how much he deserves it.

I also can't trust my bond to attempt to punish him with more pawing at his delicious skin, so it's really, *really* off the table.

Silence takes over the room again while they all eat and I mope about not being able to do a freaking thing about this stupid situation. My hand rubs over the little raised scar on the back of my neck again, an unconscious movement that I do every time I want to run.

Nox is the first one to break the silence and I'm not expecting the perfectly sedate tone of his voice or the topic at all. "Any leads on the bomb?"

North grimaces into his plate and shakes his head. "The Resistance have sent out scouts again. The bomb was a distraction, it wasn't a real attempt to take us out."

A shiver runs down my spine and Atlas' hand finds mine under the table. There's no way I can eat now, no way I can choke down the perfectly cooked lobster, no matter how delicious it is.

Gryphon shrugs at them both. "They wouldn't have been mad if it had killed half the community though. It was powerful enough to destroy the stadium, they weren't pulling punches."

I slump back in my seat and pull out my phone to text Sage, anything to block them all out and get some distance from the conversation, and Atlas' hand moves to rest over my knee. He squeezes my leg gently as he eats but doesn't try to talk to me about why I suddenly look as though I want to vomit.

It's sweet of him.

Gryphon leaves the table as soon as he's finished eating, his phone glued to his ear as he barks out orders to his team about surveillance rounds. Nox takes a little longer to eat, drinking his entire way through the meal, and when he leaves, Brutus rumbles under my ear in a little whine.

Gabe leans down to kiss my cheek softly, the barest hint of his lips against my skin, before he heads out. He'd warned me that he was popping back to his house to check in with his mom. I feel awkward about it because I haven't met the woman, or know anything about her really, but he also doesn't seem to want us to meet yet.

I try not to think too much about it.

Atlas finishes his plate and pushes it away from himself but doesn't make any attempt to get up. He's waiting for me to speak to North, and while I know that's what he's doing, it doesn't make it any easier to force the words out of myself.

Deep breath, Oli.

"So where am I sleeping tonight then? Who drew the short straw?" I can't even attempt to hide the sarcasm dripping from my words and North pegs me with a look that has my insides squirming.

"Gryphon. He's the only one you didn't get contact with last night, so we thought you should start there. Gabe knows where his room is, you can go and study in your own room until you're ready to sleep."

How kind of him to grant me permission. I want to kick him in the teeth! Instead I turn on my heel and stomp back to my room to, very begrudgingly, do exactly that. It feels ridiculous that it can't just happen in my own bed, and I'm suspicious that the reason it's not has a lot more to do with convincing Nox to go along with this than anything else.

Atlas helps me with my history assignment and then works through our plan for the maze in TT. We know we're going to be thrown in there again soon, and we've been talking about how to get to the center first for weeks. Gabe joins us when he gets back from seeing his mom, somber and looking a little pissed.

He's just as eager to win the maze as we are.

At ten, I have to concede defeat and ask Gabe to walk me over to Gryphon's room because I have to be up at four the next morning for my training session. Skipping today was fine because my bond needed it but there's no way

Gryphon will accept me flaking out again.

Especially if the reason is that I want to become an insomniac to avoid ever going to bed with any of them.

"At least it's Gryphon first, you've already slept with him before, right?" Gabe murmurs when we step into the elevator.

My cheeks heat at his choice of words and the reminder that my entire dorm had seen him mostly naked and assumed we'd spent the night fucking like bunnies.

If only.

"It's more about the fact that none of them actually want me in their beds and that I'm invading their space because my bond can't calm the fuck down around you guys for a second and let me breathe," I grumble and he huffs at me, smirking and shaking his head.

He leads me back down to the ground floor and through the house until we're at the very back, as far away from my room as possible I think. There's a large glass wall with a view of the back garden I didn't know existed, and I take a second to stare out at the landscaping.

It's really beautiful.

Gabe watches me for a second and then murmurs quietly, "I don't think you have to worry about whether any of us want you in our beds, Oli, and I'm not talking about sex. Just... just relax and get some sleep. Gryphon won't bite."

He doesn't give me a chance to reply, he just raps his knuckles against the door and takes off back down the hallway. I make an annoyed noise at him and he glances over his shoulder to grin at me.

Asshole.

The door pops open and I'm confronted with the sight of Gryphon in nothing but his boxer shorts again. I've seen it all before but, God, it doesn't get any less breathtaking. He's muscled from head to toe, all of his tanned and solid frame just freaking glorious to look at, and my bond gets all sorts of giggly inside of me.

Down girl.

We're just sleeping, dammit!

I'm staring, but he just stares right back at me with an eyebrow raised. "You're planning on wearing all of that to bed?"

I glance down at the sweatshirt and sweatpants I'm in and shrug. "Does it matter? It's six hours, I'm sure I'll survive it."

He shakes his head at me and steps aside for me to enter. He was obviously already in bed, one side clearly slept in, and there's only a lamp on. The room is less luxurious than mine, but more homey than North's minimalist one. There's a handmade quilt on the bed, old and worn, but well taken care of, and a line of boots against the closet wall. One of the chairs has his jacket and a variety of weapons slung over it and his bedside table has a gun and a knife sheathed there too.

There's also a family photo on the dresser and I try not to stare at the younger, happier version of Gryphon grinning there with his father's arms around him. His sister is there too, both of them teenagers, and she's a mirror image of him. It takes me a second to realize that he's not scarred in the photo, his hair is shorter and his eyes are less… guarded.

He's truly happy there.

"Are we sleeping or are we snooping?" he growls at me, and I startle away from the photo. I walk over to the other side of the bed, the side that's still perfectly made up, and slip under the blankets.

When Gryphon gets in on the other side, he turns the light off and stays on his own side. The cold shoulder he's giving me is freaking frigid.

Thank God it's dark and he can't actually see how red my face is with embarrassment. I'd told Gabe, I knew it would be like this!

It takes me an hour of thrashing around before I finally pass out.

I wake before the alarm because my body is now on the

right time schedule for our training sessions. Gryphon's body is hot and hard against mine in the bed, his leg pushed between mine and his face buried into my neck as if he needs my scent as badly as I need his.

It hurts.

My chest aches with the cruelty of this situation because he went to sleep as far away from me as the mattress would let him be last night and yet in our sleep, thanks to the bonds inside us, we've wound up tangled in each other again.

I want to scream and destroy something, and for the first time in weeks, it has nothing to do with the bond haze.

I carefully untangle myself from him and pad quietly over to the bathroom to pee and get ready for the hard morning of training ahead of me. Brutus is extra attentive, coming out of my hair and padding around the bathroom with me as he watches my every move. It's calming to have him there, his big void-eyes seeing everything and nothing all at once, and by the time I'm dressed and ready to head out, my head is clear again.

I don't care if they all hate me.

Gryphon is awake and dressed, sitting on the edge of the bed as I come out of the bathroom. He barely acknowledges me as he takes his turn in there and I get my music lined up on my phone for the morning run. Atlas had loaned me his headphones to run with each morning and it has made the entire experience bearable.

When Gryphon walks out of the bathroom, he doesn't wait for me or speak to me, he just walks to the door like he's expecting me to follow and because I have no other choice, I do.

Since his bedroom is on the bottom floor, it's a little easier for me to memorize the way to the front door and out of the manor. The early morning air is colder than it has been for weeks, my lungs burning at the chill and my fingers going numb almost straight away, but there's no point complaining about it, so I just duck my head and get to it.

Gryphon sets the pace and it's brutal.

I'm not sure what I could've possibly done this time to piss him off— I'm here, aren't I?— but by the time we arrive at the gym, I'm barely holding myself back from vomiting. I haven't felt this way in months, like all of the hard work to get my fitness level up has been for nothing because he just ran me into the ground in one go.

He's also barely breathing hard.

I hate him.

"Take five to stretch out and then we're sparring," he says without even looking at me, getting the gym opened up and all of the lights on while I melt into a puddle on the mats.

I strip out of the sweater I'm wearing so I'm down to

just one of Gabe's tank tops and my running shorts, and then I get to stretching out my muscles, as though it'll help me survive this. I already know it won't and my already-fragile and bruised ego is about to be blown apart by all of his critiques.

Still, I keep my mouth shut.

He strips down to his own tank and shorts and then brings me over a bottle of water. He's never done that before, and I take it with a slight nod of my head in thanks.

It hurts to admit how much this all sucks for me.

"I always thought North was harsh on you for calling you a brat but you really are acting like one right now."

I choke on my water, spluttering it all over myself like an idiot. "Ex-excuse me? How am I acting like a brat right now? I haven't complained once!"

He tilts his head like he's agreeing that I have a point there but plows on. "You needed something and we've given it to you. Instead of being grateful that North is bending over backwards to help you avoid the Bonding, you're sulking about it."

I literally can't find words to answer him.

I have nothing.

So instead, I put the cap back on the water and stand up, shaking out my legs and moving through the stances he's shown me for his approval. He stays where he is, crouched on the mats in front of me, and I only move on to the next stance when he's satisfied with how the last one looks.

I do a lot of controlled breathing and meditation techniques to clear my head. Without the bond haze or frenzy fogging me up, it's easy to do, thank God, and by the time he stands up and moves into position to spar with me, I'm calm again.

He spends the next hour throwing me around the mats.

I learn how to fall like a fighter, how to soften the blows myself and roll to my own advantage. I learn how to carry my weight correctly and how to use momentum against my opponent. I learn how to fight even when I've been bested, how to keep fighting even when a man three times my size has me on the ground.

And then, once I'm exhausted and all types of beaten, Gryphon decides to prove a damn point because he really doesn't know how to quit when I'm down.

His body slams into mine and takes me down onto the mats, my arms pinned above my head and his legs hooking around mine so there's no way I can move or gain control of the situation at all.

I grunt and try to move but it's no use, he's got me completely at his mercy.

I don't like it one bit.

"I'll tell you everything about my gift, everything about all of our gifts, if you answer a question of mine first."

I struggle again but he's like a brick wall that's landed

on me, immovable and impossible to reason with. "I already know what you're going to ask, the answer is no."

He scoffs and shakes his head. "I doubt it, Bond. Tell me why being called a brat hurts you so much? What am I not seeing here that's pissing you off so much?"

My stomach sinks and my cheeks burn, but maybe it's a good thing, maybe I'll be able to let out some of the frustration and fury over the way that they all choose to see me.

I suck in a deep breath and then just let it all out. "Maybe it's because I'm trying my best here. Maybe it's because I've done everything, *everything*, that North has demanded of me and not once have any of you acknowledged that. Hell, he wouldn't even stop to let me grab fucking Midol! I'm here every morning without complaint. I went to TT without complaint. I go to Bond dinners and classes and council dinners and Nox's stupid classes without even being given a choice. I know you all hate me for what's happened, I know it, so when I was having trouble with my bond, I didn't want to bother any of you with it—"

"Lie. That was a lie," he interrupts and his eyes are ringed in white, not enough that I can be completely sure he's using his gift, but it's definitely something.

Hell, I hope he knocks me out and I don't have to listen to this anymore.

I shrug. "I didn't want to bother you and I also didn't

want to deal with the absolute shame and mind games of you telling me to get over it... because why would you help me? All of the things that you've helped me with so far have been about control, why would you find a non-Bonding solution for my problem?"

"We did though, didn't we? North spent the entire day grilling Gabe and Bassinger about all of the effects of your bond haze and what things they'd tried until he found something. You're acting like we're selfish fucking *rapists,* when that's the farthest from the truth, Bond."

He pushes up onto his arms so he's holding himself over me and while the bottom half of me is still pinned to the mats, I can shrug at him. "Well, that's not true either, is it? If we're talking here honestly, then Nox has already shown me how much my boundaries mean to him, why should I believe you or North are any different?"

His eyes shutter and I almost regret saying anything about it but, fuck it, it's the truth. Just because I had some choice in the situation, more than Atlas believes anyway, it doesn't mean that Nox is absolved of what happened.

I can't trust any of them.

"If I wanted to force the Bond with you, I could've done it a hundred times by now. I slept in your bed in the dorms for weeks. I've trained you here every morning for months, there's no one to stop me. No matter how hard it was to knock you out, I still managed to do it. I could have you unconscious in an instant now, and what's to stop me? Maybe it's the fact that I'm *not* a fucking monster."

He spits the word at me, and Brutus decides that he doesn't appreciate the tone of this conversation and pokes his head out to growl soundlessly at Gryphon.

He doesn't freak out at the sight of him, his eyes just flick down and take note of the fact that Nox's creature still hasn't left my side. I glance down at him, going just a little cross-eyed to see him, and jerk my head back to get him to hide again. We're slowly getting to know each other well enough that I don't need to speak to him to get him to understand what I need.

If Nox takes him off of me, I might lose my mind.

I love Brutus more than I should.

Gryphon rolls away from me and onto his feet in a swift, smooth motion that is freaking enviable with how easy he makes it look. I have to scramble to my feet like an uncoordinated idiot, huffing and red-faced.

I wait for him to go again but instead, he grabs a bottle of water, gulping it down and then handing it over to me. Mine is long gone, drained in the first ten minutes, so I take it with a murmured *thank you* and finish it off.

"I'm not a healer. Gabe said that's what you'd guessed. I wasn't healing you, or him, I was stopping you both from feeling pain. There isn't much in your brain that I can't manipulate. I can knock you out, take over your thoughts, stop your motor functions… erase your memories. Most Neuros have one specialty, but I've never found a part of the brain that I can't mess with."

Huh. "Vivian said you're a great TacTeam leader in spite of not having a physical gift— I don't think you're really at a disadvantage."

He shrugs and props his hands on his hips, glancing around the room. "That's my primary. My incidental is something else."

I meet his eye, waving a hand to get him to get on with it when he doesn't just spit it out.

He huffs out a breath and then meets my eye. "I know when you lie. I can tell when anyone is lying or omitting the truth to me."

My immediate reaction is disbelief, my face screwing up at him as I'm about to call him out for his bullshit, but then I actually think about it.

North always looks to him for confirmation.

Nox doesn't question him.

Gabe had said to me, 'Only a pro knows how to get past Gryphon like that.'

Mother. *Fucker.*

I throw my hands up in the air and splutter like an idiot, "Fuck. Perfect, so you can just manipulate every conversation we've ever had because you can ask me leading questions and find out everything you want? Great.

Perfect. I'm going back to the Draven's manor now, to the room I was assigned, to go to the college I've been forced into, and to attend the classes that were picked for me. I'll just go and live the exact life that you've all chosen for me and eventually, we'll all die because of it."

His eyes narrow at me as I stalk towards the door and he follows me. "I can tell you believe that, but it makes no sense. I can feel how much power you have, gauge it a little at least, but why does that mean we're all dead? Why did the Resistance know you? I've been going back through intel from the last five years but there's no sign of them taking you, so when did you run into them?"

Jesus.

They really have been doing their research about me, haven't they? It makes me panic a little, but if they haven't come across anything so far, I doubt there's any proof of what happened. I'm not surprised the Resistance has been thorough in keeping all evidence of me under wraps.

"If you think I'm going to say another freaking word to you now that I know what you can do, you're clearly insane. I'm leaving. I'm going to find a bathtub to drown in."

He grabs my wrist to stop me from walking off while he locks up the gym, grabbing his phone to tap out a message before he shoves it back in his pocket.

I stay with him obediently, glancing around the

neighborhood and at the early morning sun still making its way into the sky. Gryphon takes a deep breath and hands me my sweater. I forgot I'd even taken it off.

"Nox wouldn't have... taken it any further than he did. I'm not making excuses, you two have to figure that shit out for yourselves, but I don't want you panicking about being around him."

I huff and answer bleakly, "You mean like sharing his bed on a regularly scheduled time slot? I can't speak though. I guess we're even now, right?"

Gryphon scowls. "Hardly, you barely even gave him a hug."

I turn away from him to shove my sweater back over my body, trying to disguise my shaking hands. "Well he reacted like I was attacking him in the worst way, so forgive me for the miscommunication there."

"He's... got his own issues. Doesn't excuse it, just means that North and I knew we had to get you off of him before his own bond stepped up to the plate. One of you in that state was hard enough, we couldn't have handled two."

I feel like him confirming that Nox has issues is like confirming the sky is blue or that the sun will rise in the morning. Obvious and sort of stupid to even say. I get my music lined up while he gets the gym locked up, but when I put my headphones in, Gryphon tugs them back out, pocketing them so that I can't just shove them back into my ears to block him out.

When I open my mouth to argue, he cuts me off. "North and Nox's dad had the nightmare creatures. He was strong, a Top Tier, but with only that gift. It still made him the most powerful Gifted alive."

He starts to walk back, a much slower pace than earlier, and I can keep up with his long strides easily enough. I nod at him but just listen to what he has to say.

"North's mom was an Elemental. No one expected their mixing to turn into what he has... it's why he has so much influence in the community, because a man with three abilities, all of them Top Tier, is terrifying to them. He has the nightmare creatures, the same as Nox's, just a little more... rabid. Then there's his death touch. It's self-explanatory. If he chooses to, he can kill anyone he touches."

A cold drop of dread rolls down my spine. That feels a little too familiar, a little too close to home for me, but Gryphon doesn't glance my way as he continues, "I don't know which of his gifts are the primary and secondary because they're both as strong as each other. His incidental is that he can find the cause of death. Again, through touch. It's helpful and it's still more power than most people get with their primary."

He looks out at the quiet street, waving a hand at a

neighbor who is getting into his car but too far away to hear our conversation. I glance over, but there's too much going on here for me to take too much notice of details.

"Nox's mom was a Neuro like me. She could manipulate the limbic system, basically she was all about forcing emotions onto people. A powerful weapon, if wielded correctly. Nox has the nightmares, the dread, and he's still figuring out the mechanics of his incidental. The last time he spoke about it, I'm pretty sure he was close to figuring it out, but then we found you and he has barely spoken to any of us since."

I clear my throat. "What exactly is 'the dread'?"

Gryphon cracks his knuckles idly. "Have you ever felt so bad that you've hallucinated? Seen things in the dark that weren't there, just because your brain is working against you? It's a bit like that."

Jesus fucking Christ. The monster moniker is making a little more sense now. Not that I think that of either of them, but powerful Gifted are already enough to make people nervous and with the *flavor* of power they have?

Terrifying.

"Gabe is going to show you his gift. He's already gotten your pass for the night to go check it out. You probably already know about the Bassingers and their powers, we've seen what Atlas has going on during TT. There are... a lot of reasons our Bond group makes people nervous. A powerful Gifted is one thing, six though? Six who will grow and share power, work together and form a family? The council is already putting a lot of pressure on North about it. Trying to find ways to neutralize us without just coming out and saying that's what they're doing."

My heart starts to thump wildly in my chest at the very thought of it.

When we get to the bottom of the driveway, Gryphon stops and looks up at the manor. He rubs at his chin for a second, his face more serious than I've ever seen it, which is saying something because he's usually the silent and grumpy type.

"Then there's you. So much power that the Resistance said it was 'leaking out of you' even when you were hiding it. That's what the students who were taken with you said. If we can't all figure out how to get along and make peace, then things are going to get a lot worse for us all."

SAVAGE BONDS

Atlas is waiting for me on my bed when I get back to my bedroom to get ready for the day.

He's already dressed and ready, and thankfully he looks a hell of a lot better than he did yesterday. I grin at him as I head towards the bathroom and he catches my hand in his to pull me against him.

"You actually look as though you've slept," he murmurs into my hair and I press my nose against his chest to breathe him in.

"Is that your nice way of saying I've been looking like a pile of shit lately? Thanks. No, honestly, I do feel better. Gryphon was also good to start with, I've already slept next to him before, and he's quietly confrontational instead of an ass like the other two."

Atlas quirks an eyebrow at me and pulls away to look down at me with a lop-sided grin. "You've slept with him? When did I miss that?"

I blush but only because they keep saying it like that, like it's more than it was. "He helped me out with some pain and then kind of— he never left my dorm room again after that. I'd wake up with him there every morning. We never talked about it or anything, he just kept showing up and I didn't want to talk about it. He's... he's a good guy. Really good, he just also plays the devil's advocate, so I find it hard to go all in with him."

Atlas nods and then lets me go so I can get ready without us being late to class. It feels good to be able to get dressed in a cute outfit without trying to layer on as many of their scents as possible. When I step out of my closet in a dress and my ankle boots with my hair curled and a little makeup, Atlas grins at me as he clutches at his chest dramatically.

"You can't do this to me, Sweetness. I can't spend all day with you looking this fucking hot only to lose you to someone else tonight."

He says it with a grin and I know he's just flirting, but butterflies explode in my stomach at the thought of who I'm going to bed with tonight. I need to get a hold of the schedule and fast.

He locks my bedroom door for me as we leave, slipping

the key into my bag and taking my hand as we head down to the garage together. Gabe meets us down there and when he looks up from his phone at me, his smile falters a little before it turns into a grin.

"Finally, a dress I can enjoy seeing you in without having to feel like shit about it."

I grin at him and do a twirl, the skirt flaring out, and I feel hot as fuck in it with both of my Bonds' eyes drinking me in. My ego needs that today and when Gabe opens my car door for me, he ducks down to kiss my cheek as I slide in.

Atlas only waits long enough to be sure we're all buckled in, then he rolls out of the garage and down the driveway, the engine revving and loud as he gives zero shits about the neighborhood and keeping the peace with the HOA.

North will probably have kittens about it later and I know for sure that Atlas is hoping for it.

"When do I get to see this other dress? You never did send me a photo. I'm a very jealous Bond, Sweetness."

I roll my eyes at him. "Never, I didn't take photos, and then I bled all over it. I threw it out the second I got back to the dorms."

Gabe winces, but I know it's got nothing to do with the mention of my period and everything to do with North refusing to stop the car for me.

I might have ranted about it for a very, *very* long time. He's probably getting trauma flashbacks about me describing every last feeling and visual of that night.

Gabe clears his throat as Atlas' phone pings in the cupholder. "North took a couple. Can I stop feeling guilty about having it on my phone now, or are we still vicious about it?"

Atlas quirks an eyebrow and checks the photo, his eyes watching for a green light and when I huff at him he hands the phone over so I can see it.

I never noticed North take the photo.

He probably had one of his staff do it but it's at the restaurant right after we arrived, my head is tilted down a little and it looks like I'm posing, a professional model or something, when really I'm trying to discreetly check the hemline. I was sure I'd stepped on it and ripped it, and at that point of the night I was still working hard to take care in it. I was aware of how much a dress like that would cost and I didn't want North to accuse me of being a gold-digger again.

I look really good in it.

Something about it makes me look older, more refined, the version of me that I might've been if my life hadn't gone to shit around me as a teenager. I look like the version of me that might have actually pleased the councilman.

"Shit. We're going to have to delete those, aren't we?"

Gabe mutters in the back and I glance over my shoulder at him. He's watching me closely and I try to wipe my face clean of whatever the fuck it had on it.

"No. It's fine. It's just, I'm not used to looking like that. I'm not really the 'council dinners' sort of girl. I'm not into that schmoozing and political maneuvering over food that is too goddamn expensive. I guess North lucked out."

Atlas scoffs and shifts gears, weaving through the traffic like it's nothing, "Fuck North Draven, he's a pretentious dick and he needs to ease up on you or we're moving. I'm pretty sure we can evade him for a good decade or two if we work together on it. Sawyer has some good ideas on that front."

Gabe shoots him a look but I laugh at him, mostly because of course he's working on getting us out of here on the side. As if I ever doubted that.

We get parked up and find our friends already waiting for us, coffees in their hands that make me feel a little murderous until I see the tray of them in Felix's hand.

As if I could like that man any more, he's a fucking peach.

Sage grins and waves at me through the window, and all I see is the fact that she's holding Felix's free hand and *glowing* right now.

I'm so goddamn relieved to see her looking happy for once, the sad and lonely girl I'd first become friends with is nowhere to be seen. I jump out before Gabe can open my door, ignoring his grumbling, and tug her into a quick hug. Felix greets me with a smug grin and Sawyer rolls his eyes at us all, which I mostly take as him still being pissed about Gray's sabbatical thanks to his parents.

"So the— uh, bed sharing is working then?" Sage murmurs into my ear, trying not to be heard by any of the loud-mouthed guys we're surrounded by, because none of them have any clue on how to be discreet.

I nod and link our arms together as we walk, letting said guys fall in around us like a little protective bubble. "I feel human again, thank God. I can't believe how much of a little bitch my bond is being. Is yours like this? Or is it a Central thing that I need to rage at the universe over?"

She laughs at my dramatics, accepting Felix's kiss to her cheek with a light blush as he heads off to his own classes. He's in all of the Gifted pre-med lectures and I do not envy him, not one little bit.

I've seen his assignment lists.

Fuck that, mine are bad enough.

"Mine isn't quite so… forceful, but it does complain a lot. Less so, now that I'm spending time with Felix. I think it's finally figured out that a life with Riley just isn't in the cards right now and I'm being given a bit of a break."

Urgh.

I don't want to think about that asshole right now so

I change the subject. "Are your parents going to ban you from football games now? I was totally expecting you to be under house arrest. I was ready to join forces with Felix to get you out."

She giggles as we arrive at class and looks around the room, still cautious like we all are now that the world has proved to be just as dangerous as it can be with the Resistance out there. "Once again, my dad is a little besotted with you. He's been fighting with Maria a lot about you, she's still pissy about North and… all that. He knows that us being friends is keeping me safer than I would be alone, so he's become very vocal. Mom is trying to stop him from going after Riley. He's been extra pissed about that situation too. Life is getting messier."

I've never felt something so hard in my life because, yep, it's so fucking messy around here, and I don't see that easing up any time soon.

After my classes are done, I head off to the cafe, grateful that I have a shorter afternoon shift.

I change into my uniform in the back before I breeze into my role. Gloria comments on my great mood and Kitty rolls her eyes at me when I'm extra nice to everyone who comes in, but I'm so relieved to finally be feeling like myself again that I just let it all roll off of me.

Gabe and Atlas come in an hour before closing, ordering coffees and then working on assignments in one of the booths together. They actually laugh and chat together nicely enough and it makes my bond hum with contentment.

I'll be vibrating around the room with joy if I can ever get all five of them in harmony and tolerating me, I can see it now.

After we close up and I've scrubbed everything down, I change back into the dress and say bye to Gloria and Kitty at the back door and walk around to the front to find Atlas and Gabe. The Hellcat is sitting out the front with parking tickets shoved in the wipers but I already know that Atlas doesn't give a shit about that sort of thing.

He's muttering with Gabe who is, surprisingly, leaning against his bike with his leather jacket over his shoulders. He hasn't ridden it since Atlas got here, preferring to have us all ride together, and I blow out a breath in disappointment. He must be going to visit his mom again or maybe doing something for North, either way, I'm not going to get to see him tonight.

My bond grumbles in displeasure but I tamp it down again, forcing it into submission because I'm over the tantrums.

Gabe glances up at the sound of my footsteps and holds

out his spare helmet to me. "You're with me tonight. I'm taking you out."

Oh.

I take the helmet from him and I shoot him a look but he just smirks at me, threads his fingers through mine, and gives Atlas a very confrontational look. I should be used to them by now, they spend half their time together snarking out little insults and jabs, but during my meltdown, they'd banded together so well that I thought maybe we were over this phase.

Apparently not.

"You're taking me on a date? Thank God I wore the dress."

He laughs at me and shrugs. "I guess it could be called a date, but jeans would've been a safer bet. It's fine, we can make it work. Besides, it'll probably help me win."

Win?

I follow him over to his bike and look down at my dress again in dismay. Well, actually, it's doable. If I hike the skirt up a little, it's long enough to give me coverage and if I scoot up close to Gabe, I shouldn't flash anyone.

Atlas shakes his head at Gabe and snaps, "Let her go home with me and get changed."

I laugh at them both and grab his arm instead. "I can do this, can you just— can you stand there and cover me when I get on? I don't want everyone seeing my thong."

Gabe groans softly and swings onto the bike, shoving the helmet on his head so he doesn't have to deal with my sass, and then Atlas holds out his arm to help me on the back. It's awkward and a little embarrassing because he doesn't even attempt to look away, his eyes hot on my skin like he's provoking me.

I show a lot of skin until I get settled, my body tucked in tight behind Gabe. Once I've got my own helmet on, Gabe gets the engine running and gives Atlas the most sarcastic little wave ever.

It feels like classic, cocky Gabe, and it's good to have him back.

The wind is cold on my legs and I burrow into Gabe a little tighter. When we stop at a set of lights, he rubs his hands down my calves, holding the bike up with his legs alone, and I get another whole set of goosebumps because of his skin sliding against mine. I shiver and almost beg him for more right there in the middle of the road with cars all around us.

Jesus.

We drive outside of my perimeter and Gryphon's words from this morning filter back into my brain. Gabe had gotten a pass from North to show me his gift, so wherever we're going, he's going to shift.

I'm not sure what more I can see of his wolf, I'd gotten a pretty close view of it when the Resistance had taken over the campus, but the idea of a quiet night together sounds freaking perfect.

We get to the edge of the town and into the small woodland, trees lining either side of the highway. There are fewer cars out this way and while we're driving, we watch the sunset. When Gabe pulls off of the highway and onto a small side road, I'm not expecting much.

When we arrive at a small industrial area, I'm shocked at how many cars are here. I was expecting something quieter and more secluded, and when Gabe pulls up at the far edge of the cars and kills the engine, I'm slow to climb down from the bike.

I pull the helmet off and then watch as Gabe swings off of the bike in one smooth move, yanking his helmet off and grabbing mine to tuck them away into the pack on the back.

He glances at me and the slightly creased, thin fabric of my dress and slips off his jacket to tuck me into it. It's way too big on me but it's warm and smells just like him and I burrow into it, enjoying the honey rasp of his chuckle at the sight of me.

He reaches out slowly to take my hand, threading our fingers together, and he blows out a slow breath. "I probably should have asked earlier... How's your bond feeling today? Because what we're going to do, it's safe, but if you're not feeling up to it, we can come back next time."

I frown at him, still confused about what the hell is going on here, but I shrug. "I'm good. Between last night and me working on bullying my bond, I've got it under control."

His eyes shift down to my chest as though he can see the way I've squashed my bond into a teeny tiny little metaphorical box in there, and he winces. "I'm sorry it feels like that. I thought we all had it bad, but at least my bond isn't homicidal."

I snort at him, so refined and ladylike, but I can't help but poke at him. "How exactly do you have it bad? You're all doing just fine, thank you very much."

His eyes grow molten, that same feline look coming back, and when he drawls at me, it feels like a purr. "Well, right now, all I can think about is ripping that dress to shreds and pressing you into this wall so hard that you can barely breathe and then watch you squirm on my cock. While you were working, I wanted to bend you over the front counter and eat you out, just to make sure everyone there knew you were mine. I spend most of the time with Atlas arguing with him because my bond wants to prove to you that I'm better for you than him. It's not so bad with the others because I grew up with them, but Atlas? Fuck, my bond wants to tear his throat out and watch him bleed out at your feet just to make sure you like me more."

Uhm.

What?!

I splutter for a second, words failing me, and they don't come back to me until he's leading me into the building. "Since when? Since when have you been thinking dirty thoughts about me? Fuck, no more talking like that, now *my* bond is thinking about that too!"

He doesn't answer me, just gives me a dirty smirk, and leads me through the surprisingly busy building.

The warehouse is clearly abandoned, dirty and old machinery left behind everywhere like trash, but there must be a hundred people jammed in here. There's a huge, makeshift circle painted on the ground, the yellow color bright on the concrete, and Gabe squeezes my hand gently as he leads me around the outside of it. When we get to the far end, two guys step into it, wearing nothing but a pair of shorts.

The crowd is screaming at them, insults and jeering, and the sounds all bounce around the enclosed space until the noise is deafening.

I squeeze Gabe's fingers just to get his attention and he runs his free hand down my arm in a soothing motion. His eyes stay glued to the ring though and we watch as the guys begin to fight.

It starts off like any of our training sessions in TT. Hand-to-hand, nothing special, but all it takes is the first left hook to the cheek before the first signs that the guys aren't just your average guys.

They're Gifted and they're both shifters.

I stiffen a little as they both snarl, the sounds garbled and painful sounding, starting off human but ending up the savage sort of sound from wolves hunting their prey as they shift.

Fur bursts through their skin and their bones crunch as they change forms, their eyes glowing, and all at once, they've completed the shift.

Even after seeing Gabe shift, it's still incredible to see and when they go at each other, snarling and jaws full of sharp teeth snapping, I have to slow my breathing down in an attempt to not trigger my bond. It's so vicious and brutal, so much worse than anything I've watched before, and I almost sigh in relief when a siren whoops out through the din of the room to signal that the fight is over.

The guys shift back, completely freaking naked and covered in wounds and blood.

I'm ready to just quietly walk back out of the door, seeing quite enough of this for one night, but then Gabe grins at the guy in the ring and jerks his head in a challenge.

I should've known.

Oddly enough, my bond doesn't freak out at the thought of him in there. Nope, it gets excited. I realize that I didn't trust the guys fighting in the ring to keep it in there, to stay away from me, but my Bond? I know he's going to wipe the freaking floor with whoever is dumb enough to get in there with him. There's no question in my mind, he's mine, so he'll be fucking magnificent in there.

I try to keep the smirk off of my face, but I'm pretty sure I fail because the guys around us all shift nervously on their feet, clearly recognizing who I am. I'm pretty sure everyone in the Gifted community knows who I am and the mystery of what I'm capable of.

I watch as Gabe strips down, handing his clothing to me until he's naked. I very pointedly don't look down, my bond doesn't need the help visualizing him, and the moment he steps into the ring, he shifts.

I know immediately what the difference in his power is to the rest of the guys and it's not the fact that he's bigger than them. He is, but that's not it.

Nope.

When the Resistance came, he'd shifted into a gray wolf. A gorgeous, huge, vicious wolf.

The animal I'm now staring at is a sleek, black leopard.

G abe doesn't just beat the wolf in the ring.

He goes up against five different shifters, each of them worse than the last, and walks out without a scratch on him. The crowd is screaming and roaring for blood, and when he puts the last guy down, I get a little worried that they're going to storm into the ring after him.

Well, I worry until I meet Kieran's eyes on the other side of the room and realize that this isn't just some underground fighting ring. There's TacTeam guys in plain clothing everywhere, and they're obviously not just here to keep an eye on us. No one in the crowd takes notice of him or his men, so clearly they're here a lot.

Gabe walks over to me in his panther form, his feline body sleek and powerful as it parts the crowd without effort.

I'm not expecting him to shift back right there.

I'm also not expecting to be faced with him completely goddamned naked. Completely naked, his chest heaving as he catches his breath, and my traitorous eyes start to work their way down his very chiseled body. Do I want to tease myself with a look at his dick? Fuck, I don't know if I can hold myself back. Brutus huffs under my ear at my racing heart, my hair flicking out a little, and I take a deep, gulping breath to get myself under control again.

Gabe chuckles at me, as he grabs his boxers out of my hands and pulls them on before I've made the decision of whether I'm looking or not.

"It won't bite, Bond. I won't either, unless you ask me to."

I want to say something back, just to knock a little of that smug energy out of him, but I can't. I have nothing left, and all I can croak out is, "Listen, you need to put pants on. The shorts are not enough."

He chuckles at me, clearly still high on the adrenaline of the fight because he ducks down until we're eye to eye. "Are you ready to beg, Bond? I think I'm ready to hear you."

I hate him.

I don't really, my eyes roll back into my head and there's an insistent throb between my legs that doesn't want to be ignored. "You're an asshole. What part of 'we can't Bond' are you struggling with here?"

He straightens up with a smirk and pulls his shirt over his head, shoving his arms through it in a very elaborate move that feels as though he's teasing me because I swear I watch every goddamned muscle on him flex. The wolfish grin he shoots my way just proves to me that he knows exactly what he's doing. I throw the jeans at him and he catches them with a roaring sort of laugh, and I refuse to look at him until he's dressed.

He leads me back out of the warehouse, both of us ignoring all of the eyes on us as the crowd shifts out of our way. Kieran nods at Gabe as we pass him, but he doesn't follow us out, proving my theory that they're regulars here and not just attending to watch out for us.

I move to take his jacket off but he grabs the lapels and pulls it on tighter around me, zipping it up against the chill of the night. He threads our fingers together and leads me over to his bike, grabbing his keys out of his pocket with a smirk. "I can't help it. Now that I know you want me as bad as I want you, it's fucking addictive to watch you react. You do it so fucking well, Oli. I can smell how badly you want me. Do you think you can hold the Bond back if I eat you out on the back of my bike?"

He swings on as he speaks, an easy and practiced motion, and I can't even think of a reply as I climb on after him. I'm glad there's no one else around because I don't even bother trying to cover up or be modest, I just hike my dress up and get on with it.

I tuck my body into his and my nipples are hard as they rub into the stiff leather of his jacket. Fuck, I end up squirming behind him, panting a little as I convince my bond to stay back and just let me have this tiny little moment with him.

Gabe groans, his legs tense as I grind into him, "Fuck, we should risk it. I need to know what you taste like—"

Nope, I can't take any more.

I shove my hand over his mouth, pulling his head back a little with the force, and I can feel him smirk against my palm. He tilts his head back even further and after watching him fight so many times, it's so obvious to me that he's sitting here on this bike without a worry, flirting it up, and baring his throat to me.

It's the most heady thing a man has ever done to me and I'm not even sure he's aware of it.

I clear my throat and drop my hand away from his mouth, my fingers trailing down his neck absently because I don't want to lose the connection with him, and I grasp at straws to change the subject away from how badly I want his lips on me. "So how many predators can you shift into, Bond? How many creatures with big teeth are you hiding under all that skin?"

He blows out a breath and gets his helmet on, buckling

it up. "All of them. If it exists, I can shift into it."

"So you can shift into *anything*? Anything?! Fuck, that's exciting! Show me something else! Gah, that is so damn cool!"

He chuckles again and starts the engine, kicking the stand and taking off down the little winding road to get us back to the highway. It's much nicer with his jacket on. and I let the cool air over my legs calm my libido down a little. As much as I enjoy the banter, I can't take too much of it. Not when we have a whole night to get through, and I don't want to wake up underneath him with a horny bond inside clawing at him.

Or do I?

Fuck, no, Oli. We don't want that, no matter how good he seems to be with that mouth of his. I wonder if I can get away with touching myself in the shower before bed, just to take the edge off?

I haven't tried it since I started sleeping at the manor. It felt weird to get off in North's house knowing that my Bonds were sleeping under the same roof, and then since the Resistance took me, I've had Gabe and Atlas with me day and night.

Maybe I just need to release some of the tension myself and it'll ease up some.

As we pull into the garage, I already know there's no way that it would work, I'd just climb into bed with him afterwards and my bond would perk the hell up for round two.

Gabe kills the engine and tugs his helmet off. "What are you thinking about? You've been rubbing up against me the whole way home."

Fuck. "I've been thinking about how long it's been since I last got off and I might need to borrow your shower. Or lock myself in my bathroom for an hour before we go to bed."

Apparently, that's the wrong thing to say.

I forget sometimes that they're all twice the size of me, fuck, or maybe even three times, and Gabe just tucks his hands under my ass to lift me up and off of the bike with him, my legs wrapping around his waist as he holds me against his back.

I squeak in outrage but he just laughs at me, jostling me up until he's basically giving me a piggyback ride, and I dissolve into laughter at his antics.

"I'm not sharing you for the rest of the night, so you're coming to my room. Bassinger gets you tomorrow and we both know he's not going to let me within ten feet of you on his night, so if you're going to get off in the shower, it's happening in mine."

I wrap my arms around his shoulders and just enjoy the ride, praying to all things good and holy that we don't run into anyone on our way to his room. I also have no clue where his room is, so I can't just duck my head and hide from everyone.

We get into the same elevator that we usually do to get to my room but he hits the button for the second floor. I bury my face in his neck and take in a good lungful of his scent, the cold night air and just a tiny bit of the fights still clinging to him, and when my eyes fall open again, I meet Nox's eyes down the hallway right as the doors close.

Just once I'd like to see him without him sneering at me because it deflates my good mood so freaking fast.

"Ignore him, Bond. He'll... get over his shit eventually. Maybe."

I scoff at him and wriggle to attempt to get down but his arms just tighten around my legs. "He won't. I think the only part of Nox that will ever accept me is Brutus and, honestly, I'm okay with that."

Gabe grunts as the doors open again and then he's off down the hallway too freaking quickly because I've never been on this floor before, I don't think, and when he takes two different turns, I know there's no way I'm making it out of this place tonight in case of an emergency.

I really need to ask North for a map.

When we stop at a door, Gabe grabs his keys and unlocks it, pushing the door open and holding out a hand for me to go in first. It's all very gentlemanly and sweet considering the dirty mouth on him all night.

The room looks exactly how I'd expect Gabe's room to look. A ton of football and sports shit everywhere, the bed primly made because obviously one of the maids has been in here, and the closet is overflowing with his clothes. There's a huge TV on the wall and a gaming console under it, shoes everywhere, and it's clear this place has been sort of a dropping ground for him.

"I probably should have cleaned before you got here," he says, scratching at the back of his neck, and I shrug at him with a scoff.

I flop back on his bed without a thought. "What do I care about spotless rooms? Mine has been a mess of boys and pillows and bullshit for weeks."

He chuckles and drops down over me, propped up on his arms to kiss my cheek before he pushes back up and heads to the bathroom to wash up.

The second the shower cuts on, all I can think about is him in there, naked and soapy. Is he going to jerk off in there? Is he just as pent up as I am, is he thinking about me in this dress or the tiny thong that he kept getting flashed? God, I want him so fucking badly.

I start thinking about homework.

I think about the whispers of monsters and bombs in stadiums and people being taken. I think about the Resistance and what they do to people and, just for good measure, I think about my parents.

My libido finally calms the fuck down.

He comes out in a pair of sweatpants and a tank top, climbing up onto the bed next to me and tucking me into his arms without hesitation. I sigh as I melt into his embrace, happy that he's so much more relaxed than Gryphon was and actually wants me in here.

It's quiet for a minute as we soak each other up and then Gabe drawls, "You owe me something, Bond."

I let out a sigh, I've been waiting for this. I'm surprised he didn't ask the moment we got to the warehouse, payment in advance, and it warms something in my chest that he trusts me to honor our agreement.

I let my eyes slip shut and listen to the strong sound of his heartbeat as I muster up the words. I'd thought a lot about what I'm going to tell him, whether to go with a safe option or the worst possible thing, and I'd decided that I'd have to give him something bad.

Something like a warning.

"My parents moved a lot because of me. I didn't realize at the time but it makes a lot of sense to me now. I was six the first time my gift came out and… one of the boys in our neighborhood was an absolute shit to me. He was always picking on me, pulling my hair and taking my bag from me on our way to school. My dad told me to stick up for myself and to tell them if I needed help with it, but I was always such a headstrong kid."

Gabe's hands run up and down my back, a soothing motion, and he doesn't try to hum along or interrupt, thank God. I don't know if I'd be able to say it if he did.

"He shoved me at school in the playground. There was a sharp rock on the ground and I cut my hand open. My gift came out and hit him full force. I didn't slowly come into what I can do. I got all three gifts in a rush and he was on the ground, brain-dead but *writhing*, before I had the chance to even stand up. He was just a little kid, just an asshole who didn't know how to talk about emotions because... well, he was six. Now he's dead. My gift slowly ate away at his brain until his parents eventually turned his life support off when he was twelve. You guys might not be monsters but... well, I am."

I don't like talking about it. I don't like talking about any of the times I've used my gift, even the times I'm sure the person deserved it, but talking about Lucas is in my top three 'nope' topics.

Right up there with my parents' accident.

"I almost killed Gryphon the first time I shifted."

My heart stutters in my chest and I lift my head to look at him. He swallows as he meets my eye, hesitant, and it takes me a second to realize he's worried that I'm going to be angry at him.

I just told him I caused a six-year-old to die a slow and painful death, and he's worried about pissing me off.

"I was late with my gift, mostly because I had a great childhood and my parents were extra protective of me. My mom was the Central to my dad and her other Bonded, but John died in the Riots before I was born, so my parents wrapped me up in cotton wool. I didn't have my first shift until you disappeared."

Oh God. I rest my head back down on his chest and rub circles into his arm, just a little soothing motion to show him I'm here, listening and not judging him for any of this.

How could I?

"My dad was already so freaked out by me being in the Draven Bond, we'd gotten the news only the day before, and then when Gryphon came to tell us you were gone, I just... lost it. I shifted and I had no idea what was going on. I didn't understand how the shifted brain works, so I— fuck, I didn't know what I was doing. When I finally shifted back, Gryphon was torn up. My dad healed him up as best he could but he was still scarred because of it. Fuck, my parents were furious at me. Furious that their only son was a shifter and in the most dangerous Bond. I was the worst kid to them and then... my dad died. I can't remember when the last time I told him I loved him was because I was such a dick to him."

I want to cry for him.

If anyone understands the type of pain and grief that comes from regrets about your parents, it's me. Because of that, I know that there's nothing I can say to him that will make this better, nothing that can heal these types of wounds, and I tuck my face into his neck and hold him instead. We just lie there, wrapped up in each other without any judgement because who else can understand your ugly moments other than your Bond? The person destined to love you no matter what and for the first time... I maybe think about believing it. Believing that he might love all of the broken, monstrous, terrifying parts of me.

We fall asleep with the TV on, tangled up in each other, his face so close to mine that I can feel him like an ache in my chest.

I sleep like the dead, my bond satisfied that he's mine.

The only thing more torturous than waking up with a man wrapped around you that you're pretty sure can barely tolerate you?

Waking up on top of a man you're on your way to being in love with, one of his hands clutching at your hip while the other curves around your ass to pull you in tighter. Your face pressed into his chest, his thigh pressing between yours, and his dick hard against your belly.

I *never* want to move.

"You're going to be late," Gabe mumbles into my hair

when my alarm goes off for the third time, but I really just don't care.

When I tell Gabe that, he chuckles and kisses the top of my head. "You say that now, but Gryphon is a fucking nightmare if he thinks you're slacking off."

I groan as I pull away from him, my bond keening the loss of all of his warmth. "I'm not sure he could get any harsher on me. Jesus, I might die if he does."

Gabe smiles and stretches out but doesn't move from the pillows. "Better get that pretty ass of yours going then, Bond."

I hate him.

Well, I don't but honestly, I'd risk death to stay in this bed with him but it's not meant to be. By the time I'm heading out of his room, Gabe is fast asleep again. Thankfully, I find a maid cleaning some windows who gets me to the elevator and then I can get down to the gym safely by myself from there. I have to push myself to get there in time and I get to the doors at the same time as Gryphon does.

He comes from the opposite direction than I did though, and thank God my bond is docile and content in my chest because a very small and quiet corner of my brain wonders where he's been all night if it's five in the morning and he's coming from the other side of the neighborhood.

He glances over at me and his eyes flick up and down

my body quickly before he looks away and curses. I glance down but I'm just wearing shorts and one of Gabe's tanks, the same as yesterday. My stomach drops once again. I hate feeling like this, goddammit.

"How are you feeling today? Is your bond under control?" Gryphon says as he gets the door open and starts opening the gym up.

I follow him, dropping my keys and phone onto the floor by the mats and sitting down to get straight into stretching. "I'm fine. North's plan is working wonders, I have it all under control. I'll have to thank him."

I refuse to look like a brat. I'll choke on those *thank you's* but I'll get them out, even if it kills me.

He nods slowly, his head ducked, and he grabs a couple of bottles of water out of the mini fridge for us both. "Go through the stances again for me, we'll just do the same as yesterday."

He's acting weird, but my stomach is still in knots, so I just get straight into the training as though everything is fine. Fake it until I make it, it's an old but effective strategy that I'm sure would've worked if he could just do the same.

He doesn't.

We move on to sparring and I'm better already, quick at picking these things up now that I'm focused on doing well. It's amazing how things go when you're desperate not to look incompetent or lazy to your trainer.

When he throws me onto the mats for the hundredth time and knocks the air out of me, I think about dying here, just giving in and letting myself just expire. He stands over me and offers me a hand to help me up off of my ass, but he's still acting skittish and weird. It makes me feel awkward.

Because death isn't actually an option, I make myself face him and ask, "If something has happened can you just... tell me? I'd rather not deal with you acting strangely."

That gets him looking right at me. The scar over his eye stands out more to me today, mostly because I know the story behind it now. He's lucky he didn't lose his eye, and I send up a silent thank you to Gabe's dad for that.

Even if he did think my Bonds are monsters.

"It's nothing," he says and when I roll my eyes at him, he shrugs. "You look better. I was just shocked at how much better you look."

Oh, wow. *Wow*.

He's so freaking good at finding the perfect place to stick a knife in my gut and twist. I drop my hands and nod at him, pulling a face, but I can't hold back the sarcastic reply any longer, "Jeez, thanks! Am I anywhere close to your standards yet, or should I just expect to be treated like a second class citizen for the rest of time? You know what, you should laugh in my face again, that's what this situation needs!"

I glance up at the clock. We still have ten minutes left, but there's no way I'm going to just stand around for this shit. I bend down and grab my water bottle to finish it off and grab my things to get out of here. The run back should clear my head enough not to ruin everyone I run into today.

Fucking Bonds!

Gryphon catches my elbow and spins me around, pulling me into his chest with a scowl. "What the fuck are you talking about? I'm saying that you looked frazzled, tired, and completely fucking lifeless for weeks. We've been worried you were about to either drop dead or go off like Unser."

Okay, seriously, who *the fuck* is Unser?

Fuck, focus, Oli!

"I'm going home. I might be ready and willing to learn all about how to defend myself, but I'm not going to just stand around taking this shit from you. I'm done for today."

I try to pull my elbow away from him but he doesn't let me go. When I take a step back, he sweeps my feet out from underneath me, taking me back down to the mats with his body pressing back into mine. We've done it enough that I go down and land it correctly so it doesn't hurt at all, but I'm spitting mad at him for pulling it on me.

It doesn't matter, though, because I once again can't move with him pinning me.

"Just once, I'd like to be able to speak to you without

having to do this to you," he snaps, and even my bond gets pissed at that.

"I'm so fucking sorry that you have to be near me!"

He moves so he's only using one hand to pin mine above my head, grabbing my chin with the other one. "Can you make your mind up, because I don't know if you're worried about me wanting to fuck you or me not wanting you at all! I can't keep up."

I hate him.

This close to him, with his eyes bright on mine as his power kicks in, I want to scream at him for using it right now.

I chose my words carefully. "Wanting power from me and wanting *me* are two very different things. I already know which one you want, so don't start with your mind-game bullshit."

He leans forward and whispers against my lips, "You know nothing, Bond. You don't stick around long enough to know a goddamned thing. The moment anything gets real here, you run off, and that has nothing to do with what I want. You could just ask me."

I take a second to thank the universe for letting me be out of the bond haze for this conversation because I would've burst into tears a week ago over this. Ask him? Why the hell would I ask him something like that when he's made himself *very* clear on the subject.

He shakes his head at me slowly. "That's not the girl who ran right into the Resistance's arms after her friend. Where's your backbone gone?"

Red flag waving right at me, I unclench my jaw to spit out, "Why did you laugh at me? Why is it so fucking funny that I would want you while my bond was out of control? Why—"

He cuts me off with his lips.

On mine.

And my bond explodes out of my chest towards him, wrapping us up together. He grunts at the force of it but doesn't stop kissing me, his lips insistent on mine. I gasp at the sensation of us being wrapped up in each other and he takes the opportunity to deepen the kiss, his tongue stroking mine as his hand tightens over my wrist.

When he breaks away from me he murmurs, "I don't give a fuck about having more power. I don't give a fuck about what other people might want or think of our Bond group. I laughed because I spent weeks in your bed, trying to convince myself that I could be patient and wait for you to be ready, and it felt good to know that maybe you were struggling with it too. I laughed because you came here and acted as though you were above us all, and yet you were barely keeping it together around me. I didn't know how badly you were struggling. I would've never taken that situation lightly."

I swallow roughly, but when my eyes flick back down to his lips, he pushes up and away from me. "I have limits too, you know. If you don't want to Bond, then you need to get out of here."

Getting through my day is almost impossible.

I find myself both hyper-focused and distracted all at once. It's like I'm completely engrossed in my classwork and taking all of the notes I'll need to get my passing grades, but I can't hold down a conversation with any of my friends.

Sage gives me a curious look but doesn't comment or attempt to force me into getting my shit together. Sawyer attempts to tease me about it but it all just goes over my head. Felix only sits with us at lunch, so he just follows Sage's lead, politely leaving me the hell alone.

Gabe is extra affectionate and argues with Atlas over everything all day so that he can be near me. I'm grateful because after my morning with Gryphon, I feel untethered.

Like everything I'd come to know was wrong.

I'd accepted that they hated me. It was useful in keeping them at arm's length. I'd convinced myself that it was only my bond that was desperate for their approval but, well, I can't lie to myself about that anymore. Even if it brings up even more things I'll have to work through.

Like if North feels like that too?

Is he harsh on me because he actually wants the Bond or because he wants me? I feel as though he's made his displeasure at being stuck with me very clear, but am I just seeing what I want to in this situation or do I have it right?

Nox is like Pandora's box; a whole lot of 'no, thank you' because if I start thinking about him, I'll never stop. What is it about his behaviors and actions, all of them fucking terrible, that makes it impossible for me to just forget about him?

I have to consciously force myself not to think about his panicked heartbeat under my ear, the way his body had tensed at the weight of me on his lap. Brutus had even come out to watch, the closest I think he's ever been to seeing me as a danger.

"I thought the bedsharing was helping? Should I kill Ardern for doing it wrong?" Atlas murmurs into my ear and I startle back into myself. The table has cleared around us, only Gabe is left, but he's busy on his phone and not listening.

I don't even remember Sage and the others leaving.

I clear my throat. "No, it's just— I spoke with Gryphon this morning, and now I'm rethinking my entire life."

He nods slowly, his eyes bright and a small smirk stretching across his lips. "Oh yeah? How far into your life are you? Have you gotten to me yet?"

I lean forward and brush my lips against him instinctively, just a tiny connection that's over in an instant, but he tenses and chases after me as I pull away. I giggle and put a hand on his chest. "I shouldn't have done that. I don't know what's gotten into me this morning."

He quirks an eyebrow at me and glances back down at my lips. "Whatever it is, I like it. Kiss me all you want, Sweetness."

My bond purrs in my chest at the sound of his voice, coaxing Atlas' bond out to push at my skin.

"You two do realize we're in public, right? Jesus, stop that shit before North catches wind of it and we're all reamed out over dinner again," Gabe drawls, and I slap both of my hands over my face and burrow into Atlas' chest.

"Don't say reamed to me right now," I mumble and even though the words are muffled by my hands, they both hear me well enough.

Atlas barks out a shocked sort of laugh and Gabe rolls his eyes but they share a look that gets my bond humming in my chest, desperate for them both.

I groan and push up to my feet, slinging my bag back over my shoulder and giving them both a savage look. "What part of 'horny bitch bond' are you two not grasping?"

Atlas shrugs and grabs my hand. "You started it, but I will say, I'm not sharing you tonight. If you want a Bond pile, you need to pick someone else's night to have one because I want you to myself."

Gabe shakes his head and takes up on my other side, grabbing my other hand. It should be sweet, but I definitely feel as though they're about to play tug-of-war with me in a battle for dominance. "No one is going to give up their night... except maybe Nox. Fuck, we'll have to see how the first night goes and then reassess."

I've been thinking about that a lot too, because after Atlas tonight, it'll be his turn tomorrow and I'm quietly shitting myself over it.

Do I trust Nox? No, no I don't. Do I trust North's assessment of his brother? Also no, though I feel a little bad about it. He'd been so sincere about assuring me he would've stepped in, but I also get the feeling he has a huge blind spot when it comes to his younger brother.

Do I trust Gryphon? That one is harder. I believe that he believes North. It carries a little more weight because he can tell if Nox is lying, so maybe that could be a way to figure out if I can go through with this.

Gabe heads off to football training with a quick kiss to my cheek and then Atlas drives me over to the cafe for my shift. I'm expecting him to leave me there like he usually does, a little calmer about my protection now that he's aware that I can hold my own, both with my gift and physically thanks to my training, but he parks and walks me in. I roll my eyes at the grin he gives Gloria as he orders coffee and enough food to get him through my four hour shift and then sets himself up in the booth he's claimed as his own.

People come through in waves all afternoon, students and frat boys and professors alike, but clearly I've missed something major in my brain fog today because they're all talking about one thing.

One of the councilmen has been kicked off of the board.

It doesn't really register as important to me at first because I'd already know if it was North and the Council don't mean shit to me, except for the fact that they keep letting North do whatever the hell he wants with me without any repercussions. But then I hear the name.

Councilman Sharpe.

He was one of the two men Gabe had warned me about before Sage's party months ago. He said something about him rummaging through my head to find out all of my secrets... I'm curious about what would get a man kicked off of the council when their seats are reserved from birth.

Literally.

North had inherited his father's seat, apparently even killing one of your Bonds isn't enough to lose your family's chair. Gabe said that North's uncle took it over temporarily and then when he was old enough, North took it back.

I'm curious as hell about it but no one around me knows anything, or they're not openly talking about it anyway. I share a look with Atlas when I come to the table near his booth and he shrugs at me.

"I can ask my parents about it, but they'll only know the official statement."

I nod and I already know that we have access to a councilman who will know *exactly* what the reason is but I'm fairly sure North won't tell us shit.

And that just gets me thinking about my Bond issues all over again.

I wait until the cafe is quieter, the last wave of frat boys finally clearing out, and let Gloria know that I'm going to use the restroom. I grab my phone on the way and lock the door behind me, fumbling a little as I write out the text to Gryphon.

I need to ask a favor from you and it's really hard for me to do that, so please don't be an asshole about it.

I'm not sure if I'm actually expecting an answer from him, he literally never messages me, but my phone buzzes almost instantly.

Tell me what you need.

Huh. I guess clearing the air with him this morning has done wonders for us and figuring out what the hell we're doing.

Can you please speak to Nox about me sleeping in his bed tomorrow night and make sure he's actually okay with it? I don't want to get there and have him tear me to pieces about it.

He doesn't reply straight away and there's only so long I can sit in the restroom without Gloria thinking I have IBS or something, so I send one last text and then shove my phone away, getting back to work.

Please? I trust you to make sure I'm okay.

When I finish my shift, Atlas doesn't drive me right back to the manor. Instead, he drives me out to get tacos from a food truck Gabe has been talking about for weeks. I didn't know that Atlas had been watching me closely enough to see how badly I wanted to try it. Fish tacos are in my top ten favorite foods, so when we roll up there, I grin at him so wide that my teeth feel like they're going to bust out of my face.

"You're so easy to please, Bond. Shoes, food, and

sweaters I've worn… the others are fucking idiots if they can't get that right."

I roll my eyes at him. "It might be a little more complicated than that, but you've picked good places to start."

He scowls at me when I reach for my door handle, hot-footing it around the car to open it for me and help me out. Gabe is usually in the backseat and doing it for me, I didn't realize Atlas was old-school about this too. It's cute though. When we order, I attempt to pay for our food. I still haven't managed to pay him back for all of the breakfasts he's bought me, but he acts as though I'm trying to mortally wound him.

"You said you'd cover things until I had my feet under me. Well, I'm working now. I can buy us dinner," I say, waving my hand at him, but he just gives me a playfully withering look.

"Over my dead fucking body is my Bond paying for dinner. Who do you think raised me? Put that away before you embarrass me any more."

He says it in a joking tone but his eyes are the type of serious that gets your attention. I watch as he pulls out his own credit card and swipes, grinning at the girl taking our order in a very polite but frosty way.

He's always very careful about being friendly but very unavailable with people on campus, and when the girl's eyes flick down his body, she settles on where his fingers are laced with mine, and he tugs me into his side a little more securely so there's no question of whether he's taken or not.

My bond likes that *a lot*.

We wait together in the cool night air, wrapped up in each other as we watch the other patrons come and go. All of the students we see sneak looks and whisper amongst themselves about us, but I'm too content in my Bond's arms to kick up a fuss.

Once we get our food, Atlas leads me back over to the car but instead of getting in, he surprises me by lifting me gently onto the hood to sit together here and eat.

I ease my way back carefully so I don't scratch the paint or dent it. He's less fussy about it though and just climbs on up after me, handing me my drink and setting the food up between us. It's the perfect way to just be alone together without the crushing weight of the Draven manor hanging over us.

I dig into the tacos and can confirm they're the best I've ever eaten. I moan a little around my mouthful and Atlas grins at me again, shifting and readjusting himself so obviously that I laugh back at him.

"Tease! And after all I've done for you, Sweetness," he drawls, and I salute him with my food.

"I told you, you've all gotta work a little harder than

dinner and a movie to impress me, baby." I jokingly tack the pet name onto the end, but his eyes flare and I think I'll be calling him that some more in the future.

Fuck.

I can't forget myself here.

I swallow a mouthful and look away, taking in the busy night around us. There's no one close to us, no one that could overhear what we're talking about, but there's plenty happening in the early night of this sleepy college town.

The food trucks are a popular choice and the lines for each of them have dozens of people in them. Some of the students are openly drinking in the parking lot, laughing and joking loudly, and it's like we're in our own little bubble for a minute.

"You don't have to worry, Sweetness. I'm not taking you for dinner and hoping for anything. I just didn't want to have to share you at all tonight," Atlas murmurs, leaning back on his elbows and watching me intently.

I don't understand how he can be so... perfect for me. He's never asked anything of me. Not to Bond or be together, not a damn thing.

He's almost too good to be true.

My brain is all sorts of the worst because I have to push him, test him, figure out what is really going on with him because if he turns on me later, I will break in half. "What do your parents think of you moving here? What do they think of you having a monster Bond?"

The dreamy look slides off of his face but he doesn't look angry at me asking, only that it's not his favorite topic. "Neither of them were happy about me moving. I'm a trust fund baby though, so there wasn't much they could do about it. Also? No more monster bullshit, Oli. I know you. I know exactly who you are and I know a monster when I see one. That's not you."

I pick at the second taco on the tray, half eaten and still looking delicious, even if my appetite is starting to wander off thanks to my prying. "How, though? How would you know all about me if you only know about one of my gifts? Atlas, it's— the gift you know about is my secondary. It's not the big one."

He nods slowly and rubs the back of his neck. "I don't want to lie to you, Oli. There's a lot we don't know about each other, a lot that you're choosing not to tell me, and a lot that I'm not saying as well. We're both guarded and trying to keep each other while we're carrying baggage."

Well, that's true of me. I know it, and even though I know that he's had a whole life before we met, it makes my bond twitchy to hear him say he has secrets too.

I mean, duh, Oli. Of course he does, in the same way all my damn Bonds do, but still. There's something about hearing it that digs under my skin.

He looks over at me again and puts his empty tray back

down onto the hood of the car. "Your eyes, the void, it's the thing that's keeping North guessing. He thinks your power is Neuro but the voids say it's not that."

Fuck. I force a whisper out, "It's not Neuro."

He nods. "No, it's not. I know it's not. I know exactly what it is, Oli, and I'm still here. I know exactly what your gift does to people, and I'm not running away scared. You're still the exact Bond I've been dreaming about since I was a kid, the beautiful girl who I'd give my life for... except that I'm indestructible, so I don't have to worry about that anyway. See? We were made for each other."

We definitely should be talking about this and not just alluding to it, because how the hell would he know? "Have you... seen eyes like mine before? A gift like mine?"

He clears his throat. "There's no one alive today with your gift except you. I know of people who had lesser gifts like yours though. You broke the mould, Sweetness."

Fuck.

Okay, he's probably got it wrong anyway. He's probably thinking that he's got me all figured out but is way off base.

"The real question I have, Oli, is why didn't you destroy Nox when he touched you? Why not just kill him for daring to touch you?"

Fuck.

Does he know? He can't. Destroy... He's definitely talking about the soul-triggering, brain melting that I can do. It's definitely not… anything else.

I want to run away from him. I want to take off screaming into the streets as a cold sweat runs down my spine. He's watching me closely, his arms tense like he's preparing himself to chase me down.

"He's mine. I know it's stupid. I know he crossed a line, but he's mine. I'd protect him the same as I'd protect you. It doesn't mean I forgive him or want him around… I just don't want his death on my conscience."

He nods and starts packing up the mess from our dinner as though he hasn't just told me he knows what I can do and rocked my entire world on its axis while I scramble to figure out if he means it or not.

He can't.

Right?

He smiles at me as he climbs down from the hood and throws away our trash. "Draven's little spy is still hanging out in your hair. I'm not saying another word about it with it around."

Oh.

Oh shit, I forgot Brutus was even there. Jesus, what if I'd blurted something out and ended up on the Dravens' radar with the extent of how bad my gift really is?

I want to scream.

Atlas helps me down and then tugs me into his arms, resting his cheek on the top of my head. "Stop it, Sweetness.

I don't care if it takes me the rest of my life, I'm proving to you that you're everything to me, gift or not. I'd kill for you without a second thought, and I know you feel the same way. I'll prove it to you, no matter how long it takes."

I desperately want to believe him.

He helps me back into his car and then we drive back to the manor together. The garage is missing all of my Bonds' usual cars, and I raise an eyebrow at Atlas when he helps me out once he's parked.

"Did they say they were all going to something? Where would they all be going at once that we wouldn't be invited to?"

He huffs out a laugh, wriggling his eyebrows at me. "Who the fuck cares, we have the place to ourselves! We should go fuck with their stuff. What's the worst thing we could leave in North's bed? Come on, Sweetness. What's the worst you've got?"

I cackle at him, enjoying his playful mood, and I let him lead me through the house. He's far too good at directions and I'm a little pissed he's figured the maze out so quickly.

Trust fund baby.

I groan at him. "It just clicked in my head. You grew up in a house like this, didn't you? Fuck, you grew up in a mega-mansion too."

He slings his arm over my shoulder and pulls me into his body, pressing his lips close to whisper to me, "It's even bigger than this place. There are servants' quarters and separate staircases for the help. My parents are *filthy* rich. The Bassingers are the Dravens of the East Coast."

I shake my head at him with a grin. "How did I get so lucky to end up with all of these wealthy, arrogant Bonds, hm? *Blessed.*"

He chuckles at the sarcasm dripping from my tone, but I'm also not joking. My parents were well off and I know that there's an inheritance waiting for me somewhere, but the years I spent on the run have given me a real appreciation for hard work and taking care of my own shit. The very idea of living off of other people's money, their hard work, it makes me itch.

Then North's warning about me being a gold-digger filters into my brain and I'm mad about it all over again.

I clear my throat and change the subject before my bond wakes up swinging about it. "So where did North put you? If you're in the basement, we can just go sleep in my room tonight."

He grumbles under his breath and then leads me through the second floor. When he stops, I recognize the hallway straight away and giggle.

"He put you next to Gabe? How are you taking that?"

He shoots me a look of warning as he gets his door unlocked, shoving it open and flicking the lights on.

It's a barren room.

Okay, that's a little dramatic, but it has about as much of his personality in it as my room has of me. It's the same layout and color scheme as Gabe's, but the only thing of Atlas' in there are his bags, which are open but still packed neatly, and his laptop, which is sitting on the bed.

"I haven't really been doing anything but sleeping in here. If we're sticking around, I should get rid of my apartment and move in properly, but I'm waiting until you're sure."

I nod and step around him to collapse on the bed, letting myself sink into the luxurious mattress. It's the same as all of the mattresses in the manor, and I think my taste has suddenly become expensive because I refuse to sleep on anything less ever again.

"Are you... sure? Or are we lulling everyone into a false sense of security here? Gimme a sign, Sweetness," he says as he toes his shoes off and climbs up next to me.

My bond is happy with how tonight has gone and his close proximity. It doesn't even try to take over when I curl up next to him, tucking my face into his chest.

"I really need to figure out how to get the chip out. Once that's dealt with... I'll have to leave."

He nods and tucks me in even closer. "We. We'll have to leave. You're not getting rid of me, Sweetness. Not ever."

Sometime after midnight, I wake to the feeling of one of my Bonds climbing into the bed behind me. I rouse just enough to lift my head off of Atlas' chest and see Gabe tucked in behind me and Gryphon dropping into one of the ornate armchairs that he's dragged over to the door, the lines of his body tense as he gets comfortable there, watching over us.

My brain doesn't properly register what's happening, how not okay things must be if they're both here right now, so I lie back down and let myself drift back into a deep sleep, my bond pleased to have more of my Bonds close by.

I wake hours later to Atlas furiously whispering, "It's my night, what the fuck are the two of you doing in here?"

I groan a little, rubbing a hand over my face, and Atlas' arm tightens around me protectively. It's early, my alarm hasn't gone off yet, and I'm struggling to get my shit together enough to figure out what's happening here.

The TV is still on from where we'd fallen asleep with the movie playing and the backlight illuminates the room just enough that I can see Gryphon is still awake in the armchair. He looks exhausted, fully dressed in his Tac gear, and there's blood on his shirt.

"Are you hurt?" I croak, and my bond starts to hum in my chest at the very idea of him in pain.

Gryphon's eyes flick in my direction and then down at himself like it never occurred to him that whatever he's been doing last night might've left evidence behind. "I'm fine. This isn't mine, but you'll either need to avoid North or come to terms with healing him."

I struggle to sit up, pushing away from Atlas and breaking his firm hold on me. "Where is he? I'll heal him, just tell me where he is."

Gabe grunts behind me and I finally remember that he's here in the bed too, curled up on his side in a torn shirt and dirty shorts. He's not the type to ever come to me dirty. Gryphon doesn't either, something bad has happened.

Atlas comes to the same conclusion at the same time and scowls at Gryphon. "What the fuck has happened now?"

Gryphon finishes up the text he's sending, then shoves his phone back in his pocket, crossing his arms again, but his eyes soften a little when they land on me in the bed in my heavily disheveled state. I already know I look like a mess, the crappy night of sleep didn't do my hair any favors.

Did I even take my makeup off last night or do I have raccoon eyes right now?

Fuck, why am I thinking that right now? One of my Bonds is hurt, no one gives a shit what I look like.

"North's on his way. He said he's already seen a healer."

Oh.

I don't like that.

I don't know how to tell any of them that I don't like that, but Atlas glances up at me and his jaw tightens, his protective instincts sharp as always. I'm not sure I'll ever figure out how to keep my emotions and feelings hidden from him because he reads me like a damn book.

There's a quiet knock at the door and Gryphon leans over to pull the door open for North, sharing a look with him as he steps in. North's face is made up of shadows and there's even streaks on the front of his crumpled suit. He must have just gotten home from the healers, coming here instead of showering or getting changed.

There's a panic in my chest at whatever the hell has happened.

Gryphon huffs out a breath. "You look like shit. You need to clear your calendar for tomorrow so you don't lose your shit at Pen and set your nightmares on her for nagging."

Pen.

I hate that woman and I've never even been formally introduced to her, but the familiarity they all have with her sets my teeth on edge.

North rubs a hand over his eyes, groaning. "I don't have time to lose anything this week, let alone have a break."

Atlas doesn't like this conversation any more than I do and snaps, "But you still had time to head off to a healer instead of coming to Oli? Good to know."

North frowns and looks past him to me, answering me directly instead of Atlas. "I didn't want to trigger anything in you right now. We need you at full power, just in case."

Atlas looks between us both and then his temper just snaps. "In case of what? What the fuck has happened? If this is about keeping Oli safe then we need to know."

North stares at him for a second and then lets out a breath. "My uncle was murdered tonight. The Resistance apparently had a sleeper cell close to him, a member of his household that I've known for over a decade slit his throat in his sleep."

My stomach drops.

Fuck. Fuck, they're getting closer again. Can they feel

me here now? Of course they can, they have Gifted whose entire job is to find Gifted like me. Hell, after I got out of there, they probably switched to only searching for me. Now I'm back to full power and glowing like a goddamned beacon, it's only a matter of time before they find me.

Atlas slowly pulls himself up straighter on the bed, shifting in front of me a little in that way he has of always shielding me no matter who we're facing. I glance at Gabe but he's still sleeping, his chest moving steadily with an arm flung over his eyes. His bond must really trust us all to keep him sleeping soundly through all of this.

My voice is soft as I try to give my condolences, "I'm sorry... for your loss."

North stares at me but his eyes are cold and distant, like he's put up a giant wall between us to stop me from ever being able to touch him. I get it, I don't blame him, but I have to remind myself that he's just as responsible for it as I am. Gryphon chose to look past me supposedly running. Gabe did too, and Atlas. The Dravens are the ones who won't.

"How do you know it's the Resistance? Who's taking credit for the attack?" Atlas says as he climbs out of the bed, grabbing his shirt from the end of the bed and pulling it over his head. I pull my knees up and hug them to my chest, resting my cheek on them as I watch the three of them test each other.

Gryphon's eyes narrow at him. "The maid who did it left a message behind in his blood, there's no mistaking who's done this. There's been a lot of talk about shifting power in the old families. William won't be the last death."

I look over at North but he's glaring across the room at the window. I'm not sure how close he was to his uncle but there's definitely a cloud around him again.

The room stays quiet for another second as we let that information soak in, then North looks back at Gryphon and jabs a finger at me. "Watch her. They're breaking up the council families' Bonded groups, they'll be coming after us the moment they find an opening. There needs to be a Bond with her at all times outside of this house, double the TacTeam presence on campus, make sure everyone knows that this is an 'ask forgiveness' situation."

That doesn't really make sense to me but all three of them are agreeing with each other and, although I know I'll be feeling claustrophobic before dinnertime, I also would rather die than be taken by the Resistance again.

Atlas shifts again, moving a little more in front of me, but Gryphon nods and stands up. "We'll move training to the home gym. Oli, you can hit the treadmill first. Go get ready and we can start now, no point trying to go back to sleep. Bassinger, you should come down too. Being strong doesn't help if you don't know technique."

Oh God.

Atlas has the exact reaction I'm expecting from that statement and he turns to stone in the bed next to me.

Time to flee.

I scramble up out of the bed and give Atlas a quick peck on the cheek as I grab one of his sweaters to shove on over my pajamas. I wasn't expecting a room full of them when I put on the tiny tee and panties to pass out in last night, and I need a little coverage to get me back to my room.

North follows me out of the bedroom and when I step into the elevator, he steps in behind me, completely engrossed with his phone and he doesn't acknowledge me when I hit the button for the third floor. I don't blame him. Normally I would be thrilled that he's ignoring me, but there's something really gut-wrenching about this type of silence.

The type where he's lost someone and I have no idea how to say something to him without seeming insincere or petty.

The doors open again and we step out together, walking down the hallway side by side until we get to my room. I hesitate at the door, tugging at my bottom lip with my teeth as if I can gnaw through it to safety or some shit. North doesn't look up from his phone as he slows down instinctively with me, I can tell whatever is on there is important and is pissing him off from the state of his shoulders right now.

I don't want to add to that but… I also can't just leave.

"Whatever you need to say, just do it and then get on with your day. Gryphon and Bassinger are waiting for you."

I clear my throat and murmur, "Don't go see a healer next time. Healing doesn't deplete my gift and my bond doesn't… like other people healing you. It's— shit, I mean, you can do anything you want to do, obviously, but don't go somewhere else on my account. Fuck, ignore me, I'll shut my bond up."

His eyes snap up to mine but I'm already scrambling into my room and shutting the door quietly behind me. I don't want to hear the severe talking to he's about to give me for demanding things from him while he's grieving and dealing with the fallout of losing his uncle.

I wonder if he and Nox have any family left at this point, their parents are all gone and I'd only ever heard of their uncle. I forgot how little I know about them all, especially the Draven men with all of their nightmare creatures and shadows to hide in.

Gryphon doesn't go easy on me just because Atlas is there. Nope, he runs us both into the ground. Atlas might've walked into the full-sized, fully stocked, insanely expensive home gym that North has in the basement with a cocky attitude, but Gryphon destroys us both.

"I would rather die than be here each morning. No wonder Ardern was a smug fucker when I left," Atlas groans from the mats next to me, but I'm beyond conversation right now.

"Can't... talk... fuck, can't *breathe*," I pant and Gryphon scoffs at me, grabbing my hand and pulling me up to sit, and shoves some water at me.

Joke's on him, my fingers are no longer working and there's no way I can get the bottle to my lips without wearing all of it. Atlas groans and rolls to sit up with me, grabbing the bottle off of me to get it open, and attempts to hand it back to me.

I have no plans of embarrassing myself in front of either of them anymore, so I just shake my head to pass on it.

"You might want to work on your stamina, Bassinger. Wouldn't want to be the only disappointment in the Bond," Gryphon snarks, smirking even as he's forced to duck to avoid the water bottle Atlas launches at his head.

"No innuendos. That's a party foul, I don't have the energy to deal with my bond," I groan, and when I lift the bottom of my shirt to wipe at my face, they both stop to look at all of the exposed skin I've just flashed them.

Neither of them attempt to hide their reactions to me, and it's definitely an ego boost because I'm not doubting Atlas' stamina one bit. He's gone from looking half-dead to re-energized and ready for round two on the mats, except this time with less-clothing and—

"Oli, knock it off. You're glowing," Gryphon says, and I fling myself back onto the mats again.

"You both started it! Fuck, I need another cold shower."

Atlas huffs and grabs me to pull me up to my feet. "Don't talk about showers either. C'mon, we have classes to get to. Say goodbye to Shore and tell him we're never coming back because he's a sadist."

I don't have time to feel awkward as Atlas gently shoves me in Gryphon's direction. I'm openly affectionate with Gabe and I think he's assuming I'll be the same with Gryphon but… I have no idea how to do this. I have no idea how to just relax around him, even though we've managed to negotiate a cease fire of some kind.

Gryphon raises his eyebrows at me and I blush a little, but Atlas just stalks off towards the door, which helps. Without his eyes on me, I can maybe fake my way through this, act as though this isn't terrifying to me.

I'm still expecting him to reject me in some way.

He can see it too and catches my arm to pull me into him, murmuring under his breath, "I spoke to Nox. Just go to his room when you're ready to sleep tonight, after ten, and I'll grab you in the morning. I promise you, it'll be fine."

I let out a breath and nod to him, relief flooding through my veins as a weight I wasn't aware was quite so heavy lifts from me. Before I have the chance to feel awkward or shy about it, he drops my elbow and grabs my cheek to pull me in for a kiss.

He's sinfully good at it.

I usually try to stick to kissing cheeks and this is exactly why because my bond flares to life in my chest, desperately scrambling at the restrictions I have on it. His bond touches my skin, gently stroking over my shoulders and down my body, though it stops respectfully around my waist.

If it went any lower I might've just spread out on the mats and begged him to Bond with me.

He breaks away from my lips and murmurs, "Keep thinking like that and I will, Bond."

My cheeks heat and I shove at his chest to stumble away from him. "Stay the fuck out of my head, Shore! That's also a party foul, you're on thin ice."

He scoffs and turns his back on me to start clearing up the mess we've made in here. "I couldn't help it, you were practically screaming it. My gift just fell over what you were throwing out."

Jesus fucking Christ.

I flee from him, running straight into Atlas and grabbing his hand to drag him away with me.

Stupid fucking Bonds and their wicked tongues.

North wasn't joking around when he said that security had to triple around campus.

When we get to Draven, we're escorted into the building by Kieran himself, and none of our friends are allowed to meet us unless it's inside the actual buildings. When we find Sage and Sawyer waiting outside of our lecture hall arguing with another Tac guy, Kieran sends him off and takes over Sage's protection.

I'm expecting him to just see us into the room and then leave to do rounds, but he forces us to sit at the very back so he can shadow us by the wall the entire time.

Gabe takes all of this easily, happy to have another set of eyes watching out for me, but Atlas is still fuming about being left behind at the stadium when Kieran had transported me out, so he's argumentative the entire time.

I'm not at all surprised and I just leave them to figure it out for themselves.

I don't question anything until we're all at lunch, choking down the world's worst meatball sub, and that's when I grill him.

"I thought you hated being on Bond watch, why didn't you assign someone else to stalk me? Or did Gryphon say it had to be you? Did you piss him off with something?"

He raises a very arrogant and pissy eyebrow at me but I just smirk back at him as I take another gross bite of the sub.

He isn't eating but he has taken a seat at the table in the corner where he can watch everything happening in the room, and I've already noticed he's stayed within arm's reach of me all day too.

Atlas has also noticed this.

"Shore made the call, he's the lead, but I agree with him. No one else on our team, that we trust completely, can do what I can. It's a Hail Mary, but getting you out and to safety is always an option with me around."

That makes sense and I nod as I take another bite, so Atlas finally turns on him and says, "I thought you hated Oli, you're being a little too friendly for my liking now."

Sage and I share a look across the table at each other because this is absolutely typical *boy* behavior and we've taken to quietly comparing notes on our guys lately. Felix might seem like much more of a gentleman than Gabe and Atlas but he pulls the same overprotective, alpha male bullshit with her that they do with me.

I really like him, and I'm so freaking glad Sage has given him a chance.

Kieran squints at something happening in the corner of the dining hall as he answers Atlas in a bored tone, "I didn't hate her. I had no respect for a little girl who ran away from a Bond group full of good men who were ready to protect her and take care of her. I didn't respect a girl who had a lot of resources wasted on her for a five year joyride around the country just for shits and giggles."

All of the air gets sucked out of my lungs at his words and I slowly put down the sub. Atlas doesn't get the chance to rip his arm off and beat him to death with it, though I'm sure that's what he's planning on doing, because a fight breaks out on a table three down from us. I find Sage shoved at me as Gabe and Atlas form a wall between us and the vicious destruction.

I tuck her behind me as well, just for an extra layer of protection, and I meet Kieran's eye behind us all as he watches everything going down with sharp eyes and his phone at his ear.

"What the hell is going on?" I mumble and Sage grabs my hand, craning her head a little to get a better look past Gabe.

"Aw, hell. It's Jacob and Martinez going for each other's throats again. They'll get kicked out for this if they don't quit!"

So just the typical Gifted students sort of fight then, nothing to worry about, except they'll both wish they'd saved it for later because without flinching, five TacTeam guys appear out of nowhere and take them both to the ground. I hear a lot of crunching noises and I'm sure there's got to be some broken bones in that pile.

Ouch.

Kieran mutters to us both, "They're fighting over the abductions. Jacob's brother is still missing and Martinez is running his mouth about it because his daddy is on the council. He's extra fucking mouthy thanks to your protection detail, and he's been loud about council favoritism."

Shit.

I roll my eyes at Sage. "He always was a little bitch. We need to lure him into the water with the pond bitch just to give him a taste of his own medicine."

Kieran shakes his head at me as his men drag the two guys out of the dining hall, their hands cuffed behind their backs. "And that's why my opinion of you changed, Fallows."

I stiffen and he doesn't elaborate on that until we're all back sitting down and attempting to finish off our food in peace. Well, there's no such thing as peace in here anymore because everyone is whispering and glancing over at our table like it's my fault the students are losing their shit.

I can't help that I'm precious, dangerous, volatile cargo.

"TacTeam aren't picked for their powers. It helps, sure, but there's better qualities that we're looking for during the simulations and obstacle courses. You've never given up, no matter how out-matched you were. You keep showing up and giving it your all, even when you're sure to lose."

Atlas shoves his tray away from himself and crosses his arms as he listens, his jaw flexing as though he's pissed, but I know now that it's also a sign that he's thinking.

Kieran jerks his head at Sage. "You went after your friend. You heard she'd been taken and just went for her, no matter the consequences. That takes the sort of guts that you can't train a person to have. Either you've got it or you don't."

He takes one last sweeping look around the dining hall and then turns to give me another of his trademark smirks. "Then there's the small fact that the Resistance knew you. You didn't run away from your Bonds. I'll bet every last fucking dollar I have that you didn't. You ran from something else, and when you were dragged back here, you were terrified you'd been tracked. You kept saying it, over and over again. Things will go bad if you're forced to stay here. Well, we're listening now, Fallows. Let's see what's coming after you."

SAVAGE BONDS

G abe has a craving for pizza, so after my shift is over at the cafe, we pile into Atlas' car and pick some up from the small local pizzeria two streets over from the Draven campus.

There's a crowd of students already there. Gabe is buzzing from the five coffees he'd drunk during my shift, so he's practically bouncing off of the walls as he greets people and chats with them. They're all more friendly than they have been for a while and my stomach roils with rage when I figure out why.

They want information and possible leads on William's death.

They're all just scared little sheep about the Resistance, and instead of doing something about it themselves, like taking up self-defense or working on their own gifts to master them, they're sucking up to my Bonds for protection.

The same men they've been calling monsters for years.

I'm feeling extra bloodthirsty about it, so when Gabe waves me over to meet someone, I fix a bored and bitchy look on my face in their direction. He might be willing to play the golden boy of campus, but over my dead fucking body will I.

Atlas chuckles under his breath at my expression but comes with me to be introduced to the guy standing with my Bond.

Gabe quirks an eyebrow at me, but the grin doesn't leave his face as he says, "Oli, this is Gray's roommate, Shay."

That snaps me out of my anger a little bit. "Is Gray back at school yet? Shit, sorry, nice to meet you."

Shay grins at me, friendly even with my bad attitude, and shrugs. "Sawyer's doing his best to get through to Gray's parents, but they're extra cautious. He's Telekinetic, so they should trust him a little more."

Huh. "Go Ice Hockey Hottie, that's a good gift. Maybe we should go around to meet his parents, inspire a little confidence in them that we've got this under control."

Atlas jerks me around to give me a look at my nickname for Gray and I grin at him, completely unrepentant. Gabe rolls his eyes at my antics because he's heard it a million times but also, I think, because he knows I'm just hyping my friends up.

Gray's hot, but he's nothing compared to any of my Bonds... even the ones that I'm still not so sure about. That's the power of the bond, they're the only ones I can think about or crave. I think it's completely fucking rude that being the Central means I feel this way, and yet Nox could bring a different girl to dinner each week without hesitation.

Bleh.

I can't think about that right now because I'll be climbing into his bed tonight, and I can't go in there angry about him daring to touch other women when I know he despises me. Fuck. I feel as though I keep cleaning up my mess of a Bond group, only to turn around and find twice as much behind me.

"His parents aren't on the council but they are a council family. They know all about William Draven, there's no fucking chance Gray's being let out of his tower any time soon, not even with you guys at his back. Jesus, I heard about what you did to that Resistance camp last night, Gabe. I'm sure half the fucking country has at this point. You're a beast."

Uhm.

What now?

I look over at Gabe, but he's keeping a carefully blank

face and it makes me feel a little violent. I don't like being the last to know everything and now that we've found our way into this relationship of sorts, it makes me want to bleed Shay out for knowing something I don't.

Atlas grabs my hand and tugs me away from the two of them, over to the pick up counter to grab our pizzas now that they're ready. He doesn't look back to see if Gabe is following us as he leads me back out to the car, tucking me into the front seat without a word or any judgement for the seething sort of hurt bubbling in my chest.

Gabe climbs into the back seat a minute later, chuckling under his breath as he waves again at someone outside, completely oblivious to the storm rolling through my stomach in the front seat.

There's a quiet moment where only my steady breathing can be heard in the silent space. In the rearview mirror, I catch Gabe frowning at Atlas when he doesn't immediately start the car and get us on the road.

Instead, Atlas strokes my hair back from my face, his fingers gentle where they brush against my cheek, but there's none of that gentleness when he snaps at Gabe, "Did you forget Oli is *violently* volatile? You probably shouldn't keep shit from her if it's already hit the gossip mills of this place."

Gabe glances at me and blows out a breath, running a hand through his hair and tugging on the ends a little.

"I didn't know how to throw it into conversation that I'd killed eighteen men last night. How do I just come out with that without sounding—"

Atlas cuts him off, "Without sounding like you did what you had to do to keep her safe? You just say it. Oli isn't going to break, you know what she's capable of."

Does he though? Well, he does, I guess. I told him enough that he should know. "I've killed people too, Gabe. I'm not going to think differently about you for doing that."

"Yeah, but you didn't tear eighteen men apart with your bare... okay, well, paws I guess. You know what I mean, I killed them physically, up close, and that's pretty violent."

I shrug, not fussed about that distinction, and tug on my seatbelt as Atlas finally gets the car moving. None of us speak until Atlas gets stuck at a red light in the last intersection before the gated community that the Draven manor is in.

"North and Nox went hunting after they found William. Gryphon and I found out after they were already elbows deep in a Resistance camp, they were too far gone to stop, so we just had to wait out their killing fury and make sure no one got close to them," Gabe says softly, and I get the feeling he thinks he's betraying his family right now by telling us this.

Being around them almost twenty-four hours a day, I've started to figure out the dynamics that were already in place before I got here. North isn't just the oldest, he's also the one who's taken on the responsibility for them all. He makes decisions with Gryphon, both of them natural leaders. Nox is the wildcard, loyal to the others, but very much walking his own path. I don't fully understand it yet, mostly because the way they treat him and refuse to call him out on shit confuses me, but I'm getting my head around it.

Gabe is definitely the 'kid brother' in this group.

They don't treat him like he's lesser than them even though he's younger and still in college, but they definitely have the same protective, nurturing sort of relationship with him that an older sibling would have.

The fact he's talking about it with us now is an offering, it's an act of faith that we're all doing what we can to bridge the chasm that we're all staring at in the middle of the Bond group.

The light turns green and Atlas gets us moving again as I ask, "How was North injured? Was Nox okay?"

Gabe rubs a hand over his eyes. "North's creatures aren't like Nox's. They're fucking *rabid*. He pushed himself too far in his anger at what happened to William, so when it was over, he barely had the energy to get them… put away. One of them took a chunk out of his arm before he got it under control."

Holy shit.

I turn around in my seat to look at him and his eyes drop down to where Brutus is curled up behind my ear. He's so quiet and calm that sometimes I forget he's even there, only the soft vibrations of his snores are a sign of him with me always.

"Nox was fine. Exhausted because he also pushed himself past his limits, but Gryphon got him home and cleaned up. His creatures have never let him get injured, not the entire time I've seen him fight. North's kill indiscriminately, but Nox's are very well trained in keeping their master safe."

I swallow and nod, my cheek turning in towards Brutus instinctively as he nuzzles at my skin affectionately.

"How did they know where to find the camp? I find it hard to believe they just tripped over a camp in the middle of the night while they were pissed," Atlas says, changing gears and then resting his hand on my knee in his own way of supporting me and showing me that none of this is scaring him away from me.

Gabe shrugs. "North and Gryphon have been tracking and mapping out Resistance sorting camps for years. They estimate that they have around thirty percent of them under monitoring, but they're struggling to get the TacTeam numbers they need to take them out. It's a catch -22 here because the upper society families refuse to join teams and fight, but they also became pillars of our community *because* they're Top Tier gifted. The lower families are willing but don't necessarily have the gifts we need in the fight."

Jesus.

I blow out a breath and watch the night pass us through the car window. Guilt climbs up my spine about how much of a brat I've been about the TT classes because that's where Gryphon needs to be finding more recruits. Fuck, Zoey would've been handy with her knockout power.

I'll have to talk to him about getting her back in the class.

It's not like she can touch me now, and I'm sure they can beat her into a better team minded headspace.

Atlas groans and glances over to me. "You're going to force me to keep training with that sadist, aren't you?"

I give him a half smile and shrug. "Think of it as a way to prove your stamina to him. I don't doubt it, but you guys are weird about proving who's the top dog around here."

Atlas waits until the car is parked and we're heading up to my room to eat the pizza before he pulls me in close to his side to whisper in my ear, "The only person I care about proving myself to is you, and I can think of much better ways to do that, Sweetness."

I lift my hand to knock on the door but I chicken out.

For the third time.

This is getting pathetic. Honestly, what's the worst Nox can do to me for showing up to his room on the night that we were assigned, when he's already agreed to have me here? The problem is that I'm not feeling particularly rational about it and, even with Gryphon's instructions swirling around in my head, I'm feeling freaking terrified about doing it.

My bond is quiet in my chest and I think that freaks me out more than anything else, the way that it's just decided that he's never going to change his mind about me and so I need to lower my expectations down to… well, nothing.

Is it too late to argue with North about this?

I glance over at his door because *of course* there are only three bedrooms on this level of the building and *of course* those rooms belong to North, Nox, and the one they've put me in.

Right.

Just knock on the door, Oli. Man up. Woman up? Fuck, what's a better, more inclusive way of saying 'get your fucking shit together and stop being a little cry baby about this, woman'? I don't know but also, this is probably just another method of procrastinating doing this.

I force myself to knock on the damn door by imagining how scowly Gryphon would be at me right now if he knew

I was freaking out about this. He'd be insulted that I was doubting him and how confident he is that everything is going to be fine.

I wait for a full three minutes before I stomp my foot and huff like a petulant toddler, of course he's not going to answer it and actually let me in. He's probably set up a spy cam to watch me waiting around for him like some pathetic—

Okay, snap out of this wallowing self-pity, Oleander.

I try the door handle and it's not locked, so I take a breath and poke my head through to call out, "Nox? This isn't funny, can I come in or not?"

Nothing.

Fucking men, I want to murder him and bathe in his innards.

I push the door open the whole way and step into the room, kicking the door shut behind me as my arms wrap around myself nervously as I look around the dark room.

I'm fine.

This is fine.

Fuck it, I call on my gift to let my eyes adjust to the darkness and I find myself standing in a library.

Right, so it's not exactly a library because it's the same size and general layout as the other rooms on this level, but there's no bed, and bookshelves line every wall. I step forward and, yep, the ensuite is in the same spot as mine is and so is the closet, except Nox's is full of books, and I mean *full* of books. There isn't a surface here that isn't overflowing with old, leather-bound tomes.

It's a different side of the professor, one I shouldn't be so surprised at... I'm not sure what I was expecting, but it wasn't this.

I walk around the shelves and it's only when I get to the end side of the room that I find the small, narrow spiral staircase tucked around a corner that definitely doesn't exist in my room.

"Nox? Are you up there?" I call, my voice a little less thready than last time, but still he doesn't answer.

I take one last look around the room but there isn't even a couch or armchair to curl up in down here, so I have to have a look up there at the very least.

I'm slow and hesitant at first, but once I get a look at the bedroom on the second floor, my feet move a lot faster.

Nox sleeps in a dream.

Okay, that's a bit dramatic, the room is smaller than the one downstairs and once again covered in books, but it's not as orderly here. No, he's clearly reading the ones up here, piles of them on every surface. There's a set of drawers in one corner and bedside tables on either side of the king-sized bed.

It's meticulously clean but cluttered, the type of busy clutter that comes with a very active mind, and it's the closest I think I've ever come to knowing something personal about Nox.

I perch on the bed to text Gryphon to ask him what the hell I should do, but his reply doesn't exactly fill me with confidence.

Just go to sleep. I'll be there at 4am to hit the gym.

A four o'clock start, that gives me six hours of sleep so, whether Nox is here and likes it or not, I need to pass out.

I'm already dressed in a pair of sweatpants and one of Gabe's old tees, so I just climb under the covers. I don't know which side of the bed is Nox's, so I climb in the far side and curl up in a ball. I'm tired enough that even with how nervous I am about being here, I slip into sleep easily.

I wake up hours later to the soft glow of Nox's nightmare creatures.

They're everywhere.

Brutus is bigger than he usually is as he stretches out on the bed next to me. When I look past him, there has to be at least a hundred different creatures laid out all over, covering every surface in the room. Most of them are barely more than smoke outlines but I can pick out other puppies of varying sizes. They're all asleep and curled up with each other in piles, and my breathing stutters to a stop in my chest at the sight of them all.

They're beautiful, made from a killing smoke but with

a strange glow, as though even in the darkest of nights there's still the glow of millions of stars to lead you through the night. They're haunting and beautiful and I'm obsessed with them all. I want to know each and every one of them the way I know Brutus and there's a deep sort of pain in me to know that I probably never will because Nox wouldn't even let me.

With that ache in my chest, I spot him on the couch with his head thrown back, his hair a mess of dark curls as he blows out a long breath. I freeze but try to keep my breathing even and slow so he doesn't notice that I'm awake. He's wearing slacks and a shirt with the top three buttons undone. His feet are bare and he looks more exhausted than I've ever seen him, the lines of a rough couple of days all over him.

I can't comfort him but that doesn't stop the longing in my chest to be able to.

I lie there and watch him brood on the couch, his eyes a little glassy as he looks around at each of his creatures with something close to fondness. They're definitely not the rabid creatures his brother commands, all of them docile and snuffling even as they nap around us.

It's peaceful.

If I could just forget how much he hates me, it would be the perfect little moment between us. Well, not really, because he has no idea I'm awake and watching him right now. I should open my mouth and find some words for him, offer my condolences and tell him how badly I want to wipe the Resistance from the Earth, but they get trapped in my throat.

I hear the door downstairs open and shut quietly, my bond tugging at my chest to say one of mine is here, and then North comes up the stairs, his feet quiet on the carpets when he walks over to get a look around the room.

He looks a lot less calm and pleased about the creatures everywhere.

Nox doesn't look at him but his tone is snappy as he snarks, "You've come to check up on me as well? Gryph has already been very firm about what is allowed to happen here."

North takes a seat on the couch next to his brother, but it's still so dark that neither of them notice that my eyes are open.

"I'm here to check on you. I know you didn't want this, and I don't want to find you drinking during your lectures again… or running off to find someone stupid enough to fight you like last time."

Nox huffs at him, rubbing a hand over his chest. He stops and looks down at his fingers, holding them up and looking at them in the pitch black room. His gift has to be at play here.

"I don't think I'm ever going to get used to them being

straight. I'm angry at her for messing with something she had no right to."

North shrugs. "She didn't know. She didn't have any control over it, you know that. I have as many reservations about this as you do, but you have to be reasonable, Nox."

He wriggles his fingers as though he's testing them. "I don't have to do anything. You told me that when you brought me back here. I don't have to do anything if I don't want to."

North presses his lips together and I can almost see Nox giving himself a point for that little win of his. Brutus snuffles in his sleep, turning towards me, and I let my eyes slip shut again just in case they look over here more carefully at the movement.

When North speaks again, his voice is lower, softer in the quiet, "They like her. I thought you'd just sent a spy, but look at them all."

"Or they're surrounding her to make sure she can't move from that bed without them noticing."

North makes an annoyed noise at the back of his throat. "She's barely more than a kid, Nox. She's not going to do anything. She's not—"

"Don't. I'm not talking about it. If you try, I'll throw you down those stairs. She's here because she's your Bond, and Gryph's, and Gabe's. If you insist on keeping me alive and *here,* then I'll play my part, but she's not mine. She never will be."

For the first time in a long time, my bond gets upset at the thought of not having him and even as I swallow down at the bile that creeps up my throat at his words, I push it down.

He's made his decision and so have I.

I wouldn't Bond with him even if the world didn't depend on that not happening.

North slips out of the bedroom quietly and Nox collapses back on the couch, pulling the blanket back over himself as he turns to get some sleep. Three feet never seemed so far away before, but now?

Now I don't think I'll ever bridge that gap.

"I fucking hate you. I hate every little thing about you, and if you weren't in this Bond group, I would snap your fucking neck and hide your goddamn body in a dump where you belong."

Gabe snorts with laughter at the vitriol dripping from Atlas' words but the look Gryphon gives him shuts him up fast. I don't have the energy or the oxygen available to talk shit at either of them, so I just focus on getting my breathing under control.

I spent an hour on the treadmill, then Gryphon got me on the free weights with Gabe while he trained with Atlas, one-on-one. It became very clear that whoever had gone over training with Atlas on the East Coast had let him coast on his form, thanks to his gift.

Gryphon isn't that type of trainer.

I've never watched him use his ability before, other than his lie detection and the pain blocking, and there's something oddly humbling about watching him hack into Atlas' brain and shut down his gift at every turn. Seriously, every time Atlas thinks about using it to win in their sparring, Gryphon just shuts him down.

And so now we're all watching Atlas rage about it.

"If you can't beat me without cheating, then you're useless to me. If you're useless to me, then you won't be trusted to protect Oli and you'll have a chaperone with the two of you at all times outside of this manor, so go right ahead and get angry about it. I'm not risking my Bond with an amateur. I'm sure Gabe will be happy to take over your shifts with her," Gryphon says as he readjusts the tape on his hands.

Gabe is practically glowing with pride at his words. I'm sure his cheeks are going to be aching soon with how hard he's grinning, but Gryphon has never been quick to throw out the compliments with me either, so I'm sure it's just a great feeling to know he thinks so highly of Gabe's skills.

I never doubted him. I've seen him fight enough to know he's unmatched in our TT class. It's been years of hard work to build up to where he is, not just the abilities, but the control he has over his gift.

He's a real asset to not only our Bond, but to the community as a whole.

Atlas grinds his teeth but Gryphon just shrugs at him, unrepentant. "Oli has only been doing this a few months and her footwork is better than yours. Your parents should be demanding a refund for whichever overpaid, lazy trainer they sent you to."

Atlas glances over at me and I keep my face blank as I lift the weights again, Gabe hovering behind me as a spotter. I don't enjoy this at all, but I'm progressing through the sets Gryphon assigned me well enough now that I'm terrified he's going to switch things up and kill me all over again.

Gryphon watches us all carefully and when Atlas takes another deep breath, he raises his eyebrows at him expectantly.

"You've done a great job with Oli. I'll work harder."

Huh.

Not the answer I was expecting, but I'm quietly pleased that Atlas has… okay, not backed down exactly, but he's willing to admit that Gryphon is the best at this.

That says a lot about a person.

Gryphon doesn't say anything but when Atlas turns to work his way through the stances again, slower and more carefully, I can see that my scarred and surly Bond is actually impressed with him as well.

Gryphon keeps us there for twice as long as usual, but it's Saturday and we don't have classes to get to, so we have no reason to ask him to let us go.

Atlas also becomes insanely focused on getting a handle on what he's being taught and by the time Gryphon finally tells us to stretch out and disappear for the day, he's consistently holding his gift back. Gryphon is still muttering critiques at him the whole time he's going through the stances but at least he's not rummaging around in his brain anymore.

Stretching is my favorite part of these torture sessions because I do it sitting on my ass on the mats and it requires zero cardio or effort, so I take my time with it. Gabe just barely does the basics and then starts bugging me to get up, but there's a sharp pain in my back that I want to roll out, so I ignore his pleading looks.

When Gryphon finishes off wiping down the machines, he packs his bag and stalks out with barely more than a curt nod at us all. He's got a lot on his mind, I knew it the moment he'd come to collect me from Nox's room, so I'm not even a little offended that he didn't come say goodbye to me properly.

Okay, maybe my bond is a little pissy about it but my rational mind is cool.

The moment the door shuts behind him, Atlas leans over to kiss my cheeks and murmur to me, "How was your night, Sweetness? You look okay but I have to check."

I knew it was coming, so I just shrug. "It was fine."

He squints back at me. "What the hell does 'fine' mean? I feel like I need to follow you into the shower and check you for bruises or any *extra* tracking devices he might've stuck to you while you were sleeping."

I shake my head at him and then stretch back out on the mats because I have no reason to be in a rush. I have a shift at the cafe later and an assignment I need to finish up, but I have all day to organize that stuff.

Gabe walks over to us with more water, handing a bottle to me and then squatting down to brush my hair back from my neck, revealing Brutus' hiding spot. "He's still there, so I'm sure you were fine and Bassinger just needs to get the stick out of his ass about it."

I open my mouth to attempt to stop them both from starting up another argument but then there's a loud *bang* and the house shakes a little on its foundation.

Atlas is on top of me in an instant.

Gabe shoots to his feet and steps in front of me, ripping his phone out of his pocket, but there's already a message on there that has him cursing viciously.

"What? Spit it out!" Atlas snaps as he pushes up to his feet and drags me up with him.

They're both so close to me, shielding me with their bodies even though there's no danger in this room yet, and

I have to wriggle out from between them to drink down the water Gabe had handed to me.

If we're going to be fighting someone in a minute, I need to be hydrated.

"Sharpe is here. He's just openly attacked a member of the council and now he's here for North."

I'm striding across the room before Gabe is even finished and Atlas curses him out as he jogs after me. "You can't just go out there without a plan, Oli. North can take care of himself."

Gabe runs after us both. "North said to just stay here. Sharpe's woken Nox up as well, now he's dealing with two tired and irritated Dravens."

I try to stop but my bond is not having it. Not at all. If people are here after our bonds, then they'll pay. They'll all have to learn what we're capable of. I feel my eyes shift and it's game over for any chances of rational thought.

"Fuck. Call Shore and tell him we're coming in hot," Atlas snaps, but I'm moving too fast for them to give the other bonds any warning.

I might not know how to get through the house but my bond doesn't hesitate to get straight through the warren-like hallways and then we're out the front door.

The front lawn is gone.

There's a giant hole in the driveway that's going to be a bitch to sort out. It takes a second for me to realize why Atlas is clutching at my elbow, but with North's black smoke everywhere, they can't see a thing.

Thank God for the void eyesight because my feet don't falter.

There has to be at least a dozen people here, standing around the front of the house in various different Gifted forms. All of their eyes are shining white as they call on their bonds to fight, and I'm hit with the need to destroy them all. How dare they come here for my bonds?

Sharpe is right at the front and center, a sneering, vicious looking man, and three of his Bonded are with him. Fuck, okay, I recognize one of them as the telekinetic who was stirring her drink with her finger at the freaking council dinner North had dragged me to, so she's one to watch. The other two are both glowing but I can't see anything to indicate what they can do.

I don't know what the other two women are capable of but Gryphon is watching them all keenly with his Tac gear on, the goggles giving him visibility. He must have gotten the call the second he left us and dressed on his way down here.

Nox is still in the same clothes he'd slept in on the couch last night and he's sneering at the little crowd of Gifted behind Sharpe. I have no clue who any of these people are, but my bond doesn't really care anyway.

They're all on *that* side, so they're a threat.

Threats will not be tolerated.

I really need to reason with my bond but it's not fucking around today. I think there's been too many injuries and talks of my Bonds being hurt lately and it's decided enough is enough.

Kill them all.

Sharpe calls out in his arrogantly cutting voice, "There she is! The little runaway Bond you're destroying our community to protect. You dare to come after me and my family just to protect some little girl? Some worthless little low-born Bond who won't submit? She should have stayed gone."

North's eyes flicker in my direction and Sharpe's telekinetic Bonded uses the advantage to throw a giant boulder at him. Two things happen simultaneously; a nightmare creature, more smoke than form, bursts out of his chest and bats the boulder away as though it's nothing.

And my bond takes the woman to the ground.

Her scream is short but loud enough that the entire group of people around us all stop to gape at her in horror as her eyes roll back in her head. I feel nothing, not a single emotion as she falls to the ground and writhes.

Brutus decides that he doesn't like the sound of that scream and jumps down to the ground, multiplying in size so that he reaches my waist by the time he's snarling in every direction.

Sharpe's hand shakes as he reaches down to his Bonded. There's already blood starting to drip out of her eyes, and if he knows anything about me at all from his time on the council, then he knows there's no saving her.

He looks at me and my voice is all cold, merciless bond, "You should know better than to touch mine. It's the least I could do to her."

His lip curls and his eyes flash white again, but I already know I'm stronger than him. My bond is smug in my chest as his gift scrambles at me and gets *nothing*. Losing your Bonded and having them injured definitely makes you irrational though and he jumps to his feet, ready to come after me, but he only makes it one step before North's creature gets to him.

There's that damage of mine though because I'm not scared or grossed out as he's literally ripped apart, limb from limb, right in front of me. Brutus watches it all happen without joining the fray, his void eyes keen as they take it all in, and I crouch down to wrap an arm around his neck to nuzzle him.

My bond likes him *a lot*.

"Oli, please, come inside. Let the others clean this up," Atlas murmurs from behind me, two steps away from me where he'd fallen back when my bond came out. I'm glad he did, even more so when North shouts at us both.

I turn to see his creature heading our way.

With every step it takes on more of a solid form until I'm staring at a fully grown Doberman-looking creature, with void eyes and a vicious set of razor sharp teeth in his jaw on full view as it appears to pant like a real dog. Gabe's description of them all being rabid runs through my brain and Gryphon starts towards me at a run, but I just hold out my arm to him.

How did I know the creature just wanted an ear scratch like Brutus is getting? I have no clue, but he whines and vibrates in pure pleasure when I do, his tongue lolling about as his void eyes shut in pleasure at all of the attention I'm giving him.

I mumble at him as we hear the sounds of a fight behind us but my bond is completely zeroed in on the gorgeous, fearsome creature in front of me. "You are so pretty, thank you for helping out. Don't nip at your brother, he's my favorite, but you can be my favorite too, if you want? Oh, belly rubs too? Okay, you can have belly rubs too."

Brutus nudges at my shoulder because he doesn't like sharing my attention and I have to work overtime to give them both equal pets.

"What, and I cannot stress this enough, *the fuck* is happening right now?" Gabe mutters in absolute horror. I glance up to find all of the Bonds standing there watching me love on the puppies.

Okay, they're both in full-sized Doberman forms right

now, but they're still just sweet puppies.

Gryphon very slowly squats down to be at my level, eyeing North's creature the whole time like he knows it's dreaming about sinking its teeth into his throat, and speaks in a low tone to me, "Oli, I need you to stop scratching the creature and back up a little so North can get him put away."

The creature doesn't like the sound of Gryphon's voice and he turns his head to growl at him.

Brutus growls back, knocking me a little to get in between us, and I have to wade back in to stop them from fighting. There's a lot of cursing around me but I ignore them all as I grab North's creature by the muzzle and turn him to look at me. "No growling at my Bonds. That's naughty, none of that, and if you do, I'm not giving you any more scratches."

He drops his butt down to sit and his tail does that sad sort of wag that tells me he knows I'm not impressed with him right now.

I look up at North who is sweating a little and say, "What's his name? Again, if it's lame, I'm going to judge you."

He takes a slow breath and holds out his hand to the creature, his palm turning black as he summons him back. Before I can say a word, the creature is gone.

I throw my hands up and snap, "I didn't say take him

away! Now he's gone home thinking I'm pissed at him! Don't be an asshole, bring him back!"

His hand curls into a fist and he snarls at me through clenched teeth, "Calm down. Your eyes are still black and we're about to have more TacTeams here for a clean up."

Brutus knocks at my legs, unhappy that I'm ranting, but I'm pissed he's taking the creature away. "Give him back to me. If I can handle Brutus, I can handle... what the hell is his name?"

North just turns on his heel and walks away from me.

I want to *murder* him.

The moment I start after him, ready to rip him a new asshole for just bailing on the argument like I'm some underling to him, Gryphon steps into my path and holds his hands up at me. It's a very placating sort of move and it's so unlike him that I do actually stop.

"Your eyes, Oli. Take a breath, calm down, if you can't, then you need to go inside because I can't have you losing your shit and taking out my team just because you're pissed at North."

I stop and look around again, taking in my surroundings a little more now that I'm not completely focused on the creatures and, sure enough, Gryphon's TacTeam is standing around looking at me like I'm the most horrifying, terrifying monster that ever existed.

It makes no sense to me.

All I did was protect North against one woman who should've known better. They're all trained to kill Resistance and protect the Gifted community and they're going to stand there judging me for protecting my own damn Bonds?

Gryphon reads my mind again, the asshole. "No, they're staring at you for hugging a nightmare creature that they've all been trained not to ever approach or get in the way of. They've all learned a million times over to never, ever touch a Draven nightmare and you were just loving the scariest goddamn bastard North has. *That's* what has them fucking quaking in their boots."

I feel my eyes finally shift back to normal as I flick him a look and mutter, "Get out of my head. Besides, he was cute. You might need a new TacTeam if that's how easily they all scare."

Kieran, who is stalking over to us both with just the tiniest bit of hesitation, stops in front of Gryphon and raises an eyebrow at me. "You just watched it tear a man apart, you can't pretend that they're docile now."

I wave a hand back at him. "Yeah, because Sharpe threatened North! That's not killing someone, that's taking out the trash."

He shakes his head slowly and as I walk away from them, calling Brutus back over to my side, I hear Kieran mutter to Gryphon, "You're in so far over your head, she's going to eat you all alive and I'm going to enjoy the show."

I decide that I might like Gryphon's second in command, even if he is a little bit of a dick.

I have to call out of work again and even though Gloria is absolutely fine with it, I feel irritated as hell about it. Gabe is quick to point out that the entire Gifted community already knows what happened on the front lawn of the infamous Draven manor already and that there's no way Gloria would want me working for her while I'm still freaking pissed about it all, but that only reminds me of all of the spineless, weak Gifted high society who dare to judge my Bonds.

I write the angriest paper for Gifted 101 in existence and I prepare myself for the failing grade North is going to give me for it.

I also can't find it in myself to care because he was such a dick to me over his creature. I don't know why it bothers me so much, but my chest is hurting over the way they all talk about his creatures.

Why does he let them all talk like that? Why does he let the creatures go feral, why do they fight back at him and injure him when Nox has his all trained to perfection?

None of it makes sense to me, so I'm in a vicious mood.

Gabe heads home after lunch to see his mom, hesitating before he kisses my cheek because I think he's a little bit wary of my temper. Atlas spends the morning with me but then ducks back to his room to video call his sister. Once again, I had no idea he even had an older sister, and when I scowl at him, he just chuckles at me.

"It's not like I was keeping her a secret! I just forget that you haven't kept up to date with the Top Tier Gifted families. Aurelia is five years older than me and we have the same father but different moms. She's the Central of a four-Bonded group, and just so you're fully in the know, I hate three of them."

I raise an eyebrow at him and he huffs at me. "Jericho is decent but the other three are all arrogant, pompous assholes who would be of better use to my sister if they disappeared permanently. That's all I'm going to say or you might judge me for hating them so much."

"Like I'd judge you for that. Hell, I'd help you kill them if you really want to," I say, only half joking.

Well, I'm not joking about helping him at all. I'm half

joking about putting that idea on the table for us both to consider.

Once I'm alone, I take the longest bath in existence. I use bubble bath and giggle like a kid over it, and when Brutus climbs out from behind my ear to sit amongst the bubbles with me, I fall just a little more in love with him. He starts off in his smaller form and glides over the top of the water but after a minute, he grows until he's taking up more of the tub than I am.

He sniffs at the bubbles and snaps his teeth at them even though he just passes through them like a ghost, adorable and perfect in every way. I start to question how the hell I've ended up here.

Not in the tub but here, in this house, with Bonds that, despite my best efforts, I'm growing attached to. I knew that the moment I let my gift back in, my bond would only grow in strength, but I wasn't prepared for how quickly they would crawl under my skin and lodge themselves there, vital to my existence in every way.

I'm screwed.

It doesn't matter that Kieran said they'd changed tactics and they're waiting to see what comes after me, if… if *that man* comes here after us all, we're dead.

Fuck.

I haven't let myself think about him in years and for good reason, my gift starts reacting in my chest just from me acknowledging that he exists.

Brutus notices and starts to bump at my face with his nose, nuzzling me and trying to pull me out of the nightmare swirling around in my head. I've learnt a lot of tricks to deal with my trauma in my time on the run, but the most effective one has been blocking it out. Squashing down the memories until they're all squished up in a tiny box at the back of my mind, wrapped in caution tape so there's no mistaking that it's my own little Pandora's box.

My phone buzzes on the floor next to the bath and I wipe my shaking hand on the towel as I grab it.

"What's going on? I will break the door down if you can't get it under control soon," Gryphon says without any formalities or niceties.

My voice is a little thready as I answer him, "What are you doing outside my door when there's a mess out front to be dealt with? Or have you already cleaned it up? This doesn't seem very 'TacTeam leader' of you."

There's murmuring in the background but he ignores whoever it is. "I am dealing with the mess. What happened this morning has rattled you and we've done a lot to get your bond under control. What do you need to calm down? The bath isn't working."

I look over at Brutus and raise my free hand to scratch behind his ears, trying not to sigh too loudly into the phone. "The bath is what set me off; I'll get out. I can't be alone with my thoughts today."

He's quiet for a moment and then says, "If you get it under control, you can come out and sit with North and me while we process Sharpe's Bonds. It'll get you out of the house for a couple of hours."

Huh.

That actually sounds interesting and I could definitely learn some more about what the hell is going on with the council without having to speak to North about it.

I pull myself to my feet and grab a towel. "Give me five to get dressed and I'll come out."

"You have two minutes before I'm leaving, move your ass."

Freaking Bonds.

I'd come out from the bathroom to find an empty bedroom but clothes laid out on my bed, waiting for me. It's a little presumptuous but if that doesn't sum Gryphon up, nothing will.

I tug the black jeans, white tee, and leather jacket on and then shove my feet into the perfect leather boots without bothering to check out how I look. It's a very TacTeam sort of outfit and I'm sure that was the whole point of it. I'll be around fully trained soldiers while they work, a dress would've been impractical.

I send Atlas a quick text and snap my fingers at Brutus to get him to follow me. He's not so keen about tucking back into my hair, not with this many unknown people in the manor, and he stays his giant size as we stalk back down to the foyer together.

The maids and TacTeam members swarming around everywhere avoid me, flattening against the walls as we pass them, and Brutus is the perfect gentlepup about it. He doesn't snap or sniff at any of them as he sticks close to my side.

North, Gryphon, and Keiran are waiting for me in the foyer, murmuring quietly together and only looking up when they hear my footsteps on the marble floors.

Gryphon shoots me a look. "I said two minutes, and the nightmare can't come like that. He's either in your hair or staying here with Nox."

My eyes narrow at him. "I was soaking wet when you invited me down here, and Brutus is twitchy about the crowd. If you want him to hide, then you'll need to wait until we're alone again because he's on edge."

North shakes his head at me and Brutus doesn't like that either. I have to step in front of him when he starts to growl at my Bond. It kind of forces my hand a little because they all stare at me again like I have no idea what I'm doing when I've never been so sure of anything in my life as I am about the creatures.

"Honestly, I don't understand how you get on the creatures' bad sides when you're literally in charge of them! You have a real gift there, Draven," I mumble, holding my hand out to Brutus and trying to coax him back into my hair.

He doesn't want to but I hold his eyes with my own, not backing down an inch, and eventually he whines a little as he shrinks, climbing back up my arm and tucking in behind my ear like the perfectly obedient good boy that he is.

I hear the entire room exhale the moment he's no longer in sight and I'm once again questioning the strength of all of these TacTeam members if they're really that scared of my beloved Brutus.

"We've wasted enough time. Oleander, you're riding over to the council offices with me. Gryphon and Black will meet us over there with the prisoners," North says, opening the door to the garage and holding out an arm like he's ushering me through.

I raise an eyebrow at Gryphon, because this definitely wasn't a part of the deal, and he just plants one of his big hands on my lower back to gently push me in North's direction.

Bastard.

Rafe, North's driver, opens the door of one of the Rolls

Royces for me and I thank him as I slide into the backseat. I have to scoot along for North as well, but it's a lot less uncomfortable than it was the last time I was trapped in here with him.

The wonders that the last few months have done for us.

He's dressed in another suit, clean and pressed to perfection, and though he looks more weary than usual, he looks much better than he did this morning.

Rafe gets the car out of the driveway without hitting any of the giant holes in the driveway, which makes him an expert in my opinion, and I try not to freak out at how many of the Dravens' neighbors are openly out and watching us drive past.

You'd think after an attack on this very street that they'd be holed up inside their ridiculously oversized mansions, clutching at their pearls and fearing for their lives.

"You can't just jump into conflict like you did this morning. You had no idea what we had planned or whether the people we were facing were a real danger to you," North says, his eyes keen on me as I attempt to avoid meeting them.

Great.

Here's the lecture I never needed.

I keep my mouth shut and just nod along with him, hoping that my silence is enough for him to let this shit go but of course it's not. This is North Draven, the councilman and control freak extraordinaire.

He couldn't let anything go if it meant taking a break on me.

"If you're refusing to tell us anything about your gift, then you need to just stay back and let us do everything for you. Without knowing the risks, you're a liability."

I need a subject change and fast. "Why wouldn't you let me make peace with your creature? Do you really hate me so much that you're happy to have him think I'm mad at him?"

His eyes flash at me and his jaw tightens as he speaks through his teeth, "I don't hate you and he doesn't think anything while he's not here. He's a mindless nightmare, not a puppy you can name and domesticate. Even you're not naive enough to think that, Fallows."

Ah, back to my surname is it? Fuck him. "Augustine. August for short."

He shakes his head at me but I go on, "If you're not going to name him then that's what I'm naming him. August and Brutus go well together, you should let me have him. We can co-parent. I'll have him every other week. Maybe he'll be less grouchy if you're not keeping him locked up all the time. Brutus loves curling up in my bed with me, running on the treadmill, hell, bath time is his favorite, as long as I use a ton of bubble bath."

If I thought I'd get away with it, I'd take a photo of

North's face right now because I've never seen anything as perfect as the horrified disbelief on this man's face.

I turn back to the window and watch the gated neighborhood disappear and turn into the busy highway. We have no luck and hit every red light on the way over to the council offices. Gryphon and Kieran are driving a blacked-out van behind us and when I glance back at them, I try not to seethe with jealousy.

Gryphon is grinning and laughing with Kieran.

I've only seen him laugh *once* and that was him laughing at me. He might've explained it to me and I'm a little less sore about it, but he looks so much younger and hotter when he's oozing out joy at his friend. There's none of the watchful, moody tension in him and I want to bathe in Kieran's blood for having this version of him when I don't.

"Stop whatever you're thinking about and calm down. I've spent a lot of time telling the council members and workers that you're not a danger to our community. I don't need you showing up here with void eyes and proving me wrong," North mutters, and I shift back around to face the front of the car again.

Right.

Put on the facade of a perfectly obedient, placid, *boring* girl. I need to smile pretty and fake it because the information I could learn today is worth it.

If I don't want to be found by that man, then I need to get my head together and play the role.

"I'll keep my bond under control," I murmur and North's eyes are sharp on the building in front of us as Rafe takes us into an underground parking garage. There's lighting everywhere, so it's not actually dark, but the rows of luxury cars still have a lead weight sinking down in my gut.

North leans over to murmur to me again, "We're always a united front in that building. Even when I disagree with one of the other Bonds, I never discuss it in the open. It would be best if you kept your commentary to yourself until we're back at the manor."

My jaw flexes but I nod my head sharply.

It's actually a very good policy to have, because weakness is never a good thing to have on display, except that it feels a little weaponized in my direction right now.

Rafe parks the car and immediately gets out to open the door for North and me. I give myself one last breath sitting in the car to make sure I'm calm and, most importantly, blank.

A frown flits over Gryphon's face where he's waiting at the blacked-out van a couple of parking spots over as I step out of the car, but he doesn't comment or do anything about it. He just looks stern as he opens up the back with Kieran and they pull out the two women who were Bonded to Sharpe.

Right up until he was eaten alive by my precious August.

"We'll take them straight down. Are you coming with us, Oli, or going the long way with North?"

I want to run right after Gryphon but I flick my eyes up to North. I can play nice for right now.

Even if I choke on it, I can do it.

"Go with Gryphon. I need to check in with Pen and you seem to have issues with her."

Ugh, fuck him.

I think calm thoughts as I stalk over to Gryphon without a word, my boots loud on the concrete as I stomp a little. Don't do anything that might come off as 'brat-like', Oli. I'm going for the higher ground here, making sure they have nothing to throw at me later.

We step into a service elevator and Gryphon hits the button for the lowest level. I take a deep breath about once again being trapped underground and I think they both misread it.

Kieran seems to have decided we're friends now and leans down to murmur to me, "What's wrong with Penelope? She's a little bit of a nag but she's a good enough kid."

That's even more insulting because he hated me on sight. Gryphon shoots him a look and his eyes flash. "Oli's bond has taken a disliking to her. Pen didn't do anything wrong, it's a Bond haze thing."

"How many of North's secretaries has he fucked? Do we have an exact number or should I just keep guessing with how much he gets touched?" I say in a very sweet tone.

Kieran startles away from me, muttering under his breath, "Fuck wading into that fight. Draven can dig himself out."

I raise an eyebrow at Gryphon but he just shrugs at me. "You can't talk, Bond."

Oh, he has no idea. No freaking idea how much I *can* talk about it and yet none of them— nope. Stop thinking about it, Oli.

I take a breath and remind my bond that men ain't shit.

The doors to the elevator open again and Gryphon takes the lead, jerking his head at me to follow him through the concrete and steel nightmare in front of us.

Prison cells.

The council offices are built on top of prison cells, all of them filled with Gifted who I hope are Resistance and definitely not just people who can't afford their taxes or drink in public.

I try not to look into the cells. I don't want to recognize anyone in there. They all react as we walk past, screaming, yelling, banging against the glass. I want to turn on my heel and get the fuck out of here.

I force my legs to keep walking.

"Just ignore them, these are the leftovers from the camps North and Nox went after," Gryphon says, his voice pitched low to me and I glance up at him. He looks worried, especially when I startle as we come to the end and one of the prisoners is smashing her fists against the glass.

I shouldn't look.

I know I shouldn't, but the sound draws my eyes and I come face-to-face with Carlin.

She looks a lot worse for wear than she did when I'd last seen her. Her hair has grown out a little and there's bags under her eyes, but the most terrifying thing about the strongest tester the Resistance has is that she recognizes me straight away this time.

"*Render*," she hisses at me and I dart around Gryphon, shoving my way into the interview's observation room before them just to get away from her.

Kieran walks in after me, opening the door to go straight through to the interview room as though he didn't hear a thing, but Gryphon just shoves his prisoner through the door and shuts it after her, turning back around to me.

"What did she just call you?"

I blink up at him. "Don't make me lie to you."

He takes a deep breath and runs a hand through his hair. "She just called you a—"

"Please don't say it. Please don't tell North, or Nox, or anyone else. Please just, *please* don't."

He tugs at his hair, scooping it back to tie it up from where it's come out. I stare through the two-way glass as Kieran gets the women both secured into their seats. They haven't said a word or attempted to escape in any way, but the glowing of Gryphon's eyes explains that perfectly.

He's switched their brains off for now, all of the parts of them that might attempt to flee or fight, leaving behind docile, walking zombies.

There's a very tense sort of silence between us, I'm choking back the panic and fear flooding me to attempt to keep my bond at bay. It's fine. If they all know about all of my gifts, they'll either let me go or lock me up into one of those little cells.

I can stop myself from hurting people in either of those scenarios, this isn't the worst possible option. I'm going to rationalize this until the moment North walks in here and loses his mind over it all.

When the door opens again and Kieran walks back into the observation room, he looks between us. "Are we going to ignore that she just called your Bond—"

"Nothing. She didn't call my Bond a single thing,"

Gryphon says with a sharp look and Kieran nods curtly, dropping it like a great second in command does.

I almost pass out with relief but I doubt this will be the last I hear of this.

SAVAGE BONDS

It takes an hour of almost unbearable silence before North arrives at the interview room.

There's nothing obvious about his appearance that says he's furious but I've already learned his subtle tells. His hands aren't exactly fisted, but he's a slight flex away from being ready to knock someone's teeth out, and there's the smallest black dot on his thumb, the teeniest little bit of his gift slipping. It could be mistaken for a freckle but I've spent too long watching this man during uncomfortable Bond dinners not to see it all for what it is.

He's just barely keeping his shit together.

The moment Gryphon tells him about my gift he's going to unleash all of that anger out on me, I'm already cringing at the very thought of it.

Kieran, who had stood with Gryphon and talked about shit I didn't understand at all the whole time we'd waited, gets one look at North and high-tails it into the interview room. I make a mental note to give him shit about it later because he's not the big scary TacTeam guy he projects if he's running scared of a moody Draven.

"Trouble?" Gryphon says, and North scoffs under his breath.

"You mean like the council being split in half about what to do before Sharpe went insane and now they're all either running scared or coming for my throat? You could say so."

Jesus Christ, there's not enough money in the world to convince me to join the council. I mean, I'm aware that my lackluster pedigree means it's not something I ever have to worry about, but the thought of dealing with those people also gives me hives.

I'm not cut out for diplomacy.

North barely acknowledges my existence, which is fine, but when he moves over to come and stand with me, Gryphon blocks him.

"You're doing the interviews, I'm not leaving Oli."

North turns to give him a look but Gryphon just shakes his head. "I'm not leaving her right now. You said you trusted me to be sure of what she needed, well, this is what she needs. Kieran will take the lead in there and you can be on point."

I swallow roughly but don't look over at either of them. I can feel the heat in North's gaze as he glares at the back of my head, but he moves into the interrogation room without another word.

I move up to stand with Gryphon at the glass, the silence a little more comfortable between us now. We watch as North takes a seat next to Kieran and unbuttons his suit jacket so he's more comfortable.

Kieran holds up a hand and Gryphon's eyes flash brighter again and then return to normal. Both of the women blink rapidly as though the light in the room is blinding, pulling against the chains on their wrists as though they have no idea they're secured to the chairs.

The quiet and calm in the room evaporates as the women look at each other and then the men in front of them with contempt.

Gryphon leans in towards me to murmur, "They can't hear us in there as long as we're not screaming. If you have questions, now's the time to ask them."

I glance at him but he's still just standing there, staring into the room. He's closer to me now, his usual two steps away that he distances himself now down to a half step.

I know he means about the interrogation or the situation with Sharpe, but my brain is fixated on my own problems. "Why didn't you tell him?"

He quirks an eyebrow at me. "Because you asked me not to. He's also just lost someone who was very important to him and isn't thinking all that rationally. I won't tell him until you're ready and he's... thinking clearly again."

I nod and he shifts a little closer to me again, now only a hair's breadth away from touching me. "Why didn't you lie? Even knowing I could tell, there are ways around it. Gabe told me you've already figured that out."

Freaking Gabe, he's both amazing and a total nark. "You told me you couldn't stand liars. I'm doing my best to respect that even when it ruins fucking *everything*. Why did Sharpe get kicked off of the council? Why now?"

I'm aware we're just taking turns grilling each other, answer for answer, but this is the first chance I've actually had to get real answers out of him without the truth about my gift getting in the way.

Gryphon's eyes narrow at North as he reads off a list of offenses the women are being held for. It includes treason, murder, and conspiracy to break up Bonded groups, but the women just both look... smug. Satisfied, like they've been given kudos for a job well done.

It's sickening.

"We've known about Sharpe's affiliation with the Resistance for years. Bella, the telekinetic that you dealt with, comes from a known Resistance family. Sharpe spent years cultivating a reputation around here for 'saving' her, as though he'd found her and deprogramed her from the bullshit that the Resistance brainwashes their followers with, but it was all a load of shit. We knew for years. He's been responsible for deaths in the community, but he's also been the rat that we've followed to find the camps."

I nod slowly and he catches my hand in his, the first little casual touch he's ever given me. I feel pathetic when my cheeks heat at the contact, it's hand-holding for Christ's sake, but his thumb traces over mine gently and I almost melt into a puddle.

He knows what I am and he's still touching me.

That has to mean something, right?

He tugs on my hand so my body is tucked in close to his, the back of his arm resting over my chest as though he's prepared to shield me completely if something happens in that room.

I try not to fall completely in love with him for this tiny moment of affection he's showing me.

"Sharpe made a political move against North last week. It involved you and our Bond not being complete. Sharpe was a piece of shit and he thought he could push North on this issue. North was dealing with him diplomatically, but then William was killed and diplomacy went out the window. Things are going to get worse around here before they get better."

I nod slowly and try not to look morbid or obsessed

with how I watch North in the questioning. The women are both refusing to speak, sharing looks with each other that make them both look unhinged. I wonder how they feel without Sharpe around anymore. I wonder if it's even hit them yet that they've lost their Central, or if they're in some kind of denial about it.

I also wonder if they were Resistance supporters, or if Sharpe had kept them in the dark about it. Do they deserve to be locked up forever, or executed for their complicity in his crimes?

Gryphon speaks again, his voice lower than before, as though he's worried the sound will somehow get through the glass. "The Resistance took you. I don't know how or when, but they had you. That's how Carlin Meadows knows you and knows what your gift is, it's the only answer that makes sense."

I give him the slightest nod of my head, the words still trapped in my throat. Even if he knows, there's no way I can tell him anything else. Not all of the gory details of why I'm a fucking monster.

"How long?"

I swallow. "I don't want to—"

He cuts me off, "Just tell me that. Tell me how long and I'll stop asking about it… for now."

Well, I can't let this conversation go on or he's going to have everything out of me, every last detail of my life, so I whisper, "Two years."

His jaw tightens and releases over and over again as he gnashes his teeth. "Why can't I find you then? We've been over every piece of intelligence we've been able to pick up and there's a lot there, Oli. Why aren't you in it?"

I shake my head, partly because I don't know for sure, but also because my best guess gives too much away. I don't want to do this anymore. I don't want to know anything else about this fucked-up situation. I don't want him prying into my head. I don't want to think about how badly I need to get away from them all.

I'm so tired of fighting and running.

He curses under his breath again and squeezes my hand. "Okay. No more questions for now, but I'm going to have more of them, Oli. I'm going to figure it all out and fix our broken Bond group. There's no way I'm letting this go on."

We focus back on the interview room, Gryphon's hand steady in mine, and I try not to fixate on his words. I need to give him answers. I can't say a word. Can I? Could I trust him?

Maybe.

But I can't trust him to let me go if the Resistance, or *that man*, figures out where I am, so I can't tell him a thing. What if he tries to keep me here and it gets him killed?

I couldn't live with myself if that happened.

An hour later, I'm dead on my feet, the interview still going round in circles. Gryphon suggests I take a break from it and leads me over to the corner of the room. I curl up on the bench there and let my eyes fall shut.

I feel Gryphon throw his long Tac coat over me and I pull it up over my face to get some rest.

I wake up curled on the back seat of the Rolls Royce with my head in Gryphon's lap to the smell of Mexican food. I don't want to wake up or function again, but my stomach rumbles and there's no denying I would murder for something to eat right now.

So I push myself up with a yawn, stretching my arms out as much as I can in the small space right as the back door opens again and North slides in with his hands full of boxes of food from the taco truck.

I almost want to tackle him to the ground just to make sure I can eat my body weight from those boxes.

Gryphon takes a couple of the boxes and hands them to me, ignoring North's icy glare his way, and says, "Gabe said you like fish tacos here, the chef is on stress leave for the rest of the week, so we'll be ordering a lot of takeout until he's back."

I take the boxes happily, trying to contain the squirming

joy that's taken over me. It's hard, especially when it's my damned bond having the reaction over them *providing* for me, going out and getting me my favorite meal for dinner, and eating all together in this cramped backseat that was definitely not made to fit two of my biggest Bonds.

Both in size and attitude.

"Sorry for sleeping. The late nights and early mornings are catching up to me," I mumble around the food, and Gryphon shrugs back.

He reaches around me to grab my seatbelt and pull it over my chest, buckling me in, right as Rafe starts the car back up and gets us on the road back to the manor.

I'm happy munching on my dinner, demolishing three tacos in the time that it takes my Bonds to eat one each, and when I've wiped my hands and mouth, I look longingly at the rest of Gryphon's nachos.

He rolls his eyes and hands them to me without uttering a word, and I decide that I'm keeping him forever. Keeping my secrets, not loathing me for my gift, *and* sharing his food with me even when I've eaten enough already not to warrant it?

He might be it for me.

"Stop with the happy sounds, you're pushing it," he grumbles at me, and I try not to scoff at his surly mood.

I am moaning under my breath with every mouthful and that might just make me an asshole.

North ignores us both, barely eating his own serving before he sets it aside and gets back on his phone to work. I swear he's addicted to it, addicted to being busy and engrossed in anything that isn't being content or happy.

Or being with me.

When we get back to the manor it's dark, but I can make out the work that a landscaper has already done to fix the mess of the morning. The driveway is still a disaster, but the scorched grass has been dug up and replaced already, a sprinkler set up and spritzing water everywhere to get the roots to grow and establish.

It's as though with enough money, nothing is ever permanent.

I want to make a comment about it but it'll only start a fight, so I wait until Rafe has the car parked in the garage and is out of the car before I murmur, "Thank you for dinner, North."

He looks down at me but doesn't acknowledge my words, just steps out of the car the moment Rafe opens the door for him. I huff and slide out after him, rubbing my hands down over my arms just so I don't strangle the arrogant asshole.

I try to remind myself that he just lost someone. He doesn't trust me and he's grieving, but that only makes my brain latch onto the fact that, honestly, his behavior hasn't changed all that much towards me.

Well, no, there was a moment that I thought maybe he was softening a little, but I blinked and it was gone. Poof, out of existence, the man who had quietly told me he would've protected me from his brother if it came to it just disappeared.

Gryphon takes my elbow gently and pulls me back into his side. "I'll walk you to your room, there's still a lot of council staff and TacTeam around. Gabe and Bassinger will already be up there and you can stay there until you're ready to sleep."

Shit.

It's North's night.

I hadn't even thought of that the entire time we'd been out, and it's the first time this week that I've thought about asking to get out of the shared sleeping situation. Even Nox has been better, mostly because Gryphon had reassured me over it, but also because Nox had left me completely alone. He hadn't even gotten into the bed, his creatures had slept around me, but being immersed in Nox's space was more than enough to settle my bond down and give it the hit of him I needed to get my head together again.

"Is it a good idea for me to sleep in North's bed tonight if he's so... on edge?" I murmur, careful not to just blurt out our private Bond business in a manor full of outsiders.

Gryphon doesn't answer me until we're in the elevator together, and even then he chooses his words with care.

"Now that I have a better view of this entire situation, there is no higher priority to me than keeping your bond calm and sated. I… understand your reluctance a bit more, but you also need to understand that we have to keep you level. Whatever that takes, that's the *only* priority I'm seeing, other than keeping us all alive. Do you understand what I'm saying, Oli?"

I do.

I get it more than he does. I get it because I'm the one dealing with the gift and bond warring with my mind and my morals every day to stop me from just… ending everything.

Everything.

I give him a nod, my mouth setting into a firm line as I try not to let him see just how much this is tearing me apart, how much I desperately need them all on such a level that it terrifies me.

He grabs my hand again, threading our fingers together as he murmurs again, "I'm not going to let anything happen, Oli. I know you didn't choose to tell me, but I'm not going to let you down. We'll figure it out, together. You, me, the rest of the Bond group, we'll figure out how to make this work."

Jesus Christ.

I blink rapidly and nod again, fighting stupid and useless tears, but there's a guilt inside of me because he doesn't really know the extent of this gift of mine.

He doesn't know what I've done.

Murderer.

He stops me at my door with a hand on my cheek as he pulls my lips to his for a quick kiss. It's barely more than a peck, no tongue, but his teeth rasp along my bottom lip.

He pulls away from me, looking down at me with his mesmerizingly clear blue eyes, and I blink up at him like some lovesick idiot. "I'll come get you in the morning but you can sleep in. I'll be here at seven, it'll be a late night with the cleanup still going on."

I clear my throat and nod, pulling away properly and patting myself down for my keys. As I get the door open, Gabe and Atlas arrive, quiet and somber today, thanks to our day from hell. Gryphon reads them both the riot act of rules and condition changes thanks to the extra bodies in the house. I already know what's expected of me, so I leave them to it.

I change into a pair of Atlas' boxer shorts and one of Gabe's tank tops, set on being comfortable for as much of the night as I can be while I'm here, and then I put a movie on, a comfort movie I've seen a million times so that I won't get upset if the guys talk the whole way through it.

Gryphon pushes the door open again and walks over to the bed to give me one last quick kiss before he leaves, stalking back out with that same stern look on his face, and

Gabe raises his eyebrows at me.

He starts to get undressed, stripping down to his boxers to lay around with me, as he says, "What the hell happened today? He's gone from pissed surveillance to enraged protection detail on you."

Atlas doesn't question me as he also gets undressed, folding his clothes up and climbing into my side of the bed with me to tuck me into his chest before Gabe has the chance to claim the spot.

They fight over it a lot, but I don't mind it.

I swallow and try not to wince at the half truth coming out of me. "We saw someone at the council offices that I knew from the Resistance. It shook me a little, and I think he's maybe put some stuff together... it's made him extra protective."

Gabe nods as though that's completely understandable and climbs in the other side of the bed, completely unconcerned about the fact that they're both mostly naked in here with me. All of the dirty fantasies I'd love to have about them are ruined by the fact I'm not supposed to be letting my bond get over excited right now, goddammit! I'll have to save them for a shower tomorrow or something.

Atlas waits for Gabe to be busy rearranging the pillows to his liking before he smoothes a hand down my hair, pressing his lips to my ear to murmur, "He knows?"

I shrug because I don't want to talk about it with either

of them. I still don't think Atlas actually knows anything and if he does, I don't want to exclude Gabe from the conversation like that. I'm not actually the bitch they all once thought I was.

That the Dravens still think of me.

"Can we just not talk about gifts or bonds for the rest of the night? I'm not feeling great and I still have to go sleep in North's room tonight. He's in the worst freaking mood too, I'm going to spend the whole night trying not to breathe wrong and piss him off more."

Atlas scowls but nods, his hands warm as he runs them up and down my spine.

I'm asleep in under a minute.

It's dark when I wake up again, only a small slice of light coming into the room from the hallway, and I can make out North's silhouette there and mentally curse myself for falling asleep.

I have to slowly and carefully pry myself out of Atlas' arms and climb over him to get out of the bed, swiping my phone and keys from my bedside table as I go.

North is still looking pissed and when I bump into the doorframe as I rub my eyes against the harsh hallway light, he huffs at me and takes my elbow in his hand to direct me down the hall to his bedroom.

He doesn't say a word to me.

I'm more than relieved about it, happy to just be

haughtily directed to his perfectly put together, minimalist bed by his firm and unrelenting hand. He lifts the covers and tucks me in, scowling the whole time, and as insulted as I want to be about him coming to collect me and putting me into the bed like the little object that I am to him, I'm too tired to put up a fight.

The stress of the whole freaking week hits me hard.

I register that he goes into the bathroom and leaves the door open while he showers, but then my eyes flutter shut and I'm out like a light again, my face buried in pillows that smell just like him and make my bond purr happily in my chest.

I wake to the sound of a key sliding into North's bedroom door as his arms tighten around me. His chest is warm against my back and one of his hands is tucked against my upper thigh, so close to cupping my core that I actually feel flutters of excitement down there before my brain catches up to what is actually happening here.

I freeze, turned on and ready to just let my bond take what it wants, consequences be damned, but then his door flies open and his secretary walks into his bedroom.

His *secretary*.

Has a *key*.

To his *bedroom*.

She doesn't bother looking shocked or repentant at finding me in his bed, wrapped up in his limbs, she just starts opening up curtains and turning on freaking lights as she yammers on. "Good morning, sir. Your appointment has arrived here early, I've moved her into your office on the ground floor with refreshments and left her to go over her proposal one last time before she presents it to you."

North pulls me in tighter to his body for a second, squeezing me tight, and for one treacherous moment, I think he's going to tell the woman to get the fuck out of this room before we both kill her.

Then he unceremoniously untangles himself from me and gets out of the bed without a word, walking over to the bathroom as he says in a very kind tone, "I'll be five minutes, Pen."

He has *never* used that tone with me.

I lie here in his obscenely comfortable bed, surrounded by all of the intoxicating smells of him, and rage one last time about this man. One last time because I will *never* get in this bed again. I would spend the rest of my life sleeping amongst Nox's nightmares in his little burrow of books and pillows and loathing rather than step foot in here again.

The secretary, who has no clue of the catalyst she's become in my Bond, walks into his closet and starts to pull out clothing for him. Clearly, she hasn't done enough damage already and needs a little more to truly rub the salt into this wound.

She fusses over picking out his suit and a button up shirt

to go underneath it, and as the final nail in the goddamn coffin, she opens up one of the drawers and pulls out boxer briefs for him.

If it wasn't crossing every goddamn line I never knew I had for him, it would be hilarious to think of this grown man having someone dress him like a child.

There's a knock at the door and the secretary moves over to open it up, her body obscuring the room from Gryphon's view. I can feel that it's my Bond out there and I'm already absolutely fucking fuming about her being here, so the way she pops her hip and giggles at him sends me over the edge.

My eyes turn black.

Fuck.

I flop back onto the bed and take a deep breath, then three more until I can get my head back under control.

I hear Gryphon curse and then the bathroom door opens and for a second, I assume North is done in there, but then I hear Gryphon tear him a new asshole, so it's clear he's gone in there after him.

I cannot see a naked North Draven right now.

I definitely can't be in the room while his fucking secretary sees him naked either, so I push myself up in the bed and throw the covers off of myself, stalking out of the room without looking anywhere but the door.

I find Kieran outside of the room and he curses under

his breath at the sight of me. "Never a dull fucking minute with you around, is there?"

I huff at him and throw my hands in the air. "I've done nothing wrong. *Nothing*, even when I really freaking wanted to. So if that asshole comes out with a bad attitude, you can tell him to shove it so far up his ass that he chokes on it!"

That's when my bedroom door flings open and Gabe pokes his sleep rumpled head out of the door, scowling until he gets a look at me. "Fuck, what's happened now?"

"Nothing! Absolutely nothing, are you coming to training or not?" I hiss like a psycho, ducking past him and stomping over to the closet only to find Atlas in there getting changed.

I get a full view of his naked ass and almost swoon like a freaking maiden at the sight of the tanned muscle there, completely overwhelmed with all of the enraged, horny, gut-wrenching feelings swirling through me.

The man has a dump truck and I want to sink my teeth into it.

Jesus fucking Christ.

I press my palms over my eyes and mumble, "I fucking hate today. I would rather throw myself out of the window than ever deal with… any of this ever again."

Atlas chuckles and pulls my hands away from my eyes, the chuckle turning into a throaty laugh when I keep my eyes screwed shut tight. "I've got my gym shorts on now, Sweetness. I didn't think my ass would be the thing that sent you over the edge."

I huff and blink at him, double checking that he does in fact have his shorts on. They're so freaking short that they're almost obscene and I hate him all over again. Instead of saying that, or something remotely normal, I blurt out, "Can we kill North's secretary? Can I kill her and hide her body, please? Are we sure we're the good guys? Can we be bad for, like, five minutes? I don't even need five whole minutes, I'll have the bitch out in a spilt fucking second."

Gabe ducks his head around the wall to look at us both, with jeans on and a shirt in his hands. "Seriously, Bond, what's happened?"

I shake my head. "I'm not talking about it. I got pretty close to frying that woman, so I'm just going to go run on a treadmill until I can't freaking move anymore."

They share a look over my head and leave me to get ready.

When we head down to the basement gym, there's no sign of Gryphon anywhere, but I do exactly what I said I was going to do. I set the treadmill to a full-blown sprint speed, shove earphones into my ears with the loudest screaming metal playlist I can find, and then I run until I think I'm going to die.

I hit the stop button when my legs are wobbling so badly that I'm becoming a danger to myself, popping out one of the earphones to hear the furious spat happening behind me.

"—his fucking rules, if he can't follow them, then why the fuck are we?" Atlas snarls, and I hear the impact of them sparring, but I don't turn yet.

My bond is quiet in my chest, worn out from the rage-running, and I don't want it flaring back to life at the mere sight of them on the mats, so I give myself another second to get my shit together.

"I've dealt with it. We have the memorial service to go to this afternoon, he's not thinking right at the moment. I know it's hard for you, Bassinger, but think about how you would be coping with the loss of a father figure. William has been the only stable family member they've ever had, and they're both barely keeping it together. To be clear, they're only keeping it together because of Oli. Her safety and the welfare of our Bond group is the only thing keeping them from wallowing in their gifts and being the monsters the whole community think they are."

Fuck.

I swallow and step off of the treadmill, my knees buckling underneath me as I slump down onto the ground. I should stretch or something, but I have nothing left in me to do the things I'm supposed to do right now.

So I lie down and splay myself out like a sweaty, awkward starfish and stare at the ceiling, lost in my own thoughts.

I never got the chance to grieve for my parents.

There wasn't a memorial service or a funeral, no burial that I got to attend. Nothing, because the Resistance already had me. I don't even know where their bodies ended up. Was my mom buried with her Bonded or cremated separately? My chest tightens at the thought of all of their ashes being in separate little urns somewhere out there, waiting for their monster daughter to claim them.

My mom would hate that so much.

Tears quietly stream down the sides of my face but I just let them, ignoring them because they're the same old useless type that mean nothing.

I don't forgive North's actions today, or any other day, but the frigid distance between us is only going to get worse if I don't do something. Yes, I still need to get out of here. Yes, I still need to lie and omit all of the important details to them all as much as I can now that Gryphon knows what I am.

But I can choose to be a decent person to my Bond.

I take a deep breath and start to think about getting up but my body feels as though it weighs a thousand pounds. I hear footsteps and then Gabe's face appears in my eyeline as he stands over me, getting a good look at the puddle I make on the floor.

"I really wish you weren't crying over your Bonds again," he murmurs, groaning a little as he folds himself onto the ground next to me.

I swallow back the tears lodged in my throat. "I'm not. I'm crying about my parents. I can't do anything else today training-wise. I've wrecked myself."

Gabe nods and reaches out tentatively to push my hair away from my face before he slumps down onto his back beside me. "We don't have to do anything else for the rest of the day if you want. We can just go back to your room and... mope."

I scoff at him, my head lolling on my shoulders to look over at him. "Nope, we're going to the memorial. We're going and there isn't going to be a single question in anyone's minds after today over whether we're a united front or not. It doesn't matter about how I feel right now, it matters that we don't have some idiot show up here and ruin the brand new landscaping all over again."

Gabe stares at me for a second, his eyes softening and going all liquid at me in a way that pulls me into him.

He murmurs quietly to me, "You make me proud to be your Bond. Even when you hate us, your backbone, endurance, and integrity is unmatched."

I want to cry all over again but instead, I kiss him, a brief pressing of our lips together that coaxes my bond out to play, even when it's over before it starts.

I pick out one of the black dresses I'd bought on my shopping spree that, at this point, feels as though it happened years ago. I'd been hoping to wear it out with my Bonds to a party or something fun, but with a black jacket over the top and a pair of flats that Sage had lent me weeks ago, I look respectful and put-together.

I curl my hair and put on a tiny bit of makeup, just enough that I look like I'm putting effort in without being too much for such a somber event.

Gabe and Atlas both wear black slacks, button-up shirts, and polished leather shoes. Both of them look like wet dreams. Gabe's shoulders are so broad that the fabric stretching over them pulls tight as he moves, and Atlas' tattoos give him an irreverent feel.

I'm a very happy Bond to be escorted down to the main foyer by them both.

We find Nox and Gryphon already there, both of them dressed the same as the others, except Nox has a waistcoat on that should make him look overdressed in comparison, instead it just accentuates his trim waist and bulging arms. I refuse to drool over this man, so I focus on Gryphon instead.

There is nothing quite like the sight of a man in formal clothes with weapons strapped all over him. His hair is still wet from his shower and slicked back, and his eyes are hot on my body as he takes in my outfit choice, lingering on my bare legs for too long to pretend that he's not enjoying what he's seeing.

Then North stalks in from one of the doors down the hall that I've never been through and breaks the mood with his scowling, snarling rage. I tuck into Atlas' side a little closer, a small movement that they all pick up on thanks to how hyper-focused on me they all are right now.

I open my mouth to attempt to deflect from how smug Atlas is about it but Gryphon steps in and saves the day, something I'm coming to rely on.

"We're taking one car over so we can have a full escort. This is a high profile, high stakes situation, so I'm driving, with Gabe on point. We're taking the armored BMW so we're not worried about bullets, only gifts. Oli is to be with two of us at all times, no exceptions."

I nod along and follow him into the garage without question. I've already made up my mind about how today is going to go, the stuff I can control anyway. Everything I've done for the last five years has been to keep these men safe and alive. I can play the part of a subservient and placid Bond today if it helps to keep them safe.

Someday I'm sure they'll *all* appreciate it.

Just not today.

Gryphon and Gabe climb into the front seat and when North opens up the back, I can see it's another one of his modified vehicles with the two rows of seats facing each other. He holds out a hand to help me in and I take it, scooting in and arranging myself so that I'm not flashing them all my underwear.

North slides in after me, sitting next to me, and I see Atlas frown at him. "I should be sitting with her, my gift is the best protection she's got."

Nox scoffs at him, climbing in to face his brother. He doesn't so much as glance in my direction. "It's a bulletproof car, you're useless in here compared to the rest of us."

Atlas' lip curls at him and I press my foot against his, smiling at him as though this is all completely fine and not bothering me in the least.

The car ride over to the cemetery is silent.

I try not to stare at either of the Dravens but my eyes keep getting drawn back to them. Nox's hands are curled into fists and there's a small black band of smoke around his wrist that can only be seen as he moves. It's weird that he's using his gift right now in the small space of the car, but his eyes are sharp as he looks out the windows.

North is barely holding himself together.

Every inch of his body is tense, the muscles all trembling

a little with the effort he's using to not just explode on us all right now. Atlas is watching him like a hawk, poised and ready to grab me the moment North actually loses it, but I trust him more than that.

Grief is an unpredictable bitch of a feeling and it's riding him hard.

When Gryphon pulls into the parking lot filled with luxury cars, we're flanked by two TacTeam vehicles. We wait until they empty out before we get out of the BMW. It's strange to have them watching over us so intensely, like we're celebrities or royalty or something, and I've got an itchy, uncomfortable feeling about it.

North holds out his arm for me to take and I do so without hesitation, though I look around to be sure Atlas is also going to be with me. I might've made the decision to play my part today, but I still want one of my trusted Bonds with me while I do it.

North leads me through the crowd of people waiting for us to arrive, dozens of the Gifted higher society members around us, and I pick out my friends straight away.

Sage nods at me with a tight smile from where she's wedged between Sawyer and her father. I'm shocked to see Gray standing with them as well, an older Bonded group standing around them that I would guess are his family.

Riley and Giovanna are there too.

It's harder for me to keep my reaction to them standing

so close to Sage with sneers on their faces off of my own than it was for me to keep myself calm about my furious Bonds, and North's arm tenses under my own. I squeeze it a little, hoping he understands that I'm saying I'm fine, but he just keeps us moving forward together.

We walk up to the church and North greets the priest at the front, briefly thanking him for being here and holding the service, then we walk in together.

There's already a TacTeam in place and I give Kieran the same nod of greeting that I'd given Sage, acknowledging him without making a big fuss about it. His eyes are sharp as he looks around at the people coming in behind us, vetting and checking each person off in his mind, I'm sure.

I'm doing the same thing.

I didn't meet a lot of people in the camps but the ones I did meet are the worst of the worst, and if I spot any of them here today, I will take them out without a second thought.

We all sit in the front row together, North at one end and Gryphon at the other. North is careful about wedging Nox between the two of us, and I'm careful about not touching him too much without being obvious about it.

I can't get his reaction to my Bond frenzy out of my head. If my touch is so abhorrent to him, then I need to do what I can to respect that boundary... even though I'm very aware that my boundaries aren't nearly as important to him.

The service is long and detailed.

I learn more about the Draven family in that hour than I have in the months that I've lived with them, like the fact that William had custody of them both when their parents all died. Or the fact that William never found his Bonds and still managed to keep his sanity and good health.

He had started several charities to help underprivileged children and domestic violence victims. He had donated to non-Gifted and Gifted alike. He was a pillar of the community, and he was murdered by crazed, elitist zealots for daring to want good things for the world.

I'm silently crying by the end of the eulogy, and when North stands to do his own speech, he glances down at me and freezes at the sight of me dabbing my eyes dry with the tissue that Gabe had tucked into my hand, passed down from Gryphon on the far end.

When North steps away from us to walk up to the podium, his steps are more sure and steady, and when he faces everyone, he no longer looks like he is filled with rage.

"Thank you for being here today to honor my uncle, William Draven, one last time. His life will be remembered as one full of many accomplishments, but the ones that I hold closest to my heart aren't any of his most lauded achievements."

He sets down the cards and glances up at the screen behind him, a photo of William grinning there. He was a very handsome man, much like his nephews, and as I watch North swallow and turn back to his speech, I have to dab at my eyes with the tissue again.

"He didn't have to take me or my brother in. He wasn't even supposed to be our guardian, but he fought the council to have custody of us. He took the Draven seat, even though politics made him queasy, because he wanted to make sure that it would still be there for me when I was old enough. He kept us safe, loved, and in my darkest hours, he was always there to offer me an ear. He never judged us or made us feel like monsters. He put us on the right path in life, and we both plan to honor the chance he gave us by ensuring that we continue his legacy in the community to make this a better, safer, and more inclusive place for all, Gifted and non-Gifted alike."

It's a risk, a huge one, but I very slowly reach over to take Nox's hand in mine. I'm expecting him to pull away or shake me off, something subtle enough not to upset North's vision of us all being seen as a united front, but harsh nonetheless.

His fingers are warm and tight around my own.

I'm not stupid enough to think that it means something, that he'll suddenly change his mind about me, but it feels like a tiny victory anyway.

21

There is a distinct change in the community after William's memorial service.

I have no doubt that there are still many people who hate us all and think that we're monsters, but there's also a hell of a lot less whispering and gossiping about us in general. My shifts at the cafe become calm and uneventful, though there's still always at least one of my Bonds around at all times.

My training with Gryphon kicks up a notch. The very first time that I manage to tackle him to the ground, I decide that I'm basically Super Woman now, and I don't need any of my Bonds stalking me anymore because, clearly, I'm a badass who can take care of herself.

None of them agree with me.

Sharing beds with them all becomes surprisingly normal, though my refusal to sleep in North's room goes down about as well as I'd expected.

Gryphon taking my side was a pleasant surprise.

I was expecting more of a fight about it, but when I'd woken up in my own bed with North wrapped around me, Atlas snoring on my floor after being kicked out of the bed overnight, and Gryphon waiting at the door for me to get a move on to head down to the gym with him, it sinks in that maybe this was one battle I'd managed to win.

Living my life with at least two sets of eyes on me at all times becomes normal. Annoying as fuck and incredibly suffocating, but normal.

Kieran or one of Gryphon's other trusted TacTeam members gets assigned to be with me and my friends while we're attending classes during the day. I'm surprised that Kieran, Gryphon's second in command, would be assigned to Bond-sitting duty, but Gabe just looks at me like I'm an idiot when I mention it to him.

"Gryphon would be here doing it himself if it didn't get too many of us in the same public space at the same time. It's bad enough that there's four Draven Bonds in Nox's classes during the week. There have been talks about getting you to take them remotely."

I scowl at him over the dining hall table, his plate of sadness is already empty but my mountain of spaghetti is still going strong in front of me. "Why should we be worried about that shit? There's safety in numbers, shouldn't we be happy to have four of us together if shit hits the fan around here?"

Sawyer scoffs at me, leaning over his sister to grab one of my abandoned breadsticks and shove it in his mouth. Gabe and Atlas both scowl at him over it but I wave them off.

I want pasta carbs right now, not bread carbs.

"It's about the council thinking you guys are still a danger, remember? North and Gryphon are trying to keep you all together but not congregating in public where people remember how terrifying you all are. Honestly, I'm not taking my father's seat on the council. Sage can have it, or we'll just give it up because the mind games are fucked up."

I didn't know their father was even on the council. I turn and give Sage a questioning look and she shrugs. "Dad's not on it, his brother is, but he's Bondless and none of us ever see him ending up with an heir, so it'll come to Sawyer and I. We're the last of the Benson line, so if we both say no... it'll go to someone else."

Atlas nods along but Gabe groans and rubs a hand over his eyes. "It'll end up going to someone shit, so one of you two better sack up and take it."

Sage throws a balled up paper bag at him with her nose

scrunched up. "'Sack up'? You're delightful, Ardern, no wonder Oli loves me the most."

Atlas' eyes narrow at her but it's playful. "You mean after the creature, right? Don't forget we're all lower down the totem pole than the murderous wisps of smoke in her hair."

Brutus doesn't like being talked about and he sticks his nose out to snort soundlessly in Atlas' direction, my hair fluttering at the motion. I lift a hand to give him a scratch behind the ear and he settles back down, licking at the crumbs on my fingers as though he can actually taste them.

Sawyer rolls his eyes at us all and cuts in, "Enough talk about the *perks* of Oli's Bond group. Tell me that you're all going to the party this weekend so I can crawl into Gray's place on the way home this afternoon and plead with his parents. Oli, how open are you to bribery? I need you to convince North or Gryphon to back me up here. Suck one of them off for me, *please.*"

I roll my eyes back at him for being dramatic and stupid, but Atlas slings an arm over the back of my chair and levels him with a savage sort of glare. "I will cut your fucking tongue out if you talk to her like that again, Benson. I'm giving you a warning because I like Sage."

It's a lie, he also likes Sawyer and we all know it. Sawyer just pretends to look shocked and humbled at him but the sarcasm is dripping from his every movement.

Gabe's hand slips onto my knee to squeeze it under the table, reassurance that I don't need but am grateful for anyway, and I drawl at Sawyer, "I couldn't even get myself into a party right now with those two watching my every move. What makes you think I can do shit for Gray if he's in his confinement?"

"It's the end of year party! My parents have spent weeks working with North and the other council members to make sure we could still have it, no one is going to stop you from attending! We have to go," Sage says, popping a breadstick dipped in sauce into her mouth. I don't understand how she keeps her perfect figure, she eats more than Sawyer and I combined.

There's a huff behind us and we all look over to see Kieran hovering like a mother hen over us all. He's pulled down his neck gaiter and removed his helmet for the first time in weeks. The full riot gear they're all in is a little bit extreme and terrifying for the halls of the college.

Sage raises an eyebrow at him, mouthier by the day at my scowling and grumpy Bond-guard. "Am I wrong? We've all been told it's going to happen. You might have to get that stick outta your ass about it."

My eyes widen at her sass and I hold out a fist to her, this new and improved Sage, the one dating outside of her asshole Bond and living life on her own goddamn terms, she's the best possible version of my best friend.

I'm so fucking proud of her.

Kieran stares us down and then takes the seat next to Sage, looking down his nose at us all. "The party is on, but there'll be a strong TacTeam presence there. You can all drink and be stupid, we'll keep an eye on you all."

Gabe drinks his water and then chuckles back at him, "When are we stupid? I'm always on my best behavior at these things."

Kieran points at him with his comms. "The last one you went to, you punched David's son in the face."

"He insulted my Bond, leered at her in a bathing suit, and then implied he wanted to touch her. He's lucky he's still breathing."

Atlas slowly leans back in his chair and looks around the dining hall. "And which asshole is David's son? Just for curiosity's sake."

I shake my head at him but Sage smirks at them both. "Martinez. He also tried to catch Oli in the maze to feed her to the pond bitch, so feel free to ruin that dickhead."

Atlas' eyebrows damn near hit his hairline. "He tried to feed my Bond to the pond bitch? Ardern, we're going to talk about why the fuck he's still breathing a bit later, but Sage, dear, please point this asshole out to me right the fuck now."

Sage giggles and starts to look around but Kieran shoots her a look as he snaps, "His family holds a seat on the council, you can't—"

"Oh, you'd be surprised at what I can and will do, Black. You should probably run off and let that piece of shit know that he's on my shit list and, fuck, does he not want to be. I play nice here because I don't want to add stress to Oli's plate, but I'm not going to let that shit go."

Gabe's hand squeezes my knee again and I grin at him while I lean into Atlas' side. "It would probably also add stress to my plate if you go after that little asshole now, so maybe we should just add him to the TT revenge list."

He doesn't want to agree with that at all, but with a little eyelash batting, he eases up a bit.

Sage cackles at the entire move and says, "So, outfits? Let's wear more than bikinis this time around now that we know Atlas is going to wage war on your behalf."

My outfit is absolutely on point.

Months of training with my Bonds mean that my legs are freaking perfect, shapely and toned, and so I pick out a playsuit that definitely shows off a little of my ass and more than a little of my tits. I try on three pairs of my new heels and stick with a pair of simple black pumps, sexy without being too flashy.

I convince Sage and the rest of our friends to spend

the night at the manor so we can all get ready together and come home together. Gryphon likes this plan a lot because it means that we're all together for his TacTeam to protect. Even though he's not attending the party, he knows absolutely everything that is being planned for the night, from the amount of students attending to the amount of alcohol that's being snuck in.

Sage and I lock ourselves in my bathroom to get ready without all the guys breathing down our necks, a great plan because between my Bonds, her brother, and their boyfriends, there is a hell of a lot of testosterone in the building.

I can barely breathe with it all.

The white minidress Sage chooses for the night has me cackling over the thought of Felix's face when he sees it, and when she's done curling her hair and applying her makeup, I decide that maybe she's getting laid tonight.

She almost dies when I say this.

"We're not— I'm not— oh hell, I haven't done that yet. I'm happy dating, and Felix is perfect but... I still have a lot of shit in my head about how Bonds are supposed to be and my heart hurts about Riley, no matter how hard I keep trying to get him out of my head. I— I don't know how to let that life go fully yet."

I perch my ass on the bathroom countertop to watch her layer on her jewelry, lots of beautiful necklaces and pendants, and shrug at her. "So what? You don't have to have a reason to want to take things slow, if you don't want to, then just… don't."

She huffs at me and bumps my leg with her hip. "You make it sound so easy, like you haven't spent months trying to fix your Bonds' expectations because they all want to Bond. I just— I feel guilty for needing time because Felix is perfect. Completely, heartbreakingly perfect."

I nod and think of my own perfect Bonds just outside of the door, that I can hear talking shit and laughing with our friends. "The perfect man will wait. The perfect man won't do something that would hurt you, no matter how badly they want to. Felix has put himself out there for you, over and over again. I don't see him disappearing over you needing some time to figure your head out a bit. Fuck, Riley and Giovanna better not show up tonight, I will fucking destroy them both."

Sage huffs and laughs at me. "You and Sawyer both. Giovanna called my parents for help last week. My dad has finally decided to take my side over this, and when he told her to get lost, she said he was 'disrespecting' his daughter's Bond and needed to help her. Can you imagine? My dad is beyond angry about it, he's ready to spill some blood himself."

I'm still not the biggest fan of the Bensons— it should not take your kid being abducted by the Resistance to treat them nicely— but I will absolutely take this as the win it is.

The more people wanting Riley and Giovanna in the ground, the better, as far as I'm concerned.

I jump down from the countertop and give myself one last look over, making sure the tape is keeping everything in place nicely, and mutter, "What the hell did that bitch want from your parents? Fuck, can you imagine having the nerve to pull that shit? I need a drink. I need to burn this rage out somehow so I don't set Brutus on her."

Sage snorts at me, zipping her makeup bag up and posing with me for one last photo of the two of us together. We're planning on drinking enough to test out the strength of this tape holding my tits in place, so a before picture is absolutely crucial.

She tucks her phone away as she drawls, "She wants an internship at his company over the summer. She's barely passing her classes, like... by the skin of her teeth, and wants a coveted spot at his genetics laboratory. Even Sawyer had to jump through a million hoops to get his spot, there's no way my dad would give it to her, even if our Bond wasn't... completely dysfunctional."

What a fucking bitch.

I'm opening my mouth to snark some more when there's a booming knock at the door and Sawyer yells, "We're out of pre-drinks and Gabe is too scared of the

Draven wrath to go get more, so we've gotta get moving or I'll lose my buzz. If you both want me to play nicely tonight, get your asses out here."

Sage rolls her eyes and flings the door open, leveling a glare at him. "You spent two hours manscaping before we came here, Sawyer. Don't freaking start on us! Oli had to use half a roll of duct tape to make sure she didn't flash her goods and cause mass destruction at the party via Atlas and Gabe's tantrums over it."

He doesn't back down, he never does. "I did that for dick, Sage! There is no other reason to spend an hour in the bathroom, except for trimming your pubes. Maybe Oli should've just gone with a bra— holy shit, Fallows. No. You can't wear that. Gabe's gonna bust a nut."

I do a full twirl so that he can see the back of the outfit as well, and he shakes his head emphatically. "Nope. No wearing that. Oli, I'm bi, not gay, I can tell you right now that this playsuit is in the 'no' basket. Atlas! Come tell her!"

I laugh, grabbing my clutch to check that I have everything I need in there, and then I hear a groan from the doorway.

"Nope, not a fucking chance. New outfit, Bond."

I turn to find Gabe staring at my ass, or rather scowling at it like it's the best and worst thing to ever happen to him, and the shot of adrenaline that runs through me has me giggling like a madwoman.

"No man, Bond or otherwise, will ever tell me what to wear, Gabriel Ardern. So you better change your tune, and quickly," I say, waving a finger at him mockingly, but the look he gives me back has my heart stuttering in my chest.

I almost forget that all of our friends are standing around watching our exchange. I almost walk over to him and climb up that impressive body of his until I can get his lips on mine, my hands in his hair, tugging and pulling until I'm directing him down my body and getting those lips elsewhere because he needs to—

He groans again and grinds his palms into his eyes. "Stop it. You're not playing fair, and Sawyer's already giving me enough shit tonight without me pitching a fucking tent at whatever is making your bond hum like that."

He sounds miserable and I do actually feel a little bad about it. I can't help that he's fucking gorgeous, built and pretty as hell, and standing there in a pair of jeans and a tight white tee that bunches up around his biceps, he's just fucking—

"I'm out. Atlas, you need to walk her out. I'll meet you guys at the door," he mutters and spins on his heel, ignoring the way Sawyer and Gray both start heckling him.

It's easy for them, they're Unbonded and happy to just enjoy each other until they find out where they're supposed to be. The rest of us are in agony over here.

Atlas finally steps out of my walk-in closet and turns to see what all of the fuss is about. I give him a sheepish grin and he just looks me over slowly, his eyes dragging over every inch of me.

"You look perfect, Sweetness, but I'm killing any man who looks at you for longer than half a second," he says with a quirk of his lips, and the grin that grows there is wolfish and perfect.

I bounce over to him, testing out the tape a little, and I'm pleasantly surprised when nothing moves. "Deal. I just wanted to look and feel good tonight. I hope it's not too much."

He catches me in his arms and gives me the lightest peck on the lips, barely grazing me so he doesn't ruin my lipstick. "You could go there naked and I would still worship you... everyone else would just have to die. A sacrifice I'm prepared to make."

I shiver and my bond purrs in my chest again, always happy to hear about them craving death in my honor, spilling blood as an offering to the Bond we share.

I want more.

He leans down again, his eyes fixed on mine, and the grin on his face stretches even wider. "Oh, my girl likes that? You want me to kill everyone who dares to look at you? I will. I'm not a good man, not like the rest of your

Bonds. I'm good for you, and fuck the rest of them. If you want blood, Sweetness, I'll give it to you. I'll give you whatever you want."

I swallow roughly and try to find my voice again but it comes out like a croak, "You can't talk like that to my bond. It's bloodthirsty and selfish, it'll take it all. It would take *everything*."

Atlas pulls me in tight to his chest again, the world narrowing to just the two of us. "Good because I'm going to give it everything and more. The second you're ready… *everything*, and that's a promise, Sweetness."

I swallow again and try to calm my racing heart down from where it's trying to beat right out of my chest. When Atlas pecks my cheek and pulls away, only to tuck me back into his side, I see that the room has emptied out while we were talking. I didn't hear the door open or shut, and that's a little embarrassing, but I glue a smile onto my face.

"Let's get this stupid party over with then, huh?"

Atlas chuckles at the dry tone I'm throwing his way and walks us both over to the door, opening it like he's about to usher me through, but we find Gryphon waiting there for me, his arms crossed over his chest, looking pissed the hell off as his eyes lock onto mine.

I cringe. "What's happened now? Is our night over already?"

He doesn't so much as glance in Atlas' direction as he

snaps at him, "I need to talk to my Bond. I'll walk her downstairs when we're done."

It's the sternest dismissal I've heard out of him in months, but even though Atlas stiffens at the tone, he kisses me again on the crown of my head and then leaves us both.

I'm a little scared about what's about to happen here but I also know I haven't done anything wrong... not unless he's finally hunted down some background information on me and he's about to tell me he hates me now. Maybe he knows about all of the death and destruction.

Maybe—

"What the fuck do you think you're doing, going out tonight dressed like that? Over my dead fucking body—"

The relief that was quick to flood me is short-lived. "It's a freaking playsuit, and I'm not going to be told what I can and can't wear by a bunch of men—"

His body hits mine like a freight train. One second, he's across the hallway and then the next, he's pressing me back into the door, his hands clutching at my bare thighs like he's still not sure he's actually seeing the real thing.

"You think you're the only one fighting your bond? This is all mine. Know that before you walk out of here because Bonded or Unbonded, you're *mine*."

I try to breathe but he's pressing into me so much that I can't. "I know. It's just a cute outfit, I'm not trying to... I'm not unhappy with my Bonds. I can change, if it's that much of a problem."

He eases up a fraction and then steps back. "No. You're in my bed tonight, you can come to me exactly like that."

I'm drunk and I've lost all of my friends.

Okay, so Gabe and Atlas are glued to my side at all times and I can see Kieran glaring at everyone around us, but Sage disappeared into a closet with Felix half an hour ago and I haven't seen either of them since. Sawyer and Gray had both already made out in every room of this house, something about a dare that I was too drunk to listen about properly, and now I'm pretty sure that they've found a quiet flat surface to fuck on. I both love that for them *and* hate them passionately for it.

The house belongs to one of the lower families on the council, which is to say that it is still a mega-mansion with a pool and ridiculous catering, but that the council members themselves don't feel the need to attend and no one is worried about the dress code when a shit-tonne of TacTeam guys show up to watch over us all.

I'm giggly and enjoying the warm night air a little too much for Kieran's liking, but both of my bonds are watching me dance by the pool with a kind of lightly inebriated rapture that has butterflies exploding in my belly, a riot of fluttering and tingling.

The music here is surprisingly good.

"Alright, you're cut off. Any more and you're going to hate the world tomorrow," Gabe says when I finish off the last of my glass of champagne and bat my eyelashes at him for a refill.

He laughs at my pout when he shakes his head at me.

Atlas isn't impressed with anything around us. He's not obvious about it, he smiles and speaks to people when they come over to us, but there's a coldness about him that I've noticed at Draven as well, like he's looking down on all of them for their many sins against us.

I can't help but lean into him, cozying up and tucking myself as close to his body as I can get, because that kind of absolute loyalty will always mean the world to me.

I've had it for them from the moment I'd heard their names in that stupid hospital room, when my world was breaking but I still had a long way to fall. Fuck, if only I knew how far away I still was from rock bottom.

A hand smooths down my spine, a soothing motion,

and Atlas leans down to murmur into my ear, "It's okay, Sweetness. Whatever you're thinking, none of it matters now. I have you."

Gabe threads his fingers through mine but when I glance over to him, he's still talking to one of his football buddies, bitching about some shit to do with the next season. He noticed my mood change without even looking at me, another sign that I'm losing the fight to keep them all from being attached to me.

The bed sharing might be settling down my bond but it's making everything a million times more complicated.

"Let's go home, Sweetness. There's nothing left for us at this party," Atlas murmurs, and I shrug at him.

"Everyone else is having fun, we can't leave without them. Why don't you get another drink and let off some steam."

He grins and shakes his head. "If I drink, I'll end up fighting someone… possibly even Gabe for the way he keeps speaking to these spineless assholes. I've never seen so much groveling and sniveling."

I giggle at the look Gabe's friend gives us both because we're not trying to be quiet about it, but Gabe just smirks at us, lifting my hand up to his lips to kiss the back of it, like I'm some perfect treasure to him.

I'm about to drag Atlas over to the dance floor by the catered table for a dance when Sage comes stumbling out of the house, her eyes round and glassy, and my stomach drops.

I pull away from my Bonds to rush to her, my bond sluggish with the alcohol but still perking up at the very idea of destroying whoever has upset my bestie.

Kieran beats me to her.

"What's happened? I thought you were with Felix, why's he left you alone?"

She blinks at him, her lip trembling a little, and I'm ready to slit his throat for snapping at her, but she just croaks out, "He sent me out to find Oli. Gracie is... Gracie drank too much and now she's talking shit. It's not a big deal, but Felix might need some help getting her down."

Down?

Kieran gently pushes Sage towards me and stalks into the house, barking orders at the other TacTeam guys around us so that they close in on us. I wrap Sage into a hug and she immediately melts into me.

"This is why I don't go out, Oli," she mumbles into my hair. She sounds so miserable that I want to punch Gracie in the face all over again.

There's some shouting and arguing in the house and Gabe steps up closer to us both, but then Felix walks out with an absolutely vicious look on his face, dragging his sister behind him.

Gracie is trashed.

So trashed that she pukes in the potted plants by the door and whimpers when Felix snaps at her, "You never fucking learn! I wanted one night, and you couldn't just keep your shit together for *one night*."

Kieran stomps out behind them, his nose scrunching up at the foul smell of Gracie's vomit, and he locks eyes with me, jerking his head in the universal motion for 'can we please leave this fucking mess now' and I nod back.

We're done.

Atlas loses 'rock, paper, scissors' against Gabe and has to go find Sawyer and Gray to drag them both home with us. Felix corrals Gracie into one of the Tac vehicles and then leaves her there to come hold Sage, kissing her hair and murmuring reassuringly to her while she rocks a little on her feet.

When I find out what that bitch said to her, Felix's sister or not, Gracie is going to feel my goddamn wrath, and I'm going to make sure she never pulls this shit again.

Everyone needs to stop shitting on my girl.

Sawyer takes one look at his sister and the good mood he's in just evaporates into thin air. He and Gray had come downstairs, still wrapped up in each other, their hair all mussed up and their clothes very obviously rearranged. I'd been so relieved for them to have this time together.

Another mark against Gracie.

"Try not to be too harsh on her, she's not exactly the

picture of stable and mentally well," Gabe whispers to me as he gets me into Atlas' car. I'm shocked to find that Atlas didn't drink at all, his good mood had nothing to do with alcohol and everything to do with being there with me.

I scowl at Gabe but he pulls a face back. "She lost her Central Bond years ago. He was only a kid when he died. She's never really been stable since. It's not an excuse but… just keep it in mind."

Fuck.

I still hate her but at least this time around, I'll leave her to Felix to deal with. He's still scowling and pissed looking as he slides into the backseat, taking the middle spot so that Sage can tuck into his side without being up in Gabe's space.

I know it wasn't for me, but it's just another reason that I'm on Felix's side here, even when his sister is a raging nightmare that I want to deal with in the most horrifying, blood-soaked ways.

"Take a breath," Atlas murmurs, his hand resting on my thigh as he directs the car into the traffic to get us back to the manor.

I glance down and find Brutus on my lap, sniffing at my clothes like he's trying to figure out what's pissed me off so much. He's always extra cute in his puppy form, and I curl my hand around his little body to cuddle him up properly in my lap. He takes it and licks at my fingertips, the sensation weird because I can feel it, but there's no physical evidence that he's doing it, no puppy drool left behind from his big tongue.

"Jesus, fuck, I forgot you had that for a second there, Fallows," Felix says from the back, sounding a little sick, and Sage cranes her head around to get a look at Brutus who is now rolling onto his back for a belly scratch.

"He's cute! I mean, I wouldn't touch him ever, but I can admire what a good boy he is," she says and Felix shakes his head at her.

"Is it weird for you two to know that she has an extension of a Draven with her at all times? Do you guys make him sleep out in the hall at night or are we okay with him now?" Felix says and I stiffen for a second, thinking he's heard about the hallway incident, but then I remember that the entire campus knows Nox isn't a fan of mine, so of course he has some questions.

Gabe sounds very nonchalant as he answers him, "The more eyes on Oli, the better. The more eyes on all of our friends and families, the better, to be honest. Draven might be a little happy bubble for us all, but it's definitely not safe."

Sage scoffs at them both, her words slurring a little thanks to all of the champagne she's had for the night. "Oli doesn't need eyes on her, she could take us all out before we had the chance to blink in her direction. She's the biggest badass I've ever met. Nox is just spying on her because he wants to control her. You all do, at least a little bit. That's a part of being in a Bond group. None of you want her to have the freedom to be her own person, unless you're involved in the process. That's it, that's her whole life now, and even with Riley and Giovanna fucking loathing me, it's my life too. Gracie was right. I'm a freak of nature, and if my Bond doesn't want me, then I am a reject. Now I'm ruining Felix too because he's got someone out there waiting for him and I'm complicating it all. Fuck, Atlas, I'm going to throw up."

He swerves the car off of the road safely enough, but the Tac vehicles escorting us all come off of the road with us as though they're about to wage a war on whoever has threatened us.

I will fucking murder Gracie.

Kieran flies out of his vehicle and bolts towards us, coming up short when he gets an eyeful of Felix and me holding Sage up between us while she pukes. Gabe grabs her hair and twists it away from her face, wincing when she sobs into Felix's chest when the heaving finally eases up.

"Is she okay? I can get a healer here pronto," Kieran says, his eyes glued to Sage's sobbing form, and I shake my head as I point to Felix's glowing hands.

"He's got this covered. It came on too fast for him to

help before it... came to this. Sorry for the stop."

He finally looks away from them but there's a hesitancy there. "It's fine. Bassinger drives like a pro, so we all had time to get you guys covered. Do we need to stay put for much longer? I'll set up a perimeter."

Felix shakes his head, coaxing Sage back towards the car, and I get them in the front passenger seat together. Atlas helps get the seatbelt around them both but with Sage tucked into Felix's lap, it's an easy enough switch up.

I listen to Sage's rattling chest the entire way home, cursing every person in this stupid town for hurting her like this. Gabe holds my hand, scowling and bouncing his knee like he's full of anxious energy.

I don't have words to reassure him right now, I only have rage and vengeance pumping through my veins.

The car is quiet and when Atlas pulls up in the garage at the Draven manor, we all just sit there for a second to evaluate what the fuck this night has ended up turning into.

"Well... we're alive, right? All breathing and in one piece was the plan," Felix drawls, still fuming at his sister but attempting to lighten the mood.

I shrug at him and snark back, "The night is still young. I could definitely still rip someone in half, if provoked."

I'm only half joking.

I'm glad that I didn't drink too much at the party, all of the alcohol burning out of my system the moment that I step out of the Hellcat, because tonight is Gryphon's night with me in his bed. After his scorching hot demand for me to be there in this outfit, my legs want to buckle at the thought of it.

I can't Bond with him.

Fuck, I want something with him tonight though, anything. Maybe the pain of holding back the Bond will be worth being able to have him. A shiver runs through my body at the thought. Atlas wraps an arm around my shoulder, mistaking the shiver for me feeling cold, and I let him lead me into the manor to grab a drink.

Gabe starts directing people to spare bedrooms like he knows every room in this place, and I let Atlas take me back to my room for a glass of water before I head down to Gryphon.

I grab a handful of my Bond's clothes to change into in Gryphon's room, ignoring the raised eyebrow Atlas gives me when I don't just get changed before I head down there. I might implode if I have to talk about the way Gryphon had been so demanding.

It was hot as fuck, and I need a lot more of that side of him in my life.

I drink one last glass of water before I kiss him on the cheek and head down to the first floor alone, my bare feet silent against the plush carpet. The house is quiet and peaceful and when I check the time on my phone, I find a text from Gabe to say he's gotten everyone into rooms and goodnight. There's a somber tone to it and I know I'll have to talk to him later about what Sage had said.

She wasn't wrong.

I'm not saying that I mind it. If I weren't being hunted and a danger to them all, I would love nothing more than to coexist with them in that very codependent way that Bonded groups have.

But that's not the life I was given.

When I get to Gryphon's door, I have to knock twice, but there's no answer either time.

It's after midnight and his car was in the garage, so I'm pretty sure he's home, but I don't like going into my Bond's rooms without their permission. Nox is the only one who literally never lets me in, but that's also part of our routine. I get up there, pass out and know that sometime, hours later, he'll be asleep on the couch with his creatures everywhere.

Gryphon always lets me in.

I blow out a deep breath and try the door handle, letting myself into the room and closing it quietly behind me. I sigh when I hear the shower going, relieved that nothing too out of the ordinary is going on here, my Bond is just getting ready for bed.

That is until I pull the covers back on his bed and the smell of perfume hits me.

I freeze, but my bond takes full control of my body before I have the chance to process what the *fuck* I've just found.

The perfume is all over the bed.

It's on his pillows and his sheets, the perfectly pressed duvet is smothered in it, and my bond slowly descends into madness.

Who dared to touch my Bond?

How could he ever let another woman into this room, into his bed? This is all mine. *Mine.* He's mine; his room, his bed, all of it belongs to me. I'm going to find this woman and I will bleed her out, present her lifeless body to my Bond, and show him what happens to anyone who touches what is mine.

Brutus whines in my ear, a feeling, not a sound, and I reach up to pluck him out of my hair, setting him down on the carpet and firmly demanding that he go home to Nox.

I don't need witnesses for this.

The bathroom door opens and Gryphon steps out naked, the towel wrapped around his waist covering him a little, but I search his body for marks regardless. He falters and comes to a halt, lifting a hand to push back his hair. When his very muscular body ripples with the movement, my eyes narrow.

Did she see him like this too?

Did she see every inch of him tense and move as he fucked her on my bed? Did she watch as *my* Bond pumped inside her body?

"Oli? What's happened, why is your bond—"

The moment I look at him, I know that I don't want to talk to him. I want his bond, I want to deal with this directly because the man might have done something fucking abhorrent, but the bond belongs to me.

Mine.

I will prove that to the very core of him, the base and animalistic truth of him, because the man cannot be trusted right now. The man has betrayed me and everything we've built together.

A growling sort of gasp rips out of his throat as his eyes flash to white, his legs stumbling as I trigger his bond to take over, and when he looks at me again, there's nothing of the surly and scowling man left.

Only the bond.

He takes a deep breath, looking around the room as though he's not sure where he is anymore, and I get frustrated quickly, enraged that he's not taking me and claiming me right now.

"*Mine.*"

My words break his stillness, his hand dropping the

towel as he charges at me in one go, taking me down onto the bed so he's pinning me there.

I barely get a look at him but it doesn't matter, none of it matters, except that he needs to Bond with me *now*.

I grab a fistful of his hair and yank his lips down to mine, our tongues fighting for dominance as he nips at my lip like he wants to punish me. I taste blood but I can't tell if it's his or mine, and his hands scramble at my clothes, tearing and ripping at the playsuit until it's in pieces on the ground.

He growls at the tape covering half of my chest, and he's not nice about getting it off either, leaving red marks and stinging skin as he goes about baring me completely, his tongue soothing the skin afterwards.

I don't want soft.

I want him to fuck me and Bond with me so that there's never a question again about who he belongs to. I'm not some soft Central Bond who needs hand-holding. I need his cum dripping down my legs and my scent replacing that fucking perfume on his sheets and I need it *now*.

I get another fistful of his hair and shove him down my body, leaning up to strip my panties off. He grabs my legs, throwing them over his shoulders until my thighs are wrapped around his head, his tongue hot as he tastes me, tastes the slick between my legs and finds out just how ready for his cock I am. The moment he stepped into this room, I was ready for him, ready to take what is mine, and it doesn't matter how fucking perfect his lips and his tongue is on my pussy, I need more.

When my legs begin to shake, I pull at him again, demanding and moody because I need him inside me when I come, I need him to join with me to complete the Bond properly.

"Fuck me. Bond with me *now*," I snap, my voice coming out dark and venomous, and his eyes flash even brighter at the command.

If I thought for a second that I'd be controlling what was happening here, he's quick to change my mind as he shoves a pillow under my hips, a hand wrapping around my throat and holding me still as he lines his cock up and pushes in with one stroke, groaning like a dying man.

Somewhere in the back of my mind I register that it hurts, that he's too big and this is all too much, but my bond shoves out of my body and wraps around him, binding us both together until I can't breathe.

His hips push into me, the friction building until he's slamming into me, a Bond with only one thing on his mind. Claiming me, tying me to him, owning me, and having me forever because there is no me without him. We were made from the same dying star, put on this earth to search one another out and bind ourselves to one another for all of eternity.

The sound of our bodies slapping together echo around the room, obscene and fucking perfect, and when I moan into his ear, his hands tighten on my skin and he deepens his strokes until his hips grind into my clit with each thrust.

I'm so close to coming, so close to taking him as mine, and when he leans down to kiss me again, I turn my face to his neck and bite him there, marking his skin somewhere that everyone will see it and know what it means.

We come together and when my bond releases into him and takes his bond into me, it's like nothing I've ever experienced. Orgasms are incredible, but this? This is everything and more, this is my entire world coming down to a single pinpoint and then exploding into a million pieces. This is a jumble of things that make a lot of sense and exactly none, and I've never felt so *whole* in my life before.

He roars as his hips stutter in their strokes, his hand tightening around my throat, and when his head rears back in ecstasy, I can see the bright light of his bond shining through his skin now that we're Bonded. I give him a piece of my power and he returns that gift to me tenfold.

Mine.

When he collapses back onto the bed beside me, my bond leaves me all at once.

The horror of what has happened sinks into my being.

I don't have time to say a word to him because the door

flies open so quickly that it bounces against the wall, North storming into the room with an absolutely livid expression on his face. I do the most awkward and embarrassing squeal as I roll myself into a cocoon with the duvet.

I hear more footsteps but Gryphon's eyes flash and they stop at the door, two of my Bonds, who would have to be Gabe and Atlas, and I want to just die.

Die.

There's a horrified sort of silence and then North snarls, "What the fuck did you do?"

How the hell am I supposed to answer that? I don't know what I did. I didn't have any control over my bond and now I'm in a freaking mess, except I glance over at Gryphon, to gauge how he's reacting to all of this, and I find North focused on him. To my horror, Gryphon looks down at his hands and the smears of blood over them and, *Jesus*, on his thighs are bright like a freaking red flag.

This is really, *really* bad.

Then they both look over at me and I really would like to die now. The bond has cleared entirely from my head now and I'm left with the consequences of the haze, the consequences of completing the Bond and making Gryphon my Bonded.

Something about the bonding has opened up the floodgate of emotions inside of me and my stomach is a riot of nerves. I feel sick, euphoric, sad, ecstatic, and a million other conflicting emotions, all at once. My skin feels tight and sore as though it's about to burst open, and the extra power growing in my gut *terrifies* me.

I want to burst into very overwhelmed tears because I've just ruined everything. Either it's obvious that I'm on the verge of a breakdown, or they both decide at the exact same time to just put me out of my goddamn misery, because Gryphon turns his back on me as he steps in front of me, as close to giving me privacy as this hellscape I've found myself in will allow.

"Oli, do you need to sleep somewhere else tonight?" North says quietly, his eyes still cutting as he stares Gryphon down. It takes me three tries to reply but I have to force the words out.

"I need to stay here. I can't leave."

Without another word, North turns on his heel and steps out of the room, carefully blocking me from the view of Atlas and Gabe who are both still stuck at the door thanks to… whatever the hell Gryphon has done to them.

I've ruined *everything*.

J BREE

The moment the door closes behind North, I bolt out of the bed, still wrapped up tight in the duvet, and scurry into the bathroom, locking the door behind me like a complete and utter coward.

Then I take a minute to panic.

Why the hell did my bond send Brutus away? I need my little smoke friend right now to keep me company while I spiral out of my freaking mind. I'm not proud but I definitely think about filling the bathtub and drowning myself in there.

I climb into the shower instead.

It still smells of Gryphon in here, all of his soaps and shampoo bubbles still sitting in the water on the bottom of the tiled shower floor, and even though my bond gets super fucking pissy about it, I wash away the scent of him on my skin.

And from between my legs.

I'm livid at my bond. I can't believe it pulled that shit on me. I can't believe that after everything I've done to keep them all at arm's length, my bond has ruined everything in a jealous little tantrum!

I don't even want to think about the fact that I just fucked my Bond right after he'd had another woman rolling around in his freaking bed.

I was also unaware that having sex would make me want to die the second the afterglow is over with. Fuck, I barely even got an afterglow thanks to the others showing up. At least it was a great introduction to sex, I'd come so freaking hard that there's a lot more of my own wetness between my legs than just blood and his cum. Okay, so it hurt a little and it would've been better without my bond taking the wheel, but if I shut my eyes and force myself to forget about the rest of the shit going on, I can still feel his mouth on my clit, driving me freaking insane.

Are you touching yourself in my shower right now, Bonded?

The noise that comes out of me definitely isn't human and I drop the bottle of shampoo in my hands. That makes the loudest banging noise in an enclosed space ever, my ears ringing and pain shooting through my head.

Then, because tonight can't possibly stop fucking me over, the bathroom door slams open as Gryphon breaks it down.

He. Breaks. It. Down.

"What do you think you're doing?!" I shriek, and he scowls at me like I'm the one who just shattered a panel off of the door with my freaking shoulder for no good goddamn reason.

He stares at me, his eyes flicking to where my arms are crossed over my chest as though he wasn't licking and sucking his way across my tits like an hour ago, and then he steps forward to jerk the shower door open.

"There was a crash, I thought you'd fallen and hurt yourself. Move over."

I gape at him, not wanting to step back, but he just barges in and forces my body back with his own so I have no choice. I don't want to watch him clean my blood from his body and when he opens his mouth, I snap, "Don't. Don't use your gift on me right now. I'm ten different types of pissed off and I'm in here to attempt to drown myself."

He huffs at me and reaches around me to grab his soap, lathering up his hands, but then instead of cleaning himself off, he starts soaping up my legs. His hands stay in very safe spots, but now that I know how it feels to have him inside of me, this is a very heated moment.

"What set it off? Black said you all got home safe and

were happy enough in his debrief, who set your bond off? I'll kill them for doing this to you."

I snort at him and shove at his chest but he's easily three times my size and practically a brick wall, so all that happens is that he catches my hands and keeps them pinned to his bare chest.

"Let me go! My bond might be okay with just forcing us to be Bonded, claiming your bond and then going back to settle in my chest, but I'm not so quick to get over you having some other girl in your fucking bed! All of that bullshit before I went out over my outfit and then you're here with some other girl? No. I changed my mind, I'm going to sleep somewhere else," I snap, but the more words that tumble out of me in a furious rant, the more confused and pissed off he looks in return.

He ducks down to catch my eyes with his own, forcing me to hold his gaze. "What the hell are you talking about? I haven't touched another woman, not from the moment we dragged you back here and dropped you at the council offices. Oli, look at me, I swear on our Bond, I have not touched *anyone* but you since we met."

I get flutters in all sorts of places they don't belong at his words. I force myself to hold onto my anger because I didn't just imagine what I smelled. "Then why the fuck was there perfume all over your bed? It didn't just magically appear on your sheets, now did it? I came back here in my playsuit, just like you told me to, and I find your bed stinking of another woman. I didn't even get the chance to be pissed off or upset about it, my bond came out instantly and then... Everything happened so fast."

He blinks at me.

Then, cursing under his breath, he shoves the shower door open and grabs a towel. I'm expecting him to just storm out of the room because he has what he wants now, the Bond is complete between us and his power is going to increase, if it hasn't already, but he turns to shut the shower off and then wraps me up in the fluffy, luxurious fabric.

His face is thunderous, the type of pissed I'm used to seeing on North but have never seen him have before, but his hands are gentle as he gets me dry and covered. Then he carefully directs me back into his room with a firm hand and zero regard for the fact that he's still naked and dripping with water.

There's blood everywhere.

Not, like, life threatening amounts, but smears of it all over the sheets and his towel on the floor from where he'd cleaned himself up a little. It feels awkward as fuck to not talk about it but I think maybe he's assuming it was just my period.

With any luck, I'll never have to talk about it with him.

He leaves me by the shattered bathroom door and stalks forward to the bed, leaning down and frowning as he obviously gets a whiff of the perfume underneath the scents of our sex. I blush furiously, it's really fucking embarrassing to think about, but when he straightens up and grabs his phone, I want to die all over again.

"What are you doing?!" I hiss, and he speaks to whoever he's called while looking me dead in the eye, no hiding or attempts at masking what is happening.

"I need you to get every woman in this house into your office, everyone who has been here for the last two hours. Someone has been in my room and messed with my bed. It set Oli's bond off, my bond responded, and someone did it to hurt her... She's fine now, she's just furious, and so am I... I'll be there in five minutes... Oli will stay here, she's not going to be walking around the manor dealing with this bullshit tonight."

When he switches his phone off and throws it back onto the bedside table, I cross my arms and snap, "You really expect me to just believe that you didn't do anything? I don't have a built-in lie detector but I wasn't born yesterday!"

He doesn't react to me at all, just gets to work stripping the sheets off his bed and bundling them up with a vague look of disgust at handling them. I shift on my feet, my body hurting in all sorts of new places, and I edge forward to try to find the pajamas I'd brought down here with me. They're in a pile by the door, I'd obviously dropped them when my bond took the reins.

The moment I pick them up, my bond gets pissy about them being from my Bonds because now it only wants my Bonded, to drown in his scent and wallow in his space until the Bond we share is properly established. I scowl down at them and when Gryphon has the bed made back up, he comes back over to me.

"Take whatever you want from my closet, you're in… *fuck*, nesting mode. I know you don't want it, but that's what you need right now. Just grab whatever is comfortable to sleep in for you and I'll fix this."

I drop the other clothes like they're on fire, showing a complete disregard for my Bonded's space, but it doesn't bother him. He just grabs them and follows me into the closet, hovering over me until I'm dressed in a pair of his boxer briefs and a cozy, black sweater.

Once I've stepped back, clearly not grabbing anything else, he starts pulling out clothes for himself as well and I turn away. I don't want him covered up and leaving me, I want him in a bed that only smells like us and wrapped around me.

My chest tightens when he steps back out in jeans and a t-shirt, my stomach dropping, and I can't stop myself from whimpering.

His arms wrap around me and smother me into his chest. "What's wrong? I know you don't believe me, but

I'll find out who it was and deal with it. Whatever proof you want, I'll get it for you."

I shake my head, rubbing my face against his chest, and even though I'm starting to believe him, I can't find my voice. It's trapped somewhere else in my body with my savage bond and my growing, murderous gift.

There's a knock at the door.

Gryphon's hand slides into my hair, cupping the back of my head as he calls out to invite my Bond in. I've already guessed that it'll be North, it's obvious who Gryphon had called to help him find the woman, but I can't move away from his arms to hide because I might crack open and spill all of my organs out everywhere if he stops touching me right now.

Tonight is definitely cursed.

"I checked the security cameras and Gracie Davenport was in here ten minutes before Oleander came in. She had her bag with her. I went to speak to her but Felix had already sent her home for going after Sage again. Apparently she'd taken offense to something Gabe said to her when he showed her to her room and went wandering."

Fucking. Gracie.

Gryphon's hands are still warm and gentle as he rubs my back but his tone as he replies to North is anything but. "I will deal with her in the morning. You need to kick her out of Draven too, she's not allowed near Oli, or any of us, ever again. If she, or her family, doesn't take it well, I'll get rid of her."

I stiffen in his arms but he doesn't stop with the calming strokes. North doesn't answer him and I get curious about what the two of them must be communicating with their faces, so I take a deep breath and turn around in Gryphon's arms to face North.

He's staring at the pile of sheets Gryphon had shoved in the wash basket in the corner. The duvet that I'd wrapped myself in is still in the bathroom, but Gryphon had found a spare one and gotten the bed made up.

"What did she do?" North says, and Gryphon steps away from me to go into the bathroom and grab the rest of the stinking evidence of Gracie's stupidity.

I swallow back bile and say, "Perfume. She put perfume all over his bed and my bond took over before I had the chance to even speak to him. It was out of our hands because my bond is a jealous, cantankerous bitch and just took over."

Gryphon grabs the pile of dirty washing and steps out of the room to get rid of them, leaving me alone with North for a second, and I immediately want to chase after him. It's stupid, I know it is, but my bond keens in my chest like he's abandoning me.

Instead of letting myself become some pathetic Bonded weeping nightmare, I concentrate on the link between us, the small threads that are barely established but that I know will grow in time. I feel tiny beads of sweat break out on my forehead as I push two words at him, cursing at myself for how easy he'd made it look to just send through a whole damn sentence to me before.

Burn them.

There's a small moment of quiet in my head and then his answer comes through, *I'll burn the whole manor down if you want me to. We can go back into your room for tonight, and I'll move rooms in the morning.*

Fuck.

My heart does a little backflip in my chest and even though it gives me the shakes, I send back to him, *I'm not leaving this room, hurry up and come back to me.*

I don't want to climb into the bed without him but North is just standing there a few paces away, scowling around the room at everything like he's planning out a punishment for all of this. God, he probably is, and I'm grateful that it's Gryphon I found myself in this mess with because at least North believes him and trusts his word a hundred percent. I wait a second in the silence, rubbing my hands over my arms because even with the sweater on, I'm a little chilly with the air conditioning cranked so high in here, but North doesn't react at all.

North steps up closer to me, his steps hesitant but his words are sure as he says, "If you need... anything after what's happened tonight, I'll arrange it for you. Name it and it's yours."

I frown at him but he won't look at me, blowing out a breath before continuing, "I didn't know you were a virgin. I'm guessing you didn't use a condom if your bond was in control. I'll get you some emergency contraceptive if you want it… unless you're against it and are fine with the consequences?"

Jesus, fuck. "Please. I was getting the shot while I was *away* for my periods but it's been too long since my last one. Oh my God, could this get any freaking worse?"

I'm definitely panicking but he doesn't look at me or notice it, he just stands there in silence again until Gryphon gets back.

He doesn't look at North at all, just heads straight over to me and bundles me up into his arms, walking me over to his bed and doing one last sniff test to make sure the perfume is all gone and it hasn't seeped onto the mattress or something.

"We're fine, North. There's nothing else that can be done tonight," Gryphon says, a clear dismissal. I think it's kind of bold of him because no matter how hard I've tried before, North has never allowed me to tell him to leave.

He goes without a word.

It's kind of terrifying.

"Oli, is the bed okay or do we need to move? I can't

smell anything."

I blink back into myself and give it a cautious sniff, still sore enough that I'm not really up to round two. There's nothing there but the clean and fresh scent of the laundry soap that the maids use, so I climb in without another word. Gryphon climbs in after me, scooting in behind me, even though he usually sleeps on the other side, and when he hits the light and plunges the room into darkness, I let my head fall back onto the pillow with a thud.

I desperately need the night to be over.

I settle into his arms and let him move me until we're both comfortable. After a minute, his hand creeps onto my stomach, warming up until I feel his gift flow through me, the ache between my legs disappearing, and I blush like crazy.

I clear my throat and whisper to him, "You don't have to do that."

He tucks his face behind my ear where Brutus usually sleeps and murmurs, "I will tear that girl apart with my bare hands for doing this to you, but I'm a selfish asshole. I'm glad it was me and not one of the others."

I turn my face into the pillow and try not to weep like a pathetic girl in relief that maybe he isn't lying, maybe he does want me and I'm tied to someone who actually knows what I'm capable of.

"Don't cry, Bonded. We're together in this, no matter what."

I huff out a bleak laugh at him. "You're Bonded to a monster. A real one, a *murderer*. You heard Carlin, you know about it. What if it gets stronger? I can feel it growing in my stomach already, you know? I can feel it, we're all going to fucking die."

He grunts and shifts me, moving my uncooperative body around to face him as though I'm a weightless rag doll, and I try not to find it as hot as I do. It's too dark to actually look into his eyes but I blink at him anyway, as though it'll make the darkness shift.

His hands reach out to cup my cheek. "If you call yourself a monster again, I will put you over my knee and spank that attitude right out of you. You're perfect. Having a Top Tier gift, no matter how rare, doesn't make you a monster. I've known a lot of monsters, you're not one."

I'm definitely not perfect but he says it with so much conviction that I desperately want to believe him. His hand begins to move to stroke over the soft skin of my belly and I'm happy that all of my training has shrunk the little belly I have there. I still have one, probably because it's housing my uterus because, hi there, I'm a girl, but it's not something I'm self-conscious of anymore.

"Go to sleep, Oli. We can deal with everything in the morning."

I wake up with Gryphon still wrapped around me, but this is a lot different to all of the other times I've woken in his bed.

Mostly because his hand is between my legs, his thumb stroking over my clit through the fabric of the boxers I'd borrowed from him last night, his dick hard and rubbing against my ass as he groans. I can't help but wiggle back, grinding up against him instinctively, and I'm happy that the ache between my legs is gone.

If the worst has happened and I'm Bonded to him, then I might as well enjoy the ride to hell.

Gryphon's teeth are sharp as he bites down on my shoulder, drawing a gasp out of me before he eases up and kisses over the mark. "If anyone is going to hell, it's me for being so fucking smug about getting to have you, though I didn't take you for such a pessimist."

I elbow him but again, it does nothing to him. "Get out of my head, I'm allowed to be a dramatic bitch in a crisis if I want to be!"

He catches my elbow and pulls it back more, pinning my arm behind my back as he blows out a breath on the wet spot he's made on my neck, goosebumps breaking out over my body as my back arches and grinds my ass into his dick a little more.

He drops his mouth back down to my ear to murmur, "Stop squirming and fighting me so I can show you how sex is supposed to be, how it's going to be between us now."

Arrogant Bonded. "I've seen enough porn, I'm pretty sure I know where all of the parts go, and I'm not sure there's a kink you can whip out that will shock me."

He huffs at me and snakes a hand around my body, slipping his fingers under the waistband of the boxer briefs and straight into the folds of my pussy, finding me slick and ready for everything his tongue is teasing me with.

I wiggle against him just because the chase is half the fun and if he wants to show me anything about his sexual prowess, he's going to have to work for it.

His dick gets even harder against my ass as I struggle and when he lets my elbow go to catch my throat and bend me back against him again, a low moan spills out of my lips. His fingers tighten but his other hand is just playing, not actually trying to make me come as he moves them, and I wiggle again to try to force him to touch the important parts.

He gets sick of waiting for me to just lie back and be compliant, so once again, he ends up just manhandling me into the position he wants me in, a pillow under my hips and his sweater shoved up my body so that he has access to all of the parts of me he's so focused on right now.

I open my mouth to cuss him out again but he just covers it with his own, biting at my lip as though he's punishing me for acting out. If this is how he plans on keeping me in line, sign me up for ruining this man's life because I'm not ever going to give this up.

His calloused thumb is rough against my nipple, the rasp of it a delicious sort of pain, and when he pinches it, I gasp into his lips, his answering chuckle a gloating sound. I want to be angry about it but his lips are too skilled and sure as he worships me with his tongue, moving down my neck and adding teeth to the mix again. I already know he's leaving a trail of red skin, making sure there's no question of where he's been, but he's perfected the line between too much and just enough, leaving me teetering on the edge of desperation.

It's so much more intense without my bond in control

of my mind.

I can feel everything he's doing much more keenly, and his hands map out every inch of my body until I lose track of where my body ends and his begins. He finds all sorts of sensitive spots I didn't even know existed, licking and sucking at my skin until I'm writhing underneath him in a mess of delayed almost-pleasure.

When he finally moves down to strip the boxer briefs off of me, I'm ready to channel a little more of my bond again and shove his face into my pussy, but he moves decisively enough that I don't have to. The large window that overlooks the garden is lit up with the morning sun and it feels too exposed, too bright and intimate. I want to fling a hand over my eyes to hide what little I can, but Gryphon takes both of my wrists in his hands and pulls them down so I have no choice but to watch him eat me out.

And the man can *eat*.

His hands tighten around my wrists as he licks his way around my pussy, making sure to lick and suck his way over every part of my lips, and it feels amazing, but nowhere near enough to get me off. When I grunt at him like a dying woman who wants to be put out of her misery, he finally zeros in, attacking my clit like a pro, and my spine lifts from the bed as I come.

If he's trying to prove himself to me, then he's doing the greatest freaking job of it. The debauched, wet sounds of my pussy echo around the room as he finally lets go of my wrists to squeeze my thighs and pull them over his shoulders. I'm seeing an obsession here with my legs, but I'm also too busy grinding myself into his face as I come again to snark at him for it.

I'm over-sensitized and whimpering after the third orgasm. He grunts at me unhappily when I beg him to ease up, take a break, let my pussy recover from the brutal pleasure of his tongue and finally, *finally*, he lifts his head up to look at the mess he's made of me, a very self-satisfied smirk stretching across his lips.

I don't have the energy to snark back at him or kick him in the teeth for looking so smug, but when he pulls himself up onto his knees and lines his cock up, there's no pain as he pushes in, my pussy is dripping, gushing with my cum, and he groans as I suck him in.

Then his mouth starts running and I decide that he's trying to kill me, his own plans to get rid of his dangerous Bonded are a wicked and cruel thing. "Such a greedy fucking pussy, taking me all the way down like a good girl. Tell me you'll be good for me from now on, give me this pretty Bonded pussy whenever I want it. Let me fuck you raw whenever you need to be reminded of who you belong to, because this is mine. Your bond told me I belong to you. Well, baby, this is my fucking pussy to use and fill up whenever I want to as well. You want me, this is what you get."

When he pulls out to flip me over, cracking a palm over my ass as he plunges back in, I moan and writhe out another orgasm into the pillows, my voice hoarse and cracking from all of the screaming he has me doing.

His fingers dig into my hips as he comes, groaning and slamming his hips into me until I'm bracing against the headboard to stop him from fucking me into the wall. I feel the wetness of it as I turn over, realizing that once again, we've had sex without a condom, but then I guess the pill North is organizing for me will take care of that.

"Holy fucking shit," I groan, my legs still tingling and made of jelly as he sprawls out on his back next to me, his chest looking freaking bitable as he catches his breath.

"Better than porn?"

I shove the pillow that was under my ass over his face with a loud thumping noise and when he roars with laughter, I give him a very reluctant sort of smile back. "It was better, but don't let your game slip. I'm a tough girl to keep happy."

I step into the foyer tentatively, which is just freaking stupid.

After I'd taken an hour to recover from the aftermath of

Gryphon's bond-free claiming, I'd climbed in the shower to delay the inevitable, awkward, post-sex aftermath meeting. I know it's coming. I know that no matter what Gryphon and, possibly, North say to Gabe and Atlas, I'm going to have to speak to them and explain what the hell happened.

Gryphon had stood guard over me, watching my every move as though he thought I was going to hang myself from the shower if he turned his back, and when one of the maids knocked on the door with a small bag from the pharmacy, he'd answered it fully dressed and with a handgun pointed at her.

It was a little extreme.

I mean, it's nice to know that I'm not the only one feeling completely freaking insane with the effects of the Bond, but it's also strange to see my most level-headed Bond just lose his head entirely now that we've completed the Bond.

Bonded.

Jesus. Fuck.

He'd waited until I'd taken the drug, drunk water, gotten dressed in his clothes, and then he'd walked me back to my room to watch over me as I got dressed and ready for my shift at the cafe. Only once I was completely ready did he leave me alone to go down first and run damage control.

I'd sat on my bed and texted Sage like a coward.

She'd already known something had happened because when North told Atlas and Gabe what Gracie had done, Atlas had, apparently, gone on the warpath. There was an argument that ended up with North's smoke coming out to split everyone up, and if that isn't the most goddamned embarrassing thing I've ever heard, I don't know what is.

So, now I'm sneaking around like a thief in the night, terrified to run into anyone but also fully prepared to bear the brunt of everyone's anger and disbelief.

Maybe the universe decided I've suffered enough because when I get to the foyer, I find a teeny, tiny puppy made of smoke and void eyes waiting for me.

I duck down to catch him as he bounds towards me, doubling in size so that when he drops to his back at my feet, there's a whole lot of belly for me to scratch. "Brutus! There you are! I've been worried, I thought I might have to come fight Nox for you. I would've, if I hadn't seen you soon."

There's footsteps but I'm too scared to look up, so I just focus on giving the best belly scratches ever.

"You shouldn't have sent him back to me. He would've helped more if he were there," Nox drawls, and when I look up at him, he looks… drunk.

I lift a shoulder. "I didn't. My bond did, it took over and sent him off. It probably knew he would've… hell, I don't know what he would've done."

Nox walks over to where we're both crouched down, running a hand over Brutus' belly alongside mine. "He would've told me what was happening and I would have had to decide what to do. You don't look too upset about the Bonding, maybe you did the right thing sending him away so you could trap Gryphon the exact way you wanted to."

This man will never make sense to me, I swear to God. "And when you pinned me to the wall in the hallway, was that me trapping you too?"

His lip curls and his face goes from the tipsy but calm look, to the enraged Draven mask I'm more than used to seeing now. "I know better than to fall for a bond's tricks. Just because I want my powers, doesn't mean I'd let myself be chained to poison."

I take a good, long look at him, my bond staying silent in my chest at the disheveled sight of him. He looks like a very well put together, very controlled, chaotic mess. I remind myself that he's also grieving someone important to him and that only a few short weeks ago, I'd held his hand during the memorial service.

He'd also let me.

I pull my hand away from Brutus' belly and sit back on my haunches a little more, moving to scratch behind the pup's ears when he chases after my hand, eager for more love, but I keep my eyes trained on Nox's, unflinching.

"If that's who you need to believe I am right now, Nox, then I won't try to change your mind. If you need me to be the villain in your story to get through your day, then I'll accept that. You're not going to be the villain in mine though, no matter how hard you try. I have a much better view of you now and I won't give you the satisfaction of being the big bad in my world."

He reacts as though I've threatened him.

Rocking back on his heels with a defensive and aggressive look at me, his eyes flick down to where Brutus is eyeing him off. I'm not sure which way he thinks this is going to go but I've never been so sure of anything in my life as I am that Brutus won't hurt me.

I'm not sure if it's that my bond knows that his gift would never harm me, that Brutus might be the only part of Nox that doesn't wish me harm, or if I'm just arrogant about the levels of my own power, but I'm not worried here.

Too bad Atlas, Gabe, and Gryphon don't feel the same way.

"Get the fuck away from her!"

"Fuck, Oli, just come away from him."

"Don't touch my Bonded, Nox. Just walk away." Gryphon's hands wrap around my forearms and pull me up to my feet, stepping backwards before he tucks me behind him.

Brutus moves with me, ducking around Gryphon to stay at my feet, and Gabe has to hold Atlas back from trying to kick my precious puppy.

I stare him down and when he finally stops swearing, jerking himself away from Gabe, he snaps, "He's a fucking Draven spy, not a pet! You're not safe from that asshole with that thing following you around."

I hold my hand out and let Brutus climb up to tuck back behind my ear where he belongs, out of sight but close to me and giving me boundless amounts of comfort. For the first time all morning, I actually feel like I can handle the mess I've found myself in.

Nox clearly doesn't feel the same way and when he finds himself at the wrong end of one of Gryphon's viciously furious looks, he snaps, "You're really going to pretend like she's some precious little innocent Bond now that you've fucked her? It must have been—"

"Don't."

Nox laughs at him, his closest friend, and for a moment I think Gryphon is going to take a swing at him, but he just takes a deep breath and then says, "Go sleep it off. It's been a stressful night and you look like shit."

The ride over to the cafe is quiet.

Gryphon had given me a very chaste kiss to my hair as he'd left me behind with Gabe and Atlas, his phone ringing with issues that he and his TacTeam needed to sort out, and he was gone before I really got to say goodbye.

Gabe was quiet for a moment and then took a hold of my hand, pulling me to his side, and we headed out to the garage together. Atlas had followed us without a word. He hadn't tried to touch me until we'd gotten into the Hellcat and out onto the highway. I'd finally taken a breath when his hand covered my knee, his fingers rubbing at the fabric on my jeans like always.

At least he's not pissed at me.

When I hurry into the cafe, Sage, Sawyer, Gray, and Felix are all waiting for me.

They're in my Bonds' booth, coffees and sandwiches in front of them. When I walk in with Atlas and Gabe close behind me, Sage punches Sawyer in the arm when he opens his mouth with a salacious grin.

I adore that girl.

Gabe and Atlas grab extra chairs to pull up to the booth and join our friends while I duck into the back to stash my bag away. Gloria is polite but a little frosty as she greets me. My stomach drops over it but instead of letting myself spiral over what she's angry at me about, I throw myself into the busy shift.

Kitty is a freaking nightmare.

She refuses to move from the register to help out even when she's gotten through the line, so I spend the entire shift running around like a crazy person.

My friends all pile out after an hour of not being able to catch me to talk but my Bonds stay put to wait out my shift. Atlas switches to iced tea after his third coffee but Gabe just downs the lattes like he's planning an all-nighter.

I have to mop a huge portion of the floor after one of the customer's kids throws an entire milkshake on the ground. No one attempts to apologize for the mess, which gets me in my feelings, but I just plaster that sedate smile over my face like this isn't the worst goddamn shift I've had since I started here.

The afternoon drags on for what seems like days.

When we finally close up, Atlas and Gabe scowl at me when I usher them out of the building so that I can mop, and Kitty disappears out the back to sit on her phone and avoid doing any of the cleaning that's required. Gloria doesn't say a word to her about it so, once again, I just shut my mouth and get into it.

I think that I'm doing a great job of proving that I'm a good worker, an asset to Gloria's business, and considerate of the time away I've been forced to have.

Boy, am I wrong.

When I've gotten everything spotlessly clean, the register counted, and the day's deposit set aside for Gloria to take with her, Kitty finally shows up from the bathroom, dressed in her regular clothes with her bag already slung over her shoulder. She smirks at me and flicks her hair over her shoulder in a smug move that sets my teeth on edge.

"Off you go, Kitty," Gloria says, waving a hand at the girl to usher her out of the back door and ignoring the way she curses under her breath about it. No one ever calls that girl out on her attitude or poor work ethic and it eats at me a bit.

But the pay here is good, so I'm going to keep my mouth shut about it.

When the door closes behind her and Gloria turns back to me, I say, "I'm sorry about all the time off I've been having, I promise it won't—"

She cuts me off. "Those Bonds of yours are waiting outside for you, so I'm not going to keep you long. You need to leave your apron behind, you'll not be working here any longer. I have your paycheck here for what you're owed for today, no need for me to have to see you again."

My jaw drops to the goddamn floor. "I'm sorry, you're firing me? What have I done wrong?"

I'm expecting her to say my time off, I could almost understand that, but her words spark my bond's ire. "You never once asked what my Gift is. I'm an Empath, I can see what people's Gifts are. I can also see their intent. I might not be the strongest Gifted, certainly not a Top Tier Gifted, but I know evil when I see it. You're not welcome in my cafe. I didn't want to make a scene when you arrived, but I won't have you here anymore."

Evil.

Monster.

Poison.

My temper catches fire. I stop myself from yelling at her, but my words are sharp nonetheless. "You let Nox eat here! He came back here and spoke with you, surely you're not going to spout that 'monster Bond' bullshit at me!"

She shakes her head at me, clicking her tongue like it's so offensive that I cursed at her. "It doesn't matter what people say about those Draven boys, I've seen what they have in them. They're good, all the way down to their bones. A Gift doesn't make a person a monster. I can see into you too, and I don't like what's there. I wasn't sure about you before, but now that you've Bonded and it's gotten clearer to me? I'm not going to have you in my shop. Don't come back, and don't call in for anything either."

There's nothing I want to do less than sit through a Bond dinner after Gloria fired me for being *evil,* but to get out of it, I'd have to tell North what Gloria had said to me, and I really don't want to do that. More ammunition for him, more clues for him to chase down, and more chances for him to figure out what I am. I don't want to risk it.

I do, however, tell Atlas and Gabe.

Atlas stares at me from the driver seat and then without a word, puts the car back into park and turns the engine off. When he climbs back out of the car and stalks back up to the cafe, I want to call out after him to stop him but the words get trapped in my throat.

I have nothing left in me.

"Don't listen to the old bitch, Bond. She's just a

crackpot Empath who doesn't know shit," Gabe says from the backseat, but I just stare at Atlas as he tears the backdoor off of the cafe like it's nothing.

We should probably be stopping him.

"I did try to warn you guys. I told you that Bonding with me was the worst freaking option! Gracie being a fucking bitch has just ruined—"

Gabe leans forward in his seat and catches my eye, cutting me off as he says, "Nothing. She's ruined *nothing*, Oli. Stop running scared for a fucking minute and look around. Nothing bad happened when you and Gryphon Bonded. Fine, it was bad because your bonds triggered and neither of you could stop it or… fuck, consent to it. This all sounds really shitty, what I'm trying to say is that the sun still rose this morning. Both of you are still breathing, unharmed, and the apocalypse hasn't begun."

He looks furious and when there's another booming crash from the cafe, he curses under his breath and gets out of the car, slamming the door and jogging into Atlas' rage breakdown.

Why are you freaking out? Tell Gabe to answer his phone.

I startle at Gryphon's words in my head, I'm not sure I'll ever get used to it just popping in there whenever he wants to chat. He's gone from ignoring my calls and messages to having full access to my brain whenever the fuck he feels like it.

Rude.

I still have to concentrate like a motherfucker to send back the reply, but it's getting easier.

I got fired because apparently I reek of evil. Atlas went after Gloria, and Gabe is too busy trying to stop the murder that is probably happening in the cafe right now to answer the phone.

He doesn't immediately answer me but for the very first time, I can feel him the way he always seems to be able to feel me.

He's furious. Fucking livid. It makes my throat close up with the force of it, and one of my hands clutches at my chest as I try to push his feelings away from me before my bond decides to wade into the fight.

There's a popping noise from outside the car and when I look up, I find Gryphon and Kieran standing there in full Tactical gear, appearing out of thin air thanks to Kieran's Gift. Gryphon slashes his hand at the car and then takes off at a sprint towards the cafe.

Kieran steps over to me, motioning for me to roll the window down. Instead, I just open the door and stand with him. He doesn't say anything as he casts the quickest, least subtle eye over me to check for injuries.

I scoff, "I was very good about not letting the evil seeping out of me touch that woman. Atlas? Not so much."

He rolls his eyes at me and shrugs. "He's a Bassinger, what do you expect? Did you really not take a bite out of her? Just a tiny swing at the prejudiced bitch?"

Oh no, no, no, I cannot have a friendship with this man. I can't have dry wit and comforting descriptions of the violence that I wish I could enact with him. I don't have any extra capacity for friends right now, my tiny circle is a busload of people as it is.

And yet I instantly feel better at his words, even when I snark out, "Oh she can't be prejudiced, she thinks the world of my very sedate and not at all monstrous Draven Bonds. Nox wouldn't hurt a fly, according to that woman. I'm the *evil* one."

Don't ask me why that word is sticking so hard with me, but I really can't shake it.

There's another loud crashing noise from inside the cafe and Kieran snickers under his breath at it, sounding too joyful about the willful destruction of property happening here.

I roll my eyes at him. "Shouldn't you be wading in there to help?"

"No, I'm on Bond-sitting duties. Besides, Bassinger is richer than God, he can pay off the bitch to shut her up once he's done ruining her place."

Men are useless.

I'm cold and hungry, can we wrap this up please? I've

had enough public shame for one day.

It gets easier and easier to speak to Gryphon like this. His reply is instant and more fluid than mine, *Get Black to take you back to the manor and then send him back here.*

I groan as I tell Kieran the orders because I hate traveling with a Transporter. Sure enough, when Kieran lets go of my arm and I open my eyes to find North standing in front of me in his dining room, I have to slap a hand over my mouth to attempt to stop myself from vomiting all over my Bond's shiny black leather Hermes shoes.

He shoves me into a chair and then forces me to put my head between my legs to stop the world from spinning.

"One day. I would like one fucking day without having to run damage control. Tell all three of them to quit making my life harder and get back here before I come down there after them," North snarls, and I cringe at the sound of it.

There's a pop again as Kieran leaves. I wait until I'm confident that I won't puke before I sit back up.

North had shoved me into his chair and when I sit up, I find him in the chair next to it with paperwork everywhere. I keep my eyes away from it all because I don't want him snapping at me for snooping, but that only causes me to make eye contact with Nox at the other end of the table.

There's a glass of whiskey in front of him.

"Bassinger is off defending your honor again? Pathetic. He really needs to find a new mantle to take," he drawls, as he lifts the glass to his lips. North sighs and his eyes flick up to narrow at Nox, but his brother just ignores him as he stares me down.

I really want to leave.

Or at least move seats, I do not want to be sitting here at the head of the table and dealing with Nox's shitty, alcohol-fueled mood.

I rub my hands over my arms and raise my eyebrows at him. "Are you just going to be an alcoholic now? Don't you have classes to teach? Young minds to mold and all that?"

He scoffs, "I could teach them in my sleep, but I'm on administrative leave for my extra duties. Gryphon hasn't told you yet? We're leaving tomorrow to back up his TacTeam."

My bond doesn't like that at all.

I glance back at North to see if Nox is just being an asshole and trying to upset me, but without looking up from the papers he says, "Gabe and Bassinger will be staying here with you. There's been more abductions further south that we need to look into. Gryphon, Nox, and I will be gone for a week, two at most."

Nope.

Don't like that at all.

I clench my hands into fists again and then, cheeks heating, I duck back down to put my head between my legs again. When will this overdramatic bond bullshit end?

"Trouble in Bonded paradise? I thought Gryphon would have told you—"

"Stop it, Nox. If you can't shut your mouth, then leave," North snaps. It's the harshest I've heard him ever speak to his brother. The kid gloves he usually wears around him are gone.

I hear him leave the room but I keep my head down until my mind is no longer swimming in fear and panic. When I sit up again, the doors to the kitchen open and servers come out with the usual platters of food, but I don't want to eat any of it.

I just want to go lie down.

North grabs a plate and begins to fill it with starchy, boring foods, as he says, "Gryphon was in the meeting with us both when you reached out to him about Bassinger. He wasn't keeping anything from you. Nox... is thriving on creating dissent, at the moment. He'll get over it."

When he places the plate in front of me before going back to his papers, my appetite thinks about returning and the plainer foods actually look tempting enough that I pick up my fork with a mumbled thank you.

He doesn't acknowledge my words, just bundles up all of the papers and murmurs, "You'll be sleeping with me tonight... unless you're still nesting and want Gryphon instead. Nox will leave his creature behind with you and you're Bonded with Gryphon now, so it makes sense for you to stay with me before we leave."

Am I still nesting? I take a second to check in with my bond to see how we're tracking along and North watches me with a strangely blank face. He's not angry or frustrated at me for once, he's just watching what I'm doing.

I try not to blush under his scrutiny. "My bond is okay, I think the nesting part is over with. If you insist on taking August with you, then I think I— I'll need you."

It almost kills me to choke those words out but he doesn't gloat or throw them back in my face, instead he sets the paperwork aside and piles together a plate of his own.

When the others finally make it home, Atlas doesn't come to dinner, and neither Gabe or Gryphon comment on my seat change.

I wake in my bed a little after two in the morning to my phone ringing.

North's arm around my waist is like a lead weight, a million pounds of immovable man appendage, and I have to stretch out like crazy to reach the damn phone. I doubt it's a prank call, and my Bonds would just come find me here if something had happened.

That just leaves my friends.

I don't even bother looking at the caller ID. I just hit answer and croak into it, "What's happened?"

Sage's panicked whisper has me jolting up in the bed. "Oh my God. Oli, I need help! I can't believe this happened. I'm fucking cursed, cursed! I can't— Oli, it's so bad—"

North grunts as he rolls over and I take the opportunity to scramble out of the bed and over to my closet. "Where are you? Are you safe? What the hell happened? I'm about to wreck someone's shit, Sage!"

She sobs, her voice cracking, and I hear a banging, like someone's trying to take her door down. I shove a pair of yoga pants on and grab one of Nox's old cashmere sweaters from where I'd hidden my stash of them.

"I'm at the Med Halls, where Felix boards. We went on a date and—"

She's cut off by more banging and I take the chance to hiss, "Has he hurt you? I'll fucking skin him alive!"

"No! We... Oli, we had sex and I set the fucking building on fire! It was, I mean, I was totally in control of my gift, but my bond just... Oli, it felt like I Bonded with him. I couldn't have done that, that's insane to even think about, but it was like... Shit, the fire department is here, I'm so fucked, Oli!"

It doesn't make any sense but it also doesn't matter.

She's my best friend. If she needs me, then I'll be getting my ass over there to save her, no matter what the fuck has happened.

"I'm on my way, just stay where you are and keep your phone on you. I've got you, Sage. Don't worry about a thing."

She whimpers out an agreement and I hang up, turning on my heel with a plan to wake up Gryphon or Atlas to help me with my escape plan.

I come face to stunningly perfect bare chest with a tired and rumpled looking North Draven.

"Where the fuck do you think you're running off to?" he grumbles, and I hold up my phone.

"Best friend duties call. I'll take a Bond with me and I'll be back in no time, just go back to sleep." I aim for coaxing and reassuring, but clearly I fail miserably because he just stares me down, moving further into the closet with me.

"Honestly, if I were attempting to run away, I wouldn't pick a night that you were in my bed. That's just stupid. I'd pick Atlas or Nox, because he never actually gets in the damn thing. Just hop back into— what the hell are you doing?"

He ignores me as he pulls on one of Gryphon's hoodies, looking the most casual and hot I've ever seen the man. He shoves his feet into a pair of Gabe's sneakers that are in the corner and then turns to give me a look. "Well? If this is such a time-sensitive rescue, we should get a move on, right?"

Oh fuck.

I blanch but he just walks out of the closet, swiping his phone from the side table and opening the door for me so that I have no choice but to follow him.

When we get in the elevator, he taps away on his phone for a moment and I try not to fidget too much to show him just how uncomfortable I am with this.

Sage is terrified of the Dravens.

She always has been, and she's never tried to hide it from me either, so I really should send her a warning text... but that could also send her over the edge in her delicate state.

Fuck.

This is such a bad idea.

"Tell Gryphon we're heading out. He's not answering my messages but someone needs to know that we're heading out," North murmurs as the elevator doors open, and I nod as I chew on my lip.

This is getting worse and worse.

Uh, hi. Sorry to wake you up, but North and I are going on a Sage rescue mission. He told me to tell you, but we'll be back soon, so go back to sleep.

I curse myself for sounding like an idiot. I'm distracted

enough that I don't notice North taking me around to one of the Bentleys and helping me into the front seat. I startle when he slides into the front.

He always takes his driver.

He rolls his eyes at my look of shock, drawling, "I can drive, and Rafe does require time off to sleep. Where are we going? Put your seatbelt on."

I do as he says, grateful that he knows where the hell the Med Halls are because I have no freaking clue. I guess he probably owns them if they're a part of Draven.

Shit.

I choose my moment wisely, waiting until the car is stopped at a red light before I say, "So, just so you know, Sage has accidentally set the building on fire."

North turns to stare at me and snaps, "I hope you're kidding. That building is two hundred years old and houses over six hundred Gifted Healers!"

I nod and say, "Yes, and it's on fire."

The light turns to green and saves me from his furious stare, not that I did anything wrong here, but if it saves Sage from his ire, then I'll take it. I'll take it all for that girl.

I'm proud of her for getting over her own obstacles to climb into bed with Felix. If she's set the building on fire, it had to be good, right? I'm going to need all of the juicy details as soon as I rescue her.

All of them.

"What happened? I'll call the caretaker and make arrangements."

I glance over at North and his face is still all sorts of pissed off, but at least he's being forced to look at the road and not me. "She and Felix went on a date, then she went back to his room at the Med Hall... then she accidentally set the building on fire. That's the whole story."

I can't even talk to North about having sex with my Bonded, there's no way I'm talking to him about Sage's sex life.

"Was she attacked? Was her bond threatened? Give me details here so that I know what I can do to get this sorted out. She's a child of Maria's Bonded group, I can't just hang the girl out to dry."

I cross my arms and shrug at him. "She wasn't attacked. She just... had a small incident. Also, she's my best friend, the first person in this place who was kind to me. If you thought about just throwing her under the bus, I would ruin you. I might not be willing to do it for myself, but you bet your ass I would do it for her."

The trip feels as though it's taking hours to get there and when we finally turn onto the right road, I know straight away because there's fire engines and police tape *everywhere*.

The car slows down to a crawl.

I send Sage a quick text to tell her we're close and not to panic. She sends back a whole stream of panicking and freaking out. I don't blame her at all.

North interrupts me from my attempts to calm her down with the worst possible questions. "How has Bassinger taken your Bonded status with Gryphon? Are you going to Bond with him and Gabe now that you've started the Bond?"

I shrug, my heart thumping a little in my chest that he's even bringing this up right now. "Nothing has changed. I mean, no, it has, obviously. Gryphon is now in my head and my Gift is begging me to test it out now that it's gotten supercharged, but my plans haven't. I don't— I can't get stronger. I can't have more power than I have now."

North nods and drums his fingers against the steering wheel in a small display of frustration at how slow we're moving. I watch the people all moving around us, chaos that isn't touching us at all in this quietly safe space.

I startle when he speaks again. "You need to give me something. I want to believe you when you say that you did what you had to do… I know that Gryphon believes you, so you're telling the truth to some degree, but I can't tell if you're lying without him around, and he's made his boundaries with you very clear to me. I was all in before you ran away. I was ready to give you the world and destroy anyone who attempted to hurt you or, fuck, breathe wrong in your direction. You broke that. Give me a reason to believe that you did it because you had no other choice… or that you were unaware that you had them in us."

I open my mouth but nothing comes out.

What could I possibly tell him that he would believe? What evidence could I give him that wouldn't lead him straight back to the Resistance?

He continues, murmuring so quietly that I have to strain to hear him, "Do you even want to be Bonded with us all? If you weren't facing the big bad that you won't tell us a thing about, would you even want us all?"

That's easier to answer. "I did want my Bonds. I do want you all. I just… can't. I don't know how to give you what you need, but I'll figure it out. God knows how, but I will."

He turns to stare at me, his face covered in shadows thanks to the street lamps and lights from the fire engines, and when he gives me a nod, it feels like the most progress we've ever made.

When the car finally pulls up, we both take a second to stare, dumbstruck, at the giant wall of flames climbing up the eight-story building.

"You said 'incident'. Oleander, this is not an incident, this is an emergency."

I clear my throat and giggle a little hysterically. "Po-tay-toe, Po-tah-toe, right?"

J BREE

North finds the caretaker in the crowd and demands that I stay in the car while he figures out how to get Sage out of there without any of us getting hurt. I take the opportunity to call Sage again and check that she's not actually in the path of the fire right now.

She sounds miserable when she answers, "I waited until the floor was evacuated and then I holed up in Felix's bathroom. I'm keeping the fire away from here but I can't get rid of the rest of it, there's too much!"

"Okay, it's fine, don't panic! North owns the building, he's not going to give a shit about you damaging it a bit. Where's Felix? If you tell me he nutted and ran off on you, I'll kill him."

She huffs but it's more of a sob. "I'm so scared and

embarrassed, Oli! He tried to get me out of here but when the fire warden came in, he was forced to leave. I told him I called you. Oli… I can hear him in my head. He's been talking to me this whole time, telling me that it's all going to be okay. He said he was only backing down from coming back in after me because he knows you're on your way."

Icy fingers of dread work their way through my belly.

North had said it himself, the Resistance would try and split up the strongest Bonded groups and families. The Bensons are up there with the Dravens. The Davenports are too.

How the fuck have they messed with the Bonds?

Is that even possible or am I just thinking crazy right now? I feel like we're on the edge of blowing up something big and life-changing, the air catching in my lungs as my rib cage squeezes in fear of the fall.

I clear my throat. "Sage, listen to me. I'm coming up to get you. Tell Felix to just comply with everything that the fire department asks him to do and then to come back to North's place as soon as he can. There's a lot we need to talk about, but let's get you out of there first, okay? I'm not going to let anything happen to you."

I get out of the car and make my way over to North, trying not to burst into highly inappropriate giggles at how wrong he looks standing there in casual clothing that he's had to find out of my closet from the other Bonds. His face is still full of authoritarian sternness and I have to wipe the grin from mine as I sidle up to him.

The caretaker moves away from us both with barely a glance my way, and I set my eyes on the crowd as I murmur, "I'm going in to grab Sage, so if you can keep the crowd distracted, that would be very helpful."

His answer is immediate and icy. "There's no way I'm letting you go into the burning building alone, Oleander. Find a new plan right now."

I huff at him and point out the crowds of students and firefighters everywhere. "You're not going to be able to get in and out of here *discreetly*. We're aiming for discretion right now, North, not a councilman wandering around looking for a naked girl in a bathroom. Can you imagine the rumor mill? No fucking thank you!"

He stares at me for a second and then he glances around at the people closest to us, still just outside of earshot. The one advantage to this school being full of preppy, rich Gifted is that no one bats an eyelid at the Bentley, and without the suit on, North is a little less noticeable, but that won't last forever.

Someone, other than the caretaker, is going to work out that he's here.

I huff at him and whisper urgently, "Gimme August, then. Get him to come with me so that you can tell I'm safe and, you know, not running off, if that's what you're so worried about."

He snaps, "Are you insane? I can't just give you one of my nightmare creatures, it doesn't work like that."

I point at my hair where Brutus is hiding. "Don't try that bullshit with me right now, just give me the puppy and let me go get my girl before the building collapses around her and we have to explain to her parents why she was holed up in there naked and freaking the hell out."

He stares at me and I decide that enough is enough, I'm done talking about pointless shit. I take off towards the building and ignore his furious whisper at me to get my ass back over to him. I'm not sure what he's expecting, I walked into the Resistance's arms for this girl, a burning building is nothing to me.

I have to be careful, skirting my way around the crowd and all of the officials standing around the perimeter. Sage had been detailed in the best path to her, so I just duck and make a run for it, hoping North has gotten on board and is running a diversion for me.

The fire is on the east side of the building and even though Sage is also there, she'd told me to take the long route through the west wing so I don't inhale smoke the whole way. I shove my sweater over my nose, just in case, and then silently send up a thank you to Gryphon for all the damned cardio he's had me doing because I'm barely panting when I make it to the third floor.

There's the pattering sounds of more footsteps behind me and I almost squeal with joy at the sight of August bounding up behind me. He's only a little smaller than the last time I'd seen him, not at all inconspicuous, but he nudges my thigh with his big head in greeting, giving me a good sniff as though he's working out what's changed.

"I've missed you, pretty baby! I'll give you all of the belly scratches and lovies the moment we find Sage and get her out of here. You can watch my back for me. Can you do that? Yes, you can, beautiful boy."

I'm hoping that this means North is on my side now, or at the very least, not feeling murderous about me just taking off, and I break into a jog the rest of the way to the infamous bathroom of panic.

I barely knock twice before Sage rips the door open and flies at me, a sheet wrapped around her body in a very deja vu sort of way, it seems she's also a fan of the burrito escape route.

"I think I'm losing my mind, Oli! I can't stop crying and my bond is going insane about Felix not being here and I just— I'm losing my fucking mind!"

Right, now is not the time to compare burrito techniques. "Everything is going to be okay, Sage. We're going to get you dressed and out of here, like, right the fuck now. Then we can talk about the nesting."

She pulls away from me, the sheet slipping a little and

showing me all of the love bites on her shoulder which make me feel weirdly proud of her.

I'm apparently also losing my mind.

"*Nesting*? Oli, I'm not Felix's Bond, it can't be nesting! I've just gone off of the fucking deep end and now I'm in hell! This is all my own stupid fault for trying to be with someone who wasn't my Central."

I start looking for some clothes to shove on her but there's nothing in this bathroom except for a ridiculously overstocked first aid kit. "We can talk about that when we get back to the manor, there's definitely something going on here. Let's just get some clothes on you and get out of this tiny-ass bathroom for now."

August takes this as a good time to start sniffing around at the tiles, as though he's worried there's danger hiding in the grout or something. I have to maneuver my way around him to keep searching for something, *anything*, to throw on Sage.

"What the fuck is that?" Sage croaks, and I grumble under my breath at her shrill tone.

Why do they all hate him so much?

"His name is August. He's here to keep us protected while North distracts the fire wardens and the caretaker to get you out of here. Felix has been lying out of his ass for you, no one is ever going to know there was a Flame in this building. Shit, why is Felix so fucking neat? We need a shirt."

Sage blinks at me right as I find a tank top behind the wastebasket, obviously missed there from Felix's cleaning, and then she bursts into tears again. "North?! You brought the Bond that my mom works for here? That's it, I'm jumping out of the window. I'm not doing this."

I grab her arm and shove the tank top at her. "He's going to be cool about this. I've told him... *nothing* but also just enough that he's definitely working with us here. It's going to be fine."

I have to help her get the tank top on and I try to remember how delicate I had felt literally last night when I was also in the nesting phase. Soft, kind words. Slow movements and gentle hands. I got her calm again and the top half of her covered.

I already know that North is going to be royally pissed about it, but I give Sage my yoga pants to cover her a little more. I have underwear on and Nox's sweater is long enough to hit me mid-thigh, so it's not as though I'm walking out of here naked. Though I'm sure it'll still be embarrassing for him to have his Bond walking around with no pants on .

I lean down to August and scratch him behind his ears, murmuring, "Do you think you could warn him about this so he's not blindsided? Can you do that, or are you more of a guard pup and not a spy?"

His void-like eyes stare at me, unblinking, and Sage whispers, "Is he about to bite you? He looks... hungry."

I huff and give him a kiss on the head. "August would never. Are you ready? We're getting out of here before the party really starts up."

She takes a deep breath, her hands shaking terribly, and nods at me. I offer her my arm, more as comfort than support, and she takes it, eyeing August distrustfully as we follow him out.

The smoke is thicker out here now.

Sage coughs once and then lifts a hand, her eyes flashing as she clears the smoke away from us both with a simple flick of her fingers.

A very handy little skill to have in an emergency.

There are fire fighters everywhere, and we spend twice as long getting out of there than I had jogging up here, dodging them as best we can. August seems intent on eating someone tonight and I spend half my time calling him away from people. When we finally walked out of the same side entrance I'd come in, Sage gasps at the thick black smoke everywhere, clutching at my hand. The smoke leads all the way to the Bentley and, after I call on my gift to see clearly, I usher her along until we're both safe and secure in the car together.

"Explain it to me again and this time, don't leave out all of the parts you think aren't important."

I groan and Sage glances at me, her cheeks on fire. The drive-through line for coffee and ice cream is ridiculous for this time in the morning but apparently we've hit the post-party rush hour. North is using the opportunity to grill Sage in a very not-cool way.

She looks like she's planning out her suicide, and I don't blame her one bit.

"We had sex and then my gift just... got stronger. I thought I was imagining it. I had to be, but then Felix got a call to go into one of the labs because he's just started his Healer rounds there, and my gift just— it freaked out that he was leaving me, and then suddenly the building was on fire. I had no control over it, I haven't lost my control like that for more than a decade."

North nods and drums his fingers over the steering wheel again, his brows pulled down tight as he's lost in his own head, processing all of this. I try not to obsessively watch him, but this is the most human I've seen him before, besides the tiny moments of him climbing in and out of my bed.

I don't know if it was him telling me he actually wants

to be able to get over me leaving, but it feels like maybe something has shifted between us again.

I clear my throat, trying to get my head back to the crisis at hand. "She can also now hear Felix in her head. That's a Bonded thing, right? That's why I can hear Gryphon."

North scowls and glances back at Sage again. "That's a very rare occurrence for Bond groups, only a very small percentage of Top Tier Bonded share that sort of connection."

Sage nods and mumbles, "That's when I decided to call Oli and get help. God, my dad is going to murder me when he finds out."

I glare at North but he doesn't even bother looking my way before he answers, "He won't find out. I'll clean this all up and have it passed off as an electrical fault. I'll make sure Maria is kept out of it. We have more important things to focus on, like how the hell you've Bonded with someone who isn't your Central."

I *almost* forgive him for putting August away now. The moment he sat in the car, he'd held out his hand, black-stained palm up, and called my precious pup back into himself. I'd refused to talk to him for a full ten minutes in a pout over it, holding in all of the snark I wanted to throw at him for how long his eyes had gotten stuck on the long lines of my bare legs.

I don't get their fascination with them, Gryphon is the same way.

Get your mind off of your drop-dead gorgeous, controlling asshole Bond, Oleander!

I clear my throat again, subtle as fuck, trying not to blush when North pulls a bottle of water out of the center console for me. "Bonds don't nest, only Centrals do. Sage was definitely having some *very* strong reactions to this whole mess. She was acting the same way I was. There's no way for a Bond to just... switch to a Central, is there?"

North frowns and pulls the car forward, rolling down the window to order for us all. The fact that he had asked Sage for what she wanted but already knew what I would order is bossy, controlling, and, curse my soul, a tiny bit hot.

He's converting me to his bullshit, but I'm not going down without a fight.

It's also sneaky as hell because I've never drunk a coffee around him before, how the hell does he know my exact, over-the-top, frilly sort of drink order? He gets me the exact drink that I'm too embarrassed to tell Atlas or Gabe that I want whenever they order me a coffee.

Even Sage's eyebrows shoot up as he rattles off the list of ingredients and extra shots.

She leans forward and murmurs to me, "What the hell kind of coffee is that?"

I side-eye him and scoff, "North is very secure in his masculinity, he doesn't mind us both knowing that he prefers a venti shaken quad espresso with five pumps of brown sugar syrup, two pumps strawberry syrup, dash of heavy cream, with caramel drizzle and extra whipped topping."

He doesn't say a word as we both cackle like children, enjoying the hell out of each other's company on such a shitty night.

Sage obviously relaxes about having North hearing our conversations and leans back in the back seat to groan, "Sawyer is going to be so pissed that I called you before him. Fuck, he's going to be a nightmare. He's been texting me about cornering you all damn day, the gossip whore."

I huff and rub my hands over my bare legs, watching as North starts fussing with the car's heating for me. "I have no doubt he's going to be a nightmare for us both. Atlas will definitely murder him if he asks me anything with him around."

My stomach drops at the thought of Atlas, his disappearance at dinner last night is still at the forefront of my mind. I don't know if I'm upset that he's upset, or pissed off that he's acting out like this over something I had no control over.

Then I feel guilty because he literally destroyed Gloria's cafe for her daring to comment about my morality, so he's not at all a bad guy.

It's a mess.

Sage hums under her breath, huffing a little at how damn slow the line is. "Felix is back at North's place. Everyone is awake there, by the way. He called Sawyer and told him that we're both safe, and now he's heading over there too. I guess this mind communication stuff is handy."

I groan at her, "Yeah, until you're stuck in front of your ex-workplace while your Bonds are going freaking mental on it for your honor and when you call in for backup, your Bonded just joins in."

North edges the car forward so we're only one car away from caffeine and sugar, and Sage bounces against the seat due to the momentum and her shock. "What do you mean, ex-workplace? You quit? Jesus, did Atlas finally kill some frat boys for stalking you?"

North's head snaps over to stare at me and I wave him off. "They're not stalking me. They've just made a game out of coming in to whisper about me, thanks to Nox making that idiot Branson shit himself publicly. I think they're all trying to psych themselves up to try again but they're too freaking soft."

Then I turn in my seat and give Sage a very serious look. "So Gloria? She's an Empath. No one told me, and when I went in there for my shift, apparently she saw who I really am now that I Bonded to Gryphon and got a little kick of power. You should be warned that your bestie is evil. Her words, I'm seeped in evil apparently. The Dravens aren't though, so there's some great news. We should really spread that around campus; Gloria gives her seal of approval, so stop with the monster bullshit. But, yeah, maybe you should rethink your friendship with me."

Sage blinks at me and then turns on North. "And what are you Bonds doing about this? I hope she's dead now. I hope you killed the old prejudiced bitch, because if Oli is evil, then I am too. Fuck, I just burned down a million-year-old building. I'm like demon-levels of evil, clearly."

I scoff at her, but North is looking right at me, his eyes too dark in the car for me to get a read on what he's thinking. Shit. "Gryphon's debrief was missing some of the finer details of the situation, but I'll be taking care of it. She's not dead, but she's about to find things a lot harder for her around here."

Sage doesn't look satisfied by that but when he finally gets our drinks and hands her an extra-large cup, she murmurs a thank you and calms down a little.

Only until he hands me the ultimate girly drink, then she bursts out laughing at my expense, curling in half and not stopping until there's tears in her eyes.

The rest of the drive back to the manor is quiet, all of us sucking down the caffeine like our lives depend on it, and when North pulls into the garage, I'm ready to just lay down and die for a few hours.

Sage takes a second to pull herself together, staring North dead in the eye through the rearview mirror as she says, "Thank you for coming to get me, the coffee, and for— the clean up. I am in your debt."

Over my dead body.

I open my mouth but North cuts me off before I can say a thing. "No debt. I owed you for taking care of Oleander when we didn't. Gryphon, Nox, and I will be gone for a week. When we get back, we're going to get to the bottom of your Bonding. Discreetly. I mean it, neither of you two or Felix should speak to anyone about it until we can get a handle on this."

Sage nods and then we follow him back into the house, ready to face the chaos waiting for us here.

We're met at the door by one of the maids, who hands me a pair of yoga pants with her eyes on the ground, as though looking at my bare legs is a sentence worse than death. I'm insulted about it for half a second, until I see North's face.

He's staring at her like she's a threat to me.

I'm reminded that his uncle was just murdered in his bed by one of his staff, a message left in his blood, and okay, yeah, I can see why he's being a little extra about this.

I also feel sorry for the poor woman, she looks like she's trying not to keel over from a heart attack right now.

"Thank you! I should really learn to take an extra set with me while out moonlighting with North. He was such a brute with my last pair, don't let the suits fool you," I say with a smirk, and Sage slaps a hand over her mouth, desperately trying to keep her giggles in at the withering stare North directs my way.

"I was unprepared for what a friendship with you would look like. I'm not sure I want it."

I smirk back at him, this shit is like fuel to the fire for my sass. "Liar, you love it. You'd have me 'chained in the basement' by now if you didn't. And, well, if she is a plant from the Resistance, they'll get some great information about how *connected* and *unified* we are."

He grimaces at the reminder of his threat to me and I enjoy the hell out of seeing it; a point to me finally. I'm going to wipe the floor with this man by the time I'm done proving myself to him and the rest of my Bonds.

I think— I think maybe I want to keep them all, and that's the most terrifying thing I've admitted to myself in a very long time.

To hope to figure out a way to have them all without my gift detonating like a freaking bomb and destroying everyone and everything in my path seems like too much and yet… I'm really thinking about it.

Fuck, it's all I can think about right now.

I don't even know if that's possible but, fuck, I need to try it.

As soon as I have the yoga pants on, North leads us

through the manor in a direction I've never been before. I'm expecting to arrive at his office or a conference room, something very formal and prestigious for the debrief he's going to give us and the others before he leaves on the mission, and I'm shocked when we get to a huge theatre room instead.

It's like a whole goddamn cinema in his house.

The lights are still on and there's nothing on the massive projection screen that covers one whole wall, but all of my remaining Bonds, Sawyer, and Felix are all sitting around with varying degrees of worry on their faces. It's kind of cute to think about them all sitting around waiting for us, and when we walk in, their heads all snap our way.

The second Sage sets eyes on Felix, who looks incredibly frazzled, she bursts into tears and throws herself at him.

I instantly feel better about my own messy reactions to, like, *everything* Bond related over the last few months. It's good to see that the crazy hormones and crying over freaking nothing was actually my bond's fault and not just because I was going insane. Fuck, am I glad to be back to normal... almost.

Sawyer takes one look at her and then turns his glare on North. "What the fuck did you say to her that has her crying? I don't give a fuck about your nightmare creatures, I'll kill you."

I step in front of North and point to Sawyer with my own frosty glare. "He got up in the middle of the night to chauffeur a rescue mission, didn't nark on her, and then bought her coffee on the way back. So simmer the fuck down, Benson, before I decide to take a chunk out of you, no precious puppies required."

Gabe's eyebrows hit his hairline and a ghost of a smile crosses over his face before he smothers it, coming over to me to throw an arm over my shoulders and stare Sawyer down with me. North huffs at us both, like it's incredibly insulting for the two of us to be protecting him like this, but we ignore him.

Sawyer looks between us and then throws his hands into the air. "Well, someone tell me what the fuck is going on then! Felix told me there was an emergency and now Sage is crying. I'm getting really fucking sick of watching people make her cry."

Jesus.

How do I tell him anything without saying too much, with this many big opinions in the room?

Gryphon cocks his head in my direction and then his words filter into mine, *don't say anything to him, Bonded. Just wait until we get back and we'll sort it out together.*

What, so I'm supposed to just stand here awkwardly in this heated silence? That sounds like torture and when Sawyer swings around to scowl at Sage, I can't help myself.

Gryphon should know better than to try to stop me from diving in front of Sage when she's threatened.

I aim for a soothing tone and probably fail miserably at it. "There was a very small incident. Sage called me because she knew I'd come save her without chewing her out like you would, and North came to use his name to smooth things over."

North scoffs at my use of the word 'incident' again but doesn't interrupt, and Sawyer doesn't call me out for my bullshit.

Thankfully, Gryphon comes to our rescue. "We have two hours until we roll out. We can debrief properly when we're back."

North checks his watch and sighs, brushing past me and letting his hand graze mine as he passes. It's such a tiny movement, the smallest brush of our skin, but it feels like a promise.

A promise we've made to each other if I can just find *something* to prove that he was wrong about me.

Gryphon bumps Nox's shoulder with his own as they follow North out of the room, murmuring to each other quietly, and I try not to stare longingly after them. Mostly at the loss of my Bonded, but also at the obvious closeness between them and the easy way Nox interacts with Gryphon.

I'll never have that.

From across the room, Atlas finally looks at me, and I finally feel as though I'm not about to have a breakdown over him because he looks at me with the same open expression as he always has.

I smile at him and he stalks over, taking my hand and murmuring to me, "Come sleep between Ardern and me while the others are getting ready to leave. You should get some rest in before we have to face the real world again."

I nod and lean forward to press my face into his chest, breathing easy for the first time in days.

Sawyer grunts unhappily and stretches out on one of the recliners, eyeing Felix as he stretches out on another one next to him with Sage pressed against his chest.

I already know that he's starting to put things together.

There's no way we're going to be able to keep this from all of our friends.

Atlas leads me over to the pallet-style seats at the back, up on the platforms, with a perfect view of the screen, where Gabe is already waiting for us with blankets for me. I duck down to give him a kiss, a small peck on the lips, and he's careful about wrapping me up and tucking me into his chest. Atlas slides in behind me, throwing one of the blankets over himself as well and then pulling my hips back so my ass is rubbing against him in a very suggestive way.

I sigh, content to be squeezed between the two of them,

and let my eyes drift shut.

I'm woken up by Gryphon's hand stroking over my cheek, his face close to mine as he murmurs quietly to me, "Wake up and kiss me goodbye, Bonded."

I feel groggy and disoriented, like my brain is swimming in my skull and bouncing around a little too much, and when I pull myself to sit up, Atlas grunts unhappily at me.

Gryphon scowls at him from where he's crouched down next to me but by the time his eyes swing back to mine, he just looks calm again. "I spoke to my sister. She's been looking for some help at her cafe and she says she'll give you a trial there. Forget about Gloria. We have a plan for that old bitch, no need for it to be upsetting you."

I nod and lean forward to kiss him, my tongue moving against his in a very PDA moment, but my bond demands it. He doesn't seem to mind it either, his hand coming up to cup the side of my neck and squeeze just a little.

Possessive Bonded is quickly becoming my favorite type.

I feel a little dazed when he pulls away, my hand clutching at his shirt like a lifeline. He watches my glazed eyes with a very smug male air about him, the type I'm starting to get used to seeing on him.

I glance away from him, the smolder in his eyes too much for me to handle right now, and I find North and Nox waiting by the door, dressed and ready to leave. Neither of them notice me looking their way, thanks to the quietly intense conversation between them, which I'm grateful for because my jaw drops.

Good god*damn*.

I've been brainwashed into thinking the Tac gear is hot, thanks to Gryphon, but there's something else entirely about the Draven boys decked out in the protective wear.

Fuck me.

Men.

Because there's nothing boy-ish about either of them. If North is sexy in a suit, he is fucking devastating in a bulletproof vest and a neck gaiter. My God, the gloves kind of fit his personality.

Is that too dirty?

Probably.

I'm absolutely, without a doubt, objectifying them both in my head right now and if Gryphon can read my mind about it, I will never live this down.

If you're a good girl, I won't tell them, his words filter into my head as he kisses me one last time before he pushes away from me.

Then I watch as my Bonds walk away from me and pray that they all come back to me, no matter how fraught our relationships might be.

Atlas is extra attentive over the next morning.

I'm wedged between him and Gabe in the dining room with Sage, Felix, and Sawyer facing us on the other side of the table as we talk over the extravagant food that the chef has put together for our late breakfast.

It takes me too long to figure out what the hell I want to eat and when I grumble under my breath about my Bonds being gone, Gabe cackles at my shitty attitude.

He drawls, "You mean you miss North serving you? I can't believe you hadn't figured out what he was doing, old-school tricks to endear him to you."

I shoot him a look and Atlas leans in closer to me, his hand warm over my knee as he gives it a squeeze, a small show of support and affection that calms my bond. He doesn't get pissed at Gabe's little jab and that settles me even more.

We're finding our way through this together, as a complete Bond group. I just need to figure some shit out first.

Wait.

"What the fuck does 'old-school tricks' mean? Why didn't you say something about it sooner?"

Gabe just laughs harder at me and shakes his head like

I'm an idiot, which I don't appreciate. Atlas murmurs to me, "You might hate it, but your bond? All it sees is that you're having your needs taken care of by your Bond. I would've told you, I thought you knew. It's a sign of respect... it was one of the reasons I backed off a bit about them all."

Huh.

What a freaking asshole.

The fact that he finds sneaky, manipulative ways to show my bond respect without showing it to me? I want to poke at my bond and tell it not to be swayed so easily, but it's also been my best judge of character. The thing has gotten me out of every shitty situation I've ever found myself in, so there's a part of me that warms at the knowledge that he's been doing that.

Dammit.

Sneaky, manipulative freaking Bonds.

I get back to my food and silence falls over the table. Sage eats like she's been starving to death, just shoveling protein and carbs into her mouth at an alarming rate.

Setting buildings on fire takes serious amounts of power.

Gabe and Atlas struggle to keep their hands away from me the entire time they eat, a hand on each of my thighs and their bodies leaning into mine as they basically turn me into a sandwich. I'm not sure what prompted the change but I'm into it.

Sawyer's eyes work their way around the room, flicking from me and my Bonds and then over to where Felix and Sage are wrapped up in each other, suspicion darkening his gaze.

I've already come to terms with the fact that we're not going to be able to keep last night a secret from our friends. There's no way that Sawyer is going to let it drop, and I already know that Atlas will be all over me for answers the moment we're alone again.

I just don't know how to do it without throwing Sage under the bus or gossiping about her business, which I would *never* do.

Like always, Sawyer forces our hand, waiting until his plate is clear before he leans back and drawls, "Are you guys going to tell us what the fuck went down last night, or am I dragging Sage home to pick apart everyone and everything possible until she cracks and tells me? Because we all know she will eventually."

Felix turns to give Atlas a look and I'm reminded that he is actually also a football player that enjoys tackling people into the dirt. He's built like the rest of them, a little smaller than Gabe but wider than Sawyer is, but his gift as a Healer always makes me think he's... above that brawling kind of thing.

Obviously, I'm wrong about that.

Sage can tell he's about to go off about her brother's sass and so she just blurts out, "Felix and I had sex and we Bonded. I set the Med Hall on fire. North is covering it up for me because Oli charged down there like it was her ass on the line and rescued me. Felix had to lie and cover up about a million things for me so I could have a panic attack in the bathroom without the fire warden breaking in the door. Oli walked into a burning building with two nightmare creatures to get me to calm down and get out of there. She also gave me her pants and walked out basically bare from the waist down, then argued with North about how best to clean all of this up without Mom, Dad, and the Parental Bonds finding out, so if you could please give us all a break, that would be fucking great. We're all running on no sleep and all-consuming anxiety right now... or at least I am."

Gabe and Atlas both turn to stone next to me and I have to assume they get exactly what Sage isn't saying right now.

Sawyer's face does about a million different things to show all of the emotions and thoughts running through his head. He finally lands on his default, cheeky bullshit. "You mean to tell me that Davenport's dick was so good that you almost killed his entire dorm? I kinda want to high five him but that seems... wrong."

Sage groans, her cheeks flushing, and I roll my eyes,

gesturing to him like he's the idiot he's looking like right now. "I don't think you're getting it, Sawyer. Why would North and Gryphon tell us to keep quiet about a normal loss of control? Don't be dense, it doesn't suit you."

He scowls at me and then, hesitantly, glances back to Sage. "A power jump can only happen with Bonds... that's impossible."

She blushes even more and ducks her head. "I don't understand how it *could* happen if I'm not a Central Bond, but it did. I'm not stupid. I know that Riley is my Central, he's the one who's my Bond and Giovanna's. The bloodwork showed it but... I can't think of another explanation."

Except, as she's speaking, I do because...the bloodwork.

At the lab.

That Giovanna is desperate to get an internship at.

Fuck, I knew she was a slimy, manipulative bitch! I look at Sage across the room and I can see when it all comes together in her head too. All of the pieces we have are nowhere near enough for the full picture but, *fuck*, it's a start.

I clear my throat. "Giovanna's gift is Telekinesis, right? What if she's the one messing with your Bond? What if you're the Central and she's been fucking with Riley to hide the fact that he's not?"

471

Felix curses under his breath and squeezes Sage a little tighter.

"Oli... Riley's mom called me last week. She told me he's been getting migraines and bloody noses, she was worried that it's because we hadn't Bonded. What if— prolonged usage of mind control can deteriorate brain mass," Sage croaks, and I groan back.

"I don't want to think about saving that asshole," Sawyer snaps.

Felix cuts him off. "But if she's messing with his head, then he's not an asshole. He's a victim. I fucking hate to say this but... Gabe, you remember, back me up. He was obsessed with Sage, the same as I always have been. He protected her and did everything with her. We all knew that they'd end up together... just like I thought I would. His change was instant, and it was the second Giovanna showed up."

Sage bursts into tears.

Felix scoops her into his chest, pressing her face into his neck, and I'm jealous for a second that she's all wrapped up in her Bonded scents right now while Gryphon is off dealing with the Resistance camps.

Gabe lets out a groan, rubbing a hand over his face in frustration. "How the fuck are they watching us all so closely? How are they finding their way into our families and fucking with our Bonds? We're fighting a losing fucking game here until we figure that out."

Atlas' jaw clenches and releases as he grinds his teeth and then says carefully, "We need to figure out how deep this goes. Giovanna has a sister on the council, right? What else doesn't make sense? Who is suspicious there? What doesn't add up? Those are the places we start."

There's a moment of silence and then Sawyer pipes up, "You mean something like the signal from Oli's GPS chip going to the East Coast?"

Silence.

Dead fucking silence for half a second before all hell breaks loose.

Atlas turns to Gabe with a glare. "What the fuck is he talking about?"

Gabe's lip curls and he snaps, "And you didn't think to say something about it before now? What the fuck is wrong with you?!"

I butt in before they can continue screaming at him from across the table, "What the hell are you talking about? How could you know something like that?"

Sawyer holds his hand up and a spark of electricity jumps between his fingers. "I'm a Technokenetic. When we first met, I could feel the chip in your spine, it felt *wrong* to me. I hated Sage being around you because that sort of tech shouldn't be inside someone... Then, once I got to know you, I realized it wasn't your fault, and I got over it. I thought… I thought you all knew."

"This is vital fucking information, Benson. It's not that hard to mention it to one of us!" Atlas snarls, and I throw myself in his direction to stop the bloodshed that I think is about to happen.

I also can tell how fragile Sage is right now because she doesn't move away from Felix even with the threat of violence to her brother, but her face does crumple a little. More reasons to calm the hell down about how messed up I've been.

Sawyer throws his hands in the air. "You were on the East Coast and I assumed you were keeping an eye on her too! Then I just… I forgot about it. It just became the weird aura around Oli. I'm sorry! Fuck, if I'd have known, I would've said something!"

This is all irrelevant. "If you're a Techno, you can manipulate it, right? You can stop it from blowing my brains out if I take it out… right?"

"Blow your brains out?! What the fuck are you talking about?" Gabe shouts, and I glance up to see him looking very green.

"That's what they told me when they put it in. They said it would trigger a small explosion, just enough to kill me, if I tried to take it out."

"I'm going to fucking puke," Gabe says, as he pushes away from the table, grabbing his phone out, probably to call North and chew him out.

Except…

Atlas says it before I can. "You can't call him. You can't tell anyone. We need to get it out, *without* killing Oli, and then we need a list of everyone who was involved in getting it put in her in the first place. We need a game plan to clean house. There's a reason North is losing the battle against the Resistance and it's because the poison has already taken root here."

"You have a med pack in this place somewhere, right? Let's get it out now," Felix says, standing up and walking through to the kitchen without hesitation as Gabe jumps up to find what he's asking for.

I stare after Felix in shock as the door swings shut, and I see him scrubbing down his hands like he's a freaking surgeon about to crack me open and take a look inside and… Well, how badly do I want this chip out?

Really, really fucking badly.

I take a deep breath. "Fuck it, let's do this."

What I wouldn't give for Gryphon and his pain manipulation, brain-mojo while Felix slices me open with nothing but a tiny bit of worthless numbing cream on my skin.

Ironically, he feels the bolt of pain through our Bond and immediately floods me with his own bond to figure out what the hell is going on. I have to work overtime to cover it up, sticking to things that are completely true.

I'm fine! Don't freak out, I'm just clumsy as hell sometimes.

His reply is instant, *What the hell is going on? We're only a few hours out, I can get Kieran here to bring me back.*

I try not to puke at the intense look of concentration on

Sawyer's face as his eyes flash white, all of his focus on stopping the killing chip from, you know, *killing me.*

I swallow and work at keeping my reply steady and sure, *No need. Felix is about to patch me up, so I don't need any extra mother hens around here. Forget about me, just focus on your job.*

His bond stays with me, the pain lessening by the second even with the tweezers digging around under my flesh. When the chip finally pops out of my neck, Felix removes one of his gloves to press his palm to the side of my neck until the wound is completely healed up.

The entire room exhales.

No more hurting yourself, I'll come back and there will be hell to pay, Bonded. Just stay at the manor and study until you go see Kyrie. She's expecting you sometime before lunch. Straight home after, promise me.

I have to be really careful about how I answer so he doesn't know that something is happening here, his ability to tell if I'm lying is a complete fucking nightmare. *I promise that I'll only leave here with my Bonds and your TacTeam protection detail.*

His bond slips away from me, slowly and like a caress, and I take a deep breath. Lying to him, even in this sort of round-about way, makes me feel like the worst goddamned Bonded in existence, but I'm sure if we told him, he'd be on his way back here in a freaking second.

Whatever help we can be to get rid of the Resistance, we're going to do it.

When Felix finally moves away from me, taking the other glove off and wrapping up all of the used medical supplies, I look over to find Sawyer holding up the tweezers with the GPS chip in one of his hands as his glowing-white eyes squint at it.

"Is there anything you can tell about it? How does your gift work? Give me something here, Benson," I say, and he shrugs.

"It's still transmitting. There's nothing to say that it's been doing anything except to track you, but I'll run home to get my laptop and I'll trace the signal. Once we know where it's going… we can go from there."

I nod and glance at my watch, finding that it's still early enough for me to grab a shower and look half decent before I meet my Bonded's sister.

I feel sick to my stomach about it.

Gabe is still a little quieter, a little subdued, thanks to the killer GPS chip reveal, but I thread our fingers together as we head back up to my room. Atlas takes a call from his mom and agrees to meet us up there, pressing a kiss to my cheek and striding ahead of us to his own room.

Gabe waits until we're alone in the elevator before he speaks. "I feel like a complete piece of shit. No wonder you fucking hated us all. I can't believe they put that in you."

I shrug and lean into the solid weight of him, letting my face tuck into his chest as I breathe him in. "Honestly? I thought it was all North. I didn't even think about the rest of you guys being in on it. The guy who did it, he just kept talking about how great North was and how embarrassing this was for him. He was the one... he told me that I just had to lay down and submit to you all. He seemed very pro-force-the-Bond."

A nerve in his jaw flickers and when I look up at him again, he shakes his head. "I'm trying not to lose my fucking shit in a tiny elevator, but it's pushing it. North will... fuck, North is going to tear the council apart over this. To find out that most of your anger and pushing back at us was over some bullshit that Noakes did? Fuck, North will let his nightmares devour the slimy fuck for this."

I desperately want to believe that but... "North once told me he'd chain me to his cellar by my throat if I tried to run, so I want to believe you, but I still have some reservations there."

Gabe curses under his breath as the elevator doors open, rubbing a hand over his face as if he hoped he could rub this entire conversation away if he applied enough pressure.

I get it.

"We don't deserve you. None of us do. We're all

fucking this entire Bond up, and you deserve so much fucking more," he murmurs, his voice breaking, and I swallow around the lump in my throat.

"Don't think like that, Gabe. You don't know about all of the terrible things I've done."

It doesn't matter that I'm dressed to absolute perfection, my hair and makeup done by Sage before we'd left, my hand shakes as I reach for the door handle of the Hellcat to get out and meet Gryphon's sister about a job.

What if she hates me?

Just meet her, she's not going to bite.

I huff and cross my arms over my chest, pouting like a child. *Well, if she's not so scary, then why haven't I met her already? She probably hates me! Fuck, I'm not doing this. I'll just start mooching off of you.*

His power is unreal because he sends me through a chuckle, perfect in pitch, and goosebumps break out over my skin at the sound of it.

We both know you won't. I'm pretty sure you have a running tally in your head with everything you owe North so far. If you don't want a job, then I'll call Kyrie and cancel it. You can meet her when I get home, she's been asking about you. I didn't want you meeting her until I was sure about you.

I swallow at the implication that he's sure about me now, that something more than just our Bonding has swayed him to think that I'm worth meeting his sister.

Fine. If she hates me, I'll never forgive you for sending me in there alone though.

"Stop flirting with him and let's go get some decent coffee," Gabe grumbles, still on edge about our conversations today. I get it. I'm not going to give him shit over it because clearly it's on my behalf.

Atlas shoots him a look though, not happy about the tone he's using in my direction, and I get a hand on his wrist to settle him down. Tensions are high and we need each other more now than ever before.

When we all get out of the car together, Atlas checks his pockets to make sure the GPS chip is still there, specially wrapped by Sawyer so that no one realizes we've taken it out yet. I'd offered to carry it, because there's nowhere I'm going that I haven't already been so far, but Atlas and Gabe had both shot that idea down fast.

Neither of them want me touching it.

Gabe does another once-over of my outfit, simple black jeans and the leather jacket Gryphon had left me over a tight black tee with my long-lost-loves boots, before he throws an arm around my shoulders and murmurs into my hair, "Kyrie is cool, stop freaking out over this. She'll only give you shit for not working with her in the first place."

I scoff at him, dragging my feet a little. "I tried! The lady I tried to give my resume to said I wasn't allowed to work here."

Atlas shakes his head at Gabe's roar of laughter, stealing me off of him and dragging me over the threshold of the cafe.

It's only a billion times better in here than in Gloria's place.

Okay, so I've seen it before and I'm totally prejudiced about it, thanks to her firing me, but the entire feel of the place is clean, warm, and inviting.

It's also bustling with a lunchtime rush of people buying sandwiches and coffees, the tables are all full and the takeout line is overflowing. I almost feel bad for interrupting the busy shift by coming in here.

"Hey, Vicki! Is Val in? Gryph sent us," Gabe says, a warm smile on his face as he approaches the same older woman who'd sent me away last time.

I try not to hold a grudge about it because I know for sure it was North's directive, but my bond still isn't happy about it.

Vicki nods and points towards the back, opening the section of the counter for us to make our way back there.

"Who is Val?" I murmur and Gabe smirks at me.

"Valkyrie. Gryphon always says his parents were

sadists for naming them both, but Kyrie is better about it. She's Val to the general public but Kyrie to family."

Holy shit.

Okay, but they're cool as fuck names. At least they're not named after poisonous flowers, an omen of what was to come for me. My mom once told me that she'd dreamt about me for years before I was born and my crib was always filled with oleander flowers.

I always wondered if she was a little bit psychic.

Gabe leads us through and pushes his way into the back room where we find Kyrie moving giant bags of coffee beans for grinding. Atlas moves over to her immediately, taking the bags from her and moving them to where she's directing him.

She watches him as she catches her breath, an apron wrapped around her waist with an order book half falling out, and she looks the same as that picture in Gryphon's room, just a little bit older.

She wipes a hand over her forehead. "Perfect timing, we're about to drown under orders. I fucking hate that old hag Gloria, but at least with a second option around here, I didn't have to deal with frat boy trash. Now I'm up to my armpits in stinking misogyny."

She glances over at me, a quick once-over like she's assessing me, and then she ducks down to grab an apron. "You can start now, right? Gryph promised you were good for the old bitch, so I'm sure you'll be good here too. I told him he should've sent you earlier, but he's a secretive little dick."

I snort with laughter, slapping a hand over my mouth as I reach out with the other one to grab the apron. "That about sums the situation up. I'm Oli, by the way. It's nice to finally meet you."

She gives me an assessing look and then her eyes soften the tiniest bit. "Kyrie, don't ask me how my parents came up with it because it's full of trauma for me that we don't have time to unpack. Gabe, can you and Mr. Strong here unload the boxes for me please, usual places. Oli, if you can follow me out and start running orders, that would be amazing."

Atlas' eyebrows rise at her no-nonsense demands but I'm not at all fazed by it. She sounds just like Gryphon to me, and I really need this job, so there's not going to be any complaints outta little ol' me.

The cafe runs like a well-oiled machine.

Kyrie has five other employees and they all accept me into the fold without a problem, helping me out whenever I have questions and complimenting how quickly I pick everything up. There's signs all throughout the kitchen to show where things go and the proper way of doing things and I'm incredibly grateful for them.

After they unload boxes, Kyrie has Gabe and Atlas put

together furniture in her office and then help to restock the kitchen fridges from the cool room out the back, and they both do it all without complaint.

I forget about all of the problems we'd run into over breakfast and just enjoy working my ass off somewhere where it's not only noticed but appreciated too. There's no Kitty trying to weasel her way into my Bonds' lives, no frat boy bullshit, and instead of having watchful Bonds in the booths, there's a TacTeam protection detail discreetly waiting outside to vet people as they come in.

I enjoy myself.

I should really know better by now.

When the power goes out while I'm elbows deep in dishwater, I'm not too worried about it. The cook, Marigold, doesn't seem fazed either as she turns off all of the burners and the oven as a safety precaution and moves the half-cooked foods over to the side to wait for the power to come back on.

Gabe walks into the kitchen, sweating from all of the manual labor, and Atlas comes in behind him looking unruffled and as clean as he was when we left the manor this morning. Super strength comes in handy, I guess.

"Do you guys know what's happening?" I say, and Gabe shakes his head.

"Let's find Kyrie, see if she needs any help keeping the customers calm and not stampeding out of here."

I nod and dry off my hands, moving with them both right as the windows at the front of the shop are blown out, screams and bullets flying everywhere around us.

My back hits the ground as Atlas covers me, his arm softening the blow a tiny bit, and Gabe drops to his belly beside us. I stare into Atlas' eyes, stunned at whatever the hell is going on, and then the screams get louder around us.

The Resistance is here.

There's a popping sound and Kieran appears in a crouch next to us, holding out his arms for us to grab and when I squirm away from him, he just grabs my wrist to drag me along too.

We leave Kyrie behind.

The moment we appear again out in the back alley, I'm ready to chew him out but he just slashes his hand at me. "I'm going back for her now, Fallows, calm the fuck—"

"Too late," Atlas says, and I jerk my head up to see Kyrie struggling between two Resistance soldiers.

My power explodes out of me and they're both dead on the ground in a flash, one of them knocking Kyrie down. I exhale and start to move towards her when there's another two pops, so close together that I don't have a chance to see it.

A Transporter has taken her.

She's fucking *gone*.

Kieran curses under his breath and gets onto his

comms, barking out orders and directives but *fuck that*, I'm going after her.

Atlas' arms band around me like iron bars, utterly immovable as he snaps, "Don't even think about it, Oli. I'm not going through your savior complex all over again. Leave it to the trained professionals."

I let my rage out, just enough that my bond gets some release without coming to the party. "They can't kill me! You know it, I know it. Fuck, if they got an eyeful of me, half the fucking Resistance would know it too! But they're taking people again, I can't just sit by and let that happen."

His arms don't ease up in the slightest. "There's enough TacTeam here to take care of it, I'm not letting you go."

I want to kill him and I have to forcibly stop my bond from reacting to him as I hiss at him, "There's not enough TacTeam and we both know it! Let me go right the fuck now, Bond! I wish I could be the Bond that lets you guys all protect me, but that's just not who I am. I'll keep in touch with Gryphon, but we're losing this battle because… because we're not using the best weapon we have. Fuck it, I'll be the goddamned weapon!"

Gabe looks between us and then looks at the line of men moving through the street towards us, guns raised and masks over their faces. His hands unclench at his side like he's about to shift and throw himself at them, but I'm not playing around.

I accept that I'm not going to be scared anymore.

I'm going to face my gift and I'll let it protect us all, I can wrestle with the consequences and my morality later, because we already know that we're fighting a losing game right now and I'm not going to let that happen. Not to my Bonds and not to our friends and family, not if I can help it.

My eyes shift to the voids, everything becoming clearer, and then I kill them all. No more incapacitation, no more brain melting horrors, I kill them instead. I let my gift touch all of their souls, gripping them tightly and feeling the agony they all experience as I rip them out.

Kieran doesn't react, Carlin's one word of warning enough to have him steady in his boots with nothing but a rough gulp.

Gabe? Not so much. "What the fuck is that?! Oli, what the fuck—"

Atlas snaps at him, "She's a Soul Render, asshole. The brain melting? It's a parlor trick to her, the lesser of her powers. It's how she leaves people to wallow in all of the shittiest parts of their souls. Her real shit? Ripping their souls the fuck out. Instant death, a billion times more powerful than North fucking Draven because he's limited to touch. Oli has no limit. Nothing. The infinite weapon."

My skin crawls at those three words but Kieran curses under his breath before my mind can really process what's being said. "Blind. We're all fucking blind, of course you were in the documents. Codename: IW. Don't burn out, let's save that gift for the big guns for now because no gift is really infinite."

Fuck the big guns.

I cast my gift out until I can feel every person on the block. All of their thoughts and emotions are too complex for me to decipher, but I can tell if they're supposed to be here. I can tell if they're here to murder and pillage.

And I kill them all.

Gabe's eyes flash at me as he stares at the bodies as they hit the ground, their eyes all staring sightlessly from where I've torn their souls clean out of their bodies.

If I wanted to, I could tell the exact number of lives I've just taken, but even though my gift is writhing with joy inside my chest, I don't want to think about it.

Or the small fact that I can't even tell that I've used my gift; no exhaustion, no shaking hands, no lagging from the sheer amount of power it takes to soul-rend.

It's barely touched the edges.

"Get the fuck behind me, Fallows, and stop with the void eyes."

I scoff and throw my hands out around me, gesturing at everything I've just done. "I don't think I need to cower behind you, Kieran. I think you should really be behind me."

He shoves his gaiter down his face and snarls at me,

"Over my dead fucking body, now get your ass moving. We're getting you back to the manor, it's more defensible than being in the open."

Atlas nods and says, "Transport us all. Ardern, get your ass over here and let's just get out."

Gabe makes it two steps before the explosions start again and Atlas dives at me to crush me under his hulking weight, pressing me against the building behind us until I can't breathe.

There's more Resistance here, waves of them arriving as they attempt to take the campus. There's screams everywhere around us, the sounds of them weird to my ringing ears thanks to the explosion.

"Fuck, they're taking more Gifted from the streets. They knew the Dravens were gone, we're being butchered from the inside out," Gabe spits out. His eyes shift into his wolf eyes and Atlas' eyes flash white with him.

We're on the edge of losing control; there's a big decision to be made here and I've already made my choice.

No one is going to like it.

I have to take control of my thoughts and emotions immediately so Gryphon doesn't catch wind of what I'm planning, but my bond thrumming inside me helps with that. I feel regret at leaving them all again, even for such a short time, but I can't let this go.

I can't just sit on my hands and do nothing.

I wait until my Bonds are busy looking around the street for more immediate threats before I lean into Kieran and murmur, "Are you really going to be cool with telling Gryphon that you watched them take his sister and did nothing about it? Because I'm not."

He curses under his breath, his eyes still watching every angle he can see from where we're wedged in. "No, but I got you out. My instructions are to protect you at all costs and I've done my job."

"Wrong. You know what I can do, take me to the sorting camps. Don't try to lie, I already know that you've found the new one. Just drop me off there and I'll get her back," I mutter and he stares at me like I've been mentally compromised.

Except he also looks relieved and I already know I've won.

He shoves his gaiter over his mouth, glancing around us, and murmurs, "Fallows, there is no fucking way that I'm taking you somewhere and leaving you there. Even if you weren't Shore's Bonded, I'd never do that… but we're going to get Kyrie and then we're coming back. You're only coming with me because you're handy in a fight thanks to your gift, and I swore I'd keep you within arm's reach at all times outside of the manor. In and out, that's it. Kill anyone who comes within five feet of us."

No matter how low he'd pitched his voice, Atlas still

hears him and turns to grab me but it's too late. Kieran's hand is already wrapped around my wrist and then the whole world is spinning as he transports us, the shouts of my Bonds lurching after us both ringing in my ears.

My heart hurts for a second but I push it away, regret won't do me any good right now, I can feel shit about it later when Kyrie is back safe.

Kieran is a well-trained TacTeam member, a second-in-command, so he gets us to the edge of where the camp is without completely blowing our cover, but when I cast my gift out like a net to find Kyrie, I realize we're fucked for about a million different reasons. I wasn't prepared for the changes that have obviously happened since I was last in the Resistance's captivity.

Olivia is here and immediately raises the alarm.

That's not a huge problem, I could take that bitch out without fucking trying, but she's standing with the strongest Shield I've ever met and I'm not totally sure I could kill Franklin, even with my extra kick of power thanks to my Bond with Gryphon. I was not expecting him to be in the sorting camps, he's usually too far up the food chain for this sort of work, and my heart clenches in my chest in fear.

But instead of screaming and running like my life depends on it, I wait.

I'm willing to risk capture, torture, and death to get my

Bonded's sister out of this camp. That photo on his dresser told me a lot about him and his relationship to his family because it was the only personal item he had in the room.

He's not losing her.

"Leave. Leave now before they get here. Go, I'll find Kyrie and bring her home safe," I murmur, but Kieran just shakes his head at me, shoving his gaiter back over his mouth as he grabs my wrist again.

Except he can't transport us back.

Franklin has already pinpointed us and stopped us from moving, the welcome wagon is on its way to us. My legs get heavy, my gift recoiling at the feel of someone else's power taking over my limbs, and the panic at who is coming pools in my gut.

Deep breaths, Oli. Don't let Gryphon know about this too soon or you'll lose them all.

I feel freaking terrible for doing this to Kieran and, knowing they'll be the last words we'll have together for a very long time, I mumble, "I'm sorry. Stay strong. Don't tell them anything, and don't worry about me. I've survived it before, I can do it again. Find Kyrie and get her out the second you have a chance to."

He blinks at me but they're already here, stomping through the longer grass as though a beacon is leading them to us. I guess that's exactly what my gift is, a beacon for corrupt men to follow and attempt to own.

And then they appear in front of us, smirking like they've won something.

I thought that seeing Silas Davies again, the man responsible for all of my torture and degradation at the hands of the Resistance, would be the greatest punch in the gut possible... and it *is* bad.

But finding Atlas' father standing next to him is worse.

SIGN UP FOR MY NEWSLETTER TO HEAR ABOUT UPCOMING RELEASES

Also by J Bree

The Bonds That Tie Series

Broken Bonds

Savage Bonds

Blood Bonds

Forced Bonds

Tragic Bonds

Unbroken Bonds

The Mortal Fates Series

Novellas

The Scepter

The Sword

The Helm

The Trilogy

The Crown of Oaths and Curses

The Throne of Blood and Honor

The Mounts Bay Saga

The Butcher Duet
The Butcher of the Bay: Part I
The Butcher of the Bay: Part II

Hannaford Prep
Just Drop Out: Hannaford Prep Year One
Make Your Move: Hannaford Prep Year Two
Play the Game: Hannaford Prep Year Three
To the End: Hannaford Prep Year Four
Make My Move: Alternate POV of Year Two

The Queen Crow Trilogy
All Hail
The Ruthless
Queen Crow

The Unseen MC
Angel Unseen

About J Bree

J Bree is a dreamer, writer, mother, and cat-wrangler. The order of priorities changes daily.

She lives on the coast of Western Australia in a city where it rains too much. She spends her days dreaming about all of her book boyfriends, listening to her partner moan about how the lawns are looking, and being a snack bitch to her three kids.

Visit her website at http://www.jbreeauthor.com to sign up for the newsletter or find her on social media through the links below.

f 　 ⊙ 　 ♪